"Ambitious, energetic . . . [This] densely plotted, often hilarious attempt at the Great American Post-Enron Novel . . . is a bold departure for thriller writer Willett."
—*Entertainment Weekly*

"A sharply drawn satire of life in post-9/11, pre-Enron America . . . The locations, lifestyle, the rarified ambience, will be familiar to many readers, which may make this novel all the more hilarious to some and especially biting to others. . . . It's also instructive, laced with information about the stock market and the law."
—*The Boston Globe*

"This Beantown *Bonfire of the Vanities* tracks Tom Wolfe closely . . . but in his breakthrough third novel, Willett . . . is nearly as hilarious as the master. And he adds something *Bonfire* lacks: someone to root for."
—*People*

"Willett's most engaging tale is slightly reminiscent of Tom Wolfe's *Bonfire of the Vanities*, with more heart and sentiment than Wolfe could ever suggest. . . . Willett's exploration of fiscal manipulators is, at once, hilarious and harrowing. . . . Because of his rich sense of humor and a touch of social outrage, Sabin Willett is able to give us a first-rate novel, one that should please folks from Wall Street to Main Street."
—David Rothenberg, WBAI Radio

"Remarkable: hilariously nasty, morally driven, sweetly romantic. . . . In an ambitious satire of post-9/11 America, the author of two previous legal thrillers manages to skewer our financial, political, and social institutions with vicious glee while offering a nuanced portrait of his tragicomic hero (and supporting heroines)."
—*Kirkus Reviews* (starred review)

"This ambitious novel is reminiscent of Tom Wolfe and Jonathan Franzen's recent works . . . and is every bit as entertaining. One can hope that Willett will produce a sequel so readers can revisit these mostly likable characters."
                                                                    —*Tampa Tribune*

"Comic . . . reminiscent of Tom Wolfe's *Bonfire of the Vanities* . . . a well-written, well-plotted morality tale for the Enron era."   —*Yankee* magazine

"A witty morality tale . . . Willett's new style has bite."   —*The Deal*

SABIN WILLETT is a partner with the law firm of Bingham McCutchen LLP. He is the author of two previous novels, *The Deal* and *The Betrayal*. He graduated from Harvard and Harvard Law School and lives near Boston.

ALSO BY SABIN WILLETT

The Deal
The Betrayal

PRESENT VALUE

PRESENT VALUE

SABIN WILLETT

a novel

Random House Trade Paperbacks • New York

2004 Random House Trade Paperback Edition

This work was originally published in hardcover by Villard Books, an imprint of
The Random House Publishing Group, a division of Random House, Inc., in 2003.

Library of Congress Cataloging-in-Publication Data
Willett, Sabin.
    Present value : a novel / Sabin Willett.
        p.   cm.
    ISBN 0-8129-6955-3
    1. Insider trading in securities—Fiction.   2. Boston (Mass.)—
Fiction.   3. Toy industry—Fiction.   4. Executives—Fiction.
I. Title.
PS3573.I4454P74   2003
813'.54—dc21   2003041103

Random House website address: www.atrandom.com

Printed in the United States of America

9 8 7 6 5 4 3 2

For Pete Willett
1929–2001

Values mattered to Dad, and value too:
but he cared nothing for money.

ACKNOWLEDGMENTS AND
AUTHOR'S NOTE

FIRST AND DEAREST, as wife, counselor, conscience, reader, critic, researcher, and steadfast partner, was you, Matty. Forever and always, I cannot thank you enough.

Many friends and loved ones read and advised: thanks to Stephanie Cabot, Errol Willett, Jennifer Gandee, Beth Thomas, Alicia Carrillo, Tom Rando, Ellen Bassett, Lea Anne Copenhefer, Paul Robertson, Julia Frost-Davies, Owen Laster, Susanna Porter, and Sybil Pincus. Partners and colleagues at Bingham McCutchen were, as always, immensely supportive and indulgent. I am grateful to all of them (none works at Elboe, Fromme & Athol, by the way).

Oh, one more thing—about Paradise. It really exists. It's even on the map now. The locals say to ski it if you can. Fine for them—I find the trail more congenial in fiction.

CONTENTS

PART I

1 A DELIVERY OF PRECIOUS CARGO

HEAT! The heat was steamy and suffocating, a humid pall that antici-pated the dawn and left everyone a little sluggish, a little vulnerable. It was so hot that the day itself seemed dazed, as though it had got lost from July somehow, made a wrong turn off the calendar, then wandered fitfully in the ether until it stumbled into September. In the suburbs west of Boston that Monday morning, it was not autumn at all; there was no hint or whisper of New England charm to come, nothing of the crisp anticipation of a new school year. It was just a sizzler—a white-sky mug-ging. And in the car-pool lane at the Chaney School, it was Cairo at noontime.

"Car-pool lane" was one of the school's many charming euphe-misms, for there wasn't much pooling evident. The fewer the kids, the bigger the vehicle. The SUVs idled in rank, pumping out pizza-oven blasts of superheated exhaust, inching forward toward the alcove, where each would discharge from seventy-eight cubic feet of cargo space its seven cubic feet of Precious Cargo.

At just after eight A.M., behind the wheel of his wife's forest-green 2001 Lincoln Navigator, Fritz Brubaker took his place at the back of the line. In front of the Navigator was a shiny black Chevrolet Yukon XL with a 2500 cc Vortex engine, its powerful air conditioner cooling Precious Cargo by means of an asphalt-melting heat transfer from the tailpipe. In front of the Yukon was a white Mercedes SUV; in front of the Mercedes a Suburban, in front of the Suburban a pearl-gray Range Rover, in front of the Range Rover an Audi A6 all-wheel-drive Quattro feeling smugly and environmentally righteous in this brigade of half-tracks, and in front of the Audi a line of seven-foot SUVs broken only once by a minivan that looked as though it were being held hostage.

They didn't wait impatiently, mind you—they advanced smartly, even eagerly, the moment they could, but not *impatiently*. No impatience would be expressed as the SUV at the front of the line stopped at the alcove and the driver hopped down from the front seat; none as she (usually but not always, either Mom or the nanny) came around to the passenger side to unbelt the cargo with a cheery wave to the vehicle behind; none as she greeted the welcome teacher (this morning it was Mavis Potemkin, one of the team-teaching second-grade pair); certainly no one would express vehicular urgency as the parent straightened the Patagonia backpack on the child's shoulders (the backpack must be an *approved* backpack: while the $79.99 JanSport would do in a pinch, a good parent really ought to spring for the $109 Patagonia number); no one in line would be so gauche as to rev a three-hundred-horsepower engine as the parent checked the water bottle (children must be properly hydrated at all times); and then, perhaps most important of all, as the line of idling SUVs pumped remorseless cubic meters of carbon monoxide into the hot morning air, *no impatience would be expressed* as the parent escorted the Precious Cargo thirty feet across the gravel and through the doorway of Fielding Hall.

Not that the crushed-stone path between the alcove and Fielding was perilous country. Mishap there was about as likely as, say, a holdup in the Oval Office. Still, this daily station of the parenting cross was vitally important. The car-pool-laners were eager—they wanted to move smartly (but not rudely) and efficiently (but not impatiently) through this process, *but no one would rush this event*. Because escorting one's children into Fielding Hall at the Chaney School was a Good Parent Ritual. At the turn of the millennium in tony Wellesley, Massachusetts, just west of the city that liked to call itself the Hub, churchgoing was off, but Good Parent Rituals were the new sacraments. Particularly when other hawkeyed good parents were watching with raptorial intent from their sport utility perches.

Fritz looked at his car phone, thought about calling the office, and thought better of it. He'd be at Playtime—the international toy, video game, and software conglomerate—soon enough. And on the ninth floor of the company's Burlington headquarters, there would be a different kind of heat. A bad wind was blowing at Playtime: a hot and angry meltemi.

Fritz lowered the automatic window and leaned out of the Navigator, craning his neck to count the cars in front. Waves of heat rushed in. Jesus, it was hot.

"*Jesus*, it's hot! Shut the window, will you?"

Thus spake 50 percent of the Precious Cargo. Among the more abrasive habits—and there were many—of Michael Brubaker was the thirteen-year-old's uncanny knack of sinning openly in precisely the way and at precisely the moment that his father was sinning in private. Only two weeks ago they had been in the Natick Mall, father and son, when Fritz and Michael passed a little hottie with exposed navel and groaningly tight bustier pulled across a diabolical set of grapefruit breasts. At the moment that the words "God, what tits!" were forming in Fritz's brain, Michael said loudly, "God, what tits!"

Only thirteen! The disrespect of it, the contemptuous disrespect! And the uncanny way that Michael had figured out how to mimic his father's own failings—to impose on his father the cost of hypocrisy whenever discipline should be asserted.

Fritz knew—the reasons were vague and rather difficult to articulate, but nevertheless he knew—that Michael was too young to be dropping profane epithets around a parent. True, other than for the annual worship-of-children service held at the First Congregational Church of Dover each Christmas Eve (in which children gave piano recitals and then were paraded in as stars, angels, sheep, and wise persons, and tumultuous applause was heard from a large crowd of adoring parental magi, right in the sanctuary), neither he nor Linda had been to services in—how long had it been? So objecting to an infraction of the Third Commandment struck Fritz as a little bit hypocritical. Still, it left him feeling vaguely uncomfortable.

He couldn't see the alcove yet, even leaning out the window. Twelve cars? Fifteen? Of which maybe eleven were as massive as Linda's Lincoln Navigator LX, with its leather seats and side-impact air bags (not that anything would dare broadside this mountain of metal), its surround-sound Blaupunkt audio, and the drop-down DVD screen. On the latter Michael even now was immersed in Death Vault, his latest video game. Fritz could hear stereophonic punches and kicks, stunning groans and grunts, and a glup-glup-glupping that he took to be the sound of arterial blood. When Michael severed a head or a limb, which he did rather frequently, DVD blood spurted from open wounds with anatomical verisimilitude. Michael liked this feature.

"Da-ad, he's been playing that stupid game since we left home. Can't he turn it *off*?"

This from the balance of the Precious Cargo, Fritz's sixth-grade daughter, Kristin.

"Shut up, queer," said Michael.

"Da-ad!"

"Michael!" Fritz barked, but to what syntactic end was uncertain. *Michael* in the general vocative. *Michael* in the undeclined emphatic. *Michael* in the will-you-stop-being-a-jerk-for-ten-more-minutes.

The mission statement of the Chaney School avowed a commitment to nonviolence, tolerance, and economic justice and affirmed the value of every human being, regardless of race, creed, religion, belief, national origin, gender, sexual preference, or physical, mental, or emotional disability. Michael, an eighth-grader, had been a student there since preschool.

The mission statement hung in a glass frame in the Welcome Center just inside Fielding Hall. It was also printed in the school brochure. Prospective parents lauded the school's commitment to these important values. They thought this an excellent environment for students of tender years. For the parents of a five-year-old, nonviolence and tolerance often appeared to be exotic goals. Only later would these parents' educational goals expand to things like chemistry and getting into Andover.

The parents also liked that the Chaney School had been around for a long time. In fund-raisers and at alumni functions, the headmistress, Harriet Tichenor, a stout and jolly lady, always mentioned that the school had a proud heritage. It had been established in 1912. This would bring nods of appreciation. Almost ninety years ago! Founded back when Wellesley was a simple country town! People liked that.

Chaney did have a proud heritage, but it avoided boastful displays. On the contrary, Chaney observed a remarkable and commendable discretion, even reticence, as to the details of the whole heritage thing, mentioning that the school had indeed been founded in 1912 by Louise S. Chaney, a spinster educator, and leaving it at that. Miss Chaney, as she was known, had bought the old Fielding Mansion overlooking the

Charles River that year, and four years later graduated the first class of sixteen students. But her father, Lounsford Chaney III, had more to do with the real establishment of the place. It was from his will that Miss Chaney had inherited a special bequest of $2 million. Lounsford had made these millions, and many more besides, as chairman of the Trans-Atlantic Mineral Corporation, which profited handsomely in the years before World War I by the systematic rapine of the mineral wealth of Liberia. Through his shrewd backing of local warlords, Lounsford achieved substantial savings in labor costs (the company subcontracted the actual mining to the warlords, who in turn used slaves). This effective management tool gave the company a competitive advantage, which it exploited to loot the country of much of its aluminum, copper, lead, and gold. After the war, Trans-Atlantic Mineral closed the mines, thanked the slave drivers for their good work, and left behind a wasteland pocked with slag heaps and leaching pools of chromium and arsenic. But by that time Lounsford had a fortune in excess of $14 million.

Although the school featured an African Appreciation Week and welcomed players of African drums and carvers of African masks, and although two months of the fifth-grade curriculum were devoted to the deplorable legacy of apartheid in southern Africa, the swashbuckling African business career of Chaney *père* was not a focus of study.

It was going to be a while before Fritz got to the alcove. Only there might he safely discharge his own Precious Cargo from the Navigator's restraint harnesses, check the backpacks and water bottles, wave jauntily and cheerily to the other good parents, and leave. Nothing—well, nothing except Linda—was less forgiving than the car-pool lane. There were no shortcuts. It would have been unthinkable simply to evacuate the Precious Cargo *before* reaching the alcove. This would be to commit poor parenting, and at the Chaney School, poor parenting was scandalous. (A child might be hit by an SUV, though none of them seemed to be moving. Still, it might happen.) So Fritz idled, crept forward, idled, and pumped hydrocarbons into the atmosphere.

This stifling Monday morning had already been more than a match for Fritz. It gave him renewed appreciation for his wife. Linda could rise at four-thirty, run four miles on her contact-free gyrotreader, spend a half hour in the bathroom, rouse the kids, rouse the nanny, rouse Fritz, preside over the choices of clothing and healthful cereal, inspect the backpacks, oversee the correct brushing and flossing of teeth, find the shoes, and bellow "Move out!" right on schedule. Linda LeBrecque was the George S. Patton of morning.

But Linda hadn't been around for this particular reveille, and neither was her usual NCO. The new nanny had vanished almost the moment she appeared—within forty-eight hours of her arrival last week, in fact. Poor Nina had been sent back to Ecuador, Linda commenting vaguely that "it just wasn't going to work out." Fritz found his wife's insight impressive, if somewhat opaque, for Nina had barely emerged from the taxi and hadn't done any child care or housework yet. The only data available as of the time Nina was cashiered was that she had a tidy little figure and a certain way of walking that Fritz kind of noticed. From the moment he was able to appreciate that salient point, Fritz suspected that poor Nina was toast.

So now they were nanny-free. To top it, on Sunday afternoon Linda had gone off to San Francisco to some kind of board meeting, leaving Fritz to do morning himself.

Which began, after the toss-and-turn night, with Fritz sleeping through the alarm. Finding Kristin's J. Crew flip-flops had been a crisis (she used to wear sneakers, he thought. Why all this new tension about finding the right flip-flops? And what was with forty-eight-dollar flip-flops?), and then nobody could find Michael's backpack, and then Kristin started wigging out about sunscreen, of all things (at the Chaney School, children must be equipped with sunscreen, without which it would be unsafe to play at recess). So Fritz, who rarely lost patience, and who almost never worried about anything, was in a uniquely uncomfortable state that morning of September 10, 2001. You could almost say he was getting nervous.

The car phone chirruped.

"Fritz, where *are* you?" It was Luce, Fritz's administrative assistant.

"Hey, Luce. I'm in car pool."

"What?"

"Car pool. Dropping the kids off. You know."

But Luce didn't know, couldn't possibly have known. Lucy O'Reardon was a single mother who lived on the top floor of a shingled double-decker in Hyde Park. In her world, kids were still capable of locomotion, as opposed to Dover, where no self-respecting kid ever walked or rode his bike anywhere. Billy, Luce's ten-year-old, left the kitchen by the back stairs each morning at six-fifty, walked six blocks on his own, then rode a school bus across town. Uzbekistan would have made more sense to Luce than the car-pool lane of the Chaney School.

"Frank is calling every ten minutes for you."

"Frank?"

"Yeah, he just came down here. You know—like, I was lying to him when I said you weren't in yet? He didn't believe that you weren't here. Needed to see for himself."

Fritz sighed. Frank Pitts, Playtime's controller, was one of those guys who needed to be worried about something to get his day started. Often he accomplished this by getting to the office at six A.M., making a to-do list, then stomping a lap around the floor, taking note of who hadn't arrived yet.

"What's he want?"

"Something for the board meeting. Is there an Eduvest P&L we were supposed to have?"

"Doesn't sound familiar."

The 2500 cc black Yukon melting asphalt in front of the Navigator inched forward, and Fritz crept up behind it. He remembered school trips to museums and wondered briefly if the Chaney School grounds might become a sort of La Brea tar pits, and schoolchildren a thousand years hence would marvel at the spot where a line of mastodons sank, waiting to complete the Good Parent Ritual. But Luce was talking.

" 'Does he know the board meets today?' Frank asks me. 'Does he know that?' "

Good question. Fritz had gone down to Marion for a morning of sailing yesterday, before Linda left for the coast. He'd forgotten the board meeting was exactly today, so he let the question pass. "They already got the board package last week. What's the problem?" he asked, then said, "Never mind, I'll call him."

Playtime. That's what forty-five years had come to for Fritz Brubaker, a job as senior assistant controller at the toy giant. Playtime did everything from strollers to Action Men, from board games to golf equipment, and they were the biggest video-game manufacturer in the world. They'd made a lot of money on Death Vault, for example. In 2000, the company was sixty-three in the Fortune 100.

"Check it out, douchebags! Level three, *yes!*"

Precisely at this moment in the car-pool lane, Michael Brubaker had reached an important milestone in his young life: level three in Death Vault. This required that he hack off a prodigious number of limbs and heads, then execute a twisting back flip and kick to the jaw of a particularly nimble gorgon near the end of the game. Very few players reached level three in Death Vault.

"You want me to connect you?"

"No, I, uh, I'll call him in a minute. Thanks, Luce." As she clicked off, Fritz muttered, "Shit."

"Da-ad," Kristin protested, again employing the two-syllable variety of the word, useful for marking infractions of parental etiquette.

"That's enough from you." He punched in the office voice mail, optioned through the menu, and sent a message to Frank: "Frank, Fritz, on my way in, see you soon. Try me on the cell."

Fourteen words: two lies and a deception. The first lie was implicit, that he had tried to call Frank; the second explicit, that he was on his way in, for he was motionless in the car-pool lane of the Chaney School (although the alcove was now in sight, and only five mastodons stood between him and enactment of the Good Parent Ritual). The deception was his invitation for Frank to try him on the cell, which Fritz now turned off.

The line oozed forward. Fritz waved jauntily at the other good parents, who waved jauntily back. His cell phone flashed a message, advising him that one call had gone unanswered. "Glup glup," went the DVD. "Yes!" Michael exulted, decapitating a gorgon.

When they reached the alcove seven minutes later, the welcome teacher sang out, "It's a beautiful morning!"

Sprinting around the car, Fritz agreed that it was indeed a beautiful morning, and because good parents should express good cheer at all times, he nodded cheerily at the lipstick-red BMW X5 behind him. He opened the door and said, "Michael. Gotta go, son."

Kristin popped out of the vehicle, backpack slung, water bottle in hand. Without waiting for her brother, she flip-flopped over to the doors. This caused a quiet commotion among the moms in the car-pool lane. As always, they were monitoring the gravel path to Fielding with the cold scrutiny of fashion writers along a Milan runway.

"Is that . . . is that *Kristin?* Well—hasn't she *grown up* over the summer!"

"Only a sixth-grader, and . . . hmm!"

"Cute bob. Not sure I'd let Sara wear pants cut like that, though. Awfully low."

"Isn't she *growing up in a hurry*, that Kristin Brubaker! Wasn't she over at our place for a play date—when was it—last year? Several times, in fact, because her mother *works*, of course."

"Seems a little young to be wearing those J. Crew platform flip-flops. I suppose her mother isn't around to see what she's putting on in the morning."

"It does happen quickly, doesn't it!"

"Her mother is never around, works downtown or something."

"It's too bad about the boy. They say he has a number of issues."

"Wonder if the Brubakers are going to get her into modeling . . ."

Thus went the mental notes being made by the watchful mothers in the SUV line, as the unsuspecting sixth-grader entered Fielding. Back inside the Navigator, there was nothing cute about Michael. He was in the video zone, locked on Death Vault. Hacking a progress through a heap of limbs, more than halfway through level three, Michael had reached a trancelike higher state of digital agility. He was one with the joystick. He felt a surge of unearthly power. Every back flip severed a gorgon head. He had a shot at level four. He could feel it.

"Michael, school time, big fella, let's go." A tight-lipped urgency.

"Wait," the boy commanded in that perfunctory manner so endearing to parents.

"Michael." Very firmly now. Water aboil, lid on but rattling.

"Dad, I'm going for level—"

"Michael!" In a kind of helpless, shipwrecked way, Fritz realized right then that he was losing it. He felt the very chipper but very firm, very attentive gazes of the good parents in the Chaney School car-pool lane. He felt the very courteous but very concerned smile of Mavis boring into his shoulder blades. He felt the blast furnace of a steel mill at his back. God, it was hot.

"Michael!" he shouted again, caught himself, turned to smile at Mavis, tightly, no longer jaunty, a good parent trying to cope with a spirited child.

At the Chaney School, each individual child was valued and cherished. Among its students were no bad children, and no stupid children, and no lazy children. There were only children with issues. Certain children had processing issues, and appropriateness issues, and sensory integration issues, and executive functioning issues. Michael Brubaker had his issues, as was generally and earnestly agreed in the staff room. But violence is never the solution (being, in fact, its own issue), nor is losing one's temper. Fritz was losing his grip on this principle.

Leaning into the Navigator, he spoke in a clipped cadence through set teeth: "Michael, turn that fucking thing off and get out of the fucking car now. NOW!" He was not smiling anymore.

Michael began a calculation. He had inherited his father's quick mind for figures. To Michael, "quantitative analysis" (which was what the Chaney School called math) was a snap. So he began to do the quantitative analysis. He knew that the word "fucking," when directed toward children, was rare—his father's word of last resort. It was the last clear chance before violence. On the other hand, violence at the alcove of the Chaney School, in the full view of the welcome teacher and a line of good parents, would be uniquely profane: roughly equivalent to rape on an altar during church services. It was extremely tempting. To be the victim of such violence would be almost heroic.

Unfortunately, in doing the quantitative analysis, Michael neglected his zone of digital brilliance. Sensing weakness, a gorgon lashed out and snapped his head off, destroying the last of his protective lives and erasing his chance for level four.

The gazes of the other good parents were now fixed on this interesting activity that seemed to be delaying things—just a little!—in the alcove. Perhaps the child had not been properly prepared, properly parented, so that he would issue smartly from the car, well nourished and happy, ready for the school day. Perhaps he had not been properly hydrated?

Michael watched blood glup rhythmically from his warrior's neck with anatomical verisimilitude. "You . . . *asshole*!" he muttered.

"What?"

Michael unbuckled his restraint harness (which was what they called seat belts at the Chaney School), glowered, turned his head away.

"WHAT?"

Fritz turned to the cheerful second-grade teacher and said, "Excuse me." He was no longer losing it. "It" was now lost. He clambered into the Lincoln Navigator and pulled the door shut behind him. This was an unusual development, and the good parents in rank behind were not impatient, exactly, but keenly interested. Was the child in the vehicle all right? The tinted glass impaired their view, but there seemed to be shapes moving actively—perhaps even violently—within the SUV idling at the very threshold of the Chaney School.

Two missed calls had now registered on Fritz's cell phone.

Inside the Navigator, he did not actually strike the child. Heaven forbid that. But Michael, wincing, thought maybe his number was up when he saw his father commit violence on the factory-installed DVD screen, tearing it from the roof of the Navigator and breaking it across his knee (a mistake, because the liquid crystal leaked out on his freshly pressed chinos and stained the new glove-leather seats). Fritz ripped the PlayStation joystick from his son's hands and crunched it under his heel.

This activity made an impression on Michael.

A moment later Fritz escorted his son to the front doors (with more of the drawn and haggard look of the humiliated parent than the cheerful confidence of the good parent) and, returning to his car, waved curtly to the other good parents, some of whom were wondering what that stuff on his pants was. At 8:35 he put the Navigator in drive.

He drove off with Michael's backpack, which contained the children's sunscreen.

2

MAIL BONDAGE

AT THE MOMENT that Fritz Brubaker was completing his Good Parent Ritual by engaging drive in the Lincoln Navigator and preparing to leave the car-pool lane of the Chaney School, a very different ritual was concluding three thousand miles away. Marvin Rosenblatt, fifty-three, an equity partner in the Boston/New York/Chicago/London/Brussels/Tokyo/Fort Myers law firm of Elboe, Fromme & Athol LLP, was achieving climax in the king-size bed of a suite on the twenty-first floor of the Fordyce Hotel in San Francisco. Marvin had completed four and one half minutes of intercourse with Linda LeBrecque, Fritz's wife.

Marvin gasped, collapsed, and rolled over. "God!" he said.

"God!" Linda agreed, to be polite. She was not winded at all.

Breathing heavily, Marvin Rosenblatt lay on his back and (as was his habit after sex) folded his hands on his chest, as though composing himself for an open casket. His breathing slowed. He became calm. His breathing slowed some more, until it seemed like he was barely breathing at all. He breathed in. She waited. And waited. He breathed out. She waited. Then she really waited. Then she told herself not to get alarmed like she had before, that time when he had simply stopped breathing, as though he had forgotten how to breathe at all and it was alarming because he definitely WAS NOT BREATHING and so she simply had to look over and . . .

Then he breathed in again.

Early in the affair this behavior had alarmed Linda, but now she had grown more accustomed to it, although those forty-second pauses still got to her. At last, at peace, Marvin opened his eyes and squinted at the digital clock. Upon this clock the large blue numerals 5:36 now appeared, but Marvin, who was profoundly nearsighted, was not wearing his glasses and could see only blue fuzz.

There was no further postcoital discussion, for each of them was in need of the twenty-first-century cigarette—e-mail.

Marvin fumbled on the night table for his glasses and his BlackBerry remote wireless. Linda reached over to the other bedside table as though to fumble for *her* BlackBerry remote wireless. In fact, her BlackBerry was already in hand. It had occurred to her that it might actually be possible to receive e-mail while having sex, and so, as Marvin got going, she had surreptitiously grabbed the hand-sized plastic lozenge. However, the eensy buttons proved too difficult to work. She also realized that her idea might be misconstrued by Marvin as some kind of insult. So she hid the device in her palm while urging on her lover. But that was over now, and she was rather impatient to get her messages. After all, it was already eight-thirty on the East Coast. People might be e-mailing her.

So, BlackBerry in hand, Linda sat up and joined Marvin Rosenblatt, leaning on the overstuffed pillows piled against the gold brocade of the headboard. Her little fingers began working the eensy buttons. His fingers began working his own eensy buttons. These useful devices enabled the lovers to review their many messages (which contained important news, such as Fred "got your e-mail" and Dave "will call you tomorrow") and to message back with other vital bulletins (such as "Thanks" and "That will be fine" and "Let's be sure to talk to Joan about that"). After the rush of passion, this instant access to the vital business matters in their lives helped calm the lovers and ready them for the day.

To all appearances, Marvin and Linda were an unlikely couple, a fact that had helped them conceal their affair. She was blond, lanky, still possessed of the lovely, delicate bone structure that had made her so striking at thirty, although she had hardened a little. Linda had obliterated fat from her forty-six-year-old body with a ruthless regimen of aerobic exercise, all of which she carried out alone, indoors, in the dark, on expensive machines. She also fought a determined rearguard against age through an array of facial oils, creams, and unguents. This strategy was hard on her, but it worked. First impressions of Linda were generally things like "babe" (so slim!) and "probably lives in Dover" (correct), "smart" (correct), "probably skis at Vail" (incorrect), and "sure seems confident" (quite incorrect).

Marvin was short and aggressively homely. He was a large-featured but quite small man with a narrow chest and arms like No. 2 pencils; except for carrying the wicker hamper from his Mercedes to the lawn at Tanglewood each Friday evening in July, then carrying it back again, he never exercised. His glasses were as thick as Orrefors crystal. He was the shortest man Linda had ever slept with and one of the shorter adult males she had ever kissed. He wore pajamas, even when they were, well, you know. First impressions of Marvin generally were "lawyer" (correct).

But these were trifling limitations. Within the rarified world of Elboe, Fromme & Athol, Marvin had put them to rout. He chaired the corporate department and was regarded as something of a giant. Associates whispered in the halls about his towering intellect, his brilliant deal structuring (also his money); junior partners noticed how learned he sounded when he spoke to boards of directors, without ever actually committing himself to a declarative sentence. Clients weren't sure what he was talking about, but they took comfort from having a genius on their team. Within Elboe, Fromme, Marvin had cemented his key-player status with a paneled office that commanded an unobstructed harbor view, in the center of which Marvin sat at a walnut desk with a desktop of Carrara marble. From this thirtieth-floor stronghold, he spent his days on conference calls, giving careful, immensely detailed, but noncommittal recitations of law to boards of directors, then dispatching teams of associates and junior partners to prepare documents. When he ventured out, it was usually to steering committee meetings.

Physically, you never would have said they belonged together—not the way Fritz and Linda seemed to. Fritz and Linda were both lean, both fair, his face too narrow to be called conventionally handsome but with short-cropped curls framing such an easy and confident smile. She was more distant, though with those model's looks that still turned your head. His sunny smile was a foil for her reserve; his contentment took the edge off her intensity and nerves. They looked like a set. People naturally said "FritznLinda"; even the words were an easy fit. If you saw one at a cocktail party, you expected to see the other nearby. There was a regularity about him to complement her quite irregular beauty, but they looked right together. They formed almost an aesthetic composition, like a bottle of champagne standing next to a single flute. The first is sturdy and convivial and full of cheer, elegant, yes, classic in its shape and line, but familiar and earthy. It welcomes you. Not so the second: the flute is striking, but its beauty is too exquisite on its own. The composition of the two is more comforting. So it was with Fritz and Linda.

Yet the sad fact was that Linda was becoming a better match for Marvin. They were corporate lawyers to several large Boston-based firms, the grandest of which was Playtime. They were worriers, organizers, obsessors over detail, people who shot bolt upright at three A.M. because they couldn't recall if the extra copies of the contract had been FedExed to the client or only mailed. They shared a confidence that everything would go wrong if left to its own devices.

And they shared something else, a burning passion right at the core of the liver: the spirit of I Must Never Be Subject to Criticism. This was the essential element of each of their characters—that they should not be criticized. It had led each of them to a lifetime of good report cards. In schools, in entrance exams, in college; in law school, in job offers, in compensation. It led them to clothe their children a certain way and enroll them in certain schools; to live on certain streets in certain towns; to give to certain charities. (Marvin was Jewish, so he lived among elites of a different town—Newton—but the idea was the same.) It left them ever vigilant to fortifying all aspects of their lives against criticism—criticism that could come at any time from any quarter.

Linda's passion for a good report card had inspired a profound and bitter resentment over the $980,000 in compensation she had been awarded in 2000 by Elboe's management committee. Compensation was the ultimate report card. And while Linda would be the first to concede that nine-eighty was a lot of money (but not *huge* money, not something to get carried away about, not when you considered what they paid at investment banks and mutual funds, and not when you started to think about the cost of living in a place like Dover), the fact was that they paid Strickler (who'd made partner a year after Linda) a flat mil, and that guy Tor Anderssen (who was nothing more than a pretty face in the lucrative insolvency group, and who was in fact a walking malpractice liability) also got a flat mil. To cut her by a trifling $20,000—to pay her less than either one of those two—was a vicious and gratuitous slap. It was a bad report card, and she'd spent most of 2001 fuming

about it. A bad report card offended the cardinal principle. Because
there it was: there was something wrong with Linda LeBrecque, as compared to Strickler and Anderssen. In black and white: criticism.

A corollary to the principle of I Must Never Be Subject to Criticism
was I Must Always Be in the Loop. At 5:36 A.M. in San Francisco, this
was where the little plastic BlackBerries came in. A lawyer's delicate
roots depended for nutrients on loop soil. Nothing else could nourish
him. And nothing could be more dangerous to a lawyer than the desert
rumored to exist out of the loop. In the desert, there were no important
discussions, no key players. No one really knew what happened to
lawyers in the desert. Linda shuddered to think about it.

E-mail was the new loop. This made both Marvin and Linda, among
other things, BlackBerry addicts. Plastic dopeheads. Always ready for a
fix—reaching for an electronic mainline the moment an aircraft door
opened or a conference flagged. And so, although all outside the Fordyce
Hotel was blackness, in the suite there was the ghostly glow of the clock
radio and the gray screens of the BlackBerries. Click-click-click, went the
eensy plastic buttons, there in the darkened bedroom suite on the twenty-
first floor.

THREE THOUSAND MILES AWAY, Fritz was trying to make a left turn
across traffic on Route 30 so as to get on Route 128 toward Burlington.
He was thinking about California. His thoughts were focused not on
shadowy hotel suites but on shadowy numbers: the VD unit's numbers.

"VD unit" was not the approved company abbreviation (which was
VDD, for video development division, although nobody used that, not
even Peter Greene, the president), but it was what everybody called the
series of off-balance-sheet partnerships Playtime used to develop video
games. There was huge money in video games: huge money to be made
and equally huge money to be lost. It cost a fortune to develop the software, what with the immensely detailed and multidimensional images.
You might make a ton on Death Vault, but you could just as easily get
squashed like a bug on Element Master. You could spend two years in
development only to have thirteen-year-old Michael Brubaker return a
verdict in eight minutes.

"It sucks."

No matter the reason: "It sucks," from a thirteen-year-old, was death. Kiss good-bye that $24 million in development, and also the $15 million in promotion and advertising. They were gone. If the thirteen-year-olds said, "It sucks," then, well, it sucked.

The VD unit had its own accounting, out in San Mateo, and the big games were supposed to be accounted for like movie productions— separate, one-off deals, each with its own books. So if Element Master sucked, it could lose only its own shirt, not anyone else's. But more and more of these deals had been done with what was starting to look like parent-guaranty financing. And that meant if Element Master sucked, then maybe just a little bit of Playtime would suck with it. Since June, and that panicked rush to get the financial results for the second quarter in line with Wall Street's expectations, Fritz had had the growing sense that something was amiss in Playtime's numbers, and that something was the development deals in San Mateo.

Take that meeting on August 8. Larry Jellicoe, the CFO, had called them all into his office and made his speech. Frank Pitts (who, as controller, was Fritz's boss) and Rachel Ewald, one of the assistants, sat there awkwardly as Jellicoe told them they had better goddamn well find some revenue or the third-quarter numbers were going to look terrible and the board would not be happy. Then the Street would hammer the stock, which would tank everybody's options. Fritz had heard this kind of speech before, but this time there was a tremor in Jellicoe's voice that spelled P-A-N-I-C.

Last to the meeting, Fritz had taken a seat on Jellicoe's couch. "Should we look through the cushions?" he asked.

No one appreciated the joke. And after that meeting, temperatures had only risen. All through August, e-mails with paper-clipped Excel spreadsheets blinked on Fritz's laptop like fireflies. For the first time ever, he logged more cell-phone minutes than did Linda during the annual Nantucket vacation. All in an effort to find change under the couch cushions. There were weekly and then daily conference calls in which Fritz mainly remained silent, every once in a while venturing to ask, "Will Settles buy off on that?" Which was as polite a way as he could think of to say, "What you are proposing offends the accounting rules, and the auditors won't let you do it."

As the summer rolled into September, the trends at Playtime were bad and getting worse. A couple of hoped-for deals that had anchored the pro forma numbers didn't quite make it to actual sales. Fritz was hearing that charge-offs might have to be taken in the VD unit. Which meant guaranties being called and more revenue to be found under more sofa cushions. These charge-offs would show up in the third-quarter numbers due in early October, and Jellicoe was trying to figure out how to ease this news to the board.

MOTORING NORTH on Route 128, Fritz was also unaware of the unique role of the BlackBerry remote wireless in his wife's infidelity. It would have struck him as fitting, though. Fritz already had a growing sense that this BlackBerry wasn't just another electronic gizmo. There was something deeply malign about it. He'd decided the BlackBerry was the second most pernicious device invented in his lifetime (yielding pride of place only to the MIRV—or multiple independently targeted reentry vehicle—which gave the upper hand in nuclear gamesmanship to whoever fired first). It was one thing to have e-mail. But it was quite another to have e-mail that followed you everywhere, and a device that generated the expectation that you would always be reading it. Fritz had thought of writing an article, an op-ed piece or something, and might have done it if he hadn't been too busy with his cycling and sailing.

He'd had a head of steam going as recently as three weeks ago in Nantucket, when he and Linda had an argument about e-mail over dinner on the back deck of the beach house near Siasconset. The argument broke out during a particularly gorgeous sunset.

"My theory is that the BlackBerry has led to a whole new coarseness in manners," Fritz said to Linda while replenishing her wineglass.

"Hmm?"

"Yes. There are actually people who, in midconversation with you, will reach for their BlackBerries and start checking their e-mail. While you are talking to them. You see this happening all the time now."

It took a moment for the penny to drop for Linda, who was a little preoccupied. A moment earlier she had reached for her own BlackBerry remote wireless, clicking the little button to scroll down and mm-hmming as she not quite registered what her husband was saying.

Then the penny dropped, and Linda looked up. "Cute," she said.

There was a breeze coming across the sand flats to the south. It

caught her hair, lifted it. How lovely Linda was, there on the deck
beach house, in that old faded blue T-shirt she wore, with her hair p
back, and her . . . fingers working the eensy buttons.

"I wasn't trying to be cute. I'm serious. What is it about that thi
that would make you do that? In the middle of a conversation, reach
over and start clicking that thing?"

"Fritz, we were just, you know, talking."

"Right. That's what conversation is. Talking."

"I'm checking my e-mail. It's part of my job."

"During dinner?"

"Yes, during dinner."

"Well, why don't you do a little legal research over dessert? That's
part of your job, too, isn't it?"

She would not dignify this offensive remark, and so, red-faced, she
returned very deliberately to the BlackBerry.

"It's part of your job to check your e-mail right now, while we are
on vacation, during dinner?"

"I don't want to have this conversation again."

"What kind of job is that?"

"I don't think you want to *go there,*" she said with dark significance.
Not thinking you wanted to go somewhere had become a refrain of
Linda's, a phrase of increasing utility. Her conversations with Fritz were
becoming a Rand McNally atlas of places to which she didn't think he
wanted to go.

"Do you see how evil that device is, hon? It's bondage—mail
bondage!"

"I don't want—"

"It's worse than heroin."

"Fine. It's worse than heroin." "Fine" was punctuation for Linda.
Also, repeating what you just said meant that you could say whatever
you wanted and she didn't care, a kind of adult "sticks and stones may
break my bones."

But Fritz didn't let it go. "Linda, honey, the sun is setting. Look at it!
Listen to those wind chimes bong-bong-bonging away next door."

(I've always *hated* those wind chimes, she thought.)

"Here we are in this extravagantly fabulous place: on the deck, with

uini and pesto and a nice fresh chardonnay. With the
ng dinner. Husband and wife. Having a conversa-
 off the ocean. And your fingers are going tap-
pid little electronic worry beads—"

ot stupid electronic worry beads. They—"

 a senior partner in that firm! Why make yourself a slave to
ngle human being, no matter how dumb, junior, or ill informed,
o has your e-mail address? Some mail clerk is sending an e-mail an-
nouncing that the new forms for certified letters are available. And that
mail clerk *owns* you! He's pulling you out of a Nantucket sunset because
he wants you to know, *now,* that the new forms are in."

"You have no idea what you're talking about."

"He owns you. That mail clerk owns you. Why do you want to be
owned by a mail clerk? That's slavery!"

"You're being ridiculous."

But she wouldn't look at him. She was now scrolling up through
the messages she had already read. To make a point. Fritz shook his head
quietly, tried to turn and enjoy the sunset of that extravagantly beautiful
place, even if he had to enjoy it on his own. He couldn't. This was a pet
peeve of his, and he was not good about letting go of pet peeves. "Linda,"
he asked, "what is it about you lawyers? Why do you think you have to
be in touch every single second? 'Hi, look at me, I'm on my e-mail, I'm
on line! I'm in touch!' "

"It's part of the job. The job—"

"That pays for this vacation. That's what you were going to say,
right? It's always part of the job that pays for the vacation or the house
or the whatever. But does e-mail really pay for this vacation? Is that
what the clients want? Someone who's on e-mail all the time? And is it
a vacation at all if you're sending e-mail? Hon, you gotta have more confidence than that."

Oops. Mentioned the confidence thing. Shouldn't have done that.
Arctic air blasted in from Labrador, flash-freezing the linguini and raising goosebumps on the arm. "*Fine,*" she punctuated again. Conversation
over. For a lawyer, she really wasn't his match in argument. But she was
a hell of a meteorologist. She could invoke tundra at will.

Linda left the table and went back into the house through the open slider. He watched her head up the stairs to the bedroom. She took her BlackBerry with her.

"Linda, do you get my point at all?" he called plaintively after her. "Hon?"

AT FIRST it was hard to see anything that different about this BlackBerry device. It was just the latest nifty plastic thing, wasn't it—one more in a regression of smaller and smaller plastic objects? Faxes and copiers became fast and easy to use; computers came out of the word-processing center and onto Fritz's desk; then came e-mail; then cell phones and pagers, then laptops, then bite-sized cell phones and flat-panel screens; and as the stuff got smaller, it got whippet-fast: messages, e-mail, e-mail to which five-hundred-page spreadsheets could be clipped, blue-lined, and cyber-whisked to the world. The lumps of plastic shrank, the batteries got lighter, and the time delay retreated to the realm of quantum physics.

It was only e-mail without a wire, after all. But something was different. "Without a wire" was big. No more hunting in airline terminals for pay phones that would accept your phone jack; no more wondering whether to take the phone off the hook as you slid the credit card. No more waiting for modems. No half-hour seminars with the IT guy about how to boot up the computer in the satellite office. This new lozenge meant you could send a fifty-page document to Singapore and get a response in thirty seconds, all while sitting on a beach in the Maldives. All from your beach chair, all without plugging anything in or booting anything up.

Even bigger than the technology shift was the change in manners it subtly drove. Communication could be instantaneous and continuous, so it must be instantaneous and continuous. Your partner, or your broker, or your lawyer might be away from his computer terminal, he might be in a meeting and unable to take a phone call, but the lozenge was wireless and quiet and utterly portable. And so . . . there was no excuse. An immediate response was demanded. For everything.

The Berry must be read, always and everywhere. In a restaurant, for example. On the train. In the Little League dugout while Johnny was leaning in for the sign. During dinner at home. In the FastLane approaching the Newton tolls. In a theater. And, most curiously, when real people were talking to you the old-fashioned way. What happened on FritznLinda's Siasconset deck was a familiar event by late 2001: Berry talk had trumped larynx talk. All over America, lawyers and investment bankers and deal makers were still flying across the country to meet in restaurants and conference rooms, and yet after coming together in person, the first thing they were doing was checking the BlackBerry. The prospect of an electronic message was more immediate, more vital, more interesting than whatever the poor human being in the room was saying. So the speakers at such meetings found themselves, like priests among penitents, speaking to bowed heads, while the bowed heads prayed to their new god.

3

NUMBERS THE
STREET CAN TRUST

AT THIRTY-SEVEN MINUTES PAST NINE, Fritz Brubaker emerged from the elevator on the fourth floor of the Playtime Tower in Burlington, carrying, in lieu of a briefcase, an L.L.Bean canvas sailing bag with the blue piping peeling off the handles. The bag contained the essentials for the day's work: his running shorts, socks, New Balance shoes, a jockstrap, a gray and blue Patriots T-shirt, a banana, an apple, a raspberry yogurt, and a Demoulas bagel. He passed the glass-walled conference room, passed Milly Kortanek's cube (smile), passed Jerry Adler's (wave), and fetched up to Luce's cube outside his small office.

"Mornin', Luce, how'm I doing?" This was Fritz's standard greeting.

"Not good, boss."

"Where's the posse?"

"Up on nine in Mr. Jellicoe's office. They said—"

"That I should go up there the minute I got in?"

"The *second*. The *second* you got in. Fritz, what's that on your pants?"

"What?"

"That, that silvery, like . . . goop on your pant leg? It looks like glue or something."

"I had a little problem with a DVD player." He wiped at it with the bag. "What do they want, anyway?"

"Something about the board meeting."

"That's today, right? This afternoon?"

Luce nodded. She was wondering how, exactly, a person had a "problem" with a DVD player. "The board meeting is at eleven," she said.

"Oh . . . kay. Guess I'll head upstairs." Fritz turned for the elevator.

"Ah, Fritz?" she called after him.

"Yeah?"

"Maybe you want to leave that? In your office?"

She was pointing at his Bean bag. "And you might want to, you know, see if you can wipe that stuff off your pants."

"Oh, yeah. Thanks, Luce," he said.

FRITZ GOT ANOTHER couch assignment. He made a quick reconnaissance. Jellicoe was in his teak command post, with the Bloomberg units on the desk and the top-on-bottom dual seventeen-inch flat-screen computer monitors on the credenza behind him. Gathered round the eminence were Frank Pitts and Rachel Ewald. And there with them was Milt Dorfman from sales. Curious. Still more curious, Milt had brought a deflector shield with him, one of his achingly lovely but brain-dead assistants, curvaceous bottom perched just on the tippy edge of the couch. She smiled gorgeously at Fritz. Beneath her linen blazer, she wore a sheer white something or other that clung for dear life. The rest were all present and accounted for in the formal dress-down uniform of the finance department (men: pressed khaki Dockers, iron crease showing crisply on the pant leg, navy socks, penny loafers, crisply starched blue button-down shirt; women: pleated and pressed pumice cotton J. Crew trousers, pumps, blouse). Fritz tried to catch Rachel's eye, but she wouldn't look up. She was locked on spreadsheets.

Suave Milt's honey-on-the-couch deflector shield, Rachel in the bunker: these were ominous signs.

What the hell has that rascal been up to, wondered Suave Milt as Fritz took his seat. Frank Pitts noticed, too. There was some kind of . . . it looked like . . . gross! . . . on his pants. Like it might be . . .

Jellicoe looked up severely, and then he noticed it, too. What the hell?

Suave Milt didn't want to speculate about why this guy was late to the meeting, but there was this . . . oh, man! . . . right on his . . . this . . .

Christ, Brubaker!

. . . stain . . . this *stain* . . . right on Fritz's pants!

Jesus. The male minds in the room all leaped to the identical absurd conclusion, expressed loathing, then embarrassment, then envy, and then settled back down. Better focus on business.

A problem had developed with the California regents deal on Point 'n Learn!, the lead product in a suite of educational software targeted at schools. Playtime's lawyers put this venture into a bulletproof off-balance-sheet partnership known as Eduvest, part of the VD unit. The partnership had real revenues, as Peter Greene liked to say, not like all these other e-commerce vaporware companies. So Playtime's equity investment in the partnership had been conservatively valued at $75 million on the basis of a discounted cash-flow analysis—because, after all, Point 'n Learn! was a hot item, and Eduvest had real cash flow. So Playtime hadn't felt the need to show a liability on its books.

Except that there kindasorta was this timing problem with the "real" revenues, as Milt from sales was saying when Fritz joined the meeting. There was this side letter. Somebody in finance had forgotten to ask for the side letter, was the way Milt put it.

("Did they ask for it, Les?" asked Milt. "Oh, no, I don't think so!" answered lovely Les, the deflector shield.)

This was all when they were doing the Q2 numbers last June, Suave Milt explained. Finance hadn't asked for this letter that said that if the board of regents changed its mind for any reason in its sole, absolute, and mercurial discretion, then it could return Point 'n Learn! from the 2,650 high schools for a full refund and cancel the four-year contract. Finance hadn't asked for that letter, said Suave Milt, and he guessed, shrugging, that finance didn't get it into the contract file when the auditors at Settles Bartlett did the Q2 review. And three days ago some lawyer from the California board of regents had written a letter. It purported, Suave Milt was saying, to reserve rights to opt for its $17 million back and cancel the four-year, $12-million-a-year contract that constituted 43 percent of Eduvest's 2002 revenues.

"Purport?" Jellicoe demanded. "Purport? It doesn't purport to do any goddamn thing. It cancels the contract!" He rubbed his temples.

Suave Milt shook his head empathetically. No, Larry didn't understand, Larry was overreacting. Milt had talked to the California guys. Reservation of rights, this was a lawyer thing. An ass-covering thing the board of regents needed. He'd talked to the California guys and gotten the sense—the strong sense—that they would like the product. There might be timing issues, that was all.

Jellicoe pressed the cross-examination. It began to come out that one of Milt's people had mentioned that maybe on some of the other sales there kindsasorta might be a few more of these side letters out there. Kindasorta most of the Point 'n Learn! deals had to be done that way, actually. Not that anyone would cancel, it was just a timing problem. A nonissue, as they said in sales. "I mean, Missouri and Illinois talk to California, you know?" What could Suave Milt do? Everybody knew California got that deal.

Everybody except Playtime's CFO. And its auditors. And its shareholders. Jellicoe, elbows on his desk, was in double-handed temple rub. "How many?" he asked through clenched teeth. His voice had gone all quiet and flat. It was beginning to tremble a bit, the way the sky does on an August afternoon in North Dakota—the way it does just before it rips open from horizon to horizon in an arc flash of heat lightning, setting off concussion bombs of thunder and lashing the prairie with rain and hailstones.

"Well, Larry, hold on," Milt answered. "Wait a minute. You guys called up last June—who was it, Les?" Suave Milt from sales would not be so rude in this group of friends as to name names himself. So now Leslie of the bright smile and luscious little pom-poms was hoisted on shoulder-top for her cameo cheer. "We got a call from Frank," she said brightly.

"Right, anyway, whoever, we got a call," Suave Milt said, magnanimously waving off the little matter of whom he was prepared to fuck over big-time if people started pointing fingers (we're all friends here). Validated by the pert and lovely smile of Leslie the deflector shield, Suave Milt went on, "And you guys wanted to know did we have that California thing, and I said yeah, we had it, I mean, they signed, you know? You remember, Frank. I said they signed, and you guys said great, send over the contract. And I said, you want the whole file or just the—"

"How . . . many . . . of . . . these . . . are . . . out . . . there?" Jellicoe repeated, in a voice now dangerously stripped of affect. The barometer in North Dakota was headed south of twenty-nine like a number-eight lead sinker in a still pond, and women were rushing out back to gather in the washing from the line and find the dog.

"You never said did I want the whole—" Frank interrupted.

Suave, smooth Milt! Unruffled Milt! Finance guys got ruffled, but not for nothing was Suave Milt in sales. Milt's smile was unshakable. He used Frank's question to ignore Jellicoe's. "I think I did, actually, Frank. Anyway, whatever, we weren't asked for the whole contract file, I mean, all the detail and the specs and all the goddamn paperwork and correspondence. We would always send finance whatever they needed to see, wouldn't we, Les?" (An earnest nod from the tasty assistant. Absolutely! Whatever finance wants, finance gets!) "You said send over the contract, am I right? So we sent over the contract." Milt smiled his beatific, team-spirit, don't-fuck-with-me-Frank smile.

You had to say this for Milt. His smile was adamantine—nothing shook it. If you confronted Milt with evidence of fraud, he would tell you it was just a timing issue, and if you mentioned the indictment for pederasty, Milt would say he had talked to the guys in the prosecutor's office and they were actually pretty much okay with it.

At the end of the couch, Fritz hadn't been following this minitrial. He'd seen it before. The CEO says, Get me numbers (nothing else! no bad news!). The CFO says, Get me enough information to book the numbers (not so much that I *can't* book the numbers!). The controller mines for enough to book the numbers. Sales plays along. And when it blows up, corporate is shocked, absolutely shocked, at the news. It hadn't been the first time.

None of this interested Fritz. He was busy doing the math in his head. The sales guy was telling them 43 percent. That meant it was more like 60 percent. Sixty or 70. Eliminate 60 percent of projected cash flow and Eduvest was way underwater, a few atmospheres down, down with the bug-eyed lantern fish, down in the dark dank depths. You couldn't recognize the investment anymore, not without an appraisal, because of these losses. The accountants knew what the auditors would say: Playtime would have to show the loss on its books, and that would trip a bank covenant. Seventy-five-million-dollar charge, $25 million bank payment due. Ba-ding!

"Milt, for Chrissakes, I ask you for the *contract*, I expect you'll send the relevant *documents*." Frank was whining. He was bleeding and wounded, but at his flank there was only silence. How had this turned into Milt versus Frank? Where were the reinforcements? How the hell had Jellicoe dodged this again? Waiting for support that didn't seem to be coming, he pressed on, "How could you *fail* to mention—"

"It's a hundred-mil charge," Fritz interrupted. "Direct hit to the P&L."

CRACK! The storm broke. Lightning rent the Dakota sky. Cats cowered under porches, and kids ran for the kitchen. "I KNOW WHAT THE FUCK IT IS!"

And they all stopped, dead as blocks of concrete, frozen in their conversational tracks. Larry Jellicoe had gone purple. They all saw him and then averted their eyes, embarrassed. Even Fritz felt awkward. Silence. For a few moments the only sound in the room was the splishy-splash sound from Jellicoe's peace fountain, burbling faintly in the corner. (After Jellicoe's last visit to the cardiologist, his wife had installed it on the credenza.) He was . . . he was purplish still. Would he burst?

This was too much tension for the CFO of Playtime to be showing. After all, Playtime was a Fortune 100 company with a market cap in excess of $50 billion. A $100-mil charge was a bad thing, but it wasn't a meltdown. Jellicoe went back to rubbing his temples while his staff wondered what else he knew that they didn't.

"I know what the fuck it is, Fritz," Jellicoe repeated, more quietly this time. Everyone let out a breath. The storm had abated. "We're not here just to do math, for Chrissakes. Let's have a little creativity. We've got a lot of brainpower in this room. Let's put it to work."

"It's a timing issue," said Milt. "I've talked to the California guys. We talked to them . . . yesterday, was it, Les?"

Les nodded brightly.

"It was a good conversation, a *good* conversation," said Milt. "Wasn't it, Les?"

Oh yes, her eager smile and earnest nod and delectably scrumptious curves were saying, desperate to bring some sunshine back after that fearful storm. It *so* was a good conversation! The best! Everyone was totally friendly and nice throughout the conversation!

"You guys are making too much of a deal out of this," Milt said. But they weren't listening to him anymore. They had heard enough from Suave Milt.

"Got to book it," Fritz ventured.

"Book it?" They all looked at him incredulously.

"Sure. You're going to sign the Q, Larry."

"Just like that? Book a hundred-million-dollar charge?"

"This isn't that hard," Fritz said. "We've got to put honest numbers out there. The company screwed up, now we know it, so we've got to put it out there. We'll take a hundred-million-dollar charge and restate the Q2 earnings."

"That's a relief!" said Larry Jellicoe, the storm cloud massing again, purple-black and menacing. "That's *comforting*. It isn't that hard! I'm so glad, Fritz, that you've dropped in to assure us that it *isn't that hard*. Just restate Q2. Take a hundred-mil charge! Easiest thing in the world. And the stock in the toilet by morning!"

"Oh yeah, the stock will dip," Fritz agreed. "That's what happens with stock. Goes up and down. And probably the class-action sharks will have a suit filed by return mail. To add to the other ones. Two more years of motions for Elboe, Fromme. But that's not our department, that's legal. We just weigh sheep, Larry, we don't fatten 'em. This isn't a close call. We've got to take the charge."

"Do you have any idea what the board will say? In fifteen minutes when they hear about the billion-five offering Peter wants to—"

Shit. Jellicoe caught himself too late. "That's highly confidential," he said.

They all nodded obediently.

"Board-sensitive."

Oh yes, *absolutely*.

"It doesn't leave this room."

Suave Milt and Frank Pitts and Rachel and luscious Les all redoubled their obedient nods. A secret. Not a word to be breathed outside this room!

This news wouldn't just *leave* the room. It would rage across the office like a wind-borne wildfire across the August prairie. Because a $1.5 billion offering meant a new acquisition, and a new acquisition meant merging a division or two, and merging a division or two meant rifs (which was what they called firing people, a "reduction in force"). But you could be sure that not a word would be voice-mailed or e-mailed or written or otherwise communicated in any traceable fashion.

The only one who wasn't nodding was Fritz. You didn't have to be a rocket scientist to guess that Peter Greene would be filling his war chest. Peter was always one acquisition ahead of Wall Street. This made it impossible to compare one year's numbers with another's, for one thing. And you could always blame lousy financials on acquisition costs, because you were always acquiring. It was easier to conquer countries than run them—that had been known since Alexander the Great's time. The same was true of corporations.

Fritz did some more quick math. Forty percent of the company's assets were investments in off-balance-sheet partnerships like Eduvest. Have this one blow up, and Morgan and Credit Suisse, not to mention Settles, would be crawling all over every one of them. And if they started crawling all over everything, what else would they find in the VD unit? What would they find the Hare Krishnas in San Mateo had been up to?

Say there's 20 percent padding in the revenues. They'd get nervous and call it 50. That would kill the offering. Or mean really big write-offs. Or . . . worse.

"Ask *them* to sign the Q, then, Larry," Fritz said.

"They pay us to sign the Q."

The Q was the Form 10-Q, a form that the Securities and Exchange Commission required a public company to file quarterly to show the world its financial health. The chief executive officer and the chief financial officer had to sign it. But if things ever got hot later, the CEO would always say he relied on his CFO for the numbers. The next 10-Q would be due in October, after the third-quarter numbers were final.

"With all respect, Larry, they don't pay me. They pay you. So sign it if you want to."

"I appreciate your help, Fritz," said Jellicoe acidly, "I really do."

"Apparently not," Fritz said in that way he sometimes had of seeming not to understand what play had been called by the team players. Fritz had about 2 percent of his ego invested in being the senior assistant controller of Playtime and, unlike the other guys in the room, about 98 percent of it hedged in stuff they couldn't touch. Like sailing.

" 'Cause, Larry, I'm trying to help. I don't think they pay you to go to jail. This is a public company. No one in this room is going to put a misleading financial statement out there, right? I mean, this may suck for Playtime, but the decision isn't hard. We need to give the Street numbers it can trust. The revenue was bullshit, so we have to take the charge and restate it. Done. What am I missing here?"

Everything. Everything was what Fritz was missing there, and had been missing for a long time.

AT TEN-FIFTY Larry Jellicoe met with Peter Greene in the chief's office. Greene was on the couch, the bifocals at the end of his nose, his studious pose. In the Hepplewhite chair beside the couch sat Don Fink. Fink's business card said that he was Playtime's senior vice president and general counsel, but his real job was to be Peter Greene's senior vice butt-boy and general talisman.

Ten years earlier Greene had been through a nasty litigation. Three days of depositions in a frivolous lawsuit claiming that Greene had made an oral agreement. Playtime had paid millions—just millions!—to its lawyers at Elboe, Fromme & Athol, and then had to be shamed in a grubby courtroom in Cambridge. The oily little hack who represented the plaintiff, and who did not come from a decent firm like Elboe, and certainly hadn't gone to good schools like the partners at Elboe, had nevertheless survived all the motions that Elboe, Fromme—which had been paid millions!—was supposed to crush him with. And the thing went to trial. To a jury! Then millions more had to be paid out, all because the Elboe, Fromme lawyers had screwed up and handed over a couple of *totally* confidential, *totally* private memos Peter Greene had written that never should have been handed over and were *totally* misunderstood and taken out of context by the lunkheads on the jury.

Greene had learned his lesson in that case. The slightest little thing gets said or written down—you jot a note, for Chrissakes, that you might have said in passing, to be polite, you know, in conversation you said sure, something sounded like a good deal, just making *conversation*—and a gang of envious beauticians from Medford ring you up for $15 mil. But he'd learned something else, too. If a lawyer was present, then things were "privileged." That meant things stayed where they belonged: private. Outside the grasp of the Hun-like hordes of auditors, class-action shysters, shareholders, investors, media hacks, investment bankers, analysts, and other parasites who longed to destroy civilization. Fink's job was to be available twenty-four hours a day to sit next to Greene, so the meetings would be protected by the attorney-client privilege. Greene privately thought that Fink was pretty useless, although he did bring one particular virtue to the table: he'd been well trained not to be Subject to Criticism, and he thirsted to be In the Loop. That meant he didn't seem to mind that Peter Greene would give him about as much warning of plans as a man gives his dog. Like the dog, Fink was just glad to be riding in the car, too.

Don Fink, in the Hepplewhite chair, had studied his board package and was looking forward to the meeting. He had not broken it to Peter Greene that his attorney superpowers were not quite what Greene imagined—that his mere presence would not act as a heat shield against all atmospheric effects. The privilege only worked if somebody was genuinely asking for or giving legal advice, which was the furthest thing from what was going on in most of those meetings. But Fink didn't trouble Peter Greene with these nuances because, first, he *liked* being at the key meetings, and second, the explanation was too complicated and Greene wouldn't have wanted to hear it.

Greene was handsome in a New York investment-banker kind of way. He had that hot-cocoa, always-tan look. That Grecian Formula look. He looked great in videos, photo ops, earnest discussion on a shop floor, giving thoughtful, over-top-of-bifocal concern to some document the photographer had handed him, or making a dramatic point at a shareholders' meeting. He had the snappiest formal dress-downs. His shoes were shined to mirrors and his chinos ironed to attention. His shirts stood straight as cardboard. His hair was slicked back. And his voice—he could have been a radio announcer.

Then there was Peter Greene in person, the vital, active way he'd come at you physically and grab hold of your arm. He was always striding by. "Good to see ya," he'd say, shaking the hell out of your hand as he executed a three-quarter-reverse ball-of-foot pivot, which was one of the moves he used to avoid breaking stride. The other favored move was the hand pat on the shoulder, but this worked only when you were headed in the same direction and he was in the passing lane. As far as Peter Greene was concerned, it was always good to see ya, but he never stopped to catch up with ya—never even broke stride, because there was always an assistant waving him toward a car that was waiting to take him to an airport.

Peter Greene didn't like paper. The lawsuit had taught him that paper lived in files and reproduced like hamsters and you could never never kill it. Ultimately, it always fell into evil hands and then got blown out of context by ignorant judges and the gangs of beauticians they rounded up for jury duty. With a grudging exception made for financial statements, he didn't like to see paper, and he never signed anything other than the most innocuous letters or press releases written by Don Fink. Answers to Peter Greene questions had to be brief, pithy, and unwritten. "Yes!" "No!" PowerPoint slides at board meetings were about as far as he'd go. Once in a while you'd get an e-mail from Peter Greene. It would be general, and short, and in large blue letters. It would contain exclamation points, and talk about being entrepreneurial, and platforms (nothing you did had to be justified on its own merit—it was always a platform for doing something else), and thinking outside the box, and being well positioned, and getting into this or that space. It would be signed "Best regards, Peter." These Peter Greene e-mails would then become the subject of a vigorous internal debate, like the sayings of Nostradamus. What the hell did they mean?

Larry Jellicoe came into the office and nodded all round. He sat down uncomfortably.

"Larry, good to see ya, good to see ya," said Peter Greene, looking up over his bifocals and switching from scholar mode to active mode. "Okay. Don, Larry, we got the board in ten minutes. We want to get them excited about the new offering, about diversifying this company. It's clearly the right thing to do. Clearly."

The room nodded. Clearly it was the right thing to saddle Playtime's shareholders with another $1.5 billion of debt so that Peter could go buy some new company. Clearly.

"What was that voice-mail thing about Eduvest?" Greene asked.

Larry cleared his throat. "Ah, Peter, there could be a problem with the Q2 revenues."

Jellicoe got the over-the-bifocal freeze. Then the pause for effect. "How much of a problem?"

"We might have to restate."

Peter Greene leaned forward, still staring over his bifocals, like the secretary of defense upon learning that the Mexican army had stormed across the Rio Grande. That was the effect.

"Restate? Say again?" Peter asked.

"Yeah, I've just been with sales, and—"

"You shitting me? How much?"

"Could be, well . . . kindasorta a hundred or so." ("Well, it might be a hundred thousand Mexicans or so, Mr. Secretary.")

"A *hundred?* Jesus, Larry."

In Peter Greenese, "Jesus, Larry" was three declarative sentences. "Jesus" meant, "This is a very big problem." "Larry" meant, "The problem is *your* problem, Larry." The abrupt conjunction of the two words said, "I don't need to hear the details." But Larry, who understood all three statements distinctly, ignored the third and began to tell the woeful tale of how sales had hidden the side letter, and now there was this new thing from the California board of regents. "Which is just a reservation of rights letter, but—"

This showed signs of becoming too much data for Peter Greene. "Will Settles *make* us restate?" he interrupted.

"Probably," Larry said. Greene looked at Fink, and Fink nodded sagely. "Probably" was a good answer, because it was always probable that accountants would be a pain in the ass. Don Fink didn't know very many accounting rules other than that one.

"Can you roll them?"

Don gulped. He would have preferred another formulation, like, say, "Can we discuss this with Settles?"

"Can I roll them?" Larry answered. "I, I don't think so, not on something like this."

"They did fourteen mil of consulting business here last year. Is it a close call, some accounting thing? Should I call Settles's managing partner—what's the guy's name?"

"Ah, no, Peter, it's not close. I don't think. From an accounting perspective."

Not close? Don Fink awoke. If it was not close, then there must be some blame to manage. (Fink had missed the third point of "Jesus, Larry.") He harrumphed and started to say, "I'm wondering, Larry, how this—"

"Never *mind*," Greene cut him off. "Larry, do a report by tomorrow to Don on how this happened. Make it privileged and all that crap. I don't want to be copied on it. Okay?"

"Okay."

Silence. Done. Larry ventured, "Ah, Peter, how do you want to handle—"

"I'll take care of the board. We're expecting some unevenness in the numbers. The economy is uneven. Which is *exactly* why we've got to diversify this company a little bit, and raise a prudent amount of capital to do it. We'll point that out to them. I don't know if it would be material to the meeting agenda to start speculating about restatements." ("Listen, gentlemen, we're not going to get the president all riled up about a few Mexicans on the border until we've confirmed the intel on this. Maybe it's just a mariachi convention or some goddamn thing. Check it out first.")

Alarm bells were ringing in Don Fink's head. He was general counsel to Playtime. He owed allegiance to the company—an inanimate but nevertheless legal person, and this meant, roughly, that Don's client, the person or thing he was supposed to be protecting, was Playtime's board of directors, not Peter Greene. Public companies and their boards could be liable for sitting on information like this for too long. Lawyers of companies ought to tell them that, or *they* could be liable.

On the other hand, Fink knew that when Peter Greene had hired him, it wasn't to worship at an altar of legal correctness. Fink was paid $350,000 a year to cover Peter Greene's ass; specifically, to ward off evil in meetings through the privilege force field, and otherwise to be Greene's general-purpose Secret Service agent, scanning the crowd for enemies and, if it came to that, taking a bullet. If Greene detected any fastidiousness on the lawyer's part, any metaphysical lawyer bullshit about fiduciary duties to the board, Don Fink's resignation would be accepted before he knew he'd written it.

And, not that it made any difference to the issue, in the current market, Don's options were all upside down.

"Peter," Don began, clearing his throat, "I don't know if it's prudent to . . ." His voice trailed off.

Larry said, "If we have to restate, it will be out there, and—"

Greene repeated, "Larry, has Settles told us we have to restate yet?" ("Has satellite intel confirmed the precise number of Mexicans, General?")

"Well, they don't exactly know about this yet, so—"

"So they haven't told us to restate. There's nothing to report." Peter pressed the button on his intercom. "Nancy, call down to Hanscom, cancel Chicago, and tell them to get the G-IV ready for a flight this afternoon to Sacramento, okay? Thanks!" He rang off, pushed another button. "Donna, find out who we know on the California board of regents, and figure out who we've given money to, governor, senators, any congress-men, all of them. Okay? Meet me after lunch on this. Thanks!" He pushed the buttons again. "Marie? Hi, it's Peter. Find me three pet causes of the governor of California. Find out if his wife runs a charity or any-thing. I need this in an hour. Okay? Thanks!"

Peter Greene put the phone down and looked at his watch. Fink and Jellicoe rose with awkward smiles. Fink was formulating his file memo—how he would remember this conversation—basically, that he'd suggested management advise the board about problems with the finan-cials, and that they'd said the matter was preliminary, as an accounting matter, and they were pursuing it fully in an effort to understand whether the accounting issues were material. Then the CEO had made a few quick phone calls, directing his staff to investigate the, er, ac-counting issues surrounding the problem.

It was 11:01 A.M., time to pump up the outside directors for another round of bond financing. Then time for Peter Greene to go to California and roll the board of regents.

4

AMHERST COLLEGE, 1976: ECONOMICS 101 (FIRST LECTURE)

"WHAT IS 'VALUE'?"

Professor Hugh Vorblen raps his ferule sharply, three times on the lectern. Economics 101 will come to order. When the murmurs in the Red Room—the grand old lecture hall in Converse—die down, the lecturer commends himself to the students by bringing out a glass, which he places on the lectern, and a bottle of Molson Golden ale, which he places next to the glass. The students view the green bottle with interest. Then the lecturer uncaps the bottle and pours the ale into the glass. He holds up the glass for them to see.

"What is the value of this glass of beer?" he asks. Professor Vorblen wears a three-button dark green tweedy suit. And a blue bow tie. He is a short man, and the light streaming into Converse reflects off his glasses, making it difficult to see his eyes. He doesn't look like the kind of guy who would value beer very much.

"Anyone?"

There is no one.

The lecturer asks, "Is it the cost of the hops, and the cost of the barley, and the cost of the water?" He puts the beer back on the lectern and strides to the blackboard. Soon he is filling the board with figures: commodity prices for malt, hops, barley; equipment costs, labor costs, utility costs.

"Just do the math, class, and we'll have the value of the glass of beer, right? The beer is the sum of its parts. Surely."

The lecturer returns to the lectern. The glass of beer is standing tall, its head firm. "Or is it?"

It seems a trifle hot in the lecture hall this afternoon, a little . . . close. The students heard the sound that the beer made, frothing into the glass. They saw the bubbles gather into the head. They haven't taken their eyes off the glass, and now they follow it as the lecturer takes it in hand, walking up the steps to the rear of the lecture hall. The beer is golden and clear. It looks cold and refreshing.

"Maybe the beer's value is purely an aesthetic matter? Can it be calculated by asking a master brewer to critique clarity, tang, taste, color? Shall we set its value based on purely objective or even aesthetic criteria? Anyone?"

The class looks uncertain. This does not seem quite right.

"No? No aesthetes? Of course not! You're economists! Budding investment bankers, accountants, stock traders! Immune to all that sentimental rubbish. Not an aesthetic bone in your bodies, right?"

Nervous laughter.

"Well, all right then, let's see if we can understand value a different way. Anybody thirsty?"

More laughter in the auditorium.

"It is hot, after all, but my beer is cool. Your throats are dry, parched . . . you've been crawling through the desert of economics, and I hold in my hand the oasis. Anyone want my beer?"

Tentative hands are in the air. Then not so tentative. A forest of hands.

"Ah," says the lecturer. He smiles. "We have hands. Anyone know what the hands represent?"

The golden liquid flashes as the sunlight catches it, the light diffused and refracted by the forest of hands.

"The hands, dear students, are *demand*. You now understand fifty percent of the first law of economics. But we need to look at the other fifty percent. Let us now inquire into the nature of . . . *supply*. What is the current supply?"

Puzzlement. What does he mean, exactly?

"Has anyone *else* in the hall got any beer?"

More wry laughter. A searching glance from the professor, who has returned to the podium. "No? No beer at all, any of you? You've come to class unprepared!"

Laughter.

"The doors are shut. No one can enter my hall. No one can leave. Oh, dear. That means *my* beer constitutes *all* of the supply. For the balance of the lecture, I have market power in beer. Indeed, I have a *monopoly* of beer. No undergraduate cometh unto beer but by me."

Laughter. This guy is great! And that last line, some of the students think, sounds familiar from somewhere.

The lecturer smiles. "Well then, let us determine the value of this beer in the way we economists can understand. We know who wants it. Now let's explore who wants it the most."

A hand waves. Then another.

"You, sir, gentleman in the lemon-yellow golf shirt and Bermuda shorts. What will you pay for my beer?"

The lemon-yellow gentleman will pay a dollar. But blue jeans at the back of the room offers $1.25. A young lady in a green T-shirt, two dollars. And so on. In the end, the beer sells for $3.05. Congratulations to the left tackle in the tenth row.

"Now, while we were exploring the nature of value, did you notice what drove our dialogue? Was it the cost of the hops? The cost of the barley? The cost of the water? Was it the aesthetic worth of the beer? Did any of the bidders argue with me about these things?"

Heads shaking.

"No one even discussed those things. Would you say it turned rather on the question of how many people—the demand—were chasing this one glass of beer, the supply?"

Clearly it had. "Supposing I'd had six glasses of beer, or sixteen. Suppose I'd had one hundred glasses of beer. Do you think the gentleman in row ten would have paid three dollars and five cents? Yet it would have been the same twelve ounces of ale that he consumed with such *relish*."

Nervous laughter. The left tackle grins sheepishly.

"So, I ask you, what was the *value* of that beer? Was it three dollars and five cents?"

Frowns of concentration around Converse Hall. The undergraduates are wondering about that very question themselves when the professor says:

"Class dismissed."

5

A GOAT IN THE PARLOR

WHY WAS LINDA LEBRECQUE HAVING AN AFFAIR? She frequently discussed this question with her therapist, whom she saw every other week for an hour, at a cost of $400 a session. (BlueCross BlueShield would cover only $220 of this cost, but the copay was only slightly more expensive than Linda's hairdresser.) The discussion went on at some length but reduced mainly to one theme:

"Serves him right."

Dr. Helga Schadenfrau's office was an airy parlor in a rambling Wellesley Hills Victorian with pale blue shingles and white shutters. The room was painted light lemon and had a nine-foot-high plaster ceiling and lovely bay windows. The doctor had worked hard to eliminate the sterile-office feel that can be so nontherapeutic. She and her patients sat across from each other on easy chairs. Chai and other beverages were available on a coffee table. Antique-white roses were arranged in a vase of blue glass. Classical music played very faintly from two small Bose speakers in the bookshelves, surrounded not by medical tomes or journals but rather by books that would give the patients a sense of serenity. These were books about children with incurable cancer or lovers returning after twenty years: in other words, books that had been on *Oprah*.

Most of the patients were wealthy professional women in their thirties and forties. If Dr. Schadenfrau had been dosed with sodium pentothol, she might have admitted that very few of them had any confirmed diagnosis of depression or cognitive/emotional disorder. The doctor's income (around $500,000 per year) was mainly a function of her willingness to advise BlueCross BlueShield to the contrary, and to spend her days in an exquisitely comfortable living room listening to rich women gripe.

It served Fritz right. Dr. Schadenfrau found this an interesting explanation. She might have asked another patient why she justified her own conduct by its relative immorality rather than attempting to portray it—if only to herself—as moral per se. But Dr. Schadenfrau declined to pursue this line of inquiry with Linda. Confronting the patient in this manner would not have been therapeutic (and might indeed lead the patient to take the highly nontherapeutic step of canceling her biweekly $400-an-hour sessions).

So they discussed *why* it served Fritz right. This elicited a frightful bill of particulars, including that things came too easily to Fritz; that he probably was having all kinds of women himself, since women swooned around him and always had; that he was too athletic; and that Linda had to do everything to support the family. Well, not everything. He made $155,000 a year as senior assistant controller at Playtime, but what was that? Did he think $155,000 was going to pay the mortgage on their $2.1 million brick mansion? Did he think $155,000 a year and a few stock options were going to support the children's education? Linda and Fritz's retirement? The summer house in Nantucket? It barely covered the nanny and the nanny's car (when they could get a good nanny, which was getting harder and harder). Fritz had been content to float along in the assistant controller's office, not working to get ahead, when he could have been a CFO a long time ago. No, not him. He wanted to leave at five, he wanted his sailing and his latest thing, this cycling (don't get me started on that!), leaving Linda with all the responsibility in the marriage. He didn't even check e-mail on weekends. He was just lazy, and if it weren't for her, they wouldn't be able to afford Dover at all. So it served him right.

Dr. Schadenfrau wanted to explore the interesting character defect of Fritz's athleticism. Well, Linda explained, anything that had to do with a ball and bat, or a racket, you name it, was effortless for him. Which was the point—he did only what was easy. From Ping-Pong to Frisbees, golf to tennis. "He doesn't play golf that much, and he's what, a six handicap? I took a solid summer of lessons that cost me twenty-five hundred dollars, and I still can't even address the ball. Tennis? I've taken lessons for years. I play regularly in the summer. The only time he plays, as far as I can tell, is at the annual law-firm outing, where, just to make me angry, he sizes up the best young player and then crushes him."

Why was this a bad thing?

"It's bad because Fritz doesn't have to work for anything. I've had to work for everything. I still do. I run on the gyrotreader, I manage the kids, I work my fingers to the bone"—this was a figure of speech; the manicurist did an excellent job maintaining Linda's nails—"to create this effortless life that he enjoys, this . . . this . . . paradise that he's living."

"Paradise? How do you mean?"

"I mean cruising along effortlessly, living in a lovely town like Dover without a care in the world. *He never does anything he doesn't want to do.* Becoming CFO might mean playing some golf with some of the financial guys. But they aren't good enough golfers, so he's not interested. Or maybe working a little harder. Or trying to get along with the people in the organization. Or checking his e-mail once in a while. Being a member of the team. Playing the game, so to speak. But will he do that? No. So it serves him right."

This was deep, this resentment of Linda's. Dr. Schadenfrau thought that they had only begun to unearth its roots.

Linda said, "And maybe the most infuriating thing about him, the most infuriating thing of all?"

"What is that?"

"What he would say if he knew about—you know, if he knew about it."

"The affair?"

"Right."

"What do you think he would say?"

"It's not what I *think* he would say. I *know* what he would say. I know exactly what he would say and the way he would say it."

"And that is?"

Linda cleared her throat. Dr. Schadenfrau could tell that she had rehearsed the delivery.

"Here's what he would do. Suppose I came to him and said, very seriously, very gently and contritely, said, 'Darling' "—Linda hadn't actually called Fritz "darling" in about five years; this was for show—"darling, we need to talk. I've a terrible confession to make. I've—I've been seeing another man.' Right? Suppose I said that?"

"Yes?"

"He'd ask, 'Who?' And I'd say, 'Marvin. Marvin Rosenblatt.' "

"Then he'd say, 'Marvin *Rosenblatt?*' Just like that. '*Rosenblatt?*' Putting the accent on that syllable that way, you know? Like 'Not just anybody, but Marvin *Rosenblatt?*' Incredulous. Shocked. But shocked in an intellectual way. Like if someone said when you combine orange juice and rubbing alcohol in a blender, you can create cold fusion. That kind of shocked. Like 'Really? Orange juice? Cold *fusion?*' He'd go, 'You, Linda LeBrecque, are having an affair with that guy Marvin *Rosenblatt,* the one I met at that cocktail party at the Algonquin Club?' He'd repeat that a few times. Then he'd go— Well, it's what he wouldn't do. He wouldn't get angry. Or sad. He wouldn't storm upstairs or out of the house. He'd be, like, totally *fascinated.* He'd want to study it. In a scientific way. Like 'This is so interesting. I need to understand this. This is fascinating—why a woman who could have me, who in fact *has* me, would choose to sleep with Marvin *Rosenblatt!*' He wouldn't be hurt at all. 'Hon,' he'd say, 'do you find Marvin *Rosenblatt physically attractive? Is it his *mind,* do you find his *mind* compelling? I met the guy once, and he talked about revisions to the materiality standard in the SEC regulations for half an hour.' He'd say something like that. It makes me really angry, how he'd say Marvin's name."

A melody from Schubert was playing softly on the Bose speakers. Dr. Schadenfrau listened to it for a moment, digesting what she'd heard.

"Why do you think that makes you angry?"

"Because it's so disrespectful of Marvin."

"We're discussing how you imagine he would say the name?"

"Yes, of course. Because he doesn't know. But he would. If he knew."

"But he hasn't actually been disrespectful of the name?" Dr. Schadenfrau was confused and struggling to understand. It was important to get at the root of this anger, so she found herself pressing the patient rather more than usual.

"Because he doesn't know about Marvin. But he would if—" Linda paused, frowned. This wasn't coming out quite right. "It's how he would act if he knew about the affair. If he knew about the affair, he would say Marvin's name in that kind of mocking, disrespectful way. Which makes me very angry. It would be very disrespectful of . . . of Marvin."

"You're angry because you think your husband would be disrespectful of the man with whom you're having an affair," Dr. Schadenfrau repeated slowly.

"Well, when you say it like that . . ." Linda's voice trailed off. She felt that Dr. Schadenfrau had missed the point somehow.

The doctor added more notes. This matter, she could see, ran deep.

Linda went on, "If you might mention that Marvin Rosenblatt has made himself an extremely successful career, and that he has earned the high regard of some extremely distinguished corporations who trust him implicitly for advice on matters of the highest importance to their boards of directors, and that he earns a healthy seven-figure salary—earns by the sweat of his brow—if you mentioned that to Mr. Phineas Adams Brubaker, you know what?"

"What?"

"He wouldn't care."

"He wouldn't?" Dr. Schadenfrau drew the question out to express the appropriate disapproval of such carelessness.

"Not at all. Not in the slightest. A million-four a year. Big deal. 'Is he funny? Does he raise goats?' "

The doctor looked up from her notes. "I'm sorry. Goats?"

Linda sighed, rolled her eyes. The matter of the goats was another thing about Fritz that was just so vexing. "There's this man Jim Feeney in Dover with these goats," she began. "This very *unfortunate* man who's some kind of back-to-the-earth type or something, I don't know, but he wants to draw attention to himself by having these rather disgusting goats that he keeps in his yard, and the neighbors quite rightly are upset, and the town's been trying to do something about it because it's not appropriate, you know? I mean, Dover is a family community. There are children. You can't just have . . . *goats.*"

She made a face, as though a goat had entered the airy Victorian parlor in Wellesley Hills and started to nibble on the roses tastefully arranged in the blue glass vase. "Well, anyway, you know what Fritz says about this? We get a perfectly decent call from a concerned neighbor asking us to help with a petition to address this problem, and do you know what he says?

"He says, 'What's wrong with that? Jim lives on Farm Street.' And I was, well, Dr. Schadenfrau, I can tell you that I was quite shocked and

I said, 'Excuse me, Fritz, we're talking about a health issue here, we're talking about a safety issue. What does the man's *address* have to do with it?' And Fritz launches on this tirade, I mean a tirade that had me quite concerned about Fritz having a number of *issues*, and having repressed a lot of hostility, and I've been telling him for years about how he ought to think about a little therapy for himself, which of course strikes him as the most absurd thing in the world, I mean, how could Mr. Fritz Brubaker, for whom everything is so easy, how could you suggest that it might help *him* a little bit to consider some of his *own* issues and lower himself to a little therapy, oh no, not him, and—"

Dr. Schadenfrau interrupted gently. "What was . . . what was the business about goats again?"

"Oh well, the usual thing with him. How phony the town is. How false and phony everything is. He's always going on about that."

Dr. Schadenfrau felt there was a thread here, even one that could be important clinically. But she'd lost it. "I'm sorry," she said, "I don't quite follow."

"Fritz says they want to have a street called Farm Street and pretend it's all country-cute farm country, but as soon as a guy on Farm Street actually has a farm animal, there has to be a petition. So he says, 'I'm circulating a "Save the Goats" petition! If they want to call it Farm Street, then they have to let Jim have his goats!' "

The Schubert proceeded *diminuendo*. The doctor made careful notes. Linda paused, wrinkling her brow. "What were we talking about— before the goats?"

"I, I'm not sure," Dr. Schadenfrau confessed.

"Oh, I remember. Fritz would *prefer* the guy with the goats. That was it. It wouldn't matter to him that a man like Marvin Rosenblatt has worked very hard to accomplish professional success. But with some man who has smelly goats and is trying to cause trouble, Fritz would feel much more affinity."

"Than with his wife's lover."

"Right. Well, no, that's not the point."

"No, of course not. I understand perfectly," said Dr. Schadenfrau, nodding to validate her patient's correct and appropriate rejection of this juvenile behavior. "Yes, this kind of thing can be upsetting," she said kindly. It was therapeutic, she felt, and important to the course of therapy—particularly to a long course of therapy—that the patient feel some validation.

The doctor smiled beatifically, her end-of-session smile, and then she leaned forward with the earnest but formal end-of-session lean. The session had drawn to a close. "The twenty-first, then, same time?"

"Oh, is it an hour already?"

FROM THE DEEP-TUFTED LEATHER of the chair in his sumptuous corner office in the Russell Senate Office Building, the senior senator from the great state of Michigan stared out the window at the dome of the U.S. Capitol, a perfect tit gleaming in the blackness. It rose up proudly in the September night, brilliantly illuminated, taunting an old, tired, fat man with its saucy whiteness and erect nipple. He sighed. These days Jack Oldcastle saw taunts all the time. The nasty, wrenching cramps in his gut taunted him, the way he wheezed taunted him, that blotchy purple stuff on his belly and around the corners of his eyes taunted him, the damned corn on his big toe taunted every step, the investment banker the Republicans were going to run against him in two years (the son-ofabitch with the thirty-two-inch waist and the $100 mil in the bank)—he taunted him, too. That gal Nell had lined up for him two weeks ago Thursday, he knew she'd taunted him the moment he left Nell's house in Georgetown. Even the U.S. Capitol, his home for thirty years, seemed to have joined the chorus line of taunters. "Hey, Oldcastle, you fat old fool! You bag of pudding!" it seemed to be saying in the September night.

For tonight there was a venomous new taunt. A single sheet of paper rested on the dark green leather inlay of the desk, a piece of pugnacity bearding him from the blotter surface. It had penetrated his sanctum, and it lay there braying at him. Hey Oldcastle—please take notice! Hey Oldcastle—if you fail to appear, judgment may be entered against you! Hey Oldcastle, you sack of shit, we're talking *termination* here!

The nerve of this paper. Dealing like this with the senior senator from the state of Michigan? Without even a telephone call or a warning?

(Well, all right, the guy claimed he called a couple of times, but Christ, do you expect a United States senator to be available to take every god-damn call that comes in from every tin-pot landlord?) And now, to drop this in the mail to him, where any aide might open it—and one in fact had. To send it off to him as though he weren't the senior senator from Michigan! As if he weren't Old Number 31!

An eviction notice! Was he, Jack Oldcastle, some mug on the street—someone you could hire a seedy solo-shop lawyer to evict, sim-ply because he might be a month or so behind on the goddamn rent for his Washington apartment? Well, all right, a couple of months, but did he have time to read the mail from these rent grubbers when he was busy doing the people's business? And we weren't exactly talking luxury living here. It wasn't like they paid you in rubies to be a United States senator. Oldcastle had to maintain a place in Lansing and a place in D.C. The divorce had creamed him, of course, Dolly had just cleaned out all the accounts with that. And now this—what if the press got ahold of it? The fact was, he was a bit short right now. There had been some club dues to pay, almost a year's worth, in fact, and Dolly's divorce guy in Lansing was a human shop-vac: all the guy did was whine and suck money out of you. He would run to the papers in a heartbeat if Old-castle missed a payment.

There it sat, the feisty demand, threatening him from his own desk in the privacy of his own sanctum. Threatening Jack Oldcastle, Unsung Hero trophy winner, Old Number 31! Distracting him from the peo-ple's business! Well, he'd have to talk to Ralph Moldy about it. Ralph—or Rafe, as the aide preferred—was his chief of staff. He was a Boy Scout about campaign finance, which could be a problem. The guy was fas-tidious as hell, like with that Rafe business—calling himself "Rafe" as though he were some goddamn English baronet when his name had an *l* in it. He probably squats to pee, Oldcastle thought. But he could also get shit done. RafeRalph would have to get this particular shit done, and quick.

How had this happened to the winner of the 1959 Michigan State Unsung Hero trophy, a legend of the Michigan State gridiron? (Well, a letterman, anyway. And he had that trophy up on his bookcase.) A deco-rated marine (well, a graduate of boot camp at Parris Island); a giant in

Congress (and out of it, for that matter). He was chairman of the Senate Banking Committee. He was a senior senator. He was—Oldcastle caught sight of his face, reflected in the glass below the dome—a . . . *really* fat old guy.

These days Oldcastle caught sight of himself in a mirror only by accident. He wasn't merely plump anymore, wasn't portly, wasn't a big-boned man with a joe, like you might forgive in a respectable ex-jock. That thing around the middle wasn't just a beer gut. Jack Oldcastle was a goddamn hillock.

He sat alone at the desk, the pale light beneath the lamp's dark green Tiffany glass illuminating the leather on the desktop and throwing the shrill letter into pearl-gray contrast, as though it were an actor about to give a soliloquy, a raucous stage villain. Sad to say, this sanctum was the one place on earth that felt like home anymore. Dolly had taken the house. The apartment in Northwest Washington they wanted to throw him out of? If it weren't for the scandal, they could have the sonofabitch. They could have the stained beige carpet, the walls decorated in modern American motel room, the couch with sprung springs and the rest of the rented veneer furniture. They could have the single frying pan on the stove, with its quarter inch of old bacon grease. They could have the fridge with its half bottle of capers and the jars of pickled herrings and olives, the pizza boxes with ancient slabs of congealed dough and cheese fat curled into Finnish sandals. They could even have the goddamn fifth of vodka in the freezer. (It was almost empty, anyway.) If it weren't for the press, he'd say good riddance to all of it. Sure, there had been some financial problems. Those REIT investments he'd made—the ones the bankers promised him were a sure thing—he might as well have set fire to the money. The snake developers who'd gotten him into those shopping-center deals in Wayne and Pontiac, they'd diluted him down to a sliver before selling the shopping centers for a killing. These were the same bastards for whom he'd greased a few skids on brownfield permits with the EPA. Frankly, his club tab was killing him. He couldn't risk getting cut out of there, so he had to keep that one vaguely in sight of break-even.

No, this sanctum was his home. It was ornate, with its oak paneling and oxblood leather couches, its plush red carpet, its flags and burled walnut desk. On the office walls were pictures—all those pictures of young Oldcastle the fire-breather, the podium-pounding Oldcastle, the stentorian Oldcastle, Oldcastle shaking Johnson's hand, and Tip O'Neill's, and Carter's; Oldcastle with the English prime minister, Oldcastle with Anwar Sadat, Oldcastle with Kennedy and Cuomo and that idiot Clinton.

He took inventory of the photographs, searching them, as he did most nights, with the watery eyes of an old lover. Old election-night shots, shots of Oldcastle and Dolly and the kids (dutiful Dolly, always that pinched, forced smile, never once looking like she could loosen up and enjoy an evening), shots of the old gang, Oldcastle and Ned Poins, old Buddy Bardolph, a party at Ned's sister Nell's. Lots of shots of the Gad's Hill Society. Photos of Lancaster, too. Oldcastle and Lancaster on the sixteenth green at Gad's Hill, when the president was still a kid and Oldcastle was still handsome, before his face had mottled—before sagging jowls, before his proud nose exploded like a yeasty muffin (before liver spots, for Chrissakes), before his eyes got so yellow and rheumy, before the blotches began showing up on his belly, before neck paunch and extra chins and the massive gut and the blubbery buttocks and the trouser-straining thighs that rubbed so hard that he had to waddle sideways.

There again was the Christmas shot, 1974. Oldcastle before Dolly left him and the kids moved up and out. The kids . . . hadn't had a word from any of them in over a year. Dolores, with her lawyer husband and faux château in Grosse Pointe, never called anymore. Butch, the ski bum in Aspen (or was it Steamboat?), he hadn't heard from in years. The oldest son, John Jr., a fancy investment banker on Wall Street with a big spread in the Hamptons, you'd have thought there might be some gratitude for all his father had done. Maybe a stock tip or two, getting him in on one of those IPOs, anything. But no.

The senator felt a shooting pain in his gut, grimaced as he looked at his watch: nearly nine P.M. He'd been getting more of these pains, but it was time for a drink. He shot a furtive look at the doorway—empty— then swiveled around to the credenza and opened the rather cleverly disguised fridge to withdraw the Stoli. Jesus, how'd it get down to a quarter bottle? He'd have to get that stocked up again. He fished a glass out of the drawer and poured himself one. You could do only so much of the people's business in one day.

Had to be careful, though. The doctors had found ulcers and were driving him crazy about the drinking. That goddamn Moldy was a petulant wet nurse, always materializing with a look of earnest concern, always speaking so correctly. Oldcastle glanced furtively over at the doorway again—still empty—then took a hit of the vodka. He felt the happy fire, felt the warmth crawl down his throat, tickle his breastbone, and spread like a blanket across his chest. He took another drink and smiled. That felt better, more . . . fortified. The whiny lawyer letter could fuck itself. He looked up at the white tit taunting him through his window.

"And you can fuck yourself, too!"

"Senator?"

"Oh, not you, for Chrissakes, Moldy!"

The senator's senior staffer had materialized like the ghost of Banquo, right in the office doorway that a second ago had been empty. He stood there regarding the great man with a look of polite concern.

"Yes, sir?"

"Jesus, you surprised me! Don't you ever knock?"

"Sorry, sir. You know what the doctor was saying about—"

"I know exactly what the pissant doctors are saying, Rafe. Don't start with what the doctors are saying. You look like you could use a drink yourself."

"Yes, Senator. But no, thank you. I was about to check out for the evening. I thought I'd drop in to see if you were all . . . if you needed anything."

Oldcastle grimaced and settled back into his chair. He spoke conspiratorially. "Well, actually, I could use your help with a small matter, Rafe."

"Yes, Senator, certainly."

"C'mon in here and sit down, for Chrissakes." The senator frowned at his aide with the precisely trimmed beard and the receding hairline. He watched the young man walk across the office and take his seat. Goddamn gays. So correct and formal all the time. So fastidious. (And that Rafe business!) So goddamn helpful. You had to abuse them—they wanted it that way. Some kind of deep-seated psychological thing.

Oldcastle went on, "There's this misunderstanding with my landlord I need you to take care of."

"Your landlord? Ah, what kind of misunderstanding, sir?"

Oldcastle waved at the notice with his fat fingers and brushed it across the desk, not deigning it the respect of picking it up. It lay there under the green glass of the dim desk lamp.

Moldy craned his neck to read it. "Ah, if I can ask, how much do you owe, Senator?"

"How the Christ do I know, Rafe? I have the people of Michigan to worry about, not some real estate developer in Northwest Washington! It's probably a couple of months behind. Three, four months, maybe, I don't know, maybe more. It's been a goddamn busy time, as you know."

"Yes, Senator, very busy."

"So take care of this, would you, please? If the *Detroit Free Press* gets ahold of this, or the TV, or the Republicans . . ."

"I understand." But RafeRalph looked uneasy. "Senator, I . . . do you want me to run down the outstanding amount and . . . I'm a little . . . what exactly—"

"Rafe, for Chrissakes, you're my chief of staff. I want you to take care of it. Get with Jerry and take care of it. Okay?"

Jerry Rubin was the campaign finance director. The guy with access to all the DNCC money that was supposed to be spent only on campaign finances and never to be diverted to personal use.

"Yes, sir," Moldy said.

"Thank you, Rafe. Now, if you'll excuse me, I need to get ready for the hearings tomorrow."

"Yes, Senator. Good night, sir." Moldy rose and slipped quietly from the office. Had a door opened and closed? You could never be sure with RafeRalph. He sort of flickered like a hologram and then wasn't there anymore.

The hearings tomorrow—what the hell *were* the hearings tomorrow? Oldcastle couldn't remember. But it didn't matter. At last there was peace. He refilled his glass and took another warming gulp. The yammering lawyer's letter was gone. Moldy had whisked it away and was going to take care of it. The goddamn guy with the Gilbert-and-Sullivan name was going to get some shit done. The senator sat alone in the dim office, nursing the Stoli. The warmth spread across his chest and gut with a hint of burning, a stabbing around the edges, but only a hint, and if you took another gulp, the warming pleasure came back, at least at first, to overwhelm that nagging stab. He took another gulp, and began to drift off into reverie. He was staring at one of his favorites: a photograph of four guys in a golf cart, Buddy Bardolph, the three-time Oklahoma congressman, and Ned Poins, Oldcastle's old lobbyist pal, asleep in the back; Oldcastle at the wheel, smoking a cigar and holding up four fingers, and next to him, the handsome young face of the kid who had gone on to be president, holding up all five. The Gad's Hill Society.

It had been twenty years. One afternoon at the Gad's Hill golf course in suburban Virginia, they played a shot a hole (a shot of tequila, that is) on the back nine until Bardolph launched his cookies into the rough alongside the seventeenth fairway and Poins fell asleep in the cart. This left Lancaster and Oldcastle to stagger on to the last hole, which Oldcastle, using a sand wedge, four-putted for a one-stroke victory.

He sipped his vodka and smiled. Those had been the best days of Jack Oldcastle's life. Better than Michigan State football, better even than the first election night. The Gad's Hill Society's only requirements were greens fees and a strong liver. In those days the usual procession was from the Gad's Hill course to its nineteenth hole, and thence to the Georgetown "salon" of Ned's sister. Eleanor Hasty had married a venture capitalist with a town house in Georgetown. He never seemed to be around, and Nell made up for his absence with the companionship of the Gad's Hill Society and drinking bouts long into the night. They'd tell prodigious lies about their legislative and sexual triumphs and, once in a while, rely on Nell's discretion to set up an assignation upstairs.

(Two weeks ago Thursday, Nell had arranged for a daybed in a ground-floor guest room. Oldcastle wasn't managing stairs very well anymore.)

Hank Lancaster the Younger had been a member. In the late seventies, soon after the kid arrived in Congress, he'd joined this group of wastrels. His father, the elder Lancaster, was on the way to his presidency, and the name alone was enough to help his kid narrowly upset Representative Percy, the old hothead from Missouri.

Oldcastle and Lancaster had first met at the course, playing a round one Friday afternoon after each had snuck off from hearings. Lancaster was a Republican, but politics didn't matter to Oldcastle when it came to the society. After that first round on the course, Lancaster bought Oldcastle a drink and asked why it was that the guys in his own party expected him to be so serious all the time.

"They're so eager to have me succeed my father, they're like to drive the goddamn life right out of me, Jack."

From that day on, Oldcastle had a special liking for the kid. It didn't hurt that Lancaster was made of money and always good for a round at the bar. So they had struck up a friendship. There was something about Lancaster, you could tell he was headed for big things.

An old memory came again to visit. He and Lancaster have tumbled into Eleanor's house in Georgetown for insults and stories. It is Nell's voice in the old days, with the southern lilt she had before the smoker's hack overtook her. "Oh, my dear knights errant, guardians of our nation. Come you in and have a drink," she says.

"Don't give Oldcastle a drink, Nellie. He's already drunk as a Welsh Baptist."

"Drunk? Do I understand that the member from Missouri says I am as drunk as one of his back-holler brimstone hell roarers?"

The memory flickered like candlelight, then flamed brightly again: they are in the summer house, Oldcastle telling the story at Nell's, in the back garden on an evening in May . . . drinking gin in tall glasses, listening to june bugs bombard the screens, the eager faces around him hanging on his words, the taste of the gin and the sound of the merriment as he tells the story of his triumph . . .

"In one day I took eleven votes from Buckram, and you should have seen the fear in the eye of that sonofabitch when I saw him in the robing chamber that evening! I took them on one by one, man to man. I made the round of their offices, and they couldn't stand up to the force of our argument. They wouldn't look me in the eye and defend that vote. Eleven of Buckram's men I took from him!"

Hoots are heard from the other Gad's Hill regulars. "Eleven votes?" Poins asks. "It was seven votes the last time I heard this goddamn story."

Lancaster speaks—yes, there is his face, too, swimming out of memory and into the darkness: "Maybe it was seven last time, but it was four the time before that, I could swear."

And then Bardolph: "Oh yeah, it was four then, but the first time I heard this whopper, Oldcastle was saying he'd turned two votes. One of those votes was Jack's own, with the other a drunk from Arkansas whom Jack outlasted at the bar of the Mayflower, and for which vote I believe Jack promised to pick up the guy's bar tab."

"A filthy lie!" Oldcastle declares with the rumble of leadership. "It was Oklahoma." Merriment all around. Laughter and happy derision. Bardolph laughing so hard he starts involuntarily blowing his nose.

"Did he pick up the tab?"

Bardolph honking uncontrollably: "The sonofabitch is still after him for the money!"

Another rumble from the leader of the pack, and Oldcastle shouts them down. "You and all your female relatives may have carnal knowledge of each other. Which would be nothing new in Missouri. Nellie, there's a darling, I'm awfully dry . . ."

The rattle of ice cubes melting in the bucket, a fresh glass of gin, the smell of magnolia and lilac, the sound of crickets, it all came back to him, but most of all, the laughter. Laughter that he lived for. Laughter that he never heard anymore.

The candle of his memory flickered and went out. Oldcastle nodded, woke, stared down at the empty glass. He blinked, looked at the clock—Jesus, it was past midnight. Across the room, the wall of pictures stood mute in the darkness. They were the great memories of Oldcastle's life. But it had all changed. There was no Gad's Hill Society anymore. Poins was a broken-down sonofabitch without room on his night table for all the pill bottles, and listless Buddy Bardolph watched the stock quotes on the television all day. It had been years since the senator had seen him. Oldcastle could barely hoist himself in or out of a golf cart.

And Lancaster? That was the saddest thing of all.

In the early nineties, during the elder Lancaster's presidency, Hank the Younger shot to fame and fortune in Congress and then the Senate. In those years Lancaster began to slip away from Oldcastle. He was always making excuses.

"Come on, Hank, let's have a drink at Nell's."

"I can't, Jack, I've got *Nightline*."

"You're always on goddamn *Nightline*. Are you blowing Koppel?"

And it was true. (Not that he was blowing Koppel but that he was always on *Nightline*. Or *Good Morning America*. Or the Sunday-morning talk shows.) The columns were filled with predictions about Lancaster the Younger. Long analyses identified him as one of the up-and-coming Republicans, but with lots of hand-wringing about his wastrel past and whether the president's playboy son would measure up to the responsibility of higher office.

"What do you know of foreign policy, or of economics, you little diapered prince?" Oldcastle would fume. "Does Koppel know what a pantywaist you are? What a bony-buttocked little pencil dick?"

"Economics? Well, what the hell do you know about economics except that lesson about how a guy on a Senate committee that controls legislation can get greased?"

"An important lesson, young Hank the third, and one that has stood me in good stead."

"Actually, we Lancasters go back further than that. I'm the fifth, if you want to know."

"The fifth generation of dry-goods merchants, maybe. Of trust funds from ascetic Baptist skinflints with a thumb on the scale and too goddamn much money. When is that Lancaster line going to breed a man, for Chrissakes?"

Until there came a day when even the banter died. Hank wasn't playing the game the same way. He wasn't sneaking away from roll-call votes. He was always giving speeches. Whenever he'd happen to bump into Oldcastle, a rarer and rarer event, he wouldn't insult him like a real friend. He'd smile at the old man and exchange a hurried greeting, like a guy at his high school reunion, meeting an old buddy who was the coolest kid in the sophomore class and still is . . . the coolest kid in the sophomore class.

The year 2000 brought Lancaster the Younger's triumph: the presidency. Oldcastle had hoped for a cabinet post, was sure of obtaining one. Of course, Oldcastle was a Democrat and all, but the administration would need balance, a sop to the opposing party, a guy to try to line up votes in a pinch. Oldcastle would have been a perfect secretary of Housing and Urban Development. He was getting on in years, and the last few campaigns, not to mention the divorce, had pretty much shot the wad. HUD would have been the right sort of payback for a life of devoted friendship; that was the way Oldcastle saw it. Not too much spotlight, lots of opportunities to meet rich developers—it would have been perfect. Didn't friendship count for something?

But it didn't happen. All through the campaign, Oldcastle's phone didn't ring. After the election, not a word, not a goddamn word from his old pal. Oldcastle would never forget the first time he called President Lancaster, the day after the inauguration, to congratulate him. When Lancaster came on the line, Oldcastle shouted out, "Well, my boy, you've gone and done it. God help your sorry ass now!"

"Excuse me?" the president answered.

"Hank, Mr. President, I mean, it's me—Oldcastle, for Chrissakes!"

"Oh, Jack. Sorry, old buddy, didn't recognize your voice."

Didn't recognize his voice. How could you not recognize the Oldcastle voice? It was a voice like the foghorn on a ferryboat, for Chrissakes. The cold way he said it, too. Jack would never forget that, the way Hank Lancaster had cut him dead on the first day of his administration, with no more regret than a man slicing the bruise out of an apple. He couldn't have said any more cruelly that everything had changed. No more drinking bouts at Nell Hasty's, no more special camaraderie. And no one would be calling about a cabinet post.

"Sure, sure, Mr. President . . . I understand."

Oldcastle came to again and blinked at the clock. One-fifteen A.M. Another news cycle gone without a call. Even the *Free Press* and the Detroit TV stations didn't call much anymore. No Republican would ever take Michigan, but Oldcastle could almost feel a vacuum gathering around him. He reached back around to the credenza, but the goddamn bottle was empty. Old fat Oldcastle. The senior senator from nowhere. He was tired. Tired but not quite done, he thought as his head sagged. "Not quite! I've got some fire in me yet! It would be a big mistake to write me off too soon, big mistake!" His head lolled. "Some sonofabitch thinks he's going to write me off just yet, he's going to make . . ."

This was the last half thought that formed in the senatorial cerebrum before Oldcastle's consciousness simply switched off, like a lightbulb. The senatorial neck relaxed suddenly, and the outsize head of Old Number 31 hit the desk like a sack of cement. The senator never felt a thing. In a moment he was snoring peacefully.

LIKE ALMOST EVERYONE ELSE IN AMERICA, Fritz Brubaker was watching a television by the time the south tower fell to earth. A crowd had gathered in the conference room next to Rachel's office. Down the tower rumbled, and up rose that fearsome white cloud of smoke and dust. Fritz looked at his watch: a minute before ten A.M.

"Oh, God," someone said. "Oh God in heaven! Those *people*!"

Fritz looked away from the screen. Luce was crying silently.

Fritz had been to the World Trade Center only last February, for a meeting with some insurance brokers. He remembered riding that elevator. It had seemed like forever. A forever of floors filled with a forever of offices, a forever of people, people like those around him right now: secretaries and finance people and traders and fund managers and accountants and insurance agents. From Jersey and Westchester, from Manhattan and Brooklyn and Staten Island. Who had settled in with their cup of coffee a few minutes ago. Who had been on phones and in meetings. Now riding that mighty tower to earth, riding down in the horrible majesty of a white cloud of smoke and dust. Now entombed.

Luce steadied herself on a chair. Fritz put his arm around her shoulder. Next to her sat Rachel, gray as fireplace ash, also silent. Someone else was sobbing. Fritz looked beyond the television. Outside was nothing but a gorgeous autumn morning. It did not seem possible.

It was ten o'clock. On the television, the north tower stood alone, belching flames against a sky of brilliant blue, wearing a dreadful skirt of smoke and dust. Fritz did not want to be watching when history repeated itself. There was nothing to do but go home.

———◆———

ONE OF the nice reliable things about Linda was how she behaved in a crisis. You didn't have to find her or worry about her. She would find you. Even in the horrific instant when Luce appeared, stricken, at his doorway, with the news that a second plane had hit one of the World Trade Center towers—that this was some kind of attack—Fritz knew that within ten minutes his telephone would ring, and it would be Linda. And it did, and it was. Then Linda was off on her telephone rounds, off to find out that the kids were okay, that her parents were okay, that her office was okay, that no jets had crashed into the house or Fielding Hall.

They must have spoken five or six times through that day. The phone companies were deluged and saying that calls couldn't get through, but the phone companies had not reckoned with Linda Le-Brecque. She got Fritz at work and she got him in the car and later, that afternoon, she got him at home.

"Is everyone all right?" she kept demanding. Yes, he told her, they were okay; no one had strafed Dover since the last call. "By the way, hon, you're the one stranded out there. How are *you* doing?"

Well, she was fine, but she was worried sick about the kids. This was—this was awful, this was unthinkable. All those people! Wasn't Fritz down there last winter for meetings? The whole thing just gone, all those people, all those firemen and policemen, just . . .

She had to stop. She was crying. He felt his own voice choke as he told her, "Okay, baby, it's okay." He felt so foolish saying it. Of course it wasn't okay, not the slightest least bit.

"And everything's shut down!" she said. "There are no flights, there's no way to get home—it's madness, madness!"

She didn't know what she was going to do. She had to get back, but there was no way back. Somebody had said something about a bus. (This brought Fritz one of his few smiles that day—the thought of his wife on a Greyhound bus.) Maybe she'd stay out there. Did he think they'd re-open the airports in a couple of days? Nobody knew. Maybe she'd rent a car and drive.

"Well, that's not a bad idea, hon. Take a trip across the country. Spend a little time. When's the next time you'd have a chance to do that?"

Was he crazy? A trip? Take a vacation? She had to get *home*!

❦

AT FOUR in the afternoon, the telephone rang. Fritz answered, thinking that maybe Linda had figured out some way to get back. But it wasn't Linda. It was a man's voice, and familiar, although in the vague dislocation of that afternoon, it took Fritz a moment before he could place it. Then he realized it was Frank Pitts on the line.

"Oh, Frank, hello."

"Terrible, isn't it?"

It *was* terrible. Yet it seemed strange to Fritz to be standing in his kitchen, phone in hand, discussing how terrible it was with, of all people, the controller of Playtime, Inc. The morning had focused Fritz's mind on the people who were important in his life: his children, his wife, his mother, his brothers, a few old friends. And on the people in those airplanes, in the Pentagon, in those towers, anonymous to him but somehow kin. Pitts's voice, by contrast, seemed almost that of a stranger. Only this morning Fritz had been scheduled to meet with his boss. But that seemed like a long time ago. And why would this guy, of all people, be calling him to commiserate for the dead?

"Just terrible," Pitts continued. "Comes at a bad time, too."

Oh. That's why.

For all his usual equanimity, Fritz knew this conversation was going to outrage him. The little rodent would be the type of person to bring a copy of the will to a dead man's funeral.

"I suppose pretty much anytime is a bad time to be burned alive and then crushed to death in the collapse of an office building," Fritz said.

Frank hesitated, decided to leave the sarcasm alone. "No, I meant a bad time for Playtime."

"Did we have an office in the World Trade Center? I wasn't aware of that."

Frank sighed. You could never just get down to business with Brubaker. Always the smart-ass. But this had been a hard day on everyone, so Frank let it pass and began to explain. How this would lead to panic and confusion and God knows what, and that was the worst thing for a leisure company.

Fritz began to steam, and then the bubbles began forming in his brain.

Pitts went on, oblivious. Orders would fall off. Christmas would be terrible. The board would be on Larry Jellicoe. And Larry Jellicoe would be on Frank and Fritz to work the numbers hard. The third quarter was going to be a problem, a real problem. He was wondering if—

At this point Fritz Brubaker boiled over. "Frank?" he interrupted.

"Yeah, Fritz?"

"Shame on you," he said, and hung up.

WHAT WE ALL were doing, without knowing it, was taking emergency inventory that afternoon. Who is in our lives? Where are they? Are they safe? Wife, kids, mother? Brothers, sisters? Fritz had talked to Linda and she was okay. He had talked to his brothers, Andy and Hap. He'd called his mother. They were okay, all of them.

It was time for an inventory at the Palazzo (which is what he called his $2.1 million brick home), although Fritz wasn't conscious of this: he was just trotting up the staircase to the landing. He'd picked them up at Chaney before noon; they sat silently in the backseat as he drove home. No GameBoys, no KISS-108, no fighting, no insults. At the corner of Centre Street, Fritz had glanced in his rearview mirror and caught sight of his daughter biting her lip, deep in thought.

Now, three hours later, the landing was quiet. Fritz peeked up and over at the upstairs hall. The doors to the kids' bedrooms were shut. From behind one came bubblegum pop music; from the other side of the hall, muffled blasts and gurgles.

"You guys okay?" he called out.

His voice echoed down the empty hall. There was no answer. He waited and then called again, louder this time. After a few moments Kristin's door opened, and her face appeared.

"Are you—"

"Ye-ah?" asked Kristin.

She delivered "yeah" in the adolescent interrogative. It wasn't a "What did you say?" yeah; rather, a "yeah" heavy with preteen disdain: a "Why *wouldn't* I be all right?" yeah.

He loved Kristin too much, and the obviousness of his delight numbered among his many faults as a parent, for it contrasted severely with his unexcited manner toward his son. Kristin was so much like him, or at least she had been as a bouncy third-grader. Many things came easily to her. He was proud of his kindergarten soccer star, also the left wing on the Mite A hockey team. Michael, alas, had rejected all physical activity since T-ball. Fritz even took a sneaking pride in Kristin's failures. She'd been drummed out of ballet for indifference. Her Chaney School reports always noted querulously that although she had the ability to excel at school, she might do even better if she devoted a little more effort. (That's my girl! he thought secretly.) The failures were a kind of success, as far as he was concerned—they showed her natural confidence. Kristin had always been the easy kid, the one who thrived independently. She'd responded fairly well to his laissez-faire parenting, hadn't she? Kristin had always been his *heir*.

And now, without warning, on the landing of the Palazzo, on the afternoon of September 11, she'd drilled him. The condescension, the disdain of that "Yeah!"

Over the summer Fritz had noticed that Kristin was changing. His little peanut was starting to stretch on him. Or something. Puberty hadn't hit Kristin yet, had it? But she was walking differently. Whether by affectation or not, he couldn't tell. Kristin could not only lip-synch Britney Spears, she could pelv-synch. There also seemed to be something in her attitude that had changed. She'd become short, where she'd always been friendly, occasionally distant, where before she'd been gregarious. "Hon," he'd asked Linda, "it's not yet, I mean, it's too early for, I mean, with Kristin, do you think?"

Linda rolled her eyes.

"I thought it was when they were, like, fourteen."

"Honestly!" said Linda.

So it was happening. But Fritz didn't get it. He was a man: he supposed feminine puberty was about body change. Same little peanut in a different body, he thought. He was clueless. And doomed.

He stood on the landing, perhaps unaware of the inventory he was taking, but sensing, fearing, that something was wrong, something beyond terrorist attacks. Who is in your life? Surely Kristin. At least Kristin. If no one else—Kristin!

The eleven-year-old came out of her doorway, slouched into the hall. She frowned, not looking at him. She seemed distracted, pouty, morose. In her hand was a copy of *Glamour*. FIFTY TIPS FROM GUYS FOR

TOTALLY BETTER SEX! screamed a headline. What had happened, he wondered, to the kid who, eighteen months ago, would have bounded into his arms like a Labrador retriever? She stopped at the top of the stairs.

"You doing okay?"

No response. She refused to make eye contact. "So . . . is Mom coming back tonight?"

"Peanut, she can't come back tonight. They closed all the airports. But she's fine."

Was that a grimace, when he said "Peanut"?

"When will she be back?"

"We're not sure. She's going to try to drive back, I guess. With Mr. Rosenblatt."

Kristin made another face. "Great." She ran her fingertips along the polished banister that topped the sweeping staircase, her eyes still distracted. Maybe, Fritz thought, he'd been oversensitive. She was a kid, after all, at the brink of adolescence, with no context for this dreadful event. Maybe she was handling it the best way she could. As they said at the Chaney School, maybe she was having trouble processing what had happened. Yes, he could see she had been moved by it all, and was approaching it in the terms she could understand—terms like where Mom was.

"Dad," she began softly, "do you think . . ."

("Dad," he noted. Didn't I used to be "Daddy"?) "What is it, sweetheart?"

"Do you think they'll preempt the regular shows *all* night?"

Fritz felt as though he'd been struck in the sternum, as though a powerful fist had driven the bone into his lungs. He felt the blood run from his face. There on the landing of the staircase, at the center of his Dover fortress, his jaw began to move helplessly, trying to say something—anything. But there were no words. His chest tightened. Of all the long minutes of September 11, that one, for Fritz Brubaker, was the saddest.

"I mean, they've had this on the TV *all* afternoon."

Fritz Brubaker looked up at his daughter, his eyes imploring that she say nothing else. Please—don't make it worse. She wore a spaghetti-strapped tank top and a pair of capris that a catalog would describe as "oatmeal" or maybe "pumice." The magazine was in her left hand, and she stood with her right hand on her hip, wrist out, jutting her hip in a pose that for a split second might have been Linda's. It was just the way Linda would have held her hand on her hip, or the way a Wellesley mom in Bread & Circus would have stood while flaying the checkout boy because the store was out of gingerroot. With the uncanny mimetic instinct of the young, Kristin flawlessly executed a cute-but-exasperated Wellesley mom. Cute-but-exasperated with the senselessness of people. Cute-but-exasperated with an absence of gingerroot when you had a dinner party planned. Cute-but-exasperated that they'd keep showing the same building crumbling down over and over when there are important shows to watch!

To have drunk this deeply of Wellesley and Dover at the age of eleven. How had he missed this change in his daughter—was it last month? Last week?

His jaw was still flapping. He should say something, he knew. But he couldn't find words. Suddenly stiff, Fritz climbed up the stairs to the hall. He shouldered past Kristin in sad silence, unable even to look at her, and went along the corridor to Michael's room.

"Hey Mike, how ya doing, son?" Fritz asked, trying to brighten up his own mood.

Michael grunted. He was playing a video game. Well then. It looked like Michael had come through the attack okay.

"Tonight is supposed to be *Apartment 3B*!" called Kristin from the landing.

"What's for dinner?" asked Michael.

"What's *Apartment 3B*?" Fritz asked quietly.

" 'What's *Apartment 3B*?' "

"Yeah, what is it?"

"Are you serious?" Michael's fingers were flying across the keyboard. He stared intently at the computer. "Dad, focus on what's important. What's for dinner?"

"What's for dinner is what's important," Fritz repeated robotically. No answer from Michael. "Maybe we'll get Chinese."

Michael grunted ambiguously. Chinese was okay, but after all, this kid was from Dover. He preferred Thai. "*Apartment 3B* is this loser show all the girls watch," he added.

Fritz turned and retreated downstairs to the kitchen, his dreary inventory complete. All safe, present, and accounted for, but where or what was his family? Earlier in the afternoon he'd telephoned his mother, who floated in the gentle mist of her midstage Alzheimer's. Her obliviousness had a peculiar grace today. "So nice that you called," she said. It was what she always said now. His wife? At this of all times, she wasn't even there, which seemed weirdly appropriate. And on a day of national tragedy, the chief concerns of his two children were take-out food and television shows. Everyone was safe, all right. Everyone was safe as hell. Each safe and in his reinforced concrete silo here at Paradise Bunker.

He cracked open a bottle of beer and drained it in three gulps, looking out at the backyard, the perfect green expanse—not a weed or a human being to be seen all the way to the tennis court. This being Dover, a due regard for country chic required that the front acre be in field (a disciplined field, to be sure: edge-mowed and sowed with Williams-Sonoma wildflower seed but, at least to the untrained passerby, something that looked like maybe the owners had horses). But the backyard, where no neighbor's eye could pry, had yielded to Linda's real comfort zone: a martial ChemLawn where botanical indiscipline was intolerable and any stray dandelion was quickly drummed out of the corps. It occurred to Fritz, looking out at his perfect grass, that nobody spent much time on it except the gardeners.

He'd never felt more alone. A brooding, nervous energy filled him, a restlessness, a need for . . . a project. It came to him as he finished the beer, ringing in his mind like a bell. It seemed goofy and piquant and absolutely the right thing, right now, to kill a tree. He had three ash saplings in mind—those three that Linda had hired a tree service to plant above the tennis court five years ago. Any one of them would be perfect.

He searched down in the basement and in the garage for a pully, without success. But he found a two-inch electrician's pipe clasp. He bent the edges of the loop with a pair of pliers, then wrapped duct tape around it to cut friction. Beneath a pile of rakes in the corner of the garage lay a posthole digger. Nearby was the chain saw and some gas-oil mixture in a red plastic jerry can. The blade was dull and the plug fouled, but after twenty or thirty pulls, he got it to start up.

The tree looked good. It had grown straight enough—it was maybe eighteen, twenty feet high, without too many limbs. He cut it down and trimmed the branches (leaving a mess that he knew would drive Linda crazy) and dragged the trunk down the hill to the backyard, alongside the house, and down through to the front field. The clasp went in easily with an electric drill and a couple of one-and-a-half-inch number-eight screws, and he threaded its loop with a length of clothesline.

The hole was the hard part. The rich ryegrass looked like it ought to sit on top of nothing but loam, but six inches underground, he was into good old New England rocks. He got a shovel and a long crowbar from the garage to loosen the bigger ones. The rest he did with the posthole digger. He stripped off his shirt and bashed away until the digger's metal components were underground, then bashed some more until the handle was halfway down. It was warm. He felt his hands aching on the handles, and his back and arms were sore.

I've got a wife out of town and kids who don't care about anything except themselves, he thought, ramming the posthole digger into the rocky earth, clanging its metal mouth off the rocks. I've got—RAM!—two spoiled kids who are upset because their—CLANG!—fucking TV shows are—

"So, like . . . what are you doing?"

Hands on hips, Kristin was eyeing him curiously. She had come down from the house. He paused, took a breath, then asked her hopefully, "Want to help?"

Kristin looked at the ash pole lying in the field. "It's not very straight," she said.

"It's straight enough."

"It's going to look kind of lame," she said, then turned.

"HEY!"

She flinched as he dropped the posthole digger and came toward her. A momentary hint of the old Kristin, but the new one recovered in a flash. Fritz glistened with sweat, and dirt, and anger.

"What is your problem, Kristin?"

"Ex-cuse me?"

"Thousands of other kids lost their parents this morning, and you're worried about your fucking TV show?"

The word, her father's anger—it staggered her. She stared back fiercely—at first. But then her lip began to quiver.

"Like it's really going to help to have some lame flagpole that's not even painted . . ." She was crying.

"Kristin!"

". . . where everyone in the whole town can, like, see it . . ."

"Kristin Brubaker, I'm—I'm—shame on you. Go on back up to the house."

It stunned her, and it stunned him, too. Never before, in Kristin's whole life, had Fritz spoken to her that way. Christ, he thought, watching her run up the drive, that's what I said to Frank Pitts.

HE KEPT AFTER the hole, ramming the posthole digger up and down, angrily and more angrily, striking, beating, brutalizing the ground, as though he would tear it rock from rock. He got down on his knees to pull rocks from the hole. Dirt covered his hands and his arms; it ground up underneath his fingernails. His brow was smeared with it. Dirt clung to the sheen on his chest.

At length the posthole digger sank up to the handles and the hole was deep enough. He knew he ought to pour a footing in, but there wasn't time; it was already past four. So he raised the pole until it slid with a satisfying thunk into the hole. He looked up at it. Not very straight. Screw that: it was straight enough. He stuffed the bigger rocks around its base. He pushed earth around the rocks, ground and tamped the mound with his heels, and jammed it in with a shovel until the pole didn't wobble too much.

He was covered in dirt and sweat, and angry as hell.

He went up to the house to wash. Then he put on a shirt and hunted around until he found it in a Neiman Marcus box on the top shelf of the front-hall closet.

Kristin had holed up in her room again. Michael wouldn't join him, either. It wasn't going to help anything, he said. It was a stupid gesture. (Besides, couldn't anybody see he was in the middle of a video game?) So Fritz walked back down the hill alone, to the new flagpole. He tied off the clothesline to the flag grommets. Then he looked back up the hill toward the house, still hesitating, hopeful. But no one was coming. He turned back to the flag.

There was a way to do this. He'd seen soldiers do this, a pair of them, snapping the line smartly. Well, they had pulleys. And help.

Just then Fritz noticed an old gray Chevy station wagon stopped on Cottage Street, about twenty-five yards away, down at the edge of the field. He'd seen it around town, rusty on the fenders, dented on the hood, as if someone had dropped bricks on it. The driver's door opened with a metallic groan, and from it stepped a heavyset man wearing blue jeans, work boots, and a T-shirt. He looked about fifty, bald on top but with steel-gray hair falling loosely from the sides of his head to his T-shirt. He gave Fritz a friendly wave. Fritz waved back.

The man walked slowly up the drive. "Good for you," he called out.

Fritz held the flag loosely in his left hand and extended his right. "Fritz Brubaker," he said.

"Jim Feeney."

Fritz smiled. "You're the guy with the goats."

Feeney acknowledged with a wry grin that he was indeed.

"No, I admire that," Fritz said.

Feeney didn't look like a desperado. He moved slowly, and smiled easily, and his belly swelled under the T-shirt.

"You know, I was driving by a few minutes ago and saw you working. I *thought* you might be putting up a flag. Mind if I watch you raise it? It'd feel good, somehow."

"Jim, I'd be proud to have you put it up with me."

Now Fritz felt like he needed to say something. This ought to be an event, however small, and his children should have participated. If they had, he would have said something, so he shouldn't let their refusal to participate change things. He cleared his throat. "Well," he began, "some deranged people did a lot of harm today. They killed a lot of decent men and women. We never knew these victims, but they were . . . well, they were our countrymen. That's what they were. They were ours. So we'll just raise this flag in memory of them. To say we're with them in spirit. To say we feel badly for their families. Our little way of doing that. Okay?"

Fritz was looking back up toward the house. He thought he might have seen a curtain move in an upstairs window.

Feeney smiled. "That was very nice," he said.

And so, at just past four-thirty in the afternoon, September 11,

2001, two citizens of Dover stood in the front field at 14 Cottage Street. Fritz held the clothesline, and the goat runner Feeney stood by with his hand on his heart. Then Fritz raised the American flag on the ash pole. The top grommet caught on a rough spot where Fritz had left a knob in trimming a branch, but then it cleared. He raised it to the top, and then he tied the line off in a clove hitch on the pole. The flag flapped loosely.

They stood and watched it.

"You really have goats?" Fritz asked.

"Sure."

"How many?"

"Too damn many. Whole town's up in arms."

Feeney was mesmerized by the flag. "You know," he said, "there's no wind today, and look how the flag finds a little to fly by."

They watched it flap lazily in the breeze.

"Up there, that's where the best wind is," Feeney added with a twinkle in his eye.

HE HAD TO GET OUT of the house—the cavernous Palazzo, with its five thousand empty square feet, its absent wife, and its two miserably spoiled kids holed up in their extravagant playpens. Fritz ordered delivery of the Chinese and left.

But where could he go? He didn't have any friends in the town. There were guys from whom you could borrow a snowblower, and guys he knew to say hello to as so-and-so's husband, contacts through Linda. But friends? People who really knew him, people with whom he could share the sorrow of this day? There wasn't a single one.

Both of his brothers lived on the north shore, but if he drove up there and left the kids, Linda would crucify him.

He got his bike down from the garage wall and headed down Cottage Street to Parson's Lane, then along Parson's to Norfolk Street. He rode out to Route 109 and then looped out along High Street toward Sherborn Avenue. Traffic was light, and he flashed swiftly along the quiet roads. He didn't know where he was going. He was looking for the town he lived in, but there wasn't any *town* there. He passed manse after manse, each set back from the road, apart, solitary. Sometimes the blue glow of a television was faintly visible, obscured by tree branches, through a window. But there were no people.

He turned onto Sherborn Avenue and rode beneath its rank of shaggy maples, aglow in the sunset with fiery red. He followed the road into River Street as dusk was falling on that beautiful September evening. Linda would be calling the house, he knew. He could almost hear her: "Your father has gone *out*? Tonight, of all nights, he left you alone?"

It was getting dark and cooler, finally, when he found himself turning back onto Farm Street. About halfway along, he came to a ramshackle farmhouse near the road. Its yellowed paint was peeling, and some of the clapboards had pulled away from the house. The porch sagged, and its floorboards were curled at the ends. Behind the house was a barn with asphalt shingles. Something odd caught his eye: the gray station wagon was parked in back, next to a tractor, and as he flew by, he had a glimpse of something on top of the car.

He braked his bike and turned around. Approaching the farmhouse again, slowly this time, he noticed an array of solar panels on the south roof; and around the house, paddocks where the grass had been worn away to dirt.

This much peeling paint, this much dirty paddock right on Farm Street—it was an affront to the whole town. Fritz smiled, looking at the house closely for the first time. Good for *you*, he thought.

He turned into the drive and stopped. There *was* something on top of the car. Fritz stared at it, then walked the bike around back and knocked on the screen door.

"Hi," said Fritz through the screen. "Sorry to disturb, but—"

"Fritz, come in, come in," Feeney interrupted. "Nan, this is our neighbor Fritz Brubaker, from over on Cottage Street."

"Nice to meet you," said Feeney's wife, a broad-hipped woman, short, with frizzy hair and, this evening, an air of distraction. She opened the door and extended her hand, seeming to struggle for a welcoming instinct.

"And you," said Fritz. "I just wanted to tell you that—"

"Come on in," said Feeney within. "Sit down and have something. What'll you have? Soup?"

Feeney was at the long trestle table that occupied most of the kitchen. About the room there hung what would have been, on any other day, a cheerful chaos.

Feeney was having soup. His bowl was perched on a pile of papers. "I'll get some," said Nan, and she reached up in the cupboard for a bowl.

"No, thanks," said Fritz, "it's all right, I—"

She was already ladling from the pot on the stove. "I can't even believe this," she said.

"No, it's awful," Fritz said, looking around the room. It wasn't just the table that was cluttered. The countertops, too, were heaped: pots, magazines, bags, papers, what looked like a carburetor. A black cat curled around Nan's legs, and a tabby surveyed the room from the brick mantel over the woodstove. Feeney returned to his soup bowl. Spread out beneath it was a CAD drawing. Next to the bowl was a thick pamphlet entitled "National Wind Atlas."

"It was so nice to hear about the flag you put up," Nan said.

Fritz didn't quite know how to respond. "Oh, thanks. I didn't mean to interrupt your dinner, but—"

"It's no interruption," Nan said.

"None at all."

"Just soup."

Fritz tried again. "But I—"

"Would you like some bread with that?" Nan asked.

"No, no thank you, I just, I . . . I thought I should tell you—"

"Sure?"

He blurted out: "There's a goat on your station wagon."

There was a pause. Then Feeney said, "She baked it fresh this morning. It's really good with the soup. She puts this honey in it."

"Molasses," she said. "This loaf came out a little lopsided."

"I didn't think so," Feeney gently contradicted. "Tastes the same, anyway."

"Ahh," Fritz tried again. "Jim. There's . . . on your car, there's—"

"Yeah. They like to get on the cars for some reason," said Feeney.

"Or how about a beer? Would you like a beer instead?" asked Nan. "Maybe he wants a beer, Jim. You want to get one from the fridge?"

Fritz was confused. "Ah, no, well . . . maybe, sure. They get on cars?"

"Not if you leave your hood up," Feeney said. "That keeps 'em off, usually."

"Not Manny. He jumps right up on the roof," said Nan. "Get one from the back. They're colder."

Jim rooted around in the back of the fridge. Then something occurred to him. "You rode a bike over, right, Fritz?"

"Ah, yeah, I . . ."

"Oh, good."

"They won't get on a bike," Nan explained.

"No, I didn't think they'd . . . but your car, Jim. Doesn't it—"

"Forgot to put the hood up," Jim explained.

"It won't *matter*, Jim. Manny jumps straight up on the roof, like I told you."

"Are they loose?" Fritz asked. "The goats?"

"Oh, they have a pen and all. But it's hard to keep a goat locked up," said Jim. "Wonderful jumpers."

"Wonderful," Nan agreed.

The Feeneys didn't seem concerned about the goat on the station wagon, so Fritz sat down with his beer and a bowl of vegetable soup and a thick brown slice of bread, and listened to the radio. The report was talking about the Portland, Maine, connection. The hijackers had come in through Portland, Maine. They had gone through metal detectors early that morning.

It was so sad, this numbing repetition of the story. Fritz wondered if he should change the subject, or whether that would be insensitive. He noticed, on the CAD layout, a drawing of a propeller. "Jim, what's that?" he asked.

It was Feeney's latest wind-turbine design. Feeney explained that he'd use an excavator to dig a hole for a ten-foot concrete foundation. He was erecting the tower now. He planned to install batteries in the shed and run the cable underground to a junction box in the basement.

"How's the town with it?" Fritz asked.

Nan looked at him nervously. "You haven't heard?"

"Heard something about the goats is all."

"What these people have against goats, I just don't understand," she said. "They don't do anyone any harm."

"Well, they do jump up on cars, it's true," Feeney pointed out.

"They—why do they jump on cars?" Fritz asked.

"Don't know," said Feeney. "Like the view, I guess."

"What's it do to the car?"

"Oh, goats are hell on cars."

"It's not such a big deal. Once in a while is all they do it," said Nan. "You know, kids climb on cars, too, nobody gets up a petition about that."

Jim didn't answer, merely smiled lovingly at his wife. Nan was the passionate one, Feeney the voice of pure reason. "Nomar did get on Patricia's Mercedes that time."

Nan sniffed. "I told her to put the hood up. And the trunk. He'd never get up there if she would have put the hood up."

Feeney nodded. "There was also the delphiniums," he said.

"That wasn't Nomar," Nan said. "It was Trot."

Jim answered thoughtfully, "I don't think it mattered to her."

"The woman has acres of gardens. She's hardly going to miss a few delphiniums."

Jim turned to Fritz. "Anyway, the goats are a challenge."

"They're *lovely*," Nan said.

"But this wind turbine really has 'em going," Jim continued. "Building inspector was here yesterday morning, matter of fact. Town's not too happy. Going to get an injunction, he told me." Feeney shook his head. "You know what they've got against wind power?"

Fritz shook his head.

"Doesn't look good."

"Quaint," Nan corrected him. "Doesn't look *quaint*. They want to live in quaint. They don't much care for real in this town."

"It doesn't look good?" Fritz repeated. "What's it look like?"

Feeney shrugged. "Just a propeller setting up on a pole in the back field. They're also bitching about noise, I guess."

"Those delphiniums were kind of stringy, if you ask me," Nan muttered.

"Noise?" Fritz asked.

"The propeller makes a whoosh-whoosh noise. Patricia's mad about the noise, too."

"Is it loud?"

"You notice it. Loud, I don't know. You hear it. But I took a decibel reading of Patricia's SUV going by the other morning. Turbine's not as loud as that, I can tell you." Feeney laughed.

"These *people*," Nan said.

The voice of the radio announcer was relentless. It broke in again. It didn't look good for survivors. There was always the hope of a few or even one. But it was chaos at what they were calling Ground Zero. The saddest thing was this: all over the southern part of Manhattan island, doctors and nurses and paramedics had set up triage units, bracing themselves, and so far, almost no one had been brought in.

"I guess today kind of puts our piddly problems in perspective, doesn't it," Feeney said.

The two men had finished their soup. They studied the drawings again. "The bigger thing's the propeller design," Feeney said. "The key is to get to where a turbine can make kilowatts out of a class-two wind zone."

"What's class two?"

Feeney pointed at the wind atlas. "This thing is a map of wind, if you can believe it. They classify by power, which is a function of speed and consistency. Class two is pretty low, and it's what we are, all the way out to Westover."

"How much can you generate?"

"Depends on the turbine design. But you can run a house on ten kilowatts. And in a class-three wind zone, it doesn't take that much of a turbine to generate ten kilowatts. The problem is how to get the design to work in lower wind areas, like ours. And how to make it cheap."

"Yeah," said Nan. "Cheap."

Out on the Cape and the islands, they had plenty of wind, but here, in interior Massachusetts, there wasn't enough. The most efficient commercial turbine designs could never get down to useful generation below class-three wind zones. Feeney thought if he varied the shape of the propeller, he could get more of an airfoil and a more efficient machine. For months he'd been trying to design a better one.

On the radio the talk had gotten political: who might be responsible for the bombing and what the Pentagon was hinting they would do about it.

"Do you mind, for a little while?" Nan asked. "It's too much. I know I should listen, but . . ."

"It's okay," Feeney said.

She switched the radio off. It was quiet in the kitchen then, and the sadness seemed overwhelming. Fritz tried to think of something cheerier: "The goats—are they all named after Red Sox?"

"Not all," Feeney said. "Only the billies. Just a joke I've got going."

"He's been doing that since the World Series in eighty-six," said Nan.

"Kind of a play on words," Jim explained.

"He was a good old goat, Billy Buckner," Nan reminisced.

Fritz smiled, thinking back to game six of the 1986 series, when the Red Sox had been one strike away from winning the whole thing—for sixteen straight pitches. "So Dover doesn't appreciate your Red Sox?" he asked.

"They offend community standards."

"What are the community standards when it comes to goats?"

"Whatever everybody in the community does, I guess. Which, in this town, is pretty antigoat."

It was late. Fritz realized he'd better get back home. Linda would be calling every ten minutes. He rose. "Thanks," he said. "Thanks so much for cheering me up."

It was dark as he walked outside. He could just make out, hovering above the station wagon, the gleam of two interested eyes watching him as he wheeled his bike out of the yard.

FRITZ RODE HOME. Now and then an anonymous someone behind the tinted glass of a luxury car raced by and then was gone. Fritz pedaled up his drive, past the flag, which was now a shadow hanging limply on the pole. The Palazzo was dark, with light visible only from the kids' bedroom windows. He went in through the kitchen and called their names. No answer. He climbed the stairs. The upstairs hall was dark, illuminated by the pencil lines of light at the bottom of the bedroom doors. There was enough light to see, standing in the hall outside each room, the white cartons of half-finished Chinese food.

8

THE DOVER KID

ON SEPTEMBER 16, Linda would at last come home, after driving with Marvin Rosenblatt all the way from San Francisco. For her husband and children, it was a day of pacing, of looking at road maps and watches, then looking at them again and doing more math in the head; a day of counting hours and miles, and for a question from Kristin repeated irritably through the day: "When's Mom getting home?"

In the early evening the phone rang. Fritz sprinted for it.

"Hi!" It was Linda's voice, weary but with an enforced cheeriness. "Almost home!"

"Where are you, hon?"

"We're outside Elmira."

"Elmira? Where the hell's that?"

"New York, Fritz. We should be home tonight. This morning, I guess. Five or six hours."

He sat awake in the living room after the kids had retreated to their rooms. He opened a bottle of red wine and let it stand on the sideboard. Then he drank half of it and wondered if he should open another one. Which he did. He turned off the television and tried to read awhile but couldn't concentrate. Then he sat in the darkness. He nodded off, blinked awake suddenly at the night noises. At last he heard the tires crunch slowly up the gravel drive. It had been eight days since he'd seen her, but it seemed longer.

He was at the door of her rental car before she could open it and say, "Oh, God, I'm *so* exhausted. But you didn't have to wait up, Fritz, tomorrow's a workday, and—"

That was all she got out of her mouth before he sealed it up.

She pulled free, flustered. "Fritz! I've got to get the bags."

But no, she didn't need to get any bags. He could get the bags later. He had her in his arms; he carried her through the doorway; he carried her down the hall to the living room; he laid her gently on the couch. There they held each other in the darkness. He poured her a glass of wine, then another. He held her head in his hands and gently stroked her face.

"Are the kids okay?"

He decided to leave the details for later. The kids were okay enough.

"You're beautiful," he said. And she was.

"I missed you," she said. And she had.

Later, as they lay together in the warm darkness of the September morning, Linda's face glowed. Such passion! He hadn't shown her such passion in years. The way he held her and caressed her—so gently, so tenderly. This was confusing, after everything that had happened to her. But it was a delicious sort of confusion. She'd been so tired, had to pull off the road outside Springfield because she couldn't keep her eyes open anymore, and neither could Marvin—heaven knew she was going to need some sleep tonight—this morning, and had a busy day tomorrow—well, today, actually. But if it was confusing, it was a wonderful warm bath. For one night she wouldn't analyze it. She'd just feel it.

Maybe . . . the way he had. . . . She sighed. He was still a wonderful lover. She began to think that this came *so easily* to him, it wasn't something he'd *work at*, but she shooed the thought away. It was good to be home, yes, she had missed this, her home, the place she belonged. She listened to his gentle breathing. He'd fallen asleep so quickly. Linda rolled over and lay at peace, drifting and floating away to sleep on a warm and gentle current, rafting along on the flow of a quiet September morning, fading into the lullaby of the crickets, the gentle serenade of night in Dover, the soft sound of . . .

Of someone crying?

Linda blinked and was awake. A cry. Her senses were now keen and sharp, and she listened intently in the darkness.

There it was again. But not really a cry. Not one of the children, thank heaven. No, it was more like somebody clearing his throat. But not human. She sat bolt upright and listened. It was some sort of animal sound, an animal with postnasal drip, very near the house! She shuddered. She grabbed Fritz's shoulder and shook him awake. "Fritz," she whispered, "listen! Do you hear that?"

"Hmmm?"

She heard the sound again. Almost like a sort of . . . no, it couldn't be. "Do you *hear* that, Fritz?"

He roused himself, sleepily threw an arm across her shoulder.

"No, Fritz, listen, what *is* that?"

"What?"

"That, that . . . *sound*. There. You hear it? Doesn't it sound like some kind of wild animal or something? Fritz?"

"Oh, that. That's Shea. Our new kid."

"Our new *what?*"

"Kid. You know, a baby goat. He's really cute. But you gotta keep your hood up. Welcome home, honey."

LINDA HAD COME HOME just in time. At the Chaney School, new trouble was brewing. Michael Brubaker's issues had grown, gathered strength, even evolved into a proper noun. The staff referred in grave tones to the Michael Brubaker Problem. As though it were a geometrical theorem or the Heisenberg uncertainty principle. It reached a crisis point over the incident in art class.

Michael had been caught attempting to fabricate a weapon of mass destruction.

A group of the children in morning assembly was buzzing, and it was there that sharp-eared Mavis Potemkin first heard about Michael Brubaker, caught red-handed in full, flagrant production, the evidence spread out on the forming table. Instantly Mavis knew that the incident must be reported to the headmistress, Harriet Tichenor. Harriet wasted no time. She promptly called a meeting in her office with Mavis and Aubrey Fulwroth-Levinsky, the school psychologist. Philippe Iskandar was also invited, since the incident had occurred in his class.

Mr. Iskandar was late, breezing into Harriet's office at ten past the hour without apology, indeed without so much as an explanation. He was wearing his usual dusty jeans, those green plastic clog things, and a black T-shirt. The T-shirt, chalky with clay, had holes along the shoulder seam. On it was some kind of block print of white swirls. Aubrey couldn't make out what it was. Mavis, too, was wondering.

"Halloo halloo," he said. "How are all of you ladies?"

Philippe smiled at Harriet Tichenor; stared frankly (maybe a trifle too frankly) at Mavis Potemkin; didn't seem to notice Aubrey Fulwroth-Levinsky.

How are all of you ladies? Indeed! Aubrey offered a frosty professional greeting. This meeting was going to be awkward. If you asked Aubrey (and Mavis, for that matter), there were issues with Mr. Iskandar as well, and there had been for a long time.

Philippe was the school's one and only rake, its Lebanese bluebeard. The olive-skinned artist certainly looked the part, with his long, silky eyelashes and darkly romantic expression. This made him an asset to Harriet in fund-raising: the headmistress liked to wheel him out at cocktail parties. But Aubrey had seen it, that predatory look he had, the way he'd come in here late, halloo-hallooing to the "ladies," the way he'd arch an eyebrow, the ironic smile he put on when women spoke, the tone of condescension in his voice, the shameless way he'd inspect the cocktail dresses of the younger moms—milfs, as he called them. Oh, yes, the psychologist had seen it. She'd even heard Philippe use that outrageous acronym. Milfs! Not even her profound tolerance could excuse this, nor her understanding that when it came to gender issues, men of Arabic background had certain cultural issues (through no fault of their own). Aubrey Fulwroth-Levinsky worked hard to be open to persons of all cultures and sexualities, but as she sometimes remarked to her partner, Cheryl Levinsky-Fulwroth, you had to draw the line somewhere.

And the shameless heterosexuality of this man was where Aubrey drew it.

The headmistress cleared her throat and thanked them all for coming. "Something's come up, as you all know. We need to discuss the Michael Brubaker Problem," she said.

So the meeting was under way, although Aubrey was still too preoccupied with Philippe's entrance to focus on the troubled eighth-grader. Oh yes, Philippe had a number of issues, as far as Aubrey was concerned. Issue number one—how had this project of Michael's gone on under Philippe's nose for more than a week? He wasn't paying attention to the children, of course. He never paid attention to the children. He cared only about his ceramic "sculptures."

The sculptures? Six-foot pots that bulged with breastlike forms and swollen pregnant bellies. That he sold for $12,000 apiece, people said, in his gallery on Newbury Street in Boston. That he made out of clay paid for by the Chaney School! That he baked, or cooked, or what ever you called it, in a kiln that had been purchased for the use of Chaney School children! (The kiln would run all night. God knew what the school's utility bill was.) That swirled with the shapes of twining limbs and the arches of human backs, with breasts and bellies and, between the turgid forms, dark shadowy crevasses that might have been—

"Haven't you, Aubrey?"

Aubrey snapped back to the meeting. The headmistress had finished asking her something. They were regarding her politely.

"I'm sorry, Harriet?"

"I was saying that you've been concerned about the Michael Brubaker Problem for a while now, haven't you?"

"Oh, yes, Harriet, I am really *quite* concerned. Michael has a number of issues, as we all know. I was wondering if first we might ask Philippe"—just the slightest curtness, perhaps, in the way she said "Philippe," just a tremolo of disapproval?—"to relate the incident for us. That occurred in art class." (That is to say, in *your* class, you left-bank poseur. And what exactly is that . . . that *design* on your T-shirt?)

Philippe shrugged. "Not so much to tell," he said. But they were staring at him, so he told what little there was. This gave Aubrey—who had heard the gossip and knew all about the incident—more leisure to pursue her thoughts down their previous course.

On Thursday evenings Philippe taught an adult-education class in ceramics, a class particularly popular among Chaney School mothers. The women signed up because pottery was wholesome and artistic and they wanted to make bowls and vases and mugs, and also (maybe an eensy bit) because Mr. Iskandar (whom they'd met at the Chaney School fund-raiser) was so, so exotic. Such an *interesting* young man to have here in Wellesley! And wasn't it rather a thrill to be taught by the *real thing*. He had a gallery and shows and everything!

Philippe signed up because it was a milf-rich environment. The art teacher was always gratified by the inspection at the first class. Sometimes there were two, or even three, but it never failed that there would be at least one. Yes, he'd note with an inward smile, at least one mother-I'd-like-to- . . .

Philippe's usual method was to spend a month treating her with insolence, criticizing her technique, disparaging her work. Then one evening he would find her as she worked at the wheel. He would lean over her and speak tenderly. He would be impressed with the improvement she was making. With the dedication. With the insight that her work was beginning to show. But, well, here, let me show you something. Then he would sit behind her, reaching around with his long dark arms to take her fingers in his and press them just so against the wet clay. The slip would ooze between her fingers and his. And the milf would feel Philippe's arms (roped with lean muscle, etched with veins) around her shoulders, would feel his face almost alongside her face, not daring to look at him, trying to focus on the clay.

"You feel that?"

"Yes!" she might answer, more of a gasp than a word, as the soft cool clay entwined their fingers in an earthen coffee frappé.

"You must be firm."

"Firm?"

"Of course. The hand must be cupped, firm, *comme ça* . . ."

"Yes?" Another gasp—a squeak, almost.

"Yes. *Alors.* But your stroke must be gentle."

Her *stroke?* The milf often would not answer this at all. Her hands would tremble and muff the pot. She would be speechless with self-consciousness.

"You must feel the shape. Fill the mind with the shape, translate this mental picture to the hands."

The milf would redouble her efforts, lingering late after the classes. For that class and the next. Now the fingers encased in slip; then the heads intent over the glaze. At last an all-nighter. To attend the kiln. Which must be watched like a hawk, because if the temperature is wrong, then—pfft!

"Pfft?"

"Yes, pfft! Pots, work, everything ruined. Twenty degrees either way and two months of work in shards! Fit only for backfill!"

So the kiln would be watched like a hawk. And the dissonant Middle Eastern music would work like a drug. And the wine would flow like water. And there would be conversations with heads held close together, sleepy, gentle, laughing conversations, because not much would be happening with the kiln, really nothing at all, except that it would be firing, but it was good to be there in case something went wrong (which it never actually had) so all the work wouldn't go pfft. And so on until . . . until . . . in the middle of the night, right there on a forming table, amid all the clay dust and slop, right there where the children were taught art, he would . . .

Yes, Aubrey knew all about this. These milfs were living clay in the predator's hands. And the worst of it, the absolute worst? After he'd selected some random mother, plundered and ravaged her?

She'd buy one of his pots for $12,000. Buy one of his breast jugs and put it in the front hall, leaving her cuckolded husband to come home late from the office and wonder, "Honey, what *is* that thing?"

"So, it is a Kalashnikov. An AK-105 assault rifle, as he told me. He has created it from drawings. It shows some skill."

Aubrey was startled once again by the voice in the meeting. Philippe was describing the art project—the incident where Michael Brubaker had been discovered in the act of fabricating a weapon of mass destruction.

"I'm sorry?" the headmistress asked.

"Yes. His use of the fettling knife to define the shape is good. And he has been creative with the bolt head to create the perforations in the silencer. Also the—"

"I think," Aubrey said, "we were all rather more concerned with Michael's selection of a violent and inappropriate device as the subject for his art project than with his technical skill at pottery."

"It is not pottery."

"I'm sorry?"

"This is not pottery. Pottery is . . . is a pot. *N'est-ce pas?* Or a bowl, or *peut-être* a plate, something like that, on the wheel. That is pottery. This is different. A kind of clay sculpture. It requires different technique than to throw."

It was starting to bother Mavis now, too. What *was* that design on Philippe's shirt?

"Yes, well, whatever it is, I think—"

"The material is not so easy to manipulate," Philippe explained. "The textures are complex. The barrel must be a smooth cylinder, like gunmetal steel, while to mimic the texture of the gunstock, for example, is very different. The stipple. It is not so easy as it might—"

"But it was a machine gun he was making?" Harriet noted, attempting to bring the meeting to the point.

But Philippe kept going on about the artwork. And the diligence of the boy. Michael had obtained drawings from Jane's over the Internet. The painstaking care with which he used the fettling knife to inscribe the weapon with the proper detail and filigree. Philippe concluded with a nod, a grudging acknowledgment. "Pretty good, for one of the br— one of the students at this place."

Now all of the women were asking themselves the same question: how such a thing could go on under Philippe's nose for an entire week.

"The children in morning assembly were all talking about it," said Mavis.

"I'm sure it was quite upsetting for them," Aubrey agreed.

The truth was that the students Ms. Potemkin overheard chattering about Michael Brubaker's Kalashnikov hadn't sounded very upset. They thought the Kalashnikov was cool. But no one at Harriet's meeting mentioned this. One of the many upsetting, even startling, consequences of September 11 was the reaction of the children. The children, for whom these events should have been quite upsetting (going against, as they did, everything that Chaney valued, everything it stood for), were masking their pain in an extraordinary manner. To the untrained eye, they hardly appeared upset at all.

"Of course, if this were the first incident with Michael," said Harriet. The women nodded vigorously. This wasn't the first incident with Michael. Far from it. There was the time with the vampire teeth in the "Gift to Be Simple" assembly. There was the Swedish Girls porn site he had downloaded to the library's computer for his Astrid Lindgren project.

"I wonder if it isn't time Michael had some assessment," said Aubrey, giving voice to the view of all the women in the room. The Chaney School was firmly committed to the idea of assessment. This was what they called testing. Not the sort of testing that required a student to study (such testing was pedagogically unsound); rather, the kind of testing administered by psychologists.

"You were thinking a Doakley-Dingle?" Harriet Tichenor asked.

"Oh yes, a Doakley-Dingle," said Aubrey. "Certainly."

As Aubrey began to itemize the tests, Mavis stole another glance at Philippe's T-shirt. What—what *was* that? Swirling lines, white on a black background. It looked, it sort of looked like—

". . . and I really think he ought to have the Leiter Attention Sustained subtest, and a Wechsler Three. And, frankly, a round of Adler Reactivity."

"The Adler Reactivity as well?"

"Oh yes," Aubrey said. "I'd recommend we try both visual and auditory cues, as I think Michael is more likely to be a visual learner, but on the other hand, one can't be sure that . . ."

It sort of looked like a horse. Yes, it definitely was a horse, at least a horse's head on a man's body. It was snorting and tossing, its mane wild, its eye fiery. And it was . . .

". . . with acuity deficit and probably sublimation of superego issues. You know, I don't want to get ahead of ourselves, but many of the indications for an antidepressant . . ."

Mavis had had to cock her head to the side in order to make sense of the design. The snorting horse was entwined with . . . a swirling something . . . swirling and flowing, and that sort of looked like limbs. Yes, limbs, legs—a woman's legs—legs all wrapped around . . . the horse! The horse on the T-shirt was . . . He'd just come from class—his class of Chaney School students—with this T-shirt right on his chest, showing . . .

Philippe was growing bored with the meeting. He noticed the odd angle at which Mavis Potemkin was holding her head. She seemed to be flushed.

"Your neck is okay, Mavis?" he asked in a whisper.

Mavis had gone scarlet now. She straightened, shook her head, and turned away.

Mavis? Ah, Mavis! thought Philippe. Tilfing—what an interesting idea! It had not occurred to me before.

". . . and some questions of depression, frankly. But these are only hypotheses, and we'll have to reconsider the situation when we have some better data. We can have another meeting after the first round of assessment," Aubrey finished.

Harriet nodded grimly. The Adler Reactivity. This did sound serious. Still, you couldn't be too careful, not with symptoms like these. She would have to discuss the situation with Michael's parents.

THE THING ABOUT PARADISE WAS . . . it could kill you.

Fritz was acting strange, Linda confessed to Dr. Helga Schadenfrau. Well, of course, who wasn't acting a little strange since September 11? Who hadn't been devastated? But this strangeness wasn't a September 11 strangeness, exactly. Linda could tell. This was a strangeness that had been building in him. A self-indulgence on his part. Maybe September 11 was an excuse to let it out, she thought. Maybe it was an excuse he was exploiting.

Linda was right about one thing. Something was happening to Fritz Brubaker, right down to his neurons.

All the trifling lies, so content before with silence, now clamored for his attention, the way a number suddenly leaps off a busy page when dabbed with highlighter. Not that it hadn't been there before, but before it had floated along anonymous and unmentioned. Suddenly the quarterly backflips to put rouge and lipstick on Playtime's numbers, the posing as perfect parents at the Chaney School, the Farm Street that forbade farms, these mild ironies that he'd tolerated so effortlessly, the familiar clothing of his life—suddenly these old clothes mocked and shamed him.

Why? False fronts and double standards were nothing new. All his life there had been falseness all around, and he'd smiled. There'd been hypocrites, and he'd shrugged and gone sailing. There'd been ambitious nerds striving for finance jobs, and he'd said, "Take them." So why now?

Molecules. That was part of the answer. Something in his molecules, something chemical, had changed. Neurotransmitters that must have long lain dormant were sending out radio beacons. Peptides and proteins were being catalyzed.

But there was another part, a deeper, sadder explanation. Fritz knew that absentee parenting hadn't quite worked out on Michael. To be honest, he'd pretty much whiffed on Michael altogether. And things weren't going very well with Linda, he knew that, too. But he'd always had at least one corner of effortless success. One brick in the wall was always taken for granted. Now he was beginning to wonder about that brick and whether there was a wall at all.

Kristin was becoming one of them. Or had already.

You can't count on anything, he realized. He took the marriage for granted, and look what had happened to it. He had figured things would work out for Michael and Kristin, and they had become strangers.

As September waned, Fritz fell into an insomnia loop: wide awake at three A.M., crashing at three P.M. Sometimes he managed to drift off before dawn, but only briefly. He cut out coffee, he dropped wine, but it didn't matter. Some mornings he lay in bed wide awake, his mind racing as the dawn came up. Sometimes he got up in the night and went downstairs, trying to read. But the words swam before his eyes. So he'd walk barefoot through the silent house, passing like a ghost through its exquisitely decorated rooms, so dark with the shapes of furnishings and so empty of life. He wondered how he'd come to live there. These kids, these kids were my link, he thought, and, and . . . But the last thought remained unformed.

Luce noticed that he was arriving at work even later than usual. His office was even more of a mess. He seemed sluggish, mechanical. He was late to meetings or missed them altogether. In the afternoons he turned his back to the door, leaning over the computer. She watched his head droop, and as he leaned motionlessly there, she quietly pulled the door shut behind him so that others wouldn't see.

She had to give him more and more reminders. Did he want to send her the pro forma that Frank wanted? Had he done the divisional report yet?

Dark rumors were skulking about the hallways of Playtime, too. There were whispers about California. Peter Greene had made a run at them, but the Californians had not rolled. People said that the asscovering letter had not been pulled and would not be pulled. That Eduvest revenue remained as fanciful as ever.

On September 26, late in the afternoon, after the secretaries had gone for the evening, Peter Greene asked Larry Jellicoe to "drop by" his office to "discuss things." This was not a scheduled meeting. It never made it onto anybody's calendar or e-mail or Day-Timer. By the time the CFO arrived, Greene had activated his privilege force field: Don Fink was already riding shotgun in the Hepplewhite as the door slowly closed behind Larry Jellicoe.

"The Californians are being pricks," Greene said. No one needed to hear the precise details. The dinners that Greene had, the suggestions he'd made, the gentle prodding and cajoling—no one needed a bill of particulars. These were bottom-line guys. It was late in the day, the third-quarter 10-Q was going to be out soon, and the bottom line was this: the Californians were being pricks. The state was not going to waive its right to cancel the Point 'n Learn! orders. This meant the revenue was no good, and Playtime would have to come clean about it.

"Can we cover it somehow?" Greene asked.

Was there unreported revenue from Q2 they could use as an offset? Fat chance. Had so miraculous a salvation appeared, it would have already been proclaimed in Greene's e-mail. He was just covering a base. The chairman stood at the window with his back to the room, watching the headlights of the homebound traffic on Route 128. In the silence that served as an answer to his question, a word joined the three men in the CEO's office: *restatement*, and just beyond the word, the fall of the dominoes that would follow. The breathless analysts' reports. A drop in market price. Outside directors calling; shareholders roiled. And then?

"Peter," Jellicoe said, "we're gonna trip the bank covenants." When this news came out, the banks would have the legal right to stop lending.

"Don'll have to work on a waiver." The lawyer would have to negotiate a little slack from the banks.

"That'll be a challenge, Peter," said Larry. "They're already nervous. They want a meeting. Just had a letter yesterday." Jellicoe began to recite the potential outcome of the bank freeze and the obvious threat to the Christmas season.

Fink was fidgeting on the chair, feeling that he'd better say something. If everyone expected him to get a waiver from the banks, then this whole problem might later be spun as his fault, after the banks turned him down. Fink began to employ the lawyer's usual stress-management tool.

Peter Greene turned when he heard the scrawl of the pen. "I don't think we need to take notes of this meeting," he said.

Fink put the pen down.

"Banks will be banks," Greene continued, turning back to the window. "They'll have to growl a little. But they don't want to see the company fail, either. Let's not oversteer, but let's prepare for a soft landing."

Greene remained at his window for a long time. Let's not oversteer, Jellicoe thought.

At length Greene continued: "What we have to do is prepare for the inevitable. The stock is going to take a hit. And we have to best position the company, Larry, and bring her in soft. We need to give the Street a plausible explanation so that we can move on." He turned and smiled beatifically. "Gentlemen?"

LONG INTO the morning Larry Jellicoe would toss and turn, the code words bouncing around in his brain. *Let's not oversteer. Best position the company. Soft landing. Plausible explanation.* It was like everything else Greene said, ambiguous as hell. But Larry kept coming back to the last thing: "plausible explanation." The stock was going to tank. He had to come up with a plausible explanation.

IT WAS on that same morning that Fritz Brubaker had a revelation.

Along about eight-thirty, he was driving his BMW north on Route 128, on his way to work. Traffic slowed to a crawl, and then a stop-and-crawl, and just before the Trapelo Road exit, it stopped. It was a complete, far-as-the-eye-could-see, get-out-of-the-car-and-peer-ahead halt.

He stood on the highway and peered ahead but could see nothing except a half-mile line of cars, shimmering in the tailpipe heat, all the way to the next bridge abutment where the road bent to the right and was lost to view. So he got back into the car and turned up the air-conditioning. He tried the radio for a while. On the public station they were fund-raising. On the yak stations the yakkers all reminded him of guys in the locker room, and the sports yakkers reminded him of guys in the JV locker room. So he turned off the radio and sat there in the quiet of his car, with only the air-conditioner blast and the thrumming of the engine for company.

And then, to Fritz's surprise, all of a sudden he was being lectured—lectured in his own head.

"You are forty-five," the voice said.

It was a voice with a didactic tone and a lecture-hall echo behind it. A voice in a dark green three-button suit, wearing a bow tie. A voice that had lost its hair. It was Professor Vorblen!

"One way of looking at your life," the professor continued, "is that this locus—this blacktop on Route 128 North in Waltham, where traffic is stalled on a Wednesday morning—is the precise midpoint of your life. It is the geographical midpoint and the chronological midpoint and the ontological midpoint."

This brain lecturer was not very comforting. Where did he come from, Fritz wondered. Demon seed of Fritz's old penchant for math, and this new chemical soup that was sloshing around up there?

Professor Vorblen began making sardonic mathematical jokes.

"You are a circle whose center is Waltham.

"Your velocity, like a pendulum's, varies in inverse ratio with your distance from Waltham.

"You will never exceed Waltham by a distance greater than that already traversed toward Waltham."

And so on.

This was ridiculous—Waltham! But the brain lecturer had a point. Wasn't forty-five pretty much the center of his life? (The Brubakers were by nature a long-lived tribe. His father, Cabot Brubaker, had been in perfect health at seventy-four when he was killed by the Rockport Express, and Uncle Monty was still kicking hard at eighty-nine—still skiing, for heaven's sake!) Didn't Fritz swing back and forth each day, like a pendulum, between an office tower in Burlington, fifteen miles to the northeast, and the Palazzo, fifteen miles to the southwest? If this was the center of his life, then where was that center?

He looked outside at the line of stalled cars shimmering with heat. Waltham.

The brain lecturer concluded this line of reasoning with something that wasn't ridiculous at all, that was in fact revelatory. In a steady voice,

as though he had just proved a mathematical theorem, Professor Vorblen said, "You cannot possibly sit in this car on this road driving to this
company to do this job for another twenty years of your life."

There the brain lecturer left class for the day. Then the traffic
moved. It lurched, stopped, inched, stopped, moved again; it began
crawling, and then rolling, and finally Fritz went on to Burlington.

Maybe he was vulnerable. He hadn't been sleeping, after all. And
maybe he'd been weakening under the assault of the insomniac stew,
because the brain lecture scared him. Maybe, too, there was another
thing. Did Fritz also feel some intuition, some sense of danger, as to
what might be happening when Jellicoe and Greene met behind the
closed door of the executive suite—as to what (or who) might be Larry
Jellicoe's idea of a "plausible explanation" to help "best position the
company"?

If so, it was deep beneath his consciousness, for his conscious mind
was on something else altogether. Fritz had never been one to examine
himself, not one to take stock of his life. He'd never bought the pop-
psych books or stared at his navel. His New Year's resolutions didn't go
beyond things like getting his 10K time back down to forty-two, or losing four pounds. Playtime had, as part of its official annual personnel review, a self-review form, but he'd never filled it out. But these chemicals
set loose in his head had him on a different course of thinking. His life
was a scarce resource. It was finite. And he could not do this with the rest
of it. The revelation dogged Fritz, and worse, it committed him to a
whole new and more perilous way of thinking. A precipitous way of
thinking.

It was as though he were on Paradise.

Up in northern Vermont, in the Green Mountains not far from
Burlington, since time out of mind, the Brubakers had skied at an odd
little resort called Stark Mountain. It was more than a ski area, it was a
state of mind. To skiers, Stark was an approach, an attitude. Stark had
never changed. It clung fiercely to its tradition. Its ski trails were narrow,
steep, and ungroomed; there were no high-speed quad lifts, no trailside
condo developments, no convention centers, no snowboards. There was
no snowmaking. The only way to the top of Stark was to ride the last single chairlift in commercial operation in America.

In 1961 Cabot and Monty Brubaker built a ski house two hundred yards from the base lodge. For almost half a century, Stark was where Brubakers made their first turn.

Linda came to the mountain by marriage rather than birth. She had never been able to understand what she called "the whole Stark *thing*." The Brubaker gatherings at the grimy, run-down ski house (the Bruhostel, they called it) where you never knew who was going to show up at midnight with five of his buddies. The Brubakers—all of them—would go on about it being the only place to ski. It separated the real skiers from the phonies. It had the best (i.e., steepest) trails. It was almost cult-like, this sick Stark machismo. "Why would you want to wait for forty-five minutes in a lift line?" Linda would ask. "Why would you even go into that disgusting ski lodge they haven't cleaned in twenty years? And those lift attendants—that guy who's so drug-crazed at the bottom. What's he say?"

"Go go go," Fritz would answer.

"Right. Go go go! Go go go! All day long! What kind of example is that for the children?"

No, Linda had never gotten it about the Stark thing. She never found four degrees above zero charming. She never liked the rockabilly music blaring from the speaker on top of the base lodge. Her mind always went to the things that needed changing about this place. Why does it have to be so ratty? What's so bad about a faster ski lift? Is snowmaking such a crime against nature, for heaven's sake? I mean, they have plenty of snowmaking at Sugarbush! If they could only change a few things, then maybe . . .

But Stark's main virtue—its unique virtue—was that they wouldn't change a few things. In fact, they would never change anything. It was exactly the same place it had been when Fritz was seven years old, the first time he rode the single chair. It was a living museum of his youth. About how many places could you say that?

Linda never got it that this was a virtue.

The Bruhostel was the same. The same bunks, the same electric griddle whose cord you had to jiggle to keep it working, a griddle that had fried ten thousand eggs and sixty thousand strips of bacon; the same spaghetti pot, the same *World of Skiing* book (copyright 1964) in which, on page 63, Stein Eriksson demonstrated the "Wedling" turn on wood skis with cable bindings (and hadn't even cable bindings returned with the telemark skiers who flocked to Stark?); the same boot room, and in the farthest dark corner, in all likelihood, some of the same ski boots. At Stark itself, the lodge, the lifts, the Chute, the Fall Line, the Lynx, all were exactly the same. The faces in the lift line, older now, more grizzled, many of them were the same. Even the guy in the stained chamois work shirt and the untied Sorrels who said "Go go go!" as he ran the single chair up to you on the loading platform, he was the same. Fritz liked that guy. No, he *loved* that guy. Because he was the same.

Perhaps most important of all, Paradise was the same.

Most of the ski trails from the top of Stark were treacherous, but one took pride of place. If you traversed a wooded ridge from the warming hut on the summit, then followed an unmarked ski track, you reached the steepest and nastiest trail of all. There was no sign for it. It wasn't even on the Stark Mountain trail map. They figured if you didn't know about it via word of mouth, you oughtn't be there.

They called this trail Paradise.

You could kill yourself on Paradise: that was the first thing. The pitch—forget about it. The trail was no wider in spots than a footpath between the silver birches and the stunted red spruce; lose control and you were likely to hit one. Deep in their winter skirts of ice and snow, the trees stood like gnarled old trolls, scolding you for attempting this lunacy. The second thing was, once you were on Paradise, you were committed. There was no green-circle bailout, no traverse, no escape. And the third thing was what it did to your head. You had to do some desperate things on the trail just to get down it. Here and there you had to leap, or sideslip, or butt-ski, cling to an edge, grab a tree. Your thinking would get a little crazy, a little irrational, on Paradise.

You didn't really ski Paradise; you just got down it the best you could. As Fritz's revelation continued to dog him, it was like getting down Paradise. The pitch got steeper. The very first turn into it committed him to a sort of Socratic fall line.

The lecturer's conclusion wasn't a conclusion—it was only the beginning of the trail. If he could not do this for twenty years, could he do it for ten? Clearly not. Five? Three? And what was "this," exactly? Was "this" only the Playtime job that Fritz could not do, or was "this" all of it? The house in Dover, the job, the Palazzo? The marriage? The family?

Could he go on with the marriage? The marriage that was always about to turn the corner. Linda was that gorgeous flute of lead crystal, but could you ever fill it with champagne? Could you drink from it, get it to bubble and fizz? And were his own son and daughter two more Lindas?

Jesus, what was happening in his brain? He still loved her, but now he saw with vicious clarity that he loved the full glass she could be better than the vessel she was. Fifteen years on, maybe she would never get to what she could be.

It got steeper as he went down.

When the lights were off and they lay together in bed, he tried to talk to Linda about his strange feelings, his sudden uncertainty. But he couldn't get the conversation started. She kept brushing the subject away. "I've been having the strangest thoughts," he'd say, and she'd either get in a dig about the goat or there-there him about how we were all suffering from 9/11. Then he tried inching up to it by asking Linda whether she saw herself doing what she was doing for the next twenty years. That backfired: Linda went right to defense. What else would he propose she do? How else would they support the children? (Translation: pay the mortgages on the Palazzo and the Siasconset house and the school fees and the college tuitions and save for retirement and all the other necessities.)

He asked her once whether she would keep working for some positive reason—that she was proud of it, that it excited and energized her, that it was important. This brought bedroom tundra: Why shouldn't she be proud of her work? While maybe Fritz didn't think it was important, maybe the fact that other people were willing to pay so much for the work she did was some indication that—

"I didn't say you shouldn't be proud of your work. I'm asking *are* you. Are *you* proud of it. I didn't say it isn't important. I'm asking whether *you* think your work is important."

"What are you suggesting?"

It only got steeper and narrower and nastier, but he couldn't get off the trail.

October came on. He realized with sadness that it was impossible. His wife was lovely and brilliant and responsible and utterly unable to enter into this conversation. The chemical-crazed neurotransmitters were popping on and off in his mind, not hers. There rose in the back of his brain a voice that at first he could barely hear, and then he could hear a little louder, and then whose words he could begin to make out, and finally, whose words he could understand with perfect, chilling clarity.

"You want out," the voice was saying. "You want out of all of it." Could that be so? Should he listen to this voice? "Fritz, for once in your go-along, get-along life, face facts. You've screwed this up, and you don't want any part of it anymore."

It was he, not Linda, who was on the downslope. His thinking, not hers, was irrational and irreverent and dangerous. How could he expect her to understand? He was skiing Paradise, and his wife, Linda? Linda would never even see Paradise.

PART II

AMHERST COLLEGE, 1976:
ECONOMICS 101
(SECOND LECTURE)

THIS AFTERNOON there is a palpable excitement, a buzz among the students. Professor Vorblen stands at the front of the hall as before. He wears his three-button suit and his bow tie, as before. The students file in. They notice the lectern. There upon it stands a glass, filled already with golden liquid.

"Shall we have another auction? I have here this glass. Who will pay for it?"

Smiles, laughter. Economics is fun! Will it be beer every class?

Jams and flip-flops raises his hand. He asks, "Is it a Molson?"

More laughter.

"But why are you laughing? That is precisely the question that should be asked. What is in the glass? No one asked the question last time."

Now he has them thinking.

"Why not? Why didn't anyone ask me last time? Think back."

A hand. A student explains that last time they saw it. The bottle, he means. "We saw you pour it."

"But you didn't taste it. You had no guarantee. Why did you assume I had Molson Golden ale just because it was a Molson bottle?"

Confusion. Well, what else would it have been?

"Trust is very important in economics," says the professor. "Let us ask the winner of the last auction. On how many previous occasions had you had experience of a bottle of Molson Golden ale?"

Laughter. The left tackle is now a celebrity. "Maybe a thousand?" More laughter.

"A conservative estimate, I'm sure," says the professor. "And in those thousand experiences, how many times had the liquid in the bottle not, in fact, been Molson Golden ale? Leaving out, of course, those occasions when you might not have been able to distinguish."

More laughter. The left tackle rises to it. "That might rule out most of them, sir."

Riotous laughter in which, for a moment, even the professor joins. "I see. Then tell us of the experiences you can recall."

"Well, Professor, of the times I can recall, the liquid in the bottle was always Molson Golden ale."

"Always. The astute undergraduate has made a profound observation. When the bottle says Molson, the beer *is* Molson. This had always been true before. What was always true before will likely be true again. And that, class, is the basis of the only trust known to economics. The bottle said it was Molson, and it was Molson for a thousand times. So it will be again.

"Now expand your thinking. Think of the bottle as not a bottle at all. Think of it as an audit opinion from an accounting firm, say, Coopers and Lybrand or Ernst and Ernst. Telling you everything inside the bottle is what it should be. You can trust it. Why? Because of a thousand audit opinions before.

"All right, then. Last time, you saw the bottle. You saw the label. You saw me pour. And you heard me describe the contents of the glass as beer. You all believed it was beer. In fact, it was beer. And that was the basis for the auction.

"Today it's a little different. Let us examine the effect upon economics of *mis*trust. I will tell you that this glass contains a yellowish liquid. It might be beer. Or it might not be. It might be an-y-thing."

The professor draws out the last word with fiendish ambiguity. He knows his audience. Although it might be anything, these Amherst undergraduates are familiar with only two varieties of yellow liquid. From them is heard a most nervous titter.

"Now, what am I bid?"

There are no bidders.

"It might be beer," says the professor. "Or it might not."

A hand at the back. "I'll give you ten cents."

Nervous laughter again, but the professor waves it away. "Why not? He's making a bet. If it's beer, good bet; if it's not, he hasn't lost much more than a rather sheepish trip to the men's room."

When the auction is completed, the glass of liquid sells for thirty-five cents. It turns out to be beer.

"What happened here? Last time our market was efficient. Everyone in the room had all the salient facts. Everyone knew what the supply was. And everyone could gauge the demand. But today look what happened. It was a terribly *in*efficient market, wouldn't you say? You bidders had no confidence in what it was you were bidding for. So some speculators in the back"—laughter—"took the beer for much less. When markets are inefficient, the speculators always profit. They feed on fear and mistrust. It is their lifeblood.

"Last time three dollars and five cents. Today thirty-five cents. Yet it was, in fact, the very same beer. Was it worth less today? I leave you with this question: if the market is this sloppy, this inefficient, this prone to fears and alarms, is it the place where value should be determined?

"Class dismissed."

12

THE VIEW FROM
THE TERRARIUM

BY ANY OBJECTIVE MEASURE, the trading desk of U-Trade was the end of the line. After this it would be aluminum siding, or time-share condos, or maybe the local Chevy dealership. "Trading desk" was a misnomer, a sop to the crushed egos of those who took a paycheck from U-Trade: it wasn't a trading desk but a bank of telephones. The "brokers" at U-Trade were telemarketers.

This is where Jimmy Civiletti had wound up.

Most of the U-Trade brokers had washed up on this last beach after a long voyage. What high hopes they'd had, embarking on a sunny morning long ago, with a following wind in the Bear Stearns or Merrill Lynch training program. They'd weathered next a trading floor, a cold-calling desk at Oppenheimer or Nomura, where all around them—close enough to touch—were successful brokers in J. Press suits, men and women making hundreds and hundreds of thousands of dollars! It was exhilarating.

For a while. Until the trainees began pursuing their hopeless leads, until a few weeks and a few hundred straight hang-ups were under their belts. Until they began to realize that despite the fancy name of the firm and the fancy title on the business card, despite the encouraging way people at cocktail parties said, "Oh, you're a broker with Merrill!," what they really did for a living was call perfect strangers and grovel in the hope that this particular stranger would be the one in ninety sufficiently bored with life that he wouldn't hang up.

Sometime after that came the first real storm: not making the cut, being called into the glass office on a Friday afternoon while everyone outside stared. A check for two weeks, hopes for better weather in the days ahead, best of luck, sailor.

But these were brokers. They remained optimists. Things would work out. The first try was an anomaly—clearly. Still young, still eager, still intoxicated by the look of the successful ones—no older than me!— on cell phones, in snappy suits, those hotshots who, with one call, could place a sell order for a hundred thousand Intel. So they shipped out again.

For the lucky ones, there might be another berth at a name broker. Maybe they sailed awhile longer, but the result was the same.

Then began the progression of smaller and smaller, seedier and seedier vessels: the odd-lot houses, the boiler rooms in Long Island City or Hoboken. No J. Press suits here, not even a wool suit in sight—just a managing partner who never came out of his office and was one step ahead of the regulators, and a psychotic floor manager handing you two dozen previously burned leads and telling you to unload fifty thousand shares of some sketchy penny stock (in which the company was long) *or else*—with the "else" left vague.

But not for long. There were no claps on the back when the end came in Hoboken; no pep talks about how you had the talent ("You've got the knack, kid, stick with it, you had some bad timing with the down cycle, but it's all timing: you'll make it!"), no beers after work, and he's a jolly good fellow—no, none of that crap now. Just clear out your veneer desk by Monday, and by the way, the base we paid you was a loan advanced against commissions you never earned. Read your contract, you piece of dog shit. You owe us four thousand dollars. We said sell *or else*.

It's else, asshole.

For Jimmy, else had come. He had washed up on the last surf-pounded atoll in the vast financial ocean, a desk in U-Trade's walk-in office in Grand Central Terminal in New York City. They called it the Terrarium, on account of being behind the glass on display to a hundred thousand commuters a day. Not that you'd ever become a broker on train-station walk-ins and phone calls from retirees for a flat salary of $35,000 a year. Not even a broker was delusional enough to imagine that. No, this wasn't Morgan Stanley. But this job, the bosses hinted, would give you some downtime each day, a few minutes when the phone wasn't ringing and you weren't having to walk some old fart through the website, just a few minutes.

And in that few minutes, you could day-trade.

Those hapless or unfortunate brokers still hanging in, still hopeful, still refusing to read the writing on the wall, believed that this was all they needed. They could beat the market. They would find the seams, run for daylight, make a score. All while being staked to a base by U-Trade. When you looked at it like that, it wasn't so bad.

Because, after all, these were brokers. Optimists. No, it wasn't so bad at all, when you thought about it that way.

Which is how, each day at eight-fifteen A.M., Jimmy Civiletti was thinking about it as he arrived at his desk.

There were two of them there, Jimmy Civiletti and Louis Fredell, whom Jimmy referred to as Lurking Louis, on account of the way Louis would be lurking whenever you were on to something good; whenever you had a good customer on the phone, whenever you'd noticed an interesting stock in the research. Louis was a forty-three-year-old bachelor who lived with his mother, Edith, and aunt Hermine in an apartment in Queens. He had a forty-two-inch waist, and his hair was thinning. His halitosis was uniquely potent. He wore a big pair of black glasses always sprinkled with dandruff (the flakes adhered to a sheen of facial oil). Louis was profoundly unsuited to brokerage work, having neither market judgment nor sales ability. But he was a skilled eavesdropper.

U-Trade had started out reasonably well for Jimmy. The market went up, and Jimmy went up with it. Through the first quarter of 2001, he'd been on a roll. He'd taken the ten he scratched together from the Vitos (his father, Vito Civiletti, who had an electronics distributorship in Mamaroneck; and Jimmy's elder brother, Vito, who was working with Dad) and traded it up to $30,000. For a few months he felt genius surging through himself like a fire. In the forefront of his mind was the Xanadu of geometric progression. Thirty would become $60,000 by July; $60,000 would become $120,000 by October. He would have a quarter mil by New Year's Day. This was going to work.

Except that the market tanked. By July his $30,000 was not $60,000, it was $20,000. By September it would be down to $15,000. On October 3, 2001, in the aftermath of the September 11 attacks, Jimmy Civiletti's account would stand at $9,400.

During the early part of this slide, Jimmy had a quasi-religious vision. It had come to him in an unlikely way, on an afternoon in the Ter-

rarium when the uneasiness in the market and the hot days of early summer had slowed business. Nobody was trading, nobody was calling. The
afternoons were particularly brutal. He spent a lot of time staring out,
wondering about the people going by.

On the afternoon of his vision, Jimmy was staring, slack-jawed, out
of the window, when a lovely girl appeared. The crowd parted, and there
she was, hurrying from a train. She dropped a bag right outside the Terrarium glass, in full view of the Terrarium creatures, then bent exquisitely to pick it up. Jimmy watched her, transfixed. She was about twenty,
she wore a tank top and shorts, her hair was bobbed and cute, her skin
tanned and smooth as a pearl. The bag she dropped was a small canvas
number bearing the inscription "MoMA," and sunscreen and a few other
odds and ends fell out of it.

She was the girl who had always been around Jimmy Civiletti as he
grew up, when he bused tables at the Larchmont Yacht Club. There had
been a member, a Mr. Arnold, who always came to dinner at the yacht
club after sailing, a guy who lived in the tony grid of Victorians by Long
Island Sound that they called the Manor. He had a cute blond wife like
this and two perfect daughters like this, and more than anything or anyone else, he, Matt Arnold, a guy with whom Jimmy had barely spoken,
was the reason that Jimmy Civiletti had put up with all the bullshit, the
securities training programs and the cold calls and the boiler rooms. Because Arnold was a broker—a stockbroker with a fabulous Victorian
house on Maple Avenue in the Manor, and a hot wife, and gorgeous
blond girls, and a thirty-eight-foot Fields sloop, and, in the parking lot of
the Larchmont Yacht Club, a Mercedes.

Now, ten years later, Jimmy stared through the Terrarium glass at
the blonde, who might have been from Westport or Rye or even Larchmont, come into the city for an afternoon at the Museum of Modern
Art, yes, that was it, with her MoMA bag and her cute bob and—Oh
Jesus, oh my saints in heaven! The long, pure perfection of those legs!
The arch of the instep coming off the pink flip-flop, the delicate gathering of those calves, the trim brown thighs smooth as coffee ice cream,
the pert accent of that bottom, the winking invitation of those cutoff
shorts!

She was right outside the glass wall of his Terrarium, not five feet
away, just as the perfect Larchmont girl had always been five feet—and

a million miles—away from Jimmy Civiletti. He wanted to fling her onto the sand at Far Rockaway beach and rip the cutoff shorts from her. He wanted to hold her hand in Central Park. He wanted to marry her in St. Augustine's Church, right on Larchmont Avenue, on a Saturday morning during race week, and stand at the front door as the nobs drove by on their way to the yacht club. He wanted to introduce her to his brother (who was making all the money in his father's electronics distributorship). He wanted to catch her eye.

She had gathered her things back into the bag. If she turned his way, he might—

Just then Lurking Louis leaned over Jimmy's computer screen. "Check out those shorts," Louis said.

Jimmy looked up at Lurking Louis's glasses, flecked like a coconut donut. He saw Louis's troll-like grinning mug. He smelled his hot, foul breath. Gone, gone, vision gone, reverie at the Rockaways gone, and— He looked back at the window. Perky shorts, teeny tank top gone. The girl herself was gone.

The girl was gone, and the usual summer bustle had swallowed her up. The commuters hurried by in khaki suits, in chinos and golf shirts, looking up for the train times and track assignments. The crowds surged back and forth from somewhere else, to somewhere else, anywhere else. Jimmy returned to his computer screen and the occasional desultory pensioner calling in to trade a hundred shares of General Electric. The minutes dragged. The girl was gone in an instant, and his life was once again a weary second hand inching around a sluggish clock. It was another endless afternoon in the Terrarium, with the fat pathetic Louis lurking at his shoulder.

A fear had overtaken Jimmy. A gnawing panic, even, that this might be his life—his whole life might be stuck in this Terrarium, looking out at the girls from Westchester. Worse, he might mutate into something like Lurking Louis—he might become Lurking Louis! When Lurking Louis was twenty-six, did he look like me? Jimmy wondered.

It was too horrific to contemplate. Fear must have supercharged his brain, because he turned to his work with a kind of panicked desperation. And as he did so, something resonated. There is a message here, a lesson here, he thought. It came to him that this was the day, the moment, that something, someone—God—was calling him, sending a message. He had to hear it, if he missed it now, he would miss it forever. The girl, the afternoon, the Terrarium, the computer screen . . .

What had Louis said? What had that reeking, leering medicine ball said—Louis Fredell, who never in his life said anything of moment. Something. Something as he leaned over the cube, opening his mouth. Something as he lurked there, stinking like a cooler that you forgot to empty from the beach trip three weeks ago, like those garbage cans behind the lattice outside the yacht club Snack Shack in July. What had he said? *Check it out*, or something like that. Lurking Louis, staring goofily at the blond Venus outside the Terrarium.

No, it wasn't "check it out." That wasn't what he'd said, not exactly. Eyes that had been heavy a moment before were now full of wild surmise, and Jimmy Civiletti, like stout Cortés, suddenly had a vision of a peak in Darien (or a slate-roofed mansion in Greenwich). *Check out those shorts.*

Yes! That was it. He moves in wondrous ways, His wonders to reveal! Blood coursed through Jimmy's brain. This was the sign he'd been waiting for!

JIMMY CIVILETTI didn't leave U-Trade that night at five, with Louis and Florence, the receptionist; nor at six, with the boss; nor at seven, nor eight. Late into the night he worked, plotted, planned, until only the lonely commuters, the exhausted lawyers and analysts, and the drunks dribbled by the Terrarium glass. He didn't notice any of them. Yes—it made perfect sense! *Check out those shorts.* This market was heading down. Everything was going down, but some stocks would head down faster than others. Jimmy, now a hardened twenty-six-year-old, had seen the vicious side of life. He'd gotten an education in greed. This education had taught him that as the market tanked, the temptation upon guys with inside information would become irresistible. Irresistible! So Jimmy would check out those shorts. He would track short *sellers*. If he could get just ahead of this wave, he could profit.

Short sellers sold shares of stock they didn't yet own, betting that the price of the stock would drop. A short seller made a contract today in which he promised that tomorrow he would sell one hundred shares of Merck at $60. On the buy side, the buyer promised to buy the shares at the same price. The short didn't actually own the shares. If the price of Merck was lower than $60 tomorrow—say it had dropped to $58—then the short would "cover his position": he'd buy a hundred shares at $58 and sell them at $60, earning $200. A short could make a lot of money if he bet right. Of course, he could lose a lot, too. If the price of Merck was $62 when he had to cover, he'd lose the $200.

As the epigrammatic quality of the injunction weighed on Jimmy's brain—*check out those shorts*—he understood that in a down market, people inside companies, people with inside information, knowledge that those companies were about to publish bad results, for example, would try to sell short. If he followed these people, he would get his edge.

There ensued the longest period of sustained study in Jimmy's young life. He subscribed to *The Short-Sale Trader.* He installed a computer program to track market activity in short sales, and to monitor every U-Trade short sale. He studied the information, learned who the players were. Jimmy bided his time as the summer months dragged on. In July and August, he was still learning. Then came September, and Jimmy hadn't yet found the edge. But somehow, even after September 11, he remained confident.

FOUR MONTHS after Jimmy's revelation—to be precise, on October 3, at two-fifteen—an icon on his computer screen blinked. That meant a short transaction on one of the Fortune 100 companies. And this was a U-Trade short. He pulled up the detail and learned that an online customer named Phineas Brubaker (Jesus, what a name!) was shorting Playtime. He had bought a sale contract for thirty-five hundred shares. Playtime was a huge company. Jimmy noticed that its third-quarter numbers were due shortly but not out yet.

But who the hell was Phineas Brubaker?

Jimmy had been tracking the shorts for months, and he'd never heard of this guy. He quickly established that Brubaker wasn't a listed broker or an arbitrageur. He checked the account Brubaker opened at U-Trade. He'd never shorted anything; indeed, he didn't have anything but blue chips and Internet companies, which seemed to be down, and most of which he'd put into an account for a Michael Brubaker.

Jimmy's heart began to pound. He ran industry searches, I-bank searches, couldn't find anything on this Brubaker. The guy wasn't a pro.

That meant he might be . . . an insider. And Playtime was a perfect target: huge market cap, little volatility, but plugging along, a great big fat supply ship churning slowly through clear waters, begging for a torpedo.

Jimmy Civiletti picked up the telephone and called Playtime's headquarters in Massachusetts.

"Phineas Brubaker, please," he said.

"Phineas?"

"Yes, please."

"Well, we have a *Fritz* Brubaker."

"That might be him. In finance, right?"

"Yes, Mr. Brubaker's in the finance department. He's the senior assistant controller."

The words "senior assistant controller" were like an adrenaline shot to Jimmy Civiletti's carotid artery. A finance guy! A guy who knew the numbers! He thanked the operator and hung up the phone. His pulse had skyrocketed. He was hyperventilating.

Control yourself, he thought. He counted to ten, measured his breathing. He thought back to the cold-calling days, got his rap down, then punched in Playtime's number again.

"Fritz Brubaker, please," he said this time.

"One moment."

Luce's voice came on. "Mr. Brubaker's line."

"Hi, can I speak to Phineas?"

"Phineas? Ah . . . may I ask who's calling?"

"Oh, this is Louis Fredell calling. An old friend from school."

"Sure . . . would you hold on, Mr. Fredell? Funny, no one calls him by his name very often. Does he . . . know you? Mr. Fredell? Sir?"

But the phone was dead.

Five minutes later Jimmy Civiletti placed a thirty-day sale order for ten thousand shares of Playtime, at the market price of $50 per share.

When Jimmy went to the men's room later that afternoon, Louis Fredell was watching. Louis had noticed how, after lunch, Jimmy had gotten all busy and secretive. He'd been turning his back away when he spoke into the phone—Louis always noticed when Jimmy did that, because it was the only time he couldn't make out what Jimmy was saying. He'd been staring at the computer screen, running searches, making notes. And how nervous he looked, how skittish and jumpy. Lurking

Louis waited for Jimmy to go around the corner, then fished out of Jimmy's trash the order confirm. Wow, he thought.

Fifteen minutes later, Louis shorted Playtime five thousand shares. Ten minutes after that, Edith's account shorted the stock a thousand shares.

FOURTEEN BLOCKS uptown at Jamieson and Company, on the fifty-eighth floor of the Trump Tower, a bright young graduate of the Wharton School named Rodney Immerman was finishing up a report for his boss. Brad Jamieson was one of the most successful arbitrageurs in New York. In September, Jamieson had assigned Immerman to follow Playtime. He didn't particularly want Playtime stock—he thought the company was overleveraged—but he was interested in Peter Greene. He'd been watching Greene for some time. He wanted to anticipate Greene's next acquisition, buy up a 5 percent position, hold it hostage, demand ransom from Greene, and double his investment. So Immerman, eager, bright as hell, hungry to please, was assigned to profile Greene and his company, and guess where he was going next.

"Mr. Jamieson? Do you have a minute?" The tall young analyst stood awkwardly in the boss's doorway.

"Sure, Rod, come on in. Figured out Greene's next move?"

"No, I haven't, but I, well, I thought I should tell you about something I noticed today."

"Tell me."

"Something might be going on this afternoon. I thought I should tell you, anyway. Somebody's shorting Playtime."

"Really? Who?"

"Well, four trades out of U-Trade."

Jamieson frowned. "Discount brokerage is for amateurs, Rodney."

"Right, sir. I mean, that's the point."

The point? This interested Jamieson—that he didn't get the point and the kid was willing to pitch it anyway. One of the things that made him an astute investor was his lack of ego, his willingness to be taught.

"Sit down, sit down," said Jamieson, and for the first time Rod Immerman found himself admitted to the boss's corner office. He sat down gingerly, gaping at the floor-to-ceiling window with a view of the park.

"Tell me your theory."

"Well, you have four shorts so far. I ran them—the last three are registered at U-Trade—they work there or are relatives. The first trade I can't trace. Thirty-five hundred shares. So I figure some client sold short, and the brokers saw what was going on and got in immediately."

"How much did the brokers short?"

"Not much. But the brokers at these online services, well . . ."

"Yes?" Jamieson didn't understand.

"They're kind of poor. I mean, usually these guys have bombed out everywhere else. They may not have too much to spend."

It was a different world, Jamieson thought, shaking his head. But now he was even more interested. He called up the stock on his Bloomberg. No movement that he could see in volume or price. It looked like it would close off twenty-five cents on modest volume.

"What time was the first trade?" he asked.

"Two-fifteen."

"News today?"

"No, none."

"No financials, press releases?"

"I can't find any."

"Lawsuits? Antitrust? They got a Hart-Scott pending?"

"No, nothing."

"When's their quarter end?"

"September thirtieth, so—"

"So the numbers are imminent but not out yet. Anything from the analysts? Company spinning?"

"Noncommittal stuff. Market uncertain in the toy industry. Some research since 9/11 about a falloff in discretionary buying, like toys and so on, but you know, nothing dramatic. Stock's been off since 9/11, but . . ."

"Whose hasn't," Jamieson agreed. He looked at the trend graphs. Nothing obvious here. Still, it was interesting. "So we have a short from a discounter. Somebody with a computer and a long-distance phone line." The smile was spreading across Jamieson's face. "You think these U-Trade brokers spotted somebody maybe trading on some information he shouldn't have?"

Immerman nodded. "It's just a hunch," he said.

"Then maybe the stock is overvalued. Maybe the market is incorrect. And it's our job to correct the market, is that it?" They shared a conspiratorial smile. Arbitrageurs liked to point out the important public service they provided. They were the gyroscopes of capitalism, always shaving off a million here or a million there so the course of the market could be corrected. For that valuable contribution, who would begrudge a man like Jamieson the $28 million he'd made last year?

"Life goes on, I suppose, even after September eleventh." Jamieson looked at his watch. Four-thirty-five. "Tell me, Rod," he said, "I don't want any trouble here. You don't have anything inside on these guys, do you? A friend who works there?"

"No, nothing like that. I just saw these trades."

"Somebody in your frat, maybe?"

"Ah, I wasn't exactly frat material."

"No. A buddy then, your brother-in-law. Your third cousin, Rod. Come on, who's your source?"

"No, nothing, I've just been tracking the company, like you said."

"You haven't laid the CFO's administrative assistant or anything?"

Immerman blushed. It did seem unlikely.

"Rod, I understand how these things work. A guy wants to get ahead. Somebody you knew in business school passed something he shouldn't have. If that happened, tell me now. It's okay. We'll forget it."

"No, nothing like that." Immerman looked crestfallen. This had been going so well, and now he was being attacked. When he'd been trying to help.

A long, awkward silence ensued, in which the boss studied Rod. His frank, searching gaze made Rod feel hot behind the ears.

"How'd you come up with this?"

"Well, I've been studying Greene, studying the company, as you asked me. I've been following them on Bloomberg. I set up a program to track trading patterns in the stock, and to try to correlate Greene's acquisitions with activity in the stock. The program picks up all short trades. It's luck, really."

Jamieson nodded. "In this kind of work, you have to be like Caesar's wife. I get an SEC investigation once a year, and I do get tired of it. If you were to be lying to me right now, it would be me who would pay the price. Now, tell me, in the research you've been doing, you can scrape together some evidence that the company's future is uncertain, operational problems, overleverage, P/E too high, right?"

"Well, I guess, I mean not anything huge, but I suppose—"

"Rod, you're missing my point. That's the result you want to get to. Capiche?"

"Oh, I see."

"Good, Rod, because frankly, we've all been in mourning since September eleventh, and it's time to get back to work. It's time to take a chance on something. Why not an online short? Here's what you are going to do. Print out all the research, the 10K, the recent Q's, and get them up to me in the next half hour. Then go back to your office and write me a report. If you have plans tonight, cancel them. This report needs to be bulletproof. About how the stock is overvalued. About how the company is at risk. Executive summary, then detail. Write me a report, and send me that by e-mail tonight. Do you understand? Tonight. Nothing about today's shorts."

"And tomorrow?" Rod ventured.

"Tomorrow's another day. We'll think about it," said Jamieson, and he gave the kid a nod that said, "You can go now."

Immerman pulled the all-nighter. He would prepare the mother of all critiques. The company would be suffering from an invisible but fully metastasized cancer by the time he was done.

But he sealed the deal long before, at six-fifteen P.M., to be precise, when he called his boss back and said, "Mr. Jamieson, I found out something else kind of interesting."

"Yes?"

"I traced the first short. It was in the account of a guy named Brubaker. I did some checking, and the address comes up a match for a guy who works for Playtime."

"Where?

"In their finance department."

Jamieson whistled. "Okay. Let's not jump to any conclusions. Get me the report I assigned tonight. You will get an e-mail back from me saying to meet me here at seven-thirty tomorrow morning. Meet me here then. I'm still not completely sure about this play. But I'm definitely interested. At seven-thirty we'll discuss your report and decide what to do."

BOTH OF THEM worked long into the night. Another thing that made Jamieson such a successful arb was his combination of insight and discipline. He spent several hours planning this campaign. The key to the game would be panic, and the key to panic would be surprise. He must overcome logic with fear, which would require a sudden onslaught from multiple fronts. He'd need five, ten, maybe even fifteen corporations. If he goaded the market the right way, before anyone could realize the shots were all coming from one place, maybe he could stampede the sellers. Then, before the market stabilized, he'd use even more corporations to cover his position. But it would have to be big, and very, very fast.

AMHERST COLLEGE, 1976: ECONOMICS 101 (THIRD LECTURE)

BEER TODAY? Another party? They come in punctually, early even, and take their seats, looking eagerly around the hall for party favors. The syllabus said "short selling" was the subject today. The students have a vague understanding that short selling is something exotic and amoral, something clever and ruthless and financial and very Wall Street. It has to do with selling what you don't own. (Which doesn't make any sense. How can you sell what you don't own? But maybe he'll explain it.) Maybe because it was so Wall Street, there wouldn't be beer but some other party favor—something stronger? There is in the crowd an expectant buzz, almost festive. We're excited to be here, thrilled to be here. But there is no beer on the lectern today.

In strides Professor Vorblen at two P.M. sharp, and the air instantly comes out of the balloon. It is the same dark suit and the same bow tie, but something feels different. The professor looks grim, dyspeptic. Down die the murmurs.

"What is economics?" he asks. "Is it science or psychology?" He lets them ponder for a moment. Then: "You think economics is science? You think it is measurable and definitive and quantitative? You think it is objective and hard-nosed? You think it is predictable?"

Actually, they do, although that doesn't seem to be the right answer. What's with the dark mood? Some problem with the dean? Some personal thing? They like to speculate about the professor now. He is so unlike economics himself, so unpredictable.

"Let us explore this. As of this moment, each person in this class has a B grade for the course."

That's a conversation starter, all right. He has their undivided attention. This is interesting. Amusing, anyway. I mean, he is kidding. Isn't he? A B? The students cast subtle glances to the left and right, to see if their classmates think he's kidding. Which he must be.

"I'm not kidding," he says. "Each of you, right now, is holding a B. And you can sell. Right now. Just put your hand up, sell, and you'll have a B for the course. I'll write it down in the grade book, and you can walk out of here a free Amherst undergraduate. You won't have to attend another lecture, read another article, hand in another problem set. You're done. B. Then again, your grade won't get any better, either. Takers?"

Well, this is a little weird. He *is* kidding, isn't he? This is what their faces say as they look at one another in the hall. We all like to joke and all, but this is *grades*, and this is Amherst, and—

"I'm not kidding."

Silence. He says he isn't kidding. Maybe he isn't kidding. Is that possible?

But no hands go up. A B grade in economics isn't terrible, but it isn't exactly going to get you into Harvard Business School. And this is Amherst College, where people expect to get into Harvard Business School; or at least where people's parents expect them to get in.

"You don't want to sell," says the professor. "You want to hold. You think your grade may improve over time. That's a strategy, I suppose."

A strategy? What does he mean, a strategy? The way he said it like that, that irony in his voice, that didn't sound so encouraging. A *strategy*?

"Perfectly understandable. If you work steadily, if you attend class, do the readings, hand in the problem sets, if you stick with the fundamentals, you think you'll do better than a B. Surely. That is a strategy that may be logical."

Understandable? Logical? How about smart? Is it a smart strategy? Does it work? That's what we want to know. The professor is not himself today. And this has been cute and interesting and all, but let's move on to something else. Time to stop kidding around with the grades stuff. It makes us nervous.

"I'm not kidding."

And that mind-reading business. Enough with that. It's creepy.

"On the other hand, this professor of ours," Professor Vorblen says, "let's be honest. He's erratic. Bit of an odd duck. Beer in the classroom and all that? Is he reliable? Is he not just a bit mercurial? Might I actually do worse than a B with this professor? Might I end up with a C in this course? What is his grade curve, anyway? What'd they get in this course last year—what was the curve then? Should I take the B? Should I sell now?"

Never in the annals of Amherst College has a lecture hall been more scrupulous in its attention to every syllable, every nuance, from the professor.

"Now, as you ponder that, you on the left side of the center aisle, all of you, please, leave the room. Leave the room and shut the door behind you. Wait in the corridor. You will be readmitted in five minutes. Quickly, please. Five minutes, no more."

The lefts are taken aback; they look around at one another. What's this? What now? We are not liking this class today, not at all. Our grade is a B or worse, and now he kicks us out. What's his problem? They shrug, they shuffle to their feet; a buzz, a murmur, arises; they grab their notebooks and texts and head back up the aisle. When the last has gone and the door closes behind him, the professor smiles for the first time. But it is a very cold smile.

"Economics is scientific, right? Operates on predictable, measurable values, right? Let's see.

"It's now two-fifteen. They'll expect to be readmitted at two-twenty. But we're going to explore the power of psychology and, in particular, of fear. The first thing is, we're going to be late. We're not going to let them back in at two-twenty. Nor at two-twenty-five. We'll keep them stewing in the corridor for fifteen minutes. Fifteen minutes is a long time to be worried.

"As for you? You are going to be the group that has inside information. They do not have inside information. But you will. We'll explore how that makes them feel. And how it makes you feel. Let me tell you the piece of inside information I'm going to give you."

Oh, good, they are thinking. This is another game. This will be cool after all. And we're on the inside. Even better.

"Your grades are going down. All of them."

Excuse me? This isn't cool. Some game!

"What I mean is, a B will be a very good outcome. You may sell your grade this period, but the price for grades is going down. I will guarantee that. I am guaranteeing you that the price for grades is heading nowhere but down today. After today I'm not sure what will happen. No guarantees one way or the other. But the B that's on offer now will not be on offer at the end of the hour. The next price for grades will be lower, and I expect there will be more price drops in grades over the course of the hour. I want you to digest this, to think about it.

"Remember, I am not kidding. I am deadly serious about this. There is a B on the table. But it will soon be off the table. You know that. They don't. You know it will be lower than a B by the end of the hour. They don't. That's the difference between you.

"Oh, one other rule that applies to you who have this inside information. If any of you shares this information with any of them, you will receive a failing grade for the course.

"And now," he says, "we will wait."

This has become extremely, decidedly unpleasant, the whole thing. The news, the threat, the waiting—there is nothing good about this. The right-hand side of the hall is pretty unhappy, pretty nervous about all this craziness. A joke's a joke and all, but . . .

The clamor, the buzz, is all gone. The students have turned pale, many of them. Maybe Vorblen really is crazy. Maybe it will be worse later. A guy who runs around with beer in a lecture hall, he might be perfectly capable of giving you a C just to make some dramatic point. For the sake of his own ego. And then where would you be? When there was a perfectly good, perfectly respectable B on the table right now. Free for the taking. Not to mention you wouldn't have to lift a finger in this class again. You could blow off the reading, the problem sets, even class. When you thought about that, B wasn't such a bad grade. It was respectable. You could cut your losses with a B. You could take a few gut courses in English and anthropology and work your GPA up.

Not until two-thirty does the professor let the other half of the class in. They return hesitantly, like a herd of cattle being led into an unfamiliar pen, each waiting for another to go first, jamming up the entry, then tumbling in slowly. There is still some undergraduate breeziness as they enter, but it dissipates quickly. He said five minutes. Why did it take fifteen? And why are those guys on the other side of the aisle all looking down and away. What has he been telling them? Where's the joking, where's the fun? Where's the beer, for Chrissakes? What's going on?

The professor says, "I have grade B on the table. Are there any takers?"

Halfway to the back of the hall, on the right, a hand shoots up. Then, tentatively, a few more. The lefts are surprised by this. What have they cooked up? Then a few more hands go up.

"Stop!" the professor shouts. "All you in the class with your hands up, keep them up. No other hands up. Right. I'll take the names now."

He takes down seven names. To the lefts, the most disturbing thing is the tremulous way six of these rights say their names. Fearful, unhappy. This is some kind of a game that's been set up for the lefts, surely. Right? Except that it doesn't look like a game.

The professor has finished taking the names. "Okay. You seven students have a B for the course. The grade for everyone else in the course is now B minus. Any takers? Hands up, please."

B minus? He can't do this, can he? Isn't this illegal or something?

Up go the hands on the right. Six hands, eight, eleven.

"I have a question," sings out a voice from the left side of the hall. "This is just a game, right?"

The voice is ignored. "Any takers for a B minus?"

"You're kidding, right?"

The professor is ignoring the questions. "The grade for the course is going to change. Do I have takers for a B minus?"

Shyly, a hand on the left. Then another, then six.

There will be twenty-three B-minus grades.

It takes quite a while to write them all down. At last the professor finishes, and looks up. "Right. The grade for the course is now C plus. Are there takers?"

AT TEN MINUTES to the hour, the professor stops the grade auction. There are seven Bs, twenty-three B minuses, twenty-two C pluses. Thirty-two students did not sell their grade.

"We began with whether economics is science or psychology. Back at the beginning of the hour. Remember that? And then look what happened. When first I offered the perfectly respectable B, there were no takers. No one believed it. But after I divided you and the insiders got insider information—that the price for grades was heading down—they acted on that information. Seven of them decided to cut their losses.

Then look what fear did to the outsiders. As they saw the price move
down to B minus, they got in. This is how short selling can work. You
have a small number of people who believe a market is heading down.
They act. Then a greater number of people act out of fear. This acceler-
ates the effect. If one creates the right circumstances for downward
market movement, one can make money by short selling—by selling a
security at a price that tomorrow will be overmarket. In our marketplace, grades were on sale for B at the top of the hour. Fear drove the
price to C plus by the end of the hour. If grades were transferable, you
could have made a point in grades simply by offering to sell at B what
you could buy later at C plus.

"Reflect on something. Every single outsider could have had a B.
Every one of them rejected it. Yet sixteen of the twenty-three B-minus
grades were outsiders. In economics, fear is a powerful motive.

"We said earlier that economics was about value, and that markets
drive value, but today's market was a function of fear. That suggests that
fear is value, or at any rate that fear is a value. So I return to the questions we asked at the outset: What is economics? Is it science or psychology?

"And what about me and the grades? Was I kidding?"

THE RED ROOM is all but empty. The students have fled. He'd barely
said "class dismissed" and they were grabbing their things, scurrying
away like a beach crowd at the crack of thunder.

All but one of them. One student is still slouched in his seat,
halfway back on the right-hand side, a quizzical look on his face. Meanwhile, the professor has gathered up his papers and packed his satchel.
Then he notices him. "May I help you?"

"No, sir, it's all right. I was just trying to figure it out."

The professor remembers. "You were the first to sell your grade,
weren't you?"

"Yes, sir," the young man says. "That was me."

The voices echo in the hall. "You didn't hesitate," the professor says.

"No, sir."

"And now you're trying to figure out if I was kidding. Well? Was I?"

The young man smiles. He has an easy smile, an easy manner. He
gets to his feet and slings his backpack over a shoulder. "Professor," he an-

swers, "your offer was, ditch the problem sets, the paper, and the exam, and nail down a B, right?"

Professor Vorblen nods. "That was the offer."

"Well, I don't mean to be disrespectful or anything, sir, but I sure hope you *weren't* kidding."

ON OCTOBER 4, in Burlington, Massachusetts, Larry Jellicoe and his accounting staff began the day with their own seven-thirty meeting. The agenda was the auditors. Because Greene's plan to roll California had sputtered and died, Settles Bartlett was certain to make the company take the hit—once Settles found out about it. The company kindasorta hadn't gotten around to discussing this particular issue with Settles, not yet. But that was going to happen tomorrow.

The restatement would be a big blow, Jellicoe knew. A review meeting with Settles's audit manager was scheduled for the next day—they'd break the restatement to them then—so the main thing on Jellicoe's mind was how to deliver the message to the accountants. The plan was to put the numbers out on the tenth. He had gathered his accounting troops to script the meeting.

Peter Greene was away from the office. He'd taken the G-IV to Cincinnati and was at a breakfast with a big new prospect. He had a bead on an acquisition. The investment bankers were skittish, but that only meant prices would be lower, he assured them. Now was exactly the time to diversify.

AWAY TO THE SOUTH, in the Trump Tower in New York City, Brad Jamieson had been at his desk since just after six A.M. Immerman met him there at seven-fifteen, and together they sat and reviewed the e-mail report. At eight, the decision was made.

On Wall Street, the traders were at their desks by seven, checking the overnight news. None of them expected anything unusual that day. The analysts who followed Playtime had no warning of what was coming. Overnight there were no major interest-rate moves. The Asian markets had been quiet. The nation remained stunned, trying to return to work but with only half its mind on business. Work was hardest in lower Manhattan, where the gash in the sky still seemed almost to bleed, and the smoky smell had not left the air. In lower Manhattan, grown men were still crying on street corners on October 4. Their world was still in shock. It looked like another slow day in the markets.

At the New York Stock Exchange, the opening bell rang at nine-thirty A.M.

Jamieson's first artillery shell—a short sale of 200,000 shares by the New Caribbean Trade Company, Ltd., of Freeport, Bahamas, made through its brokerage account with Salomon Smith Barney in Miami—was lobbed in at 9:35. A blip hit the screens at 9:38. A few people paid attention, not many. Then a second blip hit at 9:45 (a short from a Swiss holding company) and a third (an Idaho limited-liability corporation) at 9:49. Three trades: 430,000 shares shorted.

On the floor of the exchange, the traders took notice. Something was up. At 9:46, the price of Playtime moved to $49.50. The third short triggered dozens of trading programs. Brokers began calling in orders. The price fell to $48.45.

Brad Jamieson, watching the market's initial reaction from his array of computer screens, took his finger off the trigger. Let them digest this. But not for too long.

Over on Madison Avenue, at Credit Suisse First Boston, a red icon blinked on the computer screen of a young analyst named Aaron Cohen. When Credit Suisse landed the underwriting for Peter Greene's new offering, Cohen was assigned to play cornerback, shadowing Playtime's every move. Cohen clicked through his Bloomberg. Three short trades at the opening, price down $1.55. The clock clicked over to 9:52. Another short trade registered. While Cohen was watching, the price dropped to $47.75.

What's going on? Cohen was wondering. Did those guys put the numbers out without telling us? Cohen went to his Nexis but found nothing. Playtime had not released its earnings report.

On Wall Street, the traders were now at full alert. These traders were the animals of the financial forest. Reacting to small changes in financial humidity, they sensed danger, even if they didn't understand its causes. Their noses were in the air. A storm was coming. Many of them were long in the stock—they'd bought healthy positions over time, betting on long-term price growth. Even with the September slide, they still had profit to take. They began liquidating positions.

The price went to $47.

UP IN BURLINGTON, Massachusetts, Larry Jellicoe finished his staff meeting and went to the men's room. They had their plan of attack for what they'd tell Settles. The California reservation-of-rights letter had been an ass-covering thing, and Playtime was on a path to being fine with them, and then September 11 had screwed up everything royally. In other words, shit happens.

It wasn't pretty, but it would have to do.

At 9:53, walking back to his office, he passed Louise Wu, his administrative assistant, and asked genially, "Louise, how'd we open this morning?"

"Market's up, but we're off about two dollars," she said.

That stopped him in his tracks. The market's up, and we're off two dollars? But that was old news, about ten minutes old. When Larry Jellicoe got to his Bloomberg, at precisely 9:54, the price had moved to $46.75.

"What the hell?" he asked. The only answer came burbling from the peace fountain on his credenza.

ONE HUNDRED EIGHTY MILES to the south, Brad Jamieson followed each tiny move in the price, waiting for the first sign of buyers. This stock was a mile wide and an inch deep. He had figured fifty cents or a buck in the first wave, but now it was pushing four and dropping like a stone. He had planned to cover his positions at five dollars. He checked his computer. His firm had already made $8.5 million. But this thing felt wild. Maybe the bottom was a lot farther down. Maybe, instead of covering, he should short again.

"What do you think, Rod?"

The boy blanched. He was handy with numbers but too young to have any judgment about the fog of financial war.

Jamieson looked at the screen. He decided to go with his instinct. This wasn't the bottom. He readied the next attack.

Between 9:55 and 10:15, three more short trades hit the Bloomberg screens.

IN THE TERRARIUM, Jimmy Civiletti could not believe his eyes. He'd made $50,000 already! This was staggering! He stared at his computer terminal in a wide-eyed ecstasy, feeling the gush of genius course through his veins. But when should he cover?

Lurking Louis wiped the dandruff from his glasses and peeked surreptitiously at Jimmy. He was excited, too. And he was going to cover the moment Jimmy did.

AS THE SECOND WAVE of short trades hit, volume surged. The price fell to $45. Then $44.

At just after ten A.M., Playtime stock was the biggest trader on the board. Bloomberg screens were blinking all over America. "Who the hell is shorting Playtime?" brokers asked at Goldman. "Are there numbers out on Playtime?" wondered the traders at Lehman and Merrill. "You guys got anything on Playtime?" they hollered across trading floors at Hambrecht and Salomon Brothers. They called for the research.

But nobody had any research. Nothing on the Bloomberg or Nexis, no news, no announcements, no bad earnings reports. Only what looked like a drumbeat of shorts hammering the stock, one after another, every ten minutes. At Fidelity and Teachers, at Loomis Sayles and MetLife and Travelers, they double-checked their computers, they yelled to their analysts for news, for anything. Why were the shorts killing the stock? Nobody knew. They went to the website. They double-checked the news wires.

The price dropped to $43.50.

They called the analysts, but the analysts were all on the phone with the company. And Rumor, now roused, now hungry, angry, powerful, and energized, seized her opportunity. Rumor always suggests that Bad is merely a whistle-stop on the way to Worse. You can still get off the train at Bad. But hurry! Through telephones and e-mails and shouts, Rumor had her marketplace.

"Gotta be something in the financials."

"When the hell were those numbers coming out—this week, wasn't it?"

"They got a press release out, anything? Where's the research on this company?"

"They get sued or something?"

"There's nothing on the wire. Nothing. It's gotta be the numbers. The shorts have gotten ahold of the third-quarter numbers somehow."

"It's a picture. Somebody's painting us a picture. The numbers aren't out. It's an acquisition play."

"Pretty good picture. Pretty good goddamn picture."

"It's a game. It's a setup!"

"Yeah? Then where the hell are the buyers?"

"I'm thinking of buying. This thing will turn."

"My ass it will turn. You want my position?"

"I'm cutting my losses."

"I'm outta here. The shorts have got the numbers."

"What do the analysts say?"

"Sell it. Sell the goddamn position!"

"Did they have an analyst call? When's the analyst call?"

"It's a fucking *toy* company. Who buys toys when the country's been attacked?"

"They're overleveraged. Maybe the orders aren't in for Christmas. What do the orders look like?"

"*Adios, amigo.*"

"Dump it!"

"Maybe they're not shipping—the Asians. You know?"

"It's ballast: heave it!"

"Prepare to unload, baby!"

"Down the hole!"

"Dump the fucking stock!"

"It must be the numbers. The third-quarter numbers!"

Jesus, the stock was down to $43. To $42.75. Something must be seriously wrong with this company.

WAS IT BEER, OR PISS?

THEN, just as Rumor had made her rounds and stoked the fear, just as she had unnerved the trading desks and quieted the skeptics, Jamieson sent in his third assault force to set off a full-scale rout. Five more unknown corporations, five more shorts totaling 560,000 shares. All over

America, fund managers at mutual funds, insurance companies, and brokerage houses feared the worst. This many shorts couldn't be wrong. The fund managers called their brokers and the traders. They'd seen enough. Dump it. Something had to be wrong with the third-quarter numbers.

BY 10:50 A.M., the world headquarters of Playtime was a siege bunker. They gathered around televisions like they had on that dreadful morning a month before. All thought of work was impossible. The mortar rounds thudded in with deadly, metronomic precision. The stock went to $41. To $40.50. To $40.15.

The stock was under $40. Jesus, the stock was under $40!

Fritz Brubaker had missed most of this. After the staff meeting, he'd retreated to his office, shut the door, and tried to get his brain around a vexing spreadsheet. An hour had gone by before he heard, outside his office, a commotion about the market. So he went online.

"Wow," he said to himself.

He had a sinking feeling. In his mind, he did the math, played it right to the end game. The numbers weren't out. The restatement wasn't known yet. But somebody was already making a big bet on bad financials, that was clear. Something was wrong with the VD unit's off-balance-sheet stuff, and the Street had figured it out. What would happen when they announced the restatement tomorrow? This was bad, Fritz thought. A lot of good people would be hurt. The price was dropping before his eyes.

The stock under $40, and the numbers not out yet. This could actually kill the company.

UPSTAIRS, Larry Jellicoe got Mark Engelhardt, the company's lead analyst at Morgan Stanley, on his cell phone. "What the hell is going on?" Jellicoe demanded.

"Larry, I was going to ask you the same question!"

"I have no idea, Mark. This is coming from fucking nowhere!"

"What's in your numbers? What's in your goddamn numbers?"

The Credit Suisse guys were on Jellicoe's other line. The lenders were calling, too. The hedge funds with big share positions were calling. They were all calling.

Jellicoe looked at the Bloomberg screen. $39.25. $38.75. "We're under attack!" he screamed. "Who's *doing* this to us?"

"Larry," said Mark Engelhardt, "what is in your Q3 numbers? What the hell is going on with your third-quarter numbers?"

Then what had hit Fritz hit Larry Jellicoe. The Street didn't know about the restatement. The meeting with Settles was tomorrow. Playtime hadn't put out a report yet. If they said something about a restatement now, the floor would fall out from under this thing. If he said, "Nothing," and then the numbers came out, the company could be dead meat. Misleading statements, 10b5 lawsuits.

"I'll call you back."

"Larry!"

Jellicoe hung up the phone. White-faced, his assistant stood before his desk with a fax and a stack of messages. But Jellicoe shook his head. "Get me Elboe, Fromme and Athol," he said. "Get Rosenblatt on the phone immediately."

Jellicoe got a sudden leg massage as his BlackBerry remote wireless thrummed on. He pulled it out. Incoming from Peter Greene.

JESUS, LARRY, GET A STATEMENT OUT THERE!

IN THE TERRARIUM, Jimmy Civiletti felt the essence of New York City course through him like electricity. The throb of finance, the pulse of commerce—it pounded through his veins. Yes! He had done it. He had outsmarted the Street. He had been a warrior—a warrior! He had slain the saber-tooth tiger with his bare hands. Covered in gore, he had dragged it back to his cave. He had triumphed!

Pigs could get fat, but hogs would get slaughtered. The stock price would come back. He pushed the "enter" button and covered his position at $37. Bring on Greenwich, baby! He'd made $120,000 of profit in a single morning. Jimmy Civiletti had arrived.

In the next cube, Lurking Louis covered, too.

BY 11:25, a secretary had found Marvin Rosenblatt via his cell phone, pulling him out of a meeting in an Elboe, Fromme conference room. Rosenblatt could hear the panic in his client's voice.

"And we've got this restatement that isn't out there yet, Marvin.

I've got the brokers calling me and the analysts calling me and *The Wall Street Journal* calling me, and . . . Oh, Jesus Christ, it's at thirty-five. It's at thirty-five! Jesus, it's—"

"Larry, get ahold of yourself."

"I've got to give them a statement, Marvin. I've got to give them a statement. The shorts are fucking killing us, I've—"

"Larry, calm down."

"Don't tell me to calm down! The stock's at thirty-five, how can you—"

"Larry, please. Please listen to me."

"All right. All right, I'm sorry. Help me out here, Marvin. I'm listening."

"Did you say you're going to have to issue a restatement of the second-quarter earnings report?"

"Yes."

"And that information has not been made public yet?"

"No."

"All right. I see the problem. Well, there is risk both ways, I can see that."

"Marvin, for once don't tell me there is fucking risk both ways, all right? Enough with that lawyer crap! Just give me a statement that we can—"

"Larry," answered Marvin in his agonizingly methodical way, "my advice to you for the moment would be not to make any statement."

"Are you kidding, Marvin? Are you kidding?"

"Larry, my judgment would be that I think there's a high degree of risk in this environment, a high degree of risk. I'd be inclined to give serious consideration to holding off on a statement until we can develop a better understanding."

"Marvin, I'll be in chapter eleven while you guys develop a better understanding. Anyway, Peter's just told me to make a statement."

Marvin paused. This was a problem. The CEO could be a little mercurial. "He did?" he asked.

"Yes."

"Perhaps we could conference Peter in."

"No, he's on the G-IV. He sent me an e-mail telling me to get a goddamn statement out there."

"I see," said Rosenblatt. He had that infuriating calmness, that un-shakably level tone. And all those lawyer words. "Larry, relative to a statement at this time, I would be concerned about exposure not only to the company but possibly even personal exposure to you and Peter."

"To me?"

"If you were to make statements."

"You mean—"

"Ten-b-five risk, yes. You could be sued personally."

"Oh," said Larry Jellicoe. "Well, what—what do I do? What do I say?"

"I'd be inclined not to say anything."

"I can't not say anything! How can I not say anything? I'm the CFO of this company. They're calling!"

"It might be useful at this particular time to be in, well, perhaps to be in certain high-level meetings from which you would not be in a po-sition to be interrupted to take calls," said the senior partner.

"Don't answer the phone?"

"Right."

"How will that play on the Street?"

"I don't know, Larry. Certainly from a risk point of view, there are—"

"Risks both ways, yeah."

"Let me suggest that I bring a team out to your offices this after-noon, Larry. Let's gather your public relations and investor relations people, speak to the analysts after the market closes, and try to under-stand what's happening here. The company will have to make a state-ment of some kind this evening. We'll want to work with you on that."

"Okay, I understand. Thanks, Marvin, I appreciate it."

"And for the moment—"

"I'll stay off my phone."

"You might also try to reach Peter. In light of his e-mail, I would be concerned about any statements that he might be inclined to make at this time."

WELL, MARVIN, you got that right. Peter Greene was inclined to make statements. He was inclined as hell to make statements. This criminal stock manipulation, this fraud that some Wall Street bastard was pulling, this was fucking up his company, his business plan, the potential acquisition (also his options)—everything! Not to mention having embarrassed the hell out of him at this morning's meeting. Statements needed to be made. This thing had to be set straight.

Besides, he had Don Fink with him, and that meant it basically would be privileged.

At that very moment, Greene was making statements from the cabin of the Playtime G-IV, taking matters into his own mouthpiece from twenty-eight thousand feet. He had Fink next to him, listening in (so it would be privileged or, if not privileged, exactly, pretty much okay). No one was going to encourage him to do anything because he was busy speaking his mind to anyone he could find to listen. He was somewhere over New Jersey, racing back to Boston. He was a man on the move, and he wasn't going to stop for a lot of legal mumbo jumbo with Elboe, Fromme & Athol.

"Jerry," he was saying to the reporter, "I must say we are very surprised by this. Very surprised. I think there is something fishy going on with the short sellers, and perhaps with some kind of Wall Street play for this company. We are going to press, to *press* the SEC to investigate this activity today."

Greene looked at Fink for encouragement, raised an eyebrow. Fink nodded vigorously. Yes, this was all right.

"As I believe you'll shortly see, our chief financial officer will be issuing a statement—"

"Your CFO is putting a statement out?"

"Yes, absolutely, and you'll see—"

"Is it out yet?"

"Well, I don't know if it's hit the wire yet, Jerry, I'm on a flight right now, but I'm sure it will be out any minute, and—"

"Can you fax it to us? Like . . . now?"

Fink shook his head. No, that didn't sound—

"Well, I don't *have* the statement," Greene said. "I'm on the plane, Jerry. Why don't you call our investor relations people, and they'll have it faxed to you. Anyway, this price movement, as I was saying, it has no bearing—none—on company value."

"You're confident of that, Mr. Greene?"

Fink stiffened.

"I'm completely confident of that."

"How do the third-quarter numbers look?"

Greene glanced at Fink. Fink didn't know what to do. His face was frozen somewhere between shake and nod, smile and frown.

"Mr. Greene?"

"Yes, well, they look . . . fine, fine. The third-quarter numbers are looking fine. They'll be out shortly. I understand the financial people are in their usual process of finalizing the financials. This has nothing to do with the third-quarter numbers, there are no major surprises there, this is all about somebody, some of the well-known short sellers in New York running a—"

"You're on target?"

"Sure, sure, this has nothing to do with the numbers."

Greene looked over at Fink too late. Deer in the fucking headlights.

"Okay, thanks," said the reporter.

The hell with Fink. Peter Greene stopped looking at him. He was useless. This was a goddamn crisis! It called for action! So Peter talked to Jerry the reporter for another ten minutes about how wonderful the company was. Meanwhile, Jerry was watching his Bloomberg. While Greene was telling him how wonderful the company was, Playtime lost $250 million of market value.

Jerry's story hit the Dow Jones news wire at 12:15:

Peter Greene, chairman and chief executive officer of Playtime, Inc. [NYSE: PLTM], today blasted what he called the short sellers in New York for the sudden and dramatic fall in the company's stock price. At 11:30, the bid on common stock was $32.00, down 36% from the opening. Greene denied that today's rout was prompted by financial developments. He said the company's third-quarter earnings, due for release next week, contained no surprises, and that the company was on target to meet analyst expectations, which had projected profits of $2.45–$2.75 per share for the quarter.

Oops. Did he really say "on target"? Memo to directors' and officers' liability insurers: your insured, Mr. Greene, has just handed the plaintiffs' class-action bar a blank check.

Back at the head office, the price collapse had more or less shut

Playtime down. Nobody was taking calls. Nobody was going to meetings, nobody was even canceling meetings. Paralysis had set in. Every computer was logging on to the markets, and every employee was watching his options sink, deeper and deeper into the dark underwater ooze. The entire company was grinding to a disbelieving halt. People were stumbling out of conference rooms, stunned. They were the same company they'd been yesterday, right? Making the same products, selling them to the same customers, right? How could this be happening?

Yesterday it was beer—how could it be piss today?

IT WAS RAINING in the late afternoon when the limos began to pull up to the front entrance of Playtime's headquarters. The suits spilled out: lawyers, accountants, consultants, all hurrying into the building with identical long faces. All sternly no-commenting the local TV news guys camped there, who were trying in vain to snag just one of the long faces and get it to say something.

In the boardroom, the long faces gathered late into the night. In fact, when Fritz Brubaker joined the meeting at just past five, the first person he met was his wife. She was standing next to Marvin Rosenblatt.

"Hey, hon, fancy seeing *you* here! We must *really* be in trouble."

Fritz leaned in, but Linda deftly turned to the side, lest Fritz kiss her on the lips in front of all these people, and then she laughed—her nervous "don't embarrass me publicly, Fritz" laugh. This was awkward enough. Why must Fritz make an awkward enough thing even more awkward? Couldn't he at least try to look a little concerned, a little more solemn?

"Hi, Marvin, how've you been?" Fritz greeted Rosenblatt.

Marvin extended a hand to the man whose wife he was screwing, thanking him for asking. He projected the appropriate professional demeanor. Because Fritz was in finance, Marvin gave him an earnest look of condolence, as though Fritz had lost a relative.

"It's okay, Marvin. It's only money." Fritz smiled.

Marvin wondered whether he meant the stock crash or something else.

God, why did he *do* things like that? Linda fumed. She covered her fuming with a tight smile. Fritz was bad enough as a husband, but as a client? Couldn't he look more—appropriate? For her sake?

Just then a troop of accountants filed in, and Larry Jellicoe realized they'd have to get started, even though Peter Greene had been delayed. The G-IV had been diverted to Hartford after developing an avionics malfunction. The pilot suspected that his passengers had been using their phones or sending e-mail and that the signal had corrupted his instruments. Greene and Fink denied it, although the pilot noticed that Greene swiftly pocketed some sort of black plastic device when he raised the issue of onboard communications. Anyway, Greene and Fink were now in a limo somewhere in Connecticut, heading north to headquarters.

So Larry addressed the table. The group fell silent as the CFO looked down the cold row of chubby accountant faces. The slick Power-Point presentation he'd scripted for tomorrow's scheduled breakfast meeting with the accountants, that was out the window. But Larry didn't know what the hell else to do, and Marvin Rosenblatt's warnings were still ringing in his ears.

"Well, it's been a crazy day," he said, and smiled.

The chubby accountant faces didn't smile back.

"Frank, you want to take us through it?"

Pitts, who was sitting halfway down the long conference room table, looked up with surprise. *Frank* take us through this mess? Nobody had told him this would happen. He didn't have PowerPoint slides or anything. The chubby faces turned his way. But Frank Pitts wasn't born yesterday. He resumed a poker face.

"Rachel has this issue she wants to tell you about," he said.

The buck had reached bottom. The cold row of faces turned toward the end of the table and Rachel Ewald. Poor Rachel! She blanched. She bit her lip. Then, suddenly, the words poured out in a frightened rush, substituting a terror-stricken interrogative for the declarative voice.

"You know? There was this thing? On Eduvest? Which is one of the limited liability corporations in the video development division? And there's this little problem?"

Until Fritz couldn't take it anymore that they were doing this to Rachel. Rachel Ewald was a great accountant, and a good and decent friend, extremely reliable and careful on the numbers, but public speaking shriveled her like a raisin. It was just cruel.

"Terry, look," he interrupted. "There was a huge overstatement of Q2 revenue out of Eduvest. It's a big charge. We have to restate."

Silence followed this blunt remark.

The accountants, who wore a glacial expression upon arrival, now took on the aspect of fjords in Iceland. The analysts turned grimly to the managers, and the managers turned grimly to Terry MacMullin, the engagement partner. And MacMullin, a short round fireplug, turned grimly back to Jellicoe and inquired how huge, precisely, this charge was.

"Well, kindasorta a hundred or so," Jellicoe said.

From this point the weather deteriorated. The sun set in Iceland, and the temperature dropped to about forty below, and an east wind blasted in from Spitsbergen, and the only heat remaining was an angry red glow given off by the molten lava bubbling up and about to burst out on the ice fjord. The arctic eruption occurred at just past nine-thirty P.M., when Greene and Fink returned to headquarters and joined the meeting. MacMullin actually went at it with Peter Greene, *mano a mano*—ripping the CEO in front of everybody.

"I want to know right now, Peter, when management knew about this restatement."

"Excuse me?" (As in, "Are you out of your mind talking to me, Peter Greene, this way? You—accountant? You balding little bean counter who depends on me for fifty percent of your business?")

"Right *now*, Peter. No more bullshit. When did you know?"

No more bullshit? The insolence! Calling Peter Greene on the carpet! In front of twenty-five witnesses. This actuary! This little bat turd! This bookkeeper! After all we've done for Settles!

"Excuse me?" Greene repeated. (Addressing now the gathered throng, as in, "This guy is still coming at me? This green eyeshade with a potbelly? This boccie ball with horn-rims? This mosquito whose career I can squash with a phone call?")

Chest to chest! Chin to chin! (Well, chin to chest, anyway; the fireplug accountant was shorter than Greene but feisty as hell. What a terrier!) Would Greene haul off and pop the accountant? Would the accountant haul off and pop Peter?

"And what did you mean by that idiotic statement to Dow Jones, Peter?"

"Excuse me, Terry? Ex-*cuse* me?"

"When did management know about this restatement?"

"What are you, the special prosecutor? Have you forgotten who your client is? Can I hold the press's hand and make sure they write down their quotes accurately? Can I hold finance's hand to make sure they get me all the necessary information in a timely—"

But MacMullin was mad as a hornet, a fat hornet whose nest has just been sprayed. And he wasn't buying one more shovelful of Peter Greene's bullshit. "On target? On fucking target, Peter? Are you telling me the management of this company is so inept, so clueless, so incompetent, so utterly without controls that you didn't know this restatement was coming?"

A hornet? A terrier? No—a pit bull! The accountant was a pit bull with his jaws clamped right on Peter Greene's leg.

That was just about enough of that. Who the hell's conference room was this, anyway? Whose Fortune 100 company? Not MacMullin's, that was for sure. King Peter would rally the troops. Once more unto the breach! If Settles wanted war, it would be war.

"Listen, Terry, your firm did fourteen mil of consulting here last year, and twenty-two in the audit. Mouth off like that again, and we'll see if maybe Ernst and Young would like the work."

Peter Greene looked to his left and right, looked for his troops to be sounding the war cry and leaping to the battlements. But the troops were all consulting their fingernails or musing over some interesting footnote on a piece of paper, or the view from the windows of flickering headlights on the cars driving through the rain on Route 128. The troops were about as noisy as a gang of librarians. They certainly weren't going to fill up the breach with English Dead, or even Playtime Dead, for the Playtime King.

Nice speech, Peter, but you lose.

Everyone knew it as soon as the words were out of Peter's mouth. Everyone knew that Terry MacMullin might as well have had Peter Greene's balls right in his fat little hand.

"Peter, you won't fire my firm," said MacMullin. "But after what I've seen today, we might consider resigning. And if we resign, I'd recommend you short the stock yourself. Because your company will be toast."

Silence. The troops were cowed. Pins could be heard dropping.

The cocksucker! An accountant mouthing off like that—to the CEO of Playtime! Up went Peter Greene's Adam's apple. And then down.

But nothing came out of Peter Greene's mouth. Because Mac-Mullin was right. Settles held his balls. After today's slide on the market, if the accountants resigned, it was over. The whole thing would melt down. No question about it, when a Big 5 accounting firm turned and ran from a Fortune 100 company after this kind of stock crash, then nobody would trust anything. Forget the banks, forget the bondholders, forget the equity markets, forget the vendors, forget the employees. Playtime would be a big smoky hole in the ground.

Greene turned on his heel and left the room.

But the tension remained, and it was powerful. The lawyers, the finance guys, they stood as mute as the statues on Easter Island, each wondering what came next, until a voice in the back said, in a stage whisper, "Bitch-slapped—in his own damn house!"

It was Brubaker. His colleagues turned to him, shocked at this breach of loyalty. (Oh, *God*, Linda thought.) But the joke broke the ice. There were nervous chuckles from the accountants, and then a laugh or two from the investor relations guys, and then even the lawyers smiled.

"Maybe I got a little carried away," said MacMullin.

"Everybody's jumpy tonight, Terry," Fritz said. "It's been a rough day. I think we all need a beer. It was pretty rough on Peter, too, and I'm sure it's been rough as hell on you guys. Let's all relax for a few minutes, then take this a step at a time. We need to finish the restatement, you guys need the books. Terry, give us your proctologists. We'll pull every record you want, if it takes all night and you have to climb right up into Playtime's intestines. Let's all take a deep breath and do our jobs."

THE FUNNY THING—and the thing that continued to bother Fritz as he finally headed home at two the next morning—was that the math was wrong. The actual numbers would show that the market had *way* overreacted. You ought to be able to make money by buying some stock.

But now it wouldn't matter. Nobody would read the numbers; nobody would read past "restatement." "The shorts were right," people would say. "There *was* something."

Fritz was still pondering the same question—what *was* Playtime worth?—as he drove back up through Waltham that morning, returning to Burlington after only a few hours' sleep. The company wasn't owned by one accountant with a clipboard, who knew what all the bits and pieces were and could tally them up each day. It was owned by tens of thousands of strangers who didn't know much of anything. Banks, insurance companies, pension plans—they knew a few things, they read the SEC filings and the analyst reports and kept tabs, but the moms and pops, all with their teeny-weeny pieces of ownership, they didn't know bupkus. To them, it wasn't about bits and pieces, bricks and mortar. To them, it was about what someone would pay for their hundred shares. And what somebody might pay for the stock might not have too much to do with the bits and pieces.

Now, a person might say that valuing the company based on the stock is appearance, not reality. But in the world of public companies, appearance can become reality very quickly. And it was happening to Playtime.

The stock had tumbled because of fear. People thought other people knew things—bad things—that they didn't, and people generally assume in that circumstance that the mysterious evils known by others are much more evil than they actually are. Their fear was compounded by the jitters that had never left the marketplace since the 9/11 attacks. People were still scared. This was the psychological dimension that Brad Jamieson exploited.

Still, Playtime might have recovered. Smart, greedy investors (men like Brad Jamieson, perhaps even Brad Jamieson himself) might have bought the stock as an investment, figuring it was undervalued. They had made money riding it down, and if they were convinced the price had gone too far, they would get right back on the horse and make money riding it up.

The problem was the accountants. The stock crashed on October 4. Instead of being able to announce the next day that the company was strong, was robust, that this was an anomaly, the opposite happened. The accountants made Playtime announce that its June earnings report was wrong and had to be redone: this was the dreaded restatement. This headline was all that anybody read. Nobody wanted the details, nobody cared about the details, the headline was enough. It proved the shorts right. A restatement! Problems in the books! There must be other shoes to drop.

On October 5, the price didn't climb back. It hovered at around $20, waiting for the other shoes. This led to other problems, so the perception became reality—the reality that ultimately sent the company into a death spiral.

Playtime's lifeblood was Christmas. September and October were its crucial time for shipping the hottest-selling items. Each year, to pull off its business plan, Playtime bought up billions in toys from the third-world pushers who supplied America's habit for plastic junk. *Maquiladoras* in Mexico, factories in Malaysia, China, Korea; factories in Indonesia and Ecuador, factories around the globe were poised to ship massive amounts of toys. Playtime was poised to buy them. But these factories were a long way away.

If you were in China, did you want to hope that some company in Boston would get around to paying you after the goods were shipped? Some company that might be having a little financial problem? You didn't.

If you were Playtime, could you pay cash in advance for Action Men? You couldn't.

So before he shipped his Action Men, the guy in China wanted a letter of credit, an ironclad promise by a bank he'd heard of (even in China), a bank he could trust, that once those Action Men were in the hold of the container ship, he would absolutely get paid. That would be good enough. But without it? No letter of credit, no Action Men.

Where did these letters of credit come from? New York banks, banks that had six-inch-thick agreements with Playtime. The agreements had provisions that said, If you're very very good, and if your financials are all spit-polished to a shine, we'll give the guys in China and Malaysia the LCs so they'll ship. The lawyers called these provisions "covenants." But the agreements also said, If you violate the covenants, we won't issue the letters of credit.

How many covenants were there? Pages and pages.

The stock crash turned out to violate those covenants. Precipitous stock decline was one of six dozen misfortunes that would excuse the banks from lending another penny. So the banks said no. We won't issue any more letters of credit. Because at bottom, the big sophisticated New York banks, like the simple pensioners, were scared.

"No," they said to Larry Jellicoe. (The actual letter was four pages long, and written by lawyers, and it had about fifteen defined terms in it, but what it said, basically, was no.) The letter referred to "that certain Third Amended and Restated Credit Agreement dated as of September 29, 1998 (hereinafter, the Credit Agreement)." And to section 14.1(d) of the Credit Agreement (hereinafter, "Section 14.1[d]"). And, for that matter, to sections (e), (f), and (g) (hereinafter, well, you get the idea). In breach of all of which, Mr. Jellicoe, your company now was. You need to cure these violations before we'll issue any more letters of credit.

Cure? What was Playtime supposed to cure? Playtime was the *patient*, not the doctor. How could Playtime cure itself when it was lying on a cot in the ICU, unable to choke down a soft-boiled egg and toast points? What should it do? Wiggle its nose and make the stock price go back up?

Playtime couldn't cure anything. In fact, it was doomed to get sicker. When the banks stopped issuing letters of credit, the company had to say so, publicly. That drove the stock price down again. This got Larry another letter, accelerating the debt. This meant, technically, that

Playtime was supposed to pay all the debt back in cash—wire the banks $2.4 billion the next morning. Except that Playtime didn't have $2.4 billion, or any billion, in cash. It didn't have the cash because the banks wouldn't lend it. Acceleration meant the banks might come in and take their collateral back, shutting down the company. This was the one bike too many that sends all the other bikes clattering to the garage floor. It set off the bonds one after the other: the 9 percent 2004s, the 9.25 percent convertibles due in 2006, the 10 percent issue due in 2010, and all the others. These bonds collided with the stockholders, whose shares fell still further. When the vendors saw the stock price fall away, they puckered up like a bare sphincter in a Vermont snowstorm. They demanded more onerous terms. Cash on delivery. Cash in advance. Cash the company didn't have because—guess who—the banks wouldn't advance it.

Now, banks—self-interested and nervous as they are—you can work with even in tough times, even when they write you letters with every other word a defined term. Because banks do well when the borrowers do well, and they get hurt when borrowers don't do well. But bondholders? Forget about it. At the first sign of trouble, they sell off and cut their losses. And to whom do they sell?

The polite phrase for the ladies and gentlemen to whom they sell is "distressed debt traders." Their funds are also, and more accurately, known as vulture funds. Vultures are different from banks, and they part from the relative civility of normal bondholders. Banks want you prosperous; bondholders want you alive, at least long enough for them to sell; but vultures want you dead. Actually, they want you sun-cured on a stake so they can peck at your liver. They bought your whole stinking putrid body for fourteen cents, and they happen to know that if they could rip out your spleen and maybe a nice piece of kidney quickly enough, and not have to be bothered with the rest of the festering carcass, they could get twenty cents for them.

Playtime hired the best and toughest lawyers available, and they called up the banks and the debtors and tried to work something out, but that didn't get the company anywhere. You could talk to a vulture, but mainly it was thinking about how to eat you.

ABROAD, the practical problems mounted. No letters of credit meant the vendors didn't ship. The vendors not shipping meant no product for

Christmas. And no product for Christmas meant the toy chains, the discount houses, the department stores, the video outlets didn't pay. A well-diversified company might have been able to weather such a blow. But Playtime had diversified into growth plays: the investments looked good on paper; they were, as Greene liked to tout, "platforms." But they didn't generate cash. To Playtime—with its off-balance-sheet partnerships, its heavy load of bond debt, its high leverage—the lenders' blow was mortal.

Greene and Jellicoe knew this. The Street knew this, too. Everybody knew this. *The Wall Street Journal* knew this and speculated openly about a bankruptcy filing. As Greene and Jellicoe implored the commercial banks night and day to extend a credit line, the stock price dropped, and as the price dropped, the lenders got more nervous and less willing to cut Peter Greene and Larry Jellicoe a little slack.

"But the vendors are *there*! They have the product, we have the orders! It's a no-brainer!" shouted Jellicoe. And it *was* a no-brainer. But no one had any brains at that point. There was too much fear and mistrust abroad.

Jellicoe begged them. He cajoled, he pleaded. He screamed. He threatened to sue them.

Nothing worked. The banks wouldn't lend. The vendors wouldn't ship. The stores wouldn't pay. Cash dried up. And winter was coming on.

On November 11, two months to the day after the bombings, Playtime and eighty-three of its subsidiaries filed chapter 11 petitions in the United States Bankruptcy Court for the District of Delaware. It was a sad day, a stunning day, for the company. In Burlington, people sat in their cubes and cried.

On that afternoon the terrible feeling of dislocation returned. Chapter 11—it seemed unreal in the same way the collapse of the towers out of a clear blue morning had seemed unreal. This Burlington stronghold, too, could collapse, for causes that seemed born of fantasy. As an accountant, Fritz understood the economics, the numbers, the market fear, but at no human level did it make sense.

In the afternoon, as the sun was setting, Luce stood in his doorway, her hand on her forehead. She moved heavily to the chair, put Fritz's gym bag on the floor, and sat down.

"Luce, you okay?"

It was obvious that she wasn't. In that dark afternoon she looked gray and old. And frightened.

"Fritz, what does this mean? Chapter eleven . . ." She stopped and bit her lip.

"It doesn't mean they lay you off, it's—"

"Billy's ten, Fritz. He's ten!"

He'd never seen Luce like this: tough, funny Hyde Park Lucy O'Reardon, who'd always been chipper, and ribald, and sarcastic, and supremely competent. Luce was never intimidated by management. She'd been his pulling guard and run interference for him for years. She'd always been his protector. There was a tremor in her voice he'd never heard before.

"Luce—"

"Fritz, it's just me, okay? I rent. I've got, I don't know, like, two, three months' rent saved, a few CDs put away for a rainy day." Her hand strayed up to her temple again, and she winced as though suffering from a powerful headache. "I guess it's raining, huh?"

"Not yet," he said.

She looked up at him; imploring, it seemed. "He's a ten-year-old boy, Fritz. And I'm it."

"Luce, it's not over. Tomorrow the lights come on, and the company is still in business. We're just in chapter eleven."

"How long does that last?"

Later, when he was alone again, Fritz kept remembering the gray cast of Luce's face. He'd taken her for granted, too, it seemed. He felt a terrible emptiness in the pit of his stomach. Luce was raising her ten-year-old alone, and she had a few months' rent saved. Bankruptcy—Fritz guessed it was real after all.

16

DID YOU SEE IT?
WERE YOU THERE?

"THEY GOT BRUBAKER! THE FBI!"

"So here's Nathan from security, hurrying down the corridor, and behind him these *FBI agents*! Milly Kortanek—you know Milly in finance?—she was just coming back from the ladies'. Anyway, there's four of them, wearing those blue windbreakers just like they have on TV, those windbreakers that say FBI in huge gold letters on the back. Milly said she had to, like, had to get out of the way or they would have bowled her right over. These guys went into Brubaker's office, and then there was some kind of commotion. They led him out in handcuffs, like a criminal!"

"Did you hear what Brubaker said? He gives his little wink and goes, 'We all make mistakes!' Like it was some kind of joke!"

"I heard the FBI came back down the elevator with Brubaker in handcuffs, and took him outside, and held his head down and pushed him into the backseat of a dark green sedan, and then they shut the door and drove off."

"Frank Pitts said—I heard this from Joe, he was talking to Frank's assistant—anyway, he said they came in right before lunch. They found Brubaker outside his office, talking to Luce, and he looked up at them and wasn't even surprised. You know what he said? He goes, 'I guess I made a mistake, huh?' And smiled like it was a big joke. Wasn't surprised at all."

"Really?"

"Everybody on the floor heard it. Brubaker goes, 'I guess I made a mistake.' Some mistake!"

"You know, Pitts thought something like this might happen. He'd had worries about Brubaker for a long time. The guy never took anything seriously. I guess the joke's on him now."

Did you see it? Were you there?

"You know Les in sales—Milt's AA?"

"You mean the one with the—"

"Exactly. Anyway, Les was saying that Milt told her this was going to happen."

"Really? He knew?"

"It was that Eduvest thing. Milt kept trying to tell finance they couldn't take the revenue, he kept saying the deals weren't final, and Brubaker was like, 'Screw that, we need the revenue. I'm the accountant, you do your job, Milt, I'll do mine.' You know? That's what Albert said, too."

"I heard Rachel was crying."

"Rachel Ewald, that mousy one?"

"Yeah. She was a friend of his. She was like, 'How could this happen? Fritz, the nicest guy in the whole company?' "

"Earth to Rachel!"

"No shit. They're always nice, guys like that. It's always the guys like that who have something going. But she's still trying to protect him. Rachel's like, 'Fritz never said, "I made a mistake." That never happened. That was just Pitts's bullshit.' "

"Well, I wouldn't put it past Pitts. But Greg—you know Greg in marketing—he said he was down on four, and the other guys down there were saying Brubaker looked kind of stunned when they brought him out in those handcuffs. He was, like, doped out. Like he didn't know what was going on? The guys watched him go by, and it seemed like he was on drugs. Was he—was he on some kind of medication?"

"Adler thought he was taking something. Brubaker was pretty nervous lately. Distracted. Ever since the stock tanked. Even more than normal. And somebody else was saying the other day, Brubaker's been acting kind of weird lately."

"I gotta tell you, I can't take too much more of this place. First the stock crashes, then the bankruptcy, now this."

"This is why the company had to file, Jellicoe says. Brubaker shorted the stock, and that panicked the market. He caused the whole thing. I mean, Brubaker is the sonofabitch who cratered everybody's options."

"The guy was smart as hell, you know. He was like a physics major or something. That lazy-preppy-boy thing, that was just an act."

Did you see it? Were you there?

"Brubaker resisted. He said to the FBI guys, 'What's this all about?' He goes, 'I want a lawyer.' "

"Dottie said he didn't resist at all—it was like he was waiting for them. That's what Jenny said, too. He knew his number was up! And he said, 'Sorry, I made a mistake.' "

"Yeah, I heard that part, too. But you know Milt down in sales? He said there was, like, a struggle! Brubaker wouldn't let them put the cuffs on."

"No, that was the thing of it. There was no struggle at all. It was like he was waiting for them almost."

"God, that sound when the handcuffs went on. 'Snap,' they went! Just a loud metal clunk. People said you could hear it all over the office."

"Putting the sonofabitch in chains."

"One minute you live in some mansion in Weston, the next minute, snap! See ya, preppy!"

"Snap, baby!"

"I think he lived in Dover. Or it might have been Wellesley."

"Whatever."

"Somebody was saying—I think it was Barb—that they didn't make him wear handcuffs."

"No, he definitely had handcuffs on. Denise saw it."

"They're saying Brubaker shorted fifty thousand shares. What's that, like, two mil?"

"I heard it was a hundred thousand shares."

"Jerry said Brubaker was tipping a broker. The guy did a trade of like a quarter million shares. Maloney, down in sales, heard about it, too. Been going on for years, apparently."

"I always wondered about Brubaker."

"Well, his wife's a big partner at Elboe, Fromme and Athol. She'll get him off."

"I don't know. I heard they were having trouble."

"Yeah?"

"Sure. You know Les, in sales? I heard him and her were, you know."

"Really?"

"Yeah, Brubaker and her . . . you know they showed up late to a meeting with Jellicoe one time. He's all disheveled, and he had . . . well, he had this, like—"

"What?"

"Well, I heard he had this like—"

"What?"

"Come stain. All over his pants!"

"Get out of town."

"Would I shit you?"

"Stop it."

"Ask Frank Pitts. Ask Milt. They were all at the meeting!"

Did you see it? Were you there?

"My God, the FBI arrested Brubaker?"

"He had this, like, offshore trust or something, and he shorted like a half a million shares. Maybe more."

"I can't even believe it."

"Sonofabitch with all that money, and it's never enough, is it? He has to take down the whole company, too."

IT WAS like a blowtorch on tinder. Rumor gushed through telephone lines and blazed across e-mail; she raged around the floors and up and down the elevators and into the cubes and behind the closed doors of the offices and conference rooms, and through the cafeteria on six and the mail room on one and the executive suite on nine. The FBI! Stock fraud! Fritz Brubaker had shorted the company. Or tipped a broker. Or something. Tens of thousands, or hundreds of thousands, or millions of shares. He'd done this to all of them.

Nor was Rumor bounded by the bricks of the headquarters building. She hurdled Route 128; she raced through Massachusetts and down the East Coast; she streaked around the country, and then, electronically, around the globe. Instantly, the story was on e-mail; by two it was on the wires, on Bloomberg, and on the local television stations. At just past two-thirty, a company-wide e-mail went out from Peter Greene (actually, except for its valediction, it had been written by Don Fink). Peter regretted to advise the Playtime family that the FBI had today arrested

Phineas Brubaker, the company's senior assistant controller, on charges of insider trading. The e-mail assured everyone that, as far as the company had been able to determine, Brubaker had acted alone, and the company was cooperating fully with the FBI investigation. As everyone knew, the company had a strict policy against insider trading. Employees were encouraged to review policy statement twelve on trading in Playtime securities, and to direct any questions to the general counsel's office. All queries from customers, vendors, or the like regarding the Brubaker matter should be routed to investor relations. Best regards, Peter.

An arrest—right at Playtime's headquarters! Yet within only a few hours of this electrifying event, a number of Playtime employees would have told you they weren't *that* surprised. There were Playtime employees who'd seen signs of this coming. Who had an inkling about that guy Brubaker. Who'd noticed he wasn't acting normal lately. Who didn't want to say anything before, of course (it not being their business), but who had *suspicions* about a few things. Like about the VD unit, for example. Anyway, Brubaker never seemed to work that hard, and he was always going around with that tattered sail bag, but he sure had a lot of money.

In the midst of the maelstrom, as the e-mails flew and the doors closed and the knots of employees formed to pass on breathless intelligence, Luce sat alone, reading Peter Greene's brush-off in her cube across from Fritz's now vacant office. In the days since the stock crash, her fear had hardened. How long has Fritz been here, she wondered, fifteen, twenty years? And not even a word in his defense. Not even a word to say that we have no idea whether what is alleged is true or even that a person is innocent until proven guilty. Fifteen years and more with the company, and it took the suits up on nine an hour and a half to toss him out like a sack of garbage.

Fritz's light was still on, his computer still on, his gym bag still sitting in the chair by the door. Luce held her head in her hands. How could such a thing have happened to Fritz, of all people? Luce *had* been there; she actually did see it when the two agents went into his office. She stood up helplessly from her desk, she drifted to his door, riveted, and heard the older guy, the one with the sandy hair, say:

"Phineas Brubaker, you are under arrest. You are charged with criminal violations of the Securities Exchange Act of 1934. You have the right to remain silent. You . . ." Then he read Fritz the rest of his rights, just like they do on television.

Luce, watching from behind the FBI men, saw the calm look on Fritz's face, heard his quiet, level voice and the four words he said: "This is a mistake."

The other agent drew out his handcuffs, but the sandy-haired one said, "No, I don't think we need to do that. Please come with us, Mr. Brubaker." So the agent snapped the handcuffs shut and returned them to his belt.

"Let's go," said the sandy-haired one, and they led Fritz away.

IN THE BACK of the sedan, it was mental tug-of-war. Thoughts massed and pulled at the rope of Fritz's attention, and they organized themselves into two camps. There were the practical thoughts clamoring at him—the thoughts of arrest and arraignment and how-could-this-be and lawyers and when-can-I-make-a-phone-call. Then there was the other camp of thoughts, not clamorous but determined, with a better grip on the rope. The thoughts of Boo, for example.

For the first and only time of his life, Fritz found himself grateful for his mother's developing Alzheimer's. Margaret Brubaker, or Boo, as she was known, had one of those preppy nicknames whose genesis was long ago lost to all memories but her own, and now, even that memory was but a memory itself. Boo had been as gregarious and cheerful as her son, and her sheer exuberance had overcome even the stern discipline of Cabot Brubaker. In her prime, Boo was a fire hose of warmth and laughter. Seeing her son arrested might have shaken Boo's disposition, but she was too far gone and would never know.

"Aw, for Chrissakes!"

Fritz looked up, and saw that outside, traffic had slowed on 93 South approaching the bridge to Boston. The whole city was torn up with the Big Dig, as they called it. Cars were funneling into the bridge, but traffic had come to a dead stop.

"Look at this shit," muttered the agent in the sport coat.

The FBI sedan sat motionless in the traffic. Frustrated scofflaws had opted for the breakdown lane, but it, too, was motionless. No movement was visible up ahead.

The guy in the windbreaker looked at his boss. "Should I slap on the blue lights?"

"Where the hell they gonna go?"

And he was right. The narrow isthmus of the bridge to Boston was completely jammed. The agents could make all the racket they wanted, and it wouldn't make a damn bit of difference.

So they sat. Up ahead, across the bridge, the Fleet Center was visible, and beyond it the Custom House and the other downtown towers. Fritz tried to focus on arrest, arraignment, charges, defenses, but his thoughts reverted to Boo, Michael and Kristin, Linda, Andy, and Hap. He wondered where the agents would be taking him if the traffic ever cleared. Where would he be tonight?

Back tugged the practical camp. Not too far ahead, to the right of the Central Artery, was the glass tower at Exchange Place. Behind one of those glass panels way up high was Linda's office. He would have to call Linda and arrange for a lawyer. Or rather, call Linda and have *her* arrange for a lawyer. He began to imagine how that would go. First, hysterics; then, probably, a whole platoon of her partners showing up to take over his life, with Linda making the introductions. This one would be from Harvard (Fritz, are you listening?), and that one would be in the American College of Trial Lawyers (Fritz, please, this is *important*), and this other one would know all the judges (for God's sake, Fritz, please pay attention!). He pictured Linda with her hands on her hips (wrists out) and her sternest expression; and he pictured the suits with the briefcases on their laps, and their stern expressions, the thick glasses, the associates furiously taking notes.

He looked up again. They hadn't moved.

"Never get him arraigned today, this shit doesn't let up," said the driver.

The rope was tugged back the other way, and the dark suits and briefcases vanished, and Fritz's mind slipped back to Michael and Kristin, and what this would mean for them, and how distantly their lives already seemed to have receded from his. What he needed was a little mental quiet. He needed to think. So he shelved the call-Linda-and-get-the-lawyers idea, at least for a while.

They sat in traffic for over an hour, inching across the rusted bridge, down the ramp, and moving forward by fits and profanity-laced starts to the Haymarket exit, where they finally escaped the traffic jam.

The FBI's Boston office wasn't far. When the agents had parked the sedan, they brought Fritz up out of the parking garage for booking. They smudged his fingers in the ink to get prints, then took the mug shots, frontal and profile. He sat with the desk officer while they typed up the forms, answering the questions absentmindedly and thinking about that letter he'd found a week ago from the online brokerage firm, U-Trade, pitching all the services available for the new Brubaker account. Fritz had neglected it for a week or so—until yesterday, in fact, when he'd finally called them to ask *what* new account?

"Mr. Brubaker, follow me."

One of the FBI agents was beckoning. For reasons unclear to Fritz, it was time to be taken somewhere else. They led him to a van for the trip across Boston to the courthouse, where he would be delivered into the custody of the U.S. Marshals Service.

Except that traffic was as bad as before. "For Chrissakes, I could walk to the fucking thing!" the exasperated agent shouted out, slamming his fist on the dashboard. He'd spent his whole day in a traffic jam, it seemed like. They sat motionless on the Evelyn Moakley Bridge, staring at the courthouse.

"I'd be okay with that," Fritz said.

The agents didn't answer.

Twenty minutes later Fritz had at last been remanded, as they say, to the custody of the United States Marshals Service. Again he sat in a windowless office. A deputy marshal opened the ink box and prepared to smudge his fingers.

"They did this already," Fritz said.

"Sir," said the marshal, "it's procedure."

"I know it's procedure. But they already did this procedure."

"Sir," said the marshal a little testily, "that was the FBI. This is the United States Marshals Service."

Fritz looked at her blankly. "Don't you guys work together?"

"Sir, put your thumb *there*," she ordered.

When they'd finished with the fingerprints, she said, "Please wait here, sir, while they get more film."

"More film?"

"For your folder. We need front and side shots."

"They already took those."

A sigh. "Sir, I thought I told you."

Fine, thought Fritz. Take some more pictures. It figured that there would be some kind of screwup with the camera film, without which they could not complete the vital task of taking his picture again. By the time they found some film and got the pictures retaken, it was too late to get arraigned, and not only that, the van had already left for Plymouth County House of Corrections, where they housed federal prisoners awaiting arraignment. Fritz gathered they were having some trouble figuring out what to do with him until morning. He overheard another marshal on the phone.

"Yeah, I told you, the van's gone."

A pause.

"No, they didn't . . . we didn't get him till four-thirty, at least."

It had been three-thirty, Fritz thought.

"No, I said, the goddamn van is gone. Right . . . yeah." The marshal looked over at Brubaker as though this were all his fault, then looked away again. "Yeah, well, Jesus Christ." The marshal nodded. "Uh-huh. Uh-huh . . ." He nodded some more. "I understand. I understand, but how the hell am I supposed to get him to Brockton?"

They're sending me to Brockton? Fritz thought.

"No, no, Palumbo's off today. We don't have the sedan. Right . . . right. Shit, I don't know." The marshal hung up the phone. He looked over at Fritz. "Goddamn FBI," he said.

"My thoughts exactly," Fritz agreed. "Look, can you tell me what this is all about?"

The marshal became very stern and businesslike. "You want to call a lawyer?"

"What could he tell me?"

"Excuse me?"

"What would the lawyer tell me?"

This seemed to catch the marshal by surprise. "I guess he . . . I don't know. That's what you're supposed to do."

"Believe me, I know. My wife's a lawyer. She knows all about what you're supposed to do. But what could he tell me? About what the charges are and so forth?"

"Look, sir, I suggest you call a lawyer."

That call-the-lawyer thing, you couldn't escape it. But Fritz wanted to figure out what the hell was going on before falling into the clutches of six of Linda's partners. He thought about it. "Can I talk to the prosecutor?"

"Mr. Brubaker, you're supposed to talk to your lawyer. But—"

"Yeah, we can all agree I should talk to my lawyer."

The marshal lingered. Then he answered, quietly, "Look, you want to talk the prosecutor, I can arrange it."

"Thanks. Please do."

This got their attention. Within an hour, the assistant U.S. attorney (a young guy named Feingold) was at the marshals' office, only too eager to talk to Fritz. They led him from the holding cell to a small room: Fritz, Feingold, some other prosecutor, and two of the marshals. They brought in a stenographer, they read him his rights again, reminded him he had the right to call a lawyer, in case he'd forgotten that in the last forty minutes. It seemed to Fritz that everyone was part of some grand conspiracy to get him to talk to Linda's partners. They made him sign a form to say he was waiving that right, and then they sat at a desk and the stenographer worked his machine as they spoke. It stood on a stand like a tiny, ten-key piano, and the endless sheet of stenographic paper slid through the machine and neatly folded itself into the catch box. Sometimes the man pressed single notes, other times he seemed to make chords. Fritz wondered what words were expressed by the chords. He found the machine fascinating.

Feingold looked somber and serious. He wouldn't crack a smile. "Just tell us what happened," he said. "Just tell us what happened."

"What happened was that today two FBI agents came into my office and arrested me. Beyond that, why don't we start with you telling *me* what happened?"

Which Feingold wouldn't do, not directly. But he asked a lot of questions. Questions about October 3, and U-Trade accounts, and the restatement of Playtime's earnings, and how long that had been known, and then more questions about Fritz's activities on the afternoon of October 3, and where he went, and who saw him. The stenographic paper slid through the machine, acquired hieroglyphics, then folded itself into the catch box.

"What's all that about the afternoon of October 3?" Fritz asked.

"Just tell us where you were on the afternoon of October 3. Were you home?"

"Was I home? I don't know. Was it a weekend?"

"I think you know it was a Wednesday, Mr. Brubaker. In the afternoon. Were you home? Logged on to your computer?"

"Wait," he said. "Are you guys saying this was done on my home computer?"

Feingold looked at the agent. He didn't answer.

"That's why you're asking me these questions, isn't it?"

"Look, Mr. Brubaker, your attorney can speak to us about the investigation. That's the normal procedure here, and—"

Jesus, Fritz thought, how had those guys gotten on to his home computer? He knew the Hare Krishnas in the VD unit could do essentially anything, but did that include mimicking, somehow, his home computer? Some trick they could do over the Internet to make it look like the trade was done from his home? It was true, he often logged on to the system there. Maybe they could reverse that route to tap into his private stuff. He shivered.

By the time they'd finished the interview, it was late. "I'd better call my wife," he said to one of the marshals.

The marshal shook his head. "Car's waiting. You can call her from Brockton."

ON A LONELY AFTERNOON more than a year later, Fritz would sit brooding by a woodstove, remembering this part of it. How he'd failed to telephone Linda appropriately. The telephone was a big part of her life: communication was one of his wife's core bodily functions. She was an expert at eensy buttons and demanded of her loved ones if not expertise then at least eensy-button competence. But their marriage had reached a point where so many communications went astray. He could have, should have, gotten a call to her up in her glass box earlier in the afternoon. One call, full of the appropriate remorse, and solicitude, and need—one call and perhaps the whole thing might have gone differently.

It wasn't before eleven-thirty that night, after completing his third police intake of the day, that Fritz Brubaker finally got on a pay phone inside the Brockton lockup and made a collect call to his wife. "Hi, hon, it's me," he said wearily.

By this point she'd known about his arrest for almost nine hours and, for about eight of them, had been stewing over his failure to contact her. The rumor and gossip had reached Elboe, Fromme & Athol with lightning speed, only seconds behind Don Fink's official notification to Marvin Rosenblatt. By evening it was all over everywhere. Hap had called, Andy had called, Linda's mother had called, everyone had called but Fritz. The kids were asking, "Dad was *arrested?*" Linda was beside herself.

"Why didn't you call me before, Fritz?"

"I'm sorry, honey, it's been kind of busy, I guess."

"Fritz!"

"What?"

She sighed. "I don't even know what to say to you anymore! I feel like I don't even know you!"

"Hon—"

"How could you do something so selfish, so stupid? No, don't answer that. Don't say a word to anyone but your attorneys. I've made arrangements for your attorneys. They'll be there in the morning, and you can tell them the whole story."

"I don't know, Linda, I don't know if that's necessary, I—"

"Fritz, don't be an idiot!"

And so it went, but not for long. Beneath the flickering fluorescent lights in Brockton a few minutes later, Fritz stared stupidly at the pay phone, which brayed the dial tone at him. That was it, he thought, the famous telephone call. Then he hung up the receiver, and a Brockton cop led him off to his first night in a jail cell.

The holding cell was small, and damp, and chilly. Fritz was still wearing the chinos, golf shirt, and blue blazer he'd arrived at Playtime in sixteen hours before. There was a blanket on the bunk, made of some dreadful synthetic, a frayed, puke-colored polyester. He didn't want to chance it. So he unlaced his shoes, folded the blanket, and put it at his feet, then lay gingerly back on the mattress, covering himself with the blazer. A light flickered in the corridor. The place smelled of mold and urine. From down the corridor, he heard the periodical break and static and indecipherable police jargon of a police radio.

His home computer? Playtime's VD boys were cutting-edge; the kids they had in there probably could hack in to NORAD. Still, he was having trouble understanding this. He lay in the darkness, smelling that foul brew of urine and Lysol and sweat, working through the whys and the hows, trying to figure it out, searching his memory for a clue, a gesture, a stray remark from someone in IT, an e-mail from Pitts, something. And then, in the darkness, it came to him. The math resolved itself in an unexpected way. With the brute elegance of a mathematical theorem, with all its chilling simplicity.

As he lay awake on the bunk, startled by this, Professor Vorblen returned to lecture him: "Love is the investment you haven't made."

The professor continued, "Tomorrow is the final exam. You have a higher responsibility. Will you accept it? Class dismissed."

And then the professor was gone.

Gone, leaving him lying in the Brockton cell, blinking at the flickering light in the corridor, breathing in the stale jail-cell smells, wide awake with the answer. He'd never sleep now. The molecules positively whizzed around his brain. If only he'd acted sooner. But what the hell could he have done? Maybe he should tell the judge the whole story. Certainly that would be the best way out for *him*. But no, he thought, no. Professor Vorblen was right: lying there in the urine-suffused darkness of the Brockton cell, Fritz knew he had a higher duty. His brain soup congealed around a startling proposition.

The investment he hadn't made. Could it be that things would be best this way? That given all that had happened, maybe this was the only way to put things right? And who else but Fritz could do so? Another thought hit him, more darkly this time. He could tell no one about this. Not even Linda. Least of all Linda.

Fritz hopped off the bunk and stepped over to the bars. He called out to the cop on duty, "Can we get that guy Feingold back on the phone?"

"It's past midnight, for Chrissakes. Go to sleep!"

"I'm going to plead guilty."

"You can tell it to the judge in the morning."

17

PLEADING IN VAIN

IT WAS a tough ticket, Fritz's arraignment. Playtime's meltdown was the best business story since September 11, and the press took to it joyously, the way a man kisses the granddaughter he thought would never marry. Everybody needed relief from the sheer sadness of September 11. This story was more to their liking, much more. "Preppy suits exploit workers, shareholders with crooked accounting; take down big business." Accounting scandals, shady stock deals. This was getting back to work!

They came in force, with TV satellite dishes ringing the John Joseph Moakley Courthouse on Boston Harbor, and the familiar television faces filling the pews in courtroom 14 up on the fifth floor. Don Fink was there in one corner, with two lawyers from the in-house staff at Playtime. Over yonder in the other corner was one of Mel Popotkus's associates from the famous class-action firm. Mel was already angling for the lead counsel spot in the class-action lawsuit against Playtime's directors. Around and among them were the ladies and gentlemen of the Fourth Estate. The room buzzed with expectant conversation. They were ready to party.

The buzz stopped for a moment when the marshals brought Fritz in from the lockup. He was alone. Defendants never came in alone, particularly *rich* defendants. They were supposed to arrive under a phalanx of lawyer bodyguards. Instead, Fritz sat next to a marshal on the left side of the courtroom, surveying the crowded room as though looking for a familiar face at a cocktail party, looking not so much awkward as curious. Three assistant U.S. attorneys, gathered around the government's table, fell silent.

There he is, thought the channel 4 guy, sitting in the first row of pews behind the rail. A little nonchalant—wearing a golf shirt to an arraignment? Where's his lawyer?

There he is, thought the *Globe* guy, Country Club Man. Prepare to die.

There he is, thought the *Herald* gal, what a preppy. Kind of a cute smile, actually. Nice eyes . . . is he married?

He *is* married. And to prove it, at that moment the implausibly lovely wife appeared. She was wearing a midnight-blue pleated-skirt-and-bolero-jacket number that she'd had rushed over from Armani the afternoon before, a cream-colored silk blouse, and Chanel heels, and she was carrying a Kelly handbag. Linda came sweeping into the room like a prime minister, attended by aides. With her were the lawyers she had hired for Fritz: Prentiss Wolcott, a senior partner of Daley and Hoar, and Wolcott's equerries, a his-and-hers pair of solemn associates, shiny-backed as partridges, in blue pinstriped suits, carrying black leather trial bags. They held the double doors as though they'd rehearsed the move.

Damn, thought the *Globe*.

She's got a Kelly, thought the *Herald*.

"Fritz, *there* you are!" Linda said. (Where else would he be?) Prentiss Wolcott nodded at the marshal, and he and his retinue entered the enclosure and huddled around the defendant. Linda bussed Fritz with appropriate decorum, then gave his forearm a supportive rub. "This is Prentiss Wolcott. From Daley and Hoar. Prentiss, this is my husband."

"Who's he?" Fritz asked.

"Your attorney, Fritz. Prentiss Wolcott from Daley and Hoar. He's agreed to take the case!" Linda whispered, as though that were the first good news in weeks.

"To be my lawyer?"

"Yes."

"I don't need a lawyer. I told you that."

Christened to great fanfare in 1998, the John Joseph Moakley U.S. Courthouse was an architectural marvel. Its sweeping glass front gave a stunning view of Boston Harbor. Its courtrooms were grand but simple, most of them decorated with a pineapple Shaker stencil, and well equipped with computers and the other latest toys. But they had one flaw: acoustics. Each courtroom had a slightly concave ceiling, and the result was that the rooms had an eerie, Jeffersonian acoustical property. A whisper on one side of the courtroom could plainly be heard on the other. The clarity was uncanny. Jurors soon discovered this. Those determined scrums of lawyers whispering at "sidebar"? The jurors could hear every syllable. So this earnest dialogue was being conducted for the benefit of all present.

Channel 4 looked over to New England Cable News. "Did he just say he didn't need a lawyer?"

Linda, flustered, whispered, "Fritz, for heaven's sake. You're about to be *arraigned*!"

Channel 7 turned to the *Globe* and said, "I think he just said he doesn't want the guy." The *Globe* asked Channel 5. Channel 5 in turn caught the eye of the *Herald*. Their pens were flashing across their steno pads.

Fritz wasn't even whispering. "It's okay," he said, "I don't need—"

Prentiss Wolcott, confused by this development, spoke up. "Linda," he asked, "do you and your husband need a moment?"

"He's just being *impossible*," she answered.

The press took a keen interest in this development. Up until now the case had been a suit fight, a dispute over money. It already had plenty of pizzazz. It was already a good rich-preppy-sells-out-the-little-guy kind of story. But marital strife would give it real juice. A nice angle.

Prentiss Wolcott could sense what was happening. He knew the acoustics well. He bent over, close to Fritz, and said, "Mr. Brubaker, it would be unwise to proceed without counsel."

"Why?"

"Why? Because you need representation. There are some very odd things going on here. I understand Judge Chandler herself will handle the arraignment. Usually the magistrates do arraignments."

"But this is just where they read the charges, right?"

"Yes, but why Judge Chandler is doing that could present an issue. We need to think it through tactically. It could mean a lot of different things."

"Maybe it just means she wants her name in the papers, like everybody else. But if you still need to think it through, Mr. Wolcott, why do I need to hire you again?"

"Fritz!" Linda glowered at him.

In the gallery, the press leaned forward, straining to hear every word.

Wolcott struggled to maintain his composure. "You need to know your rights," he whispered. "You need to . . . you need to know where to sit, for one thing."

"I need to pay a guy to tell me where to sit?"

"We'll make a motion to permit you to sit there, with me. It looks better." Prentiss Wolcott pointed toward the defense counsel table.

"No, thank you, Mr. Wolcott. I'd rather not focus on how things look. Thanks for coming and all, but . . ." Fritz smiled.

Wolcott, uncertain what to do, looked at Linda for guidance. She waved vigorously toward the defense table, so he went over and stood behind it.

"All rise!"

At that unfortunate moment, United States District Judge Sally Chandler came rushing in, robe flapping, laptop in hand. She took her seat on the bench.

"You may be seated," the clerk said.

Fritz, who was still in the marshal's custody, shook his head politely at Wolcott. But Wolcott, pretending not to have seen this, took the chair farthest to the right behind the defense table. His two partridges joined him.

"Criminal number 01-4599-SKC, United States versus Phineas Brubaker." "Finey-ass," the clerk pronounced it. United States versus Finey-ass Brubaker. There were a few titters in the gallery. The *Herald* smiled, made a note. "Appearances?"

What did this mean, Fritz wondered, appearances? The prosecutor was up on his feet. He had very shiny shoes. He made a good appearance. "Good morning, Your Honor. Assistant United States Attorney James Feingold for the government."

"Good morning, Mr. Feingold."

Quick as a wink, Wolcott was on his feet. "Prentiss Wolcott for the defendant, Your Honor."

"For the defendant?" Fritz asked. "You're not for the defendant."

"Quiet!" ordered the marshal.

The press craned forward. Was the guy fighting with Wolcott in open court?

"Good morning, Mr. Wolcott," said Judge Chandler. "Have you filed your appearance?"

"No, Your Honor, I was just retained. I'll be filing the appearance today."

"Very well, Mr.—" She stopped herself. "Excuse me, Mr. Brubaker. *Please be seated.*"

Judge Chandler interrupted herself because she, and everyone else, had been startled by a development at the side of the room, where Fritz had come to his feet and raised his hand, like a child in class asking for a turn to speak.

"Sorry," he said, and sat. It seemed strange that the others stood up to speak, but he was supposed to sit. He was only trying to be polite. From his seat, he said, "Your Honor."

"Be quiet," said the marshal.

"Mr. Brubaker, please let your attorney—"

"But Your Honor—"

"Mr. Brubaker, be quiet!" the judge commanded.

"Be *quiet!*" the marshal echoed.

"He's not my lawyer!" Fritz blurted out.

He's not my lawyer?

The *Herald* knew that if she could get a picture of Wolcott, she had tomorrow's headline: HE'S NOT MY LAWYER! The TV guys knew they had tonight's lead. Channel 5 grinned at Channel 7. The *Globe* shook his head, struggling to keep a straight face.

"Excuse me, Your Honor, I don't mean to interrupt. But he's not my lawyer. I don't know what an appearance is, and what filing it means, but I'd rather Mr. Wolcott not be my lawyer, if that's okay."

Poor Linda! Her eyes were wide with astonishment. Why would he embarrass her this way in front of all these dreadful newspeople?

The *Herald* craned her neck to get a look at the wife. Then the *Globe* craned his neck. Then Channel 7. They were all craning their necks to look at the wife. Linda flushed. Fritz, she thought, why *for once* can't you act appropriately?

"I see," said Judge Chandler. "Mr. Wolcott, the defendant says you are not his lawyer. Are you his lawyer?"

"Ah, well, Your Honor, I just met Mr. Brubaker before the arraignment, and I—"

"How did you come to meet Mr. Brubaker, if I might ask?"

"Ms. LeBrecque, who is an attorney with Elboe, Fromme, asked me to take the case, Your Honor. And I said I would. Mr. Brubaker and I haven't had a chance to speak before, and as you can see, Mr. Brubaker is a little agitated. Perhaps we could take a short recess?"

"I'm not agitated," Fritz said. "I'm not the one trying to be someone's lawyer."

"Mr. Brubaker," Judge Chandler answered. "Please rise when addressing the court."

"Stand *up!*" the marshal ordered.

"Oh, I'm sorry," said Fritz, "I thought you told me to sit down."

Polite smiles from the gallery. A cough or two was heard, discreetly muffling what otherwise might have been a giggle.

Fritz stood up again. "But ma'am, Your Honor, I mean, I'm not agitated. I'd just as soon get this over with. Mr. Wolcott isn't my lawyer. No offense or anything. I don't need to talk to him about it. I understand the object of today's exercise is for there to be a reading of the charges against me, so I was hoping, not to be rude or anything, we could get on with that."

Is this guy crazy? the clerk was wondering.

"Well, Mr. Brubaker, if not Mr. Wolcott, who *will* be representing you?" Judge Chandler seemed a pleasant enough sort. It was a reasonable question.

"I hadn't planned to have a lawyer, Your Honor."

"I don't think that's very prudent, Mr. Brubaker."

"That's what Mr. Wolcott said."

More laughter from the gallery. The press were looking around the seats, wide-eyed with joy.

"I'm sure he did. It was good advice, from a pretty good attorney. Mr. Feingold, is there any question of competence here?"

"No, Your Honor, I don't—"

"Your Honor?" Fritz interrupted.

"Yes?"

"Well, that—well, I think that was a little uncalled for."

Still more restrained laughter. Judge Chandler was staring at Fritz. What was with this guy? He didn't look nuts (he was kind of nice-looking, actually). Why was he acting nuts? This was the guy who had sold out Playtime, fired the first shot that ultimately sank the ship? The guy responsible for all those employees losing their 401(k)s? And he wanted to go it alone? She'd expected a Prentiss Wolcott, a whole platoon of them. She certainly didn't expect this.

"Mr. Brubaker, one of the things I'm supposed to do here is consider the question of pretrial detention. Most people like to have an attorney argue on their behalf that they should not be held before trial. There may be motions, pretrial preparation, and so on. Mr. Feingold, the government is requesting bail, is it not?"

"Yes, Your Honor, and because these are serious crimes, and the defendant is a person of means, it would have to be a substantial bail, and—"

"Yes, I understand the government's position, Mr. Feingold. I won't hear you on that just yet. Mr. Brubaker, you're going to need an attorney to help you with this, aren't you?"

"I hope not. You said bail is for pretrial detention. We don't need to worry about that here. I'm going to plead guilty, so we won't need a trial. In fact, I'm pleading guilty right now. So we can get right to posttrial detention."

There was a rustling, even an audible murmur, in the benches. Guilty? Right to the sentencing? He's pleading! He says he did it!

Oh my God, Fritz! thought Linda. You absolute raving idiot! Why are you doing this to me?

Oh my God! thought Don Fink. He's an unguided missile!

Oh my God, how great is this! thought the *Globe*, the *Herald*, channels 4, 5, and 7, NECN, and the associates of Mel Popotkus.

"And, Your Honor, I don't want to be disrespectful, but I'm competent. I don't think competence is a function of willingness to hire Prentiss Wolcott."

More titters. The press were all but wetting themselves. They were leaning down, mouths covered by their hands.

"Mr. Brubaker, that's enough. We haven't even arraigned you yet, you can't plead guilty. As for the other comments, well, it's *enough*." The judge was getting a little cross. She frowned some more. "All right, Mr. Brubaker, you want to waive counsel for this hearing, you'll waive counsel. Do you also waive the reading?" She gave him her blankest, sternest stare.

He wondered. Did he waive the reading? "The reading of what, Your Honor?"

"Of the indictment." It was common for defendants represented by good lawyers to waive the reading. One less embarrassing thing for the press to write down. All those maliciouslies and intentionallies and willfullies.

The indictment, Fritz was thinking, that meant the charges. Did he waive the reading of the charges? "No, Your Honor, people should know what the charges are. So I guess I'd prefer they be read out, if that's all right."

She scowled. This guy was officially pissing her off. "Mr. Brubaker, please rise. Read the indictment," the judge said to the clerk, shaking her head. Which the clerk proceeded to do. That the defendant, Finey-Ass A. Brubaker, on the third day of October, 2001, through the use of wires in interstate commerce, being possessed of "inside information," as the phrase is defined in the Securities Exchange Act of 1934, and so on and on. Ms. Johnson labored in monotone. She had a number of maliciouslies and willfullies and so on in there.

Judge Chandler looked at Fritz when it was over. "Now's the part when I'm supposed to ask you to enter—"

"Guilty, Your Honor."

"Don't interrupt!" the marshal barked.

"—a plea," Judge Chandler finished, and shook her head again. She had been a fine defense lawyer in her day. The government probably had this guy nailed now, based on what he'd said already. His admissions would likely come in at trial. She might herself become a witness to some later dispute about whether he had acted with knowledge of his rights.

"Mr. Brubaker, you know, we don't accept a guilty plea unless we're sure the defendant understands his rights."

"Rights should come with responsibilities, Your Honor."

"And until he understands that it is the prosecution's burden to prove each and every element of the indictment, and that he has the constitutional right to—"

"Yes, Your Honor. I'll waive that, if that's all right."

"It's not all right. You have the right to counsel, and if you cannot afford one, one will be appointed for you."

"I can afford one," he said. "Just prefer to do without, if that's okay."

"Mr. Brubaker! Look, here's what I'm going to do. I'm not going to accept your plea, at least not today. So stop telling me you're guilty!" More laughter from the gallery. The judge looked up, and they fell silent. "Which leaves me with Mr. Feingold's bail request. Why shouldn't I have you locked up today?"

"You should," Fritz agreed.

She put her head in her hands and ran her fingers through her dark hair. "You're supposed to tell me why I *shouldn't*. This would be a lot easier if you had an attorney, Mr. Brubaker."

"But you should," Fritz said. "I'm guilty, after all."

Exasperated, Judge Chandler pressed on. No defendant had ever begged her to plead guilty before. "Mr. Brubaker, I don't find that you are entering a knowledgeable plea at this time, and therefore I am directing the entry of a plea of not guilty."

"But I *am* guilty."

"Mr. Brubaker," said Judge Chandler sternly, "that's enough. You may sit down."

This left Prentiss Wolcott feeling rather . . . alone. Throughout this bizarre exchange, he had remained standing at the defense table, pole-axed, uncertain what the hell to do. Now, as Fritz took his seat, Wolcott realized self-consciously that he was the only one left standing. He wondered if he should say something. Should he sit? Leave? Speak?

Judge Chandler noticed this and said, "Mr. Wolcott, I guess you are excused."

"Yes, Your Honor," he said. He straightened himself and nodded to the partridges, who rose. He threw back his shoulders with stern dignity. The partridges had soft and drooping shoulders but nevertheless threw them back with stern dignity. The sternly dignified little entourage made its way back through the gallery to the courtroom doors. Wolcott could see all the press eyes locked on them. Smirking! Grinning! Pencils flashing! Fired in front of the entire world!

Linda rose and followed them out. She would not sit still for one more minute of this humiliation.

The heads in the gallery followed their exit, then swung back to the front of the room. The wife just walked out on him! This was theater in the round. What next?

POOR LINDA LEBRECQUE! Her world seemed to be crashing around her Cartier-beringed ears. Humiliated in public. And then, outside the courtroom, Wolcott had abandoned her with a stiff handshake and a curt "Good day, Ms. LeBrecque." Left her there just like that, to fend for herself in this asylum house full of litigators and criminals and predatory journalists. In ten minutes it would be all over Daley and Hoar what an absolute ass Linda's husband had been, what a public spectacle he had made of himself. By the end of the day, the whole city (the "whole city," to Linda, meant all of its bankers, corporate lawyers, and mutual-fund managers) would know. Subject to criticism? Subject to ridicule, more like. Linda hurried down the corridor. She found the ladies' room and locked herself in a stall, and there she sat on the toilet and sobbed.

Inside the salmon-colored sheet-metal walls of the stall, Linda was paid a visit by her life's most constant companion. Since Linda had been about thirteen, this piercing voice, a shrill commentator in the back of her head, had been her most persistent visitor. The Shrill Small Voice was occasionally convivial (for example, in joining Linda to condemn Fritz's shortcomings), but mainly it dropped in at times of temptation (as when she might otherwise have enjoyed a dish of ice cream) or moments of insufficient stress (to point out that however bad things might seem, they were about to get worse). The Shrill Small Voice, which could not be locked out of anywhere, now arrived in the rest-room stall to observe sharply that while Linda was in here blubbing and feeling sorry for herself, the arraignment was nearing completion. Once it was over, where did she think all the greasy-fingered harridans among those dreadful press hordes would be headed next?

This very rest room, that's where.

Linda dabbed at her eyes, emerged from the stall to give herself the quick once-over in the mirror, then sprinted from the ladies' room. She took the stairs to the ground floor at a trot, collected her cell phone and BlackBerry at the front desk, and then hurried outside.

Right outside the front door of the John Joseph Moakley Court-house, three TV news vans were idling with their big broadcast dishes thrust up high in the air on TV-van erections. The engines revved in the cold. A brisk onshore wind was snapping the American flag on its pole, and the dish erections swayed too. They seemed hungry, eager for an object for their attention, anxious for someone to come out of the building. A guy leaning up against one of the TV trucks looked at Linda kind of funny, like he noticed her, and then straightened. She realized she would have to *walk* back to the Financial District, across the Evelyn Moakley Bridge (Joe Moakley, the South Boston congressman, got the courthouse; his wife, the bridge). There were no cabs waiting, and she could not risk hanging around the erectile vans or, worse, standing haplessly in front of the courthouse with her hand in the air when all those people from courtroom 14 came outside. It was cold—her panty hose were little use against the wind whipping in off the channel—but she had no choice. The guy from the TV truck was now striding toward her.

She hurried away on foot. This was hard in heels, but Linda was a gyrotreader champ, and she quickly clip-clipped out of range of the press. When she'd put the courthouse and the TV trucks behind her, she began working the eensy buttons on her BlackBerry. Both hands on the buttons, she hurried along past the Barking Crab toward Seaport Boulevard.

But there wasn't any e-mail. She scrolled up; she scrolled down. *Nada.* For one and a half hours, she had gone dark inside the ghastly bowels of the John Joseph Moakley U.S. Courthouse—for over ninety minutes, she had actually relinquished her BlackBerry. And now there was no e-mail. Not a single message. Not a cc attaching a copy of a draft agreement, not a partners' circular, not the call-in data for a conference call, not an announcement of the egg-salad special in the Elboe, Fromme cafeteria, not a "Good luck, Linda" before the arraignment. Nothing.

A deathly electronic silence. A silence like that of deep space. A silence like that of solitary confinement, like that of being—Out of the Loop.

Linda's high heels quickened from clip to click speed. She popped the BlackBerry back in her Kelly bag. Hurrying onto Seaport Boulevard and the Evelyn Moakley Bridge, she was beset by a terror, the thought that—but she brushed it away and concentrated on hastening through the cold and back to the office. It wasn't a thought she'd even articulate. This was a coincidence. It was nothing. She would be back at the office in a few minutes, and there would be faxes and FedExes and phone messages. And e-mails. There would be people who had to talk to her immediately. Linda was as In the Loop as she had ever been. In fact, maybe she'd just gotten an e-mail. You never knew.

So, once again, she withdrew the BlackBerry from her Kelly bag. Just to give it a quick check. And now Linda, who was hurrying up the incline of the Evelyn Moakley Bridge, and half noticing a young man in a blue overcoat (young *black* man, not that it mattered, not that it was anything she noticed) coming the other way, and steering just to his right—between the young man and the curb—so as not to break stride, and feeling the wind whistling down the channel from Boston Harbor and up her legs, and crooking her arm to keep the Kelly handbag from slipping, and holding the BlackBerry in two hands, and working the buttons with her fingers, and trying to see the sidewalk, the young man, and the BlackBerry all at once: now Linda miscalculated.

It was only a matter of half an inch. But the heel on Linda's left Chanel shoe slipped ever so slightly as it made contact with the smooth granite surface of the curbstone. It pivoted out to the left just as her weight came down, slipped out off the curbstone, and plunged six inches toward the road surface.

Other people fall down in a hurry, but one always felt oneself as though falling on the moon, impelled by a remorseless but lesser gravity, permitted a cruel leisure to make any number of observations about one's own doom. It was this way for Linda: the splay-legged, arch-backed helplessness she felt while plunging into the traffic, the way the young man on the sidewalk began to turn, wide-eyed, the way a yellow taxi swerved, the way Linda's own hands could not swing out to protect her fall but seemed anchored by the BlackBerry. She felt her handbag rocketing up and over her shoulder, she felt a wrenching stab in her ankle, and she experienced the vertigo of free fall as she was launched into Seaport Boulevard. All of this seemed to happen at once, yet with dreadful deliberation.

Linda's hip hit the pavement first, then her elbow, and then her knees. The Kelly bag fired itself like a slingshot, scattering onto the roadbed of the Evelyn Moakley Bridge an intimate shrapnel: a compact case, a Blistex tube, several wadded Kleenexes, receipts from Louis and Bread & Circus, three tampons, her cell phone, pens, a lipstick, a walletful of credit cards, her backup book, her cell-phone charger, and two AAA batteries.

It was a mercy she wasn't killed. The taxicab in the right lane swerved and then screeched to a halt. Behind him, the other traffic screeched to a halt, the drivers all thinking one thing: Jesus, lady! We could have killed you!

Then she was lying on the cold pavement, and everything came back to real speed. She felt a chill along the back of her legs where her skirt must have come up. Her hair was in her face. Her elbow hurt. There were cars, motionless, all around, and there were voices, and people were coming toward her. She looked back at the sidewalk, and a circle of gaping pedestrians was gathering there. A circle of gawking strangers! The humiliation! She rolled to a seat. The silk lining of her cashmere coat had torn, the Armani skirt was ripped, her dark hose were rent. Her knees were bleeding.

"Ma'am, are you okay?"

She looked up, dazed, at the young man in the blue coat, who had come out into the roadway to help her. The wind was whipping her hair in her face. A crowd was gathering. Another man was coming toward her, and a third man was getting out of the yellow taxicab. She could feel mascara smudges on her cheeks; her eyes were full of tears.

"Can I help you? Are you okay? Did you break anything?"

She couldn't answer him, couldn't speak at all. The pens and tampons and Blistex were rolling across the pavement of the Evelyn Moakley Bridge. And something with them, bits of paper blowing around, familiar bits of paper. Pages—pages from her backup book! Her one infallible backup source of addresses, phone numbers, and birthdays, which she kept as a backup to her electronic records. Blowing across six traffic lanes of the Evelyn Moakley Bridge!

She had to get those pages. Those pages were her life, her whole life—every human connection in her life was backed up in those pages. She started to crawl across the pavement, grabbing the scraps of paper and further scraping her bloody knees. She pulled herself to her feet and stumbled, ran, lunging after the pages from the backup book that were blowing in the November wind across the bridge.

She had now stopped six lanes of traffic. No car was moving in either direction. At the northern base of the bridge, the driver of a sand

and gravel truck, unable to see quite what was happening over the lip of the bridge but anxious to do his civic duty, let out a blast on his air horn. It was a call to arms. The cars and vans picked up the cue and added toots, and then honks, and then an angry chorus of Boston car-horn blasts and shouts. Car-horn obscenities from cabs and panel vans and pickup trucks, all directed at Linda, whose entire life was blowing in scraps across the Evelyn Moakley Bridge!

She was lunging and scraping and dashing after the pieces of paper, peeling them off fenders and pouncing on them on the roadbed. She had to get the pages, as many as she could save. The observers were shaking their heads. The woman seemed to be raving. The car horns were reaching crescendo.

Linda reached the east side of the Evelyn Moakley Bridge. She was jamming bits and pieces—the cell phone, the BlackBerry—into the Kelly bag. She had grabbed the backup book itself, with its ring binder sprung open by the fall, and stuffed it back into the bag. Her hands were full of backup book pages. She climbed back out of the roadway to the sidewalk, and there she collapsed. Just collapsed against the railing that ran alongside the sidewalk. She sat on the cold concrete, stuffing the paper she'd recovered back into the purse, sniffling and wiping her face, stuffing the bits and waving, shaking her head against the earnest solicitations of passersby.

The man in the blue coat had followed her across the bridge. He was leaning down, offering his hand to her, his black hand (not that it mattered what color his hand was, not to a right-thinking person like Linda; it was just that he was a . . . stranger, yes, that was it, a stranger, and there was his hand held out to her without any invitation or anything, and he might be just *anybody*!). Poor Linda was all alone, leaning up against the railing of a bridge, Linda LeBrecque, a partner at Elboe, Fromme & Athol.

"Ma'am, are you sure you're okay?"

She shrank from him, shaking her head. "No, it's all right," she said. "Please."

As in "Please leave me alone," to this nice young man who was only trying to help. Linda had lost all sense of herself; she had no perception of her rudeness to this Samaritan. She tried to brush the tears from her face.

At this juncture, the Shrill Small Voice paid an empathetic call. "It's all his fault," the Voice pointed out helpfully. "He *wanted* to humiliate you."

Meaning Fritz, of course, not the nice young man, who was turning uncertainly to go, wondering if he should call for an ambulance. Now other people were stopping, stepping over her, asking if she was all right, if she needed anything. She waved them all away. She was crying and crying.

The Voice gave her some more encouragement. "You look terrible. Stop your blubbering and pull yourself together."

Linda looked up and took a deep breath, trying to do as the Voice said. Everything hurt—her knees, her elbow, her forehead. Everything was such a mess. Everything was so screwed up!

The Voice was right: she had to pull herself together. She had to stop crying. You couldn't just sit there against the balustrade of the Evelyn Moakley Bridge crying and looking like a bum, or people would stop to inquire or call for help. But she wasn't sure she could stand up steadily, either. She brushed at her eyes, then fished her cell phone back out of the purse. Her fingers were trembling as she punched in Marvin's number. Frances, his secretary, picked up.

She pressed "end." Better to take a deep breath and start over. She counted to ten. Then she counted to thirty. She brushed the hair out of her face, felt herself calming. Then she tried again.

"Hi, Frances, it's Linda."

"For heaven's sake, pull yourself together," the Voice ordered.

"Hi, Linda, how're ya doing?" said Frances.

Linda's lip quivered, and she poised on the precipice of telling Frances how she was doing. But the Voice was watching and listening, and Linda recovered. "Fine, thanks, Frances. I'm fine. Is he there?"

"Oh, he's out at Playtime this morning, Linda. Should I leave him a message?"

He's out at Playtime? The Shrill Small Voice now took complete title to Linda's head in fee simple absolute. There was a meeting at Playtime? Why hadn't Marvin told her about it? Why hadn't she been invited? Yes, of course, she wouldn't have been able to go because of the arraignment and everything, but why hadn't she been invited? Ignoring even a pretense of empathy for what she had just been through, without a nod even to her physical injury, the Voice pummeled Linda as though it were on amphetamines.

"Oh, right, the Playtime meeting," Linda said. She didn't want it thought by a blabbermouth like Frances that she was Out of the Loop. Once these rumors got started, there was no stopping them. You could never be too careful. "Tell him I called, please, Frances. I should be back in the office soon."

Linda stood. She took a breath and tried her best to recover some dignity. But her stockings were torn, and her kneecaps a mess. The toes of the $450 Chanel shoes were scuffed. The torn lining of her cashmere coat was flapping around her legs. She ripped it out of the coat and tossed it over the rail, high above Fort Point Channel, and watched the wind pick it up and carry it pell-mell up the channel toward the Boston Tea Party Ship.

She picked up the Kelly bag and set off again, at first unsteadily but then gaining speed, clip-clip-clipping her way down the Evelyn Moakley Bridge to Atlantic Avenue. As she descended the bridge, she looked up at the familiar towers—at International Place and the Pregnant Building and the other beacons of the Financial District. This meant nothing, she told the Shrill Small Voice. There was a lot going on with Playtime. They were trying to prepare for the Friday bankruptcy filing; there was a lot to do, and (thank heaven!) bankruptcy was not exactly Linda's specialty. You wouldn't expect *her* to be at a meeting to prepare the bankruptcy papers.

The Shrill Small Voice wasn't having any of that. "The directors. Senior management. The directors and senior management will be at a meeting to which you were not even invited. And your knees are a mess."

No, it was nothing. Marvin knew she had to go to that dreadful arraignment this morning, that was all.

The Shrill Small Voice was in Linda's ear. "Not even copied? Not even a cc on an e-mail, Linda? An e-mail about a meeting with the directors and senior management concerning the most pressing, the most important, thing in the life of your biggest client? Not even kept In the Loop?"

She had to get back to the office, away from this dreadful part of town with its humiliating courthouse, its rabble of journalists and erectile vans, its treacherous footing. She was Out of the Loop and needed to get back into it.

The Shrill Small Voice summed up for the jury with cruel, remorseless logic: this was Fritz's doing.

Oh, yes—Fritz. Linda wondered briefly what had happened to him. They'd probably thrown him in jail already, after that grandstanding stunt. She'd tried to do her best, she'd arranged for Prentiss Wolcott on terribly short notice, and look what had happened. There was a limit, she had to concede, to even her ability to parent Fritz, her third child. For almost fifteen years she had tried to do her best by that man. And look what she had to show for it.

Clip-clip-clip went the now scuffed $450 heels of the Chanel shoes as Linda LeBrecque descended to Atlantic Avenue. Wounded but alive after her brush with the cold forbidden frontier south of the Fort Point Channel, Linda hurried back to the safe bosom of her home in the Financial District.

BACK IN THE COURTROOM, they had not, in fact, thrown him in jail already. Fritz Brubaker was actually doing fairly well for himself.

The arraignment had carried on in courtroom 14 after Linda's departure. The ladies and gentlemen of the press snapped their attention back to the bench as soon as Linda swept out the back, afraid they might be missing something.

Judge Chandler said, "The question is, Mr. Brubaker, whether you pose a risk of flight. Whether, if I release you on your own recognizance, you can be trusted to return for trial. If I order you to return, will you return?"

Fritz stood up again. "Of course, Your Honor. Whatever you say. I just don't understand why we couldn't find me guilty today. But if we can't, then tell me whenever you'd like me to come back and plead guilty. I'll—"

"*I would not,*" Judge Chandler interrupted, then corrected herself, resuming a more judicious tone: "Mr. Brubaker, I would not like you to come back and plead guilty. I just want you to come back. Preferably with a lawyer. What plea you make will be your own decision in consultation with your lawyer. Do you understand?"

"Yes, of course. I'll come back whenever you say, Your Honor."

"I think I believe him," the judge said to no one in particular. The clerk nodded in agreement. Yeah, the guy was nuts. But he'd be back.

"Your Honor," Feingold remonstrated.

"But if you're uncomfortable about it, just lock me up," Fritz added.

"Mr. Brubaker, please be quiet. Mr. Feingold needs to offer the government's case on bail."

Which Mr. Feingold did. He adopted a stern tone and described Fritz's crime to the judge (and, he secretly hoped, the newspapers), in what he fancied would be heard as a voice of the people. Young Assistant United States Attorney Feingold, with his degrees from Yale and Georgetown, was making his play for the big time. He described in shock and outrage how the sale led to the catastrophic collapse of the company, how Brubaker was the worst kind of insider, operating with not only inside information but considerable culpability for the erroneous financial statements, how millions of shareholders had suffered while this plutocrat took his profits, how Brubaker was a person of enormous wealth, and lastly, how it would be a simple matter for him to hop a plane for the South Sea Islands and disappear forever.

"Thank you, Mr. Feingold. Let me ask you something. Has your office had any contact with the defendant before this morning?"

"Ummm . . . yes, Your Honor. Actually, he called me yesterday."

She nodded. "Now, there's a shocker. And what was the nature of this call?"

"That he wanted to meet with us. And we interviewed him, Your Honor. Of course, we advised him that he had the right not to speak to us, that he should retain an attorney, but—"

She interrupted, her old defense-counsel nose picking up a scent. "The marshals probably fixed everybody a pot of coffee. How interesting."

"Yes, Your Honor, I suppose so. But Mr. Brubaker told us he understood and waived his rights. In a call this morning, he said he wanted to come and plead guilty."

"I see." Judge Chandler sat and thought for about half a minute or so. At last she looked up. "Mr. Brubaker, I'm setting this case down for a pretrial conference on December third. According to the report, you are married, you live in the community, you have children. You apparently are eager to come here. So I'm releasing you on your own recognizance. That means you don't have to post bail. But I am imposing conditions. You will surrender your passport to the U.S. attorney's office by three P.M. today. You are not to leave the commonwealth without an order of this court. You will not trade any securities on any exchange. All right, Mr. Feingold?"

Well, it wasn't, but what could he do? "Yes, Your Honor," Feingold said.

She looked at the marshal. "Take the handcuffs off Mr. Brubaker, please. I don't think he's going anywhere, Mr. Feingold. He keeps asking me to lock him up."

"Yes, Your Honor."

"You're going to do what I've ordered, aren't you, Mr. Brubaker?"

"Yes, Your Honor," said Fritz.

"I believe him," she said.

"Only one thing, Your Honor," Fritz said.

"Yes?"

"The bit about being responsible for misleading financial statements? That wasn't true. The rest of it—"

"Mr. Brubaker. I'm begging you to shut up. No, I'm ordering you. You are hereby ordered to shut up. Got it?"

"Yes, Your Honor."

"Very well. Mr. Brubaker, I'm also ordering you to be here at nine-thirty A.M. on December third. Will you be here?"

"Yes. Yes, Your Honor."

"All right. And one more thing. I'm ordering you to consult with a lawyer." She scanned the pews. "Since I see that Mr. Pearl is here this morning on my next case, I'm ordering you to consult with Mr. Pearl. You don't have to hire him. But you have to talk to him. Mr. Pearl, will you meet with Mr. Brubaker, please?"

Attorney Max Pearl stood up in the gallery. "Your Honor, the guy's doing better than most of *my* clients. He just got released on his own recognizance." More laughter.

"Mr. Pearl, I think we've had enough comedy for one day."

"Yes, Your Honor. I'll be happy to meet with Mr. Brubaker."

"Very well, then, December third at nine-thirty. Next case."

SO FRITZ wished the marshal a good day and left courtroom 14 by the main door, a free man, at least temporarily. He looked for Linda in the hall. She was gone. But he didn't have to look hard for the ladies and gentlemen of the press. No lawyer to run interference? A lunatic defendant? Let the games begin!

"Mr. Brubaker?"

"Mr. Brubaker, could we ask you a few questions?"

"Would you come downstairs with us for an interview?"

He walked to the elevator, and the pod of reporters and sketch artists followed him, enveloping him like cytoplasm so that he became the nucleus of single-celled creature, an amoeba that changed shape as it slid down the corridor, squeezed into the elevator, then glopped out, along the main lobby to the front doors and out into the cold November morning.

They were all yelling, prodding him with microphones. Lights were in his eyes, microphones were dangling overhead. The wind blew his hair across his forehead.

"Mr. Brubaker?"

"Fritz!"

"Mr. Brubaker, are you guilty?"

He stood there with a polite smile in silence. He had guessed something like this might happen, that there might be a moment when he was ambushed by the press. So he had thought carefully about this part. He knew it would be a bad idea to get into any kind of dialogue. They'd just cut and paste the pieces they wanted.

"Mr. Brubaker?"

"Mr. Brubaker, why didn't you hire a lawyer?"

"Was that your wife's lawyer?"

"Are you having problems with your wife?"

"Did your wife try to force a lawyer on you?"

"Are you getting a divorce?"

"Why did you rip off the company, Fritz?"

"Fritz?"

"How do you feel about all the people who lost their 401(k)s, Fritz?"

"Fritz?"

A loud voice at the back of the mauling, rucking mass yelled out, "HEY, FINEY-ASS, CAT GOT YOUR TONGUE?"

He didn't respond. Instead, he waited, smiling, for them to quiet down.

"I have a statement," he said.

They jostled and mumbled and began to settle down.

He unfolded the yellow sheet of paper the Brockton cop had given him that morning. Then he looked up, which got them going again.

"Fritz, what's on the paper?"

"Did you write it?"

"Why don't you have a lawyer, Fritz?"

"Is it a confession?"

Then the surly voice again: "FINEY-ASS, READ THE FUCKING THING!"

Fritz smiled his polite, patient smile. "Whenever you're ready," he said.

This time they got it. Maybe he wasn't as stupid as he seemed in the courtroom. He wasn't going to be bullied. Anyway, he wasn't going to read the goddamn thing until they shut up. And it was cold out there.

So they shut up. And when they were quiet, he read it.

"I regret very much what has happened to Playtime and its shareholders," it began. "Had its books been kept forthrightly, the company would be healthy today. I did my best to make that happen, but I was unsuccessful. For my part, I will plead guilty to the charges brought against me. In the double-entry bookkeeping of a democratic republic, there should be no right without a corresponding responsibility. The responsibility here is mine. I feel that this will at least balance my own books. Thank you."

Fritz folded the paper and restored it to his pocket and, still smiling, began to try to ease his way through the journalistic protoplasm.

They were mumbling, scribbling, but not for long. They broke out again.

"That's it?"

"What the hell is that—double-entry bookkeeping?"

"What did you mean by that, Mr. Brubaker?"

"Why did you do it?"

"What did you mean, balance your own books?"

"Can we get a copy of that paper? You got any copies?"

"Is anyone else responsible?"

"Fritz?"

One of them said to another: "He didn't exactly say he did it, though, did he? Corresponding liabilities, or whatever the hell he said?"

"Hey, Fritz, did you do it?"

"Fritz! The hell?"

But he wasn't taking questions. He knew questions could kill you. So he kept up his smile, edged and sidled, and finally worked his way out of the amoeba. He walked briskly alongside the courthouse to the corner. They tried to follow him for a while, shouting questions, but he didn't answer.

18

THE BLACKBERRY PATCH

ON NOVEMBER 22, a frolicsome troop of lawyers and accountants gathered in the BlackBerry Patch: courtroom 6 of the United States Bankruptcy Court for the District of Delaware. Playtime had filed, and the lawyers had gathered for the first-day hearings in the bankruptcy. It was not quite Playtime anymore: from now on, the company would be known simply as "the debtor." Anywhere else it would be humiliating to be referred to as the debtor, the one that owes everybody money. But here in courtroom 6, being the debtor was big. It was power.

Bankruptcy—the very word gave you the shivers. A bankrupt was ripped apart, demolished, a ruin, a heap of masonry and broken pottery. It was . . . *rupt.* An ugly idea, an ugly sound, to be rupt. The word itself summoned fearful images—an apartment block in Gaza bombed to smithereens, a rubble of stones, big hawks of phlegm expectorated. The word held dark power: one thought of Jimmy Stewart in *It's a Wonderful Life*, handsome, charming Jimmy Stewart. How frightening the transformation he undergoes in the scene where Uncle Billy loses the money—how his lip curls and his brow darkens as he contemplates . . . bankruptcy.

"You know what this means? This means bankruptcy and scandal and jail, that's what it means, you silly old fool!"

Bankruptcy—the way the word clouded even the face of Jimmy Stewart, and turned him dark, and made him brood and thunder like an Old Testament prophet.

But things had changed since the days of Frank Capra. Bankruptcy didn't mean scandal and jail or even ruin anymore. By 2001 it meant rejuvenation. Bankruptcy wasn't poison, it was an elixir. A tonic of rebirth. America had reached her New Testament period of bankruptcy, where it meant forgiveness and a fresh start, renewal and God's love. It meant preserving jobs and restating balance sheets and renewing credit lines and revitalizing business and refreshing management and all things great and glorious. In short, it had transformed itself from *rupt* to *Bankruptcy, Inc.*

The shareholders of Bankruptcy, Inc., were lawyers, accountants, and finance wizards. Its factories were the U.S. bankruptcy courts. And the executive suite in the corporate headquarters of Bankruptcy, Inc., was right here in Wilmington, Delaware, just a few blocks from the Hotel du Pont, on the sixth floor of a nondescript office building. This is where the lawyers and accountants came. And if most bankruptcy cases meant lawyers in packs, then Playtime meant lawyers in platoons, armies of lawyers on the march toward the Wilmington headquarters; lawyers of the creditors, by the creditors, and for the creditors, so that legal fees would not perish from the earth.

The first-day hearings—the series of motions filed at the outset of a large bankruptcy case—were a kind of bankruptcy lawyers' convention. Everybody who was anybody would show up for first days in a case like Playtime, and more than fifty of them had. Wiley and Mangel was there. Scriven and Lugpaper, Adders Harpy, Shave and Crookstory, the Niekap firm, they were all there. They had come down on the Acela from New York, or they had flown in from Dallas or Chicago to spend the night in the du Pont on the corner of Eleventh and Market streets. And now they were shoulder to shoulder in the remarkably close quarters of this court-room, the executive suite and boardroom of Bankruptcy, Inc.

The pews were full, the aisles were full; the lawyers were crammed in like a football team flying coach. Here and there was an occasional, confused creditor, someone actually owed money by Playtime, wearing a dirty baseball cap that might say MARINO & SONS TRUCKING, someone so naive as to think that he should come to bankruptcy court to get the money owed to Marino & Sons Trucking. A few of these interlopers had shuffled into the room and now were crammed in among the rows of lawyers. Marino & Sons Trucking and the other creditors would be crushed in due course. But these were just the first days—Mr. Marino and his ilk did not yet understand how pervasively incomprehensible the whole business would be.

All around these stray unfortunates was the BlackBerry Patch. The lawyers had their briefcases on their knees and their papers on their briefcases, and perched atop their papers, held lovingly in two hands, their BlackBerries. At the security gate next to the elevators, the court officers had vacuumed up all the cell phones, but BlackBerries were permitted, so the ranks, shoehorned in, were all working furiously over the eensy buttons, sending to distant places e-mails that might happen to let slip that at the same moment the sender was In the Loop, he was right there, in the beating heart of Bankruptcy, Inc., for the first days in Playtime itself!

The BlackBerries were also an extremely useful tool with which the lawyers could communicate with one another. BlackBerry messages were bouncing all around courtroom 6 with dizzying acceleration. It was as though a trapdoor in the ceiling had opened, and a thousand electronic Ping-Pong balls had been let loose and were now bouncing and bounding and ricocheting in every direction—messages and replies and forwards and replies to forwards—witticisms, profanity, jokes, insults. All of this activity was generating substantial usage charges, which would later be included in the fee applications of the lawyers for "telecommunications costs."

The lawyers in courtroom 6 observed the usual canine seating conventions. In the back pews were the mutts and curs: lawyers who represented smaller creditors. The pew immediately behind the enclosure held the border collies. These were the young working dogs seconding really important dogs, ready to run laps, herd sheep, and fetch papers from the boxes at their feet. Next came the row of seats just inside the pews, show-dog seats, where lawyers for big and powerful creditors sat, and from which they would range to herd in committee business. Among the show dogs this morning were Larry Glubb, Lucinda Roth, and Jerry Nathan: very showy dogs indeed.

But the biggest dogs, the alpha dogs, the mighty lead dogs, commanded seats at the tables. These were the lawyers for the debtor and the banks. (Once the creditors' committee was formed, its lawyers would claim a seat at a table, too, but today was the first-day hearing, and no committee had been formed yet.) Occupying the seats at the tables were the great Micah Fensterwald, from Pladd and Tweed, because he had the debtors; Irv Klein, from Wiley and Mangel, because he had the banks; and Saul Herzog, because, well, because he was Saul Herzog.

Herzog! Glowering at the end seat at a table, in the red silks (wearing, in fact, a royal blue Egyptian cotton shirt with striped collar and French cuffs, a red silk tie and matching kerchief, and a gray suit with brazen chalk stripes, the trousers held up by red silk suspenders), was the undisputed heavyweight champion of the insolvency world, Saul Herzog, of the great New York firm Speel, Snapshank LLP. He was the bankruptcy lawyer you simply had to have when your bonds were in trouble. He chaired the annual New York Insolvency Institute (judge or no judge, you would not be invited onto a panel if Herzog thought your decisions inept); he edited the learned journal *Annals of Bankruptcy* (you wouldn't get an article published there unless Herzog approved it); he chaired the Speel, Snapshank bankruptcy department; he appeared in only the most mega of megacases; he wrote leading articles; he was the luminary of luminaries.

Herzog's taxonomy was complex. The lions of the bankruptcy bar came historically from two types. There were the High German Jews—men and, latterly, women who were not simply scholars of the bankruptcy code but connoisseurs of literature and art, lawyers who had personal tailors and season tickets to the Met, and had long since moved out to Westchester. Then there were the Brooklyn Jews—brawlers whose uncles were in retail. In the last part of the twentieth century, gentiles had been admitted, grudgingly, to the bankruptcy bar, but to a large extent, the lions remained Jews. This was an artifact of anti-Semitism. Jews had taken to bankruptcy two generations earlier, when it was deemed beneath the dignity of the Wall Street law firms, dominated by WASPs. But as Bankruptcy, Inc., had prospered, all the white-shoes had thoughtfully reconsidered this prejudice.

In Herzog both of the distinguished Jewish traditions were uneasily married. He did have season tickets to the Met, although Uncle Max had done pretty well in the diamond business. Herzog could read the Talmud and a put option. He could argue the merits of Matisse or Phil Rizzuto.

When Herzog was eighteen and still wearing the curls of the yeshiva student, his grandfather had summoned him.

When Zaideh summoned, you came. So Herzog rode the J train to Marcy Avenue and walked the five blocks to Zaideh's small second-floor apartment. His grandfather was in the easy chair by the bookshelf, polishing his glasses with a white handkerchief. Saul took a seat on the couch.

"What will you do with your life, my boy?"

Herzog had had a feeling something like this was coming. "Zaideh, I will be a rabbi."

Zaideh didn't react to this. He continued to polish the glasses. He worked slowly and methodically, holding them up to the lamp, then down again in his lap. Herzog shifted. The couch was formal, with an antimacassar draped over its stiff back and springs gone haywire, about as comfortable as a pile of lumber. Had Zaideh heard him? Was he ever going to finish with those glasses?

"I said I—"

"I heard what you said." Zaideh held up the glasses again, frowned a little. He went back to polishing them, the hankie describing unhurried circles on the glass. After what seemed to Saul like an hour and a half, Zaideh said, "I don't think so."

"I was first in my class!"

Zaideh held the glasses to the light. He was still unsatisfied. "Yes, you are a fine student, I think. And you have a big heart. These are two things a rabbi should have." He went back to his polishing.

"So if I have two—"

"Saul."

"Yes, Zaideh."

"Saul, you have no patience. A rabbi must be patient."

The boy stared at his hands. "I . . . I'm working on that, Zaideh."

Zaideh finished polishing the glasses and placed them carefully on his nose. With deliberation, he turned to examine his grandson on the couch. The glasses magnified Zaideh's eyes. It was brutal when he focused in on a person with his glasses on, like being under God's microscope.

"Believe me, Saul, when I tell you it's not something you can work on. I've watched you from a boy. You don't have the patience. A man should know his limitations."

Herzog, crestfallen, looked into the magnified eyes of the old man, or God, or whoever Zaideh was. "But what should I do, Zaideh?"

"Go be a lawyer, my boy."

Herzog was short and broad. His hair was on the longish side and tended toward wildness. He had the angry brow of a Beethoven, and the stocky arms of a clean-and-jerk champion, but he also owned a suit closet you could offer as collateral for a six-figure loan. What he didn't know about the bankruptcy code wasn't worth knowing. What he hadn't read in the journals wasn't worth reading. The deals he hadn't done weren't worth doing.

And he had stones. Famous in the bankruptcy bar was the story of the time in the seventies when Herzog, as a pup, a newly minted partner with Speel, represented the Knickerbocker Bank in a workout of the old Scoharie Malt Liquor Company. One night at a drafting session in Speel's offices, the head bank officer, a Brahmin swine named Brudermeier, was chatting with the borrower and hoped aloud that his "beanie boys" would finish this up, as he was late to a function. Herzog had been at the other end of the conference room, but he heard the remark. The room fell silent as he stalked over to Brudermeier. He got right in the banker's face and, in front of the entire crowd of thirty people or so, demanded, "What did you say?"

Brudermeier tried to brush off this provocation. "Those things you people wear on your head, Saul, I can never remember the name. Harmonicas?"

"We *people* wear on our head?" Herzog answered. "It's called a yarmulke, you Nazi. Now get out of my office. You're fired."

His office? Fired? Firing the client on the Scoharie deal, the refinancing of the fifth largest brewery in America? This Herzog wasn't even the engagement partner. No one fired the Knickerbocker Bank!

"You'll never work for the bank again," said Brudermeier icily.

"You've got that right. Out!"

That bit of grandstanding had probably cost Speel, Snapshank $10 million, but what it had gained them was immeasurably more valuable.

When Playtime hit the screen, it was to this man that the vultures turned. In the priority of claims against Playtime, the vultures stood behind the banks but ahead of the shareholders. The vultures were always in danger of getting shut out completely. On the other hand, they might make a score, as they'd bought their positions at a steep discount. They needed a presence to shout and threaten and insult and finally browbeat the banks into a deal. And Saul Herzog was their champion. At some time or other, he had screamed at almost every other lawyer in courtroom 6. One of them (Jerry Nathan) he had actually assaulted with a ham sandwich. Although battery was unusual, it wasn't startling: within the bankruptcy community, you weren't worth bothering about unless Herzog had, at some point, threatened to file a complaint against you with the Board of Bar Examiners. Dominic D'Oria, for example, was one of the kindest and gentlest-mannered of men, and in one meeting, Herzog declared that if Dominic stuck his nose into any more of his client's business, he, Herzog, would rip off the offending organ and eat it.

And yet Herzog's kindnesses were as flamboyant as his assaults. He was a regular visitor to the pediatric oncology ward at Mount Sinai Hospital. Not just a patron, not just a guy who'd pop $10,000 at a fundraiser and go to a dinner dance, he was an actual visitor to the ward. There were dying kids in that hospital who had felt the surprisingly soft touch of Herzog's big hands, and remembered the voice of the lawyer in the fancy suit reading to them. Once, a Speel, Snapshank associate who'd been sent on some emergency or other to find Herzog was shocked to discover the great warrior sitting alone in the waiting room in tears, because the kid he hadn't had time to visit in the last three weeks hadn't made it. There he sat, mighty Saul Herzog, bawling like a baby. And the day after Jerry Nathan got pegged with the sandwich, Mr. Ling Xi Fan, Herzog's personal tailor, showed up at Nathan's office at ten A.M. to measure Nathan for a new suit. It was measured, cut, tailored, and delivered, all courtesy of Herzog.

Mostly, Herzog turned away business. He employed two secretaries to do nothing but screen calls from potential clients. Fifty million bonds in Lastwave on line one? How'd you get this number? A hundred million bonds in American Power on line two? Please. A billion bonds in Acme Motors? Well, maybe we can talk. Send me a $1 million retainer.

They all wanted Herzog. In Playtime, the biggest filing of the year, they wanted Herzog very much indeed.

Playtime would be a feeding frenzy for hourly rates. The company needed bankruptcy lawyers. Its banks needed lawyers. A committee of creditors would be organized, and it would need lawyers. Because the case was in Delaware, each constituency would need so-called local counsel—Delaware lawyers. So each group would need two sets of lawyers.

Lawyers were only the beginning. These groups would need accountants, financial advisers, investment bankers, appraisers. The debtors would need a set; the banks a set; the committee a set. The law firms, the investment bankers, the accounting firms, the restructuring advisers would bill by the hour and travel in packs. They would have partners north of $600 per hour, and managers at $450 per hour, and associates at $300 an hour, and assorted scriveners, proofreaders, drones, drudges, box carriers, and coat holders at $200 an hour. With all of these meters running, it was conservatively estimated that a typical one-hour hearing on Playtime would run the debtor about $18,000 in fees.

TWO HOURS into the Playtime first days, visiting judge Herb Shoughler, who had been dispatched from his home in Louisville, Kentucky, to help Delaware with its groaning docket but had never in his life seen anything like this case, had reached the fourteenth item. It was a request to approve the employee-retention plan. Buried among the two dozen motions filed on the first day (which, it was hoped, the judge would rubber-stamp before much opposition could form) was a request from the company's lawyers that the court approve a plan to retain key employees (who turned out to be the boss and six of his cronies). The plan for retaining them was basically to pay them a whole shitload of money.

Craggy Micah Fensterwald, a tall, lean bankruptcy guru from New York, was at the podium, delivering his argument in the reasoned manner usually employed by debtor's counsel during first days. The spindly lawyer was making threats. If you don't approve this today, Judge, the management will resign en masse, and the ship will founder and sink before we can even lower the lifeboats, and lots of women and children will drown in three thousand fathoms of the icy North Atlantic. But hey, it's up to you.

Said in the most genteel possible way, of course.

"What's more," Micah added, "the banks have agreed to this." Irv Klein looked up from the other table and nodded. Micah was making an important point: Judge, you don't need to stick your neck out here. The banks, who have $2.4 billion at risk, they've looked this over, and it's okay with them. (The banks happened to have cut a deal with management to get Playtime to pay interest like clockwork on the first day of the month, but surely that had no influence on their judgment.)

Sticking his neck out was the last thing Judge Shoughler wanted to do in this crowd. "Any opposition to this motion?" he asked.

There was a rustle of anticipation throughout the room as Saul Herzog rose. Heads inclined, one to the other. Fingers flashed across eensy buttons. Herzog at the podium always presented the chance of a show. "Your Honor, Saul Herzog, Speel, Snapshank, on behalf of Pillar Partners, Atlas Ventures Two, Steadfast Limited Venture Funds . . ."

As Herzog went through the list of his clients, a lawyer in the back of the room typed a message on his BlackBerry and sent it to a pal across the room. It read, "Carrion Fund, Grave Robber Partners, Roadkill Investors . . ." The pal smiled and punched back this response: "Undead, LLP, Stiffs-R-Us, Morgue Venture Partners . . ." (These were more accurate descriptions of Herzog's vultures.) Pretty soon this message was being forwarded all over the courtroom, and the lawyers were gleefully adding names.

Herzog finished reading out the thirteen institutional bondholders who were his clients. The e-mails rocketed around the room behind him. He paused, dramatically. There was a moment of anxious anticipation, of fingers poised over the buttons. Would Herzog thunder? Would he rip the employee-retention plan to shreds? Would he burst with brimstone? Would he rant?

Oh, sure, he would rant. Fish gotta swim, and birds gotta fly—Saul Herzog would blast like a geyser. But not here. Here at the podium in courtroom 6, at the Playtime first days, Saul Herzog would not give voice to such harsh and combative thoughts. Here all was kindness. Here he was the caring and thoughtful rabbi Zaideh had dissuaded him from becoming. "Your Honor," he purred, leaning on the podium in an informal, almost avuncular way, "let's be practical. The committees—and I really think that in a case like this, there will be more than one, there will *have* to be—the committees haven't been formed yet. We ought to table this motion for a week or so." He smiled sweetly at the judge and took his seat. A sense of calm settled upon the masses. How practical this advice! How sound and sensible!

"I think that's a good idea," Judge Shoughler rumbled, himself relieved that Herzog had not ranted. (Also relieved that he would not have to read in the next day's papers that he had approved $1 million bonuses for the gang who drove the company into bankruptcy.)

Herzog would rant, but later. The geothermal eruption would come next week, in the privacy of a New York law office. He would assemble a vulture or two for the performance, as well as the bank lawyers. Knowing exactly what was coming, Micah would have ordered his clients to stay away. Larry Jellicoe was no match for Herzog and probably would start fibrillating right on the conference room table if exposed to the full performance. (Micah would, however, bring in five associates and a paralegal at a total hourly cost of about $2,100 to ensure that the debtors were fully protected and also, just a little bit, to enjoy the show.)

In the New York office, Herzog would be in full swing. The employee-retention plan was bullshit, it was an outrage, it was unethical and confiscatory; it stank, it reeked, it smelled; it was a foul, putrid pile of dung, it was turds floating in latrine muck, it was an embarrassment, it was criminal; an aging stripper in a Seventh Avenue peep show had more shame than to ask for this; a looter in the Rodney King riots had more shame than to ask for this; Bill Clinton had more shame than to ask for this.

This was a warm-up, to limber the vocal cords before Herzog really got going. "Micah, either this vile excrescence of a retention plan is dropped immediately, or my clients will have no choice but to crush Playtime and afterward drag Peter Greene's lifeless body out onto the mudflats of Bayonne, New Jersey, and gnaw on his genitals."

Micah was a genteel man. (He had no uncles in retail; his uncle Seth was a respected rabbi in Bronxville.) He never raised his voice, and his usual reaction to dramatic displays was a world-weary sigh. He'd known Saul for years. So, after the rousing first act, he would sigh and shrug. "Saul, c'mon, enough with the Demosthenes. Management needs the retention plan. You know, we have a Thirteenth Amendment in this country. They don't have to stay with the company. They could move on. You really want mass resignations? Not so good for business. What do you want, Saul?"

Saul would glower for a few minutes more. "Let me talk to my guys," he'd say. Act Two.

Micah would nod at his six assistants, and the youngest, trembling, would be deputized to lead the great man and his vultures along the corridor to the privacy of another conference room.

The moment the door was shut behind them, Saul would be right in their wattles, nose to beak. "You gotta take a deal here," he would say.

This volt-face might puzzle one of the newer vultures, one who had seen the opening aria and was still glorying in its epic power, still thinking about dragging Peter Greene out to the mudflats of Bayonne. He might be taken aback. He'd look perplexed. "But you said it was outrageous, and all that. That other deals weren't like this."

"Believe me, I know Delaware," Saul would answer. "The judge is going to give this to them. All we can do is negotiate for something."

"But I don't understand. Before, you were saying—"

"Listen to what I am telling you. The judge will cut your nuts off. So we will take the best deal we can get. All right?"

Herzog's face would seem to these vultures a little too flushed. No one would argue with this man, who was acting sort of deranged. Sure, he was entertaining when he was yelling at other people, but in the tight confines of this interior conference room, the guy made you nervous. There was also that disturbing business about nut cutting hanging in the air.

"All right," the vultures would chirp, crossing their legs.

Back now to the large conference room (the one with windows and a view south along a Third Avenue now lit up for the Christmas season, the one spread out with coffees and sodas and Poland Spring bottles and piles of paper). Herzog would stalk in first, the vultures filing behind. With such an audience gathered, he would not let it down by wrapping things up without Act Three. The resolution scene must be played with undiminished verve. It would begin sotto voce, with a shake of his head. A grim countenance. "Micah, my people are very concerned about this. They have no confidence in management, none." (They had bought their bonds within the past month or so and could give a shit about anything other than extracting forty cents out of a twenty-cent investment, but to hear Saul tell it, his people were deeply concerned with the ability of the management team to carry out the five-year business plan.)

Saul would build in the strings and the woodwinds and wind up with a harmonious flourish. Because they wanted to be reasonable, because they were willing to be accommodating, Herzog's clients could choke down this particular confiscatory outrage if they got their attorneys' fees paid. Micah needed to go along with the formation of an official bondholders' committee.

(And who would be the lawyer for this committee? Herzog, of course.)

Micah would consider this offer with a show of solemn reflection. Then he would have to excuse himself to go talk on the phone to Larry Jellicoe, who was stewing in his office up at Playtime.

"Another set of lawyers we have to pay to torture us?" Larry would demand. "I thought there already was a committee."

"That's the unsecured creditors. This is the bondholders."

"What's the difference?"

"Larry, I know Delaware. The judge is not just going to give this to us. All we can do is negotiate for something."

"But I thought you said it was customary, that all the Delaware cases had a plan like this."

"Larry, listen to what I am telling you. We have to take this deal. If there is substantial opposition to this plan, the judge could cut off your—" Micah was too well bred to finish the sentence. "Anyway, I think we should take it."

The CFO could fill in the blank. Larry Jellicoe was already shell-shocked. He'd seen an option package worth $12 million turn to powder and slip through his fingers, and now he was looking at his bonus, paltry as that was, showing a certain friability, and in the midst of all this goddamn dust, he'd just as soon save his nuts, thanks very much. Faced with advice like this, what could Larry do?

"Whatever you say."

At the next hearing, Judge Shoughler would approve a deal. There wasn't much he could do either—the lawyers smiled at him from every corner of the room, and not a single one of them got up to object. And this was Micah Fensterwald and Irv Klein and Herzog—the lions of the bar, people the judge had been reading about for years. Who was Herb Shoughler—a guy who mainly did chapter 13 cases where the only dispute was about whether a guy could keep his pickup—who was Herb to say no to this crowd, in Playtime, the biggest chapter 11 case in America? So Peter Greene and Larry Jellicoe would get their bonuses; and the mil-

lions of dollars in attorney time that Saul Herzog would rack up tortur-
ing Playtime on behalf of the vultures would be billed to an "official
committee," which meant it would be paid by Playtime itself.

The judge said as little as possible and hurried the agenda on to
something else, hoping that somehow this detail might sink in the mass
of papers and arguments and motions that were filed day after day in
Playtime. But he couldn't fail to notice, with a sinking heart, the reporters in the third pew scribbling away on their steno pads.

HOW HAD all of this happened? Why was her husband acting this way, Linda demanded of Dr. Helga Schadenfrau. Ever since September 11, crazier and crazier, and now this awful stock business. He'd traded on inside information, which is illegal, you can go to jail for it! And he probably would—Michael and Kristin's father would actually go to jail—when they sentenced him early in the New Year. Linda would be married to a felon. How could he put her and the children at such risk? And he did it on their home computer—what could possibly have been more stupid? Not to mention that Playtime was Linda's biggest client, how did it look to the Playtime board—your own lawyer is married to a man making illegal stock trades. "I made almost a million dollars last year. Wasn't that enough?"

In the Wellesley office, Dr. Schadenfrau tried to slow Linda down, tried to calm her. She sought to focus the patient on how she was reacting to these stressful events. But Linda was far from able to rationally assess her feelings. That was plain to Dr. Schadenfrau. This pain was too raw.

"And the kids, it's just killing me what this is doing to the kids. Poor Kristin doesn't know what to do, she came home from school the other day in tears, all her friends at school are saying her daddy's a criminal. And Michael won't even leave his room!"

It was a cold December afternoon, with winter sunlight playing wanly through the bay windows. Five days earlier it had snowed hard through the night. The snow had melted, but then the melt froze and left angry steel-gray lumps lining the curbstones and sidewalks, a glum precursor of the long winter to come. Dr. Schadenfrau had selected Chopin for the session. Today called for something gentle, if tinged with darkness. Something melancholy. A tinkling of keys as backdrop to the clinical evaluation.

"Just before this all erupted, I came home and found Fritz and Michael upstairs in Michael's room—Fritz probably hasn't been in that room in years—and they had the door shut, and I opened it suddenly, and both of them looked like children caught up to some mischief or other (well, they both *are* children, for heaven's sake, that's the whole *problem!*). Michael was sitting on the end of his bed with his head between his hands, the poor child, and his father was squatting on the floor, like he was pleading for Michael's forgiveness or something, and they both looked up at me and stopped talking. Fritz said to me, 'Excuse me, Linda, can you give us a few minutes,' too ashamed for his own wife to hear him beg for forgiveness, and Michael just kept his head in his hands. I said, 'Michael, darling, are you all right?,' and he just shook his head. Imagine it—wrestling with all the problems of adolescence and having your father come into your room and beg for your forgiveness like that. Imagine how it would shake your world!"

"Yes, it must be quite a burden for your son."

"The way Michael looked." Linda dabbed at her eyes. "Since that day I can barely get him out of his room."

The doctor shook her own head. It was extremely ill advised for adults to place children in the middle of such problems. "Generally, an adolescent is not ready to process information of this kind."

"He bolts down to the car two minutes before we leave for school, and he rushes back to the room and slams the door the moment school is out. All he does is play computer games. I ask him if he wants to talk about it, I try to encourage him to let it out, but he's completely traumatized. These feelings about his father—he's got to let them out!"

Dr. Schadenfrau was in complete agreement. Such feelings needed to be released from psychological bondage—with the assistance of professional help, of course.

"Things between Michael and his father haven't been that good. It's obvious to Michael that Kristin is Daddy's favorite, and as soon as he wasn't interested in lacrosse, Fritz abandoned him, that was years ago, but imagine wrestling with that problem and then having your father come in to ask your approval for his own criminal conduct."

It was all terribly sad. Dr. Schadenfrau frowned and subtly placed a fingertip to her tongue and flipped over a page in her notebook. "Did you ask Fritz about their conversation?"

"He refused to talk about it."

"I see." Denial. A common sign, the doctor thought. Counseling was strongly indicated. "You might want to consider setting up an appointment for Michael," she said. All things considered, a number of appointments for Michael would be the appropriate thing, and there had been a convenient cancellation by one of Dr. Schadenfrau's regular Thursday-afternoon patients. "It would help Michael to begin to process some of his feelings."

LIKE A JAPANESE
MONSTER MOVIE

IT WAS time for a drink: an ice-cold vodka in a frosted highball glass, with a twist of lemon. One little drink to mark a fine day of conducting the people's business. Because on the whole, omitting two or three passing gut stabs (he got the goddamn pains more frequently now), Senator Oldcastle had been feeling good since about three this afternoon, when he'd wrapped up his emergency session of the Senate Banking Committee in the Russell Senate Office Building. While it was too early to celebrate, it was not too early to plan a celebration over a drink. He hadn't exactly gained the yards, but he'd seen daylight ahead. And that was all Old Number 31 from Michigan State had ever needed before.

When Playtime's stock had plummeted, Senator Oldcastle's office got a few letters. Michigan pensioners who'd lost money, the usual whiners, not enough to matter. Then the story came out about the insider who sold stock, and his office got a few hundred calls. Oldcastle started to notice that this Playtime thing was different. It was getting a helluva play in the papers and on TV. But when, on December 4, *The Wall Street Journal* reported that the senior management of Playtime had been awarded bonuses by some bankruptcy judge in Delaware, all hell officially slipped its mooring. Oldcastle's office got five thousand letters. And they couldn't count all the e-mails, because the server crashed.

The last thing changed the feel of it, made Oldcastle's constituents and everybody else's angry as hell. This had been a big company. The stock could crash, and it would make people sick with fear or angry; they might feel stunned or betrayed. But when they heard on TV that some bankruptcy judge had given the management bonuses, then by God, heads needed to roll.

I think the committee will be the place to bring the tumbrel, thought Senator Oldcastle.

THERE WAS a threshold difficulty. The Michigan Democrat chaired the Senate Banking Committee, and it wasn't precisely clear what the Playtime problem had to do with banking per se. Playtime was about people's pensions, about accounting, about the trading of securities. Banks didn't seem to have a lot to do with it. But difficulties of this sort never stopped Oldcastle for longer than ten seconds. Because if he let them stop him for twenty seconds, then that rat bastard Phil Purse, Republican congressman from Tennessee and head of the House Commerce Committee, would get the jump on him. Or maybe Senator Gobbel (chairman of Administration and Finance) or Senator Braytrump (Senate Commerce). And by the time *his* committee got to grill people, they all would have taken the Fifth and television would have grown bored with it all.

So Senator Oldcastle had convened an emergency meeting of the Banking Committee and instructed his staff to prepare subpoenas.

Now, the constitutional role of the Congress, as the first branch of government, is to legislate. In support of its legislative powers, Congress has the power to subpoena witnesses and documents. The idea is that evidence from real life will help the legislators draft useful laws. But the use of subpoenas in Playtime would have nothing to do with drafting laws: subpoenas were for the purpose of hearings, and hearings were for the purpose of television. This was a vital issue for Congress to get right into, for practical reasons, important reasons. Item: Senator Oldcastle had five thousand letters from constituents who were mad. Item: those constituents would get a chance to see Oldcastle pummeling the financial guys responsible for the company's collapse, which could help Oldcastle get reelected. Item: there was no ticklish political issue here. The stockholders were Democrats and Republicans alike, so it was safe for Senator Oldcastle to come out against the financial guys and in favor of the common man.

As far as the legislation was concerned, he would get staffers to work on that (someone like Ursula Fratangelo, that smart new intern on his staff, might do nicely). Anytime you had a law about accounting, it would take so long to draft and comment and haggle and amend and horse around that by the time it was ready, people would have forgotten about whatever the hell grievance had inspired it in the first place. So the law could quietly disappear, which was a good thing. There wasn't much danger of having to stick your neck out in favor of a law the business guys wouldn't like. It was a tricky balance. To keep their money coming, you had to keep big business worried about what you might do. You had to make them fret. You could yell at them, call the lobbyists into your office and say, "Goddammit, guys, I've got constituents whose retirements are cleaned out by this thing! If you can't keep your house in order, you're goddamn right we're going to get some federal oversight into accounting!"

You could make those speeches, you could rail at them, but you couldn't actually enact an oversight law or the PACs would conclude that you weren't just having a tantrum: you really had become a communist. If that happened the money would dry up. The thing was to have the tantrum but keep it vague: keep them guessing that you'd come around in the end. Oldcastle was a master at this. He knew he could milk the thing for a couple of years, sucking in good money from the accounting firms and industry groups worried about what he might do. All around, it was a win.

He finished his vodka appetizer. It was eight-thirty and time, after a long day of seeing to the people's business, to get a real drink or two. The burning pain in his gut had returned, and he had some goddamn soreness around the knees that maybe a drink would remedy. Maybe a couple of drinks, and then a visit to Nell's. Before dismissing them for the night, Senator Oldcastle decided to inspect his troops, to give them a few words of encouragement for the fight to come. His staffers and interns had geared up for a long night of drafting subpoenas. Also, he was worried about one detail that he needed to check on with his chief of staff, so he began his rounds with Ralph Moldy.

"Good evening, Senator."

"How are you, Rafe? Say, did you have a chance to look into that little issue on Playtime?"

The "little issue on Playtime" was the delicate question he'd pulled Moldy out of a hearing to investigate. How much dough had Playtime given his campaign?

"Yes sir, I did. They pretty much maxed out," Moldy said. "CEO and six other executives and five directors all did a thou for each of the last three years. And big givers to our PAC. Looks like a hundred or so. We're still running down names."

"Okay, well, can't be helped. Nice to see you."

It wasn't all that nice to see RafeRalph, if the truth be told, but this was Oldcastle's default greeting. The senator saw hundreds, if not thousands, of people every day, and "Nice to see you" was his standard line, whatever the hour. It was a handy salutation and valediction all in four quick syllables; you didn't have to linger and chat if you didn't want to.

Which he didn't. Not that Oldcastle didn't appreciate what the staffer had done for him with that landlord problem. The senator was very grateful indeed, but on a personal level, gays made Jack Oldcastle squeamish, although he'd matured on the subject. Gays voted like a sonofabitch, so Oldcastle tiptoed down the middle of the road on gay issues. He'd learned never to have a chief of staff who wasn't gay, because gays were ideal for the job. They didn't have wives and kids and need to keep some semblance of reasonable hours. You could flog the shit out of them—you could work gays eighteen hours a day, and as long as you respected their sexual preference, it was not required that you respect anything else. The best of them also got protective and not only could take care of shit but would fight like a mongoose with the media, and worry about how you'd look in a photo, and stuff like that that bored the hell out of Oldcastle but unfortunately was necessary. (Actually, getting Oldcastle to look like anything other than a fat bastard had become a job for Madison Avenue, and RafeRalph was pretty good at it.)

But most important of all: gays were discreet couriers. Getting laid was a most cumbersome business for a United States senator. You had to get to a place, you had to get the girl to the place, and then you had to get away from the place and get the girl the hell away from the place, all without anybody taking pictures. You also had to get this done without the courier, who in all likelihood was going to be closer to the girl's age—much closer—trying to scoop the girl for himself. For obvious reasons, nobody was better suited to this task than RafeRalph, who probably squatted to pee and definitely used that ridiculous name but nevertheless could get shit done. Not that Oldcastle had needed this service too frequently in the last year or so.

He lumbered over to another desk. Jesus, how that corn on his big toe screamed at him, made him limp. "Nice to see you, Jeffrey. How's the family?"

"Well, Senator. Very well, sir."

Oldcastle liked the way they all senatored him, even the ones who'd been there for years. The dignity of it.

"Good evening, Senator."

"Nice to see you, Jeanine."

The senator was now huffing and puffing. It was embarrassing how out of breath he got. He could barely walk through an airport anymore. He wasn't far from needing a seat with the old crones on those irritating electric wagons that beep their way through the terminals. Jack Oldcastle, who gained 160 yards against Auburn in the Sugar Bowl! (Technically, Glidden, Michigan State's fancy-boy halfback, had been the ballcarrier, but without Old Number 31 lead-blocking for him, Glidden sure as hell wouldn't have gained all that yardage.) But anyway, those were details from a long time ago. He'd been a mountain of a fullback, cut from flint and able to run through linebackers as though they were sofa cushions. But he'd become a mountain of flesh who couldn't run through a pile of leaves.

His tour of the plantation led him to three desks crammed near the back of the office, next to the kitchen and toward the interns, and in particular, past the new intern, that smart young Ursula Fratangelo, who might be helpful in drafting some accounting legislation.

"Good evening, Senator."

"Nice to see you, Ursula."

The senator's salutation was wholly true and, in all likelihood, the only moment of complete veracity in Oldcastle's entire day. It was exceedingly nice to see Ursula, whose sultry skin was the color of cocoa and whose dark hair shone with invitation. Ursula had a coy smile and a curvaceous set of sultry ta-tas, and on many occasions, including this one, she wore for a blouse a thriller featuring the improbable heroism of a lone button. Ursula's silk blouse was only an eyedrop away from transparency. Often (and, the senator saw, tonight) the lone button defended this tissue from being thrust apart by powerful hydraulic forces. The senator found Ursula's button compelling viewing. How mightily it strained!

"How's the family?" he asked.

"Very well, thank you, Senator. How are you this evening?"

I'm hale and fit! I'm a former Unsung Hero trophy winner coursing with earthy desire and vital male juices, ready on a moment's notice to run rampant through your backfield! That's how I am!

Senator Oldcastle didn't say any of this, of course. He was transfixed by the button, so what he said was "I'm very well, thank you, Ursula. How's your but—your butter?"

"My butter, Senator?"

"Yes, yes, your *brother*," he recovered. "How's your brother?"

She looked confused. "I . . . I don't have a brother, Senator."

"Oh, I thought you did. Thought you did. How's the family?"

She smiled politely. Hadn't he asked her this already? He seemed to be lingering.

Goddammit, the senator was thinking, the hell with the family! The whole wretched horde of Fratangelos, the sisters and the cousins and the aunts, the goddamn brother who didn't even exist—he was interested in the *button*, for Chrissakes. And now he was starting to wheeze louder, keeping up with this conversation. He would have liked to give vent to his true thoughts on the matter of the button in a nice hotel room somewhere, and he quite longed to liberate the heroic button and bury his massive jowls deep within Ursula Fratangelo's nubile young— But no. Ever since that fool Clinton had made such a hash of things, adventures like these were damn near impossible. Snitches and bluenoses lurked everywhere, and every kid who showed up with a résumé and an aptitude for licking envelopes was a potential lawsuit. So, "How's the family?" was about as close as he could get.

"They're fine, thank you, Senator, my mom and my dad, I mean. I'm, you know, single myself!"

Oh, that delicious little just-single giggle, with its wanton hint of an apartment somewhere free from a spouse and perhaps even free from the prying eyes of the press!

But he felt a stab in the gut right then, a sharp, searing pain, and the stab quickly erased any thoughts of luring Ursula Fratangelo into an evening of pleasure, or any pleasure at all. He'd better get a drink to take the sting off. Maybe he needed to see the goddamn doctor.

"Are you all right, sir?"

He forced a smile. "Oh yes, thanks. Long day. Have a good evening, Ursula." Old Number 31 waddled off to the office lobby, thinking, Maybe I'll skip Nell's and go home. Get some rest. Feel better tomorrow.

Ralph Moldy had already gotten the usual shit done. The limo was idling at the curb, waiting to take the senator to his apartment in Northwest Washington, where the lease had recently been brought up to date.

"LIKE A Japanese monster movie, huh?" asked Max Pearl at lunchtime the next day up in Boston. Pearl was carrying out Judge Chandler's order by welcoming a potential new client to his cluttered third-floor office near the center of town, on Tremont Street.

"I don't follow," said the potential new client.

"Phineas Brubaker of Dover meets Pearl the Jew. You wanna sandwich?"

Pearl was standing behind the desk, which overflowed with heaps of papers and cardboard files. A paper plate clung precariously to the summit of the highest pile. On the plate an island of seafood-salad wraps was separated from potato chips by a moat of white drippings. Pearl was eating a half sandwich, holding the soggy wrap like a cigar and leaning over the plate so the juice would drip on the plate. His tie was tucked into his shirt.

The sounds in the office were of car horns from Tremont Street, clanks and bangs from the radiator, and munches from Pearl's jaw. He was a loud eater.

Scattered everywhere on the floor were files, in stacks, in heaps, in piles. Behind Pearl, a dusty window gave half a view of the Old Granary Burying Ground. A graveyard, thought Fritz Brubaker, not a good omen. He sat in one of the two tired wooden chairs parked in front of Pearl's desk. The other chair held a suit jacket and three files. In the corner of the office was a leaf bag full of soda cans.

Fritz declined the offer of lunch.

"Me, I would have done just what you did," said Pearl.

"Meaning?"

"Firing that dope Wolcott. A putz if there ever was one. Guy needs a script to wish a judge good morning."

"Oh. Well, I didn't fire him, exactly."

"Always lugging those librarians around with him, too. Personally, I thought that was a good move. I liked the part where he had to admit to about a hundred people that he didn't actually have a client. And then, with all those reporters watching, had to slink out of there. That was a nice touch."

"I didn't mean to insult the man. I just hadn't hired him."

"I know. Your brilliance was accidental. That would be consistent with everything else you did, which happens to have been dumber than rail grease. Sure you're not hungry? You're thin as hell, Fritz." Max held out the seafood cigar. Fritz shook his head politely. "No? Fine. But the arraignment? It won the Oscar, Fritz, for dumbest speech by an adult male not under the influence of a hard-on."

The guy was direct, Fritz had to give him that. "Is this the part where you make your pitch for a new client?"

"I'm getting to that."

"Oh, good."

"Here it comes." Pearl put on a caring, empathetic look. "Hey, whaddayagonna do? Could have happened to anyone."

"That's it?"

Pearl shrugged. "I lied, actually. Should have said 'Anyone not a Jew.' "

"Why not a Jew?"

"Only a WASP is that stupid," said Max Pearl. He finished the wrap and began to eat the now soggy potato chips. "I love seafood salad. You like seafood salad?"

Fritz shook his head.

"Didn't think so. You'd rather catch the fish on the fly rod, then have Chester grill it whole over mesquite, am I right? You great white chiefs and this fishing thing. It's very primitive, Fritzie."

"I do like to fish," Fritz conceded.

"Please," Pearl replied, dismissing with a wave of his hand the whole aboriginal business of standing in the cold in the hopes of hooking up a fighting, scaly, clammy creature with a length of filament. "Me? Gimme the processed."

He fished out another wrap from the paper plate. "You know, Fritzie, all those times you said you're guilty, the prosecution can use that, probably. And the statement to the papers. Ouch. Even Prentiss

Wolcott might have advised against it. All that shit about being responsible and double-entry whatever the hell it was? Nuts." He shook his head. "Very hard to get a good jury now."

Pearl straightened up suddenly, held his arms out. The wrap dripped white juice on the carpet. "But I was forgetting. You're dying for a federal condo. Escape the urban blight of Dover. Free meals for three to six. Saturday night in the prison showers, all the dates a girl could want. Homosexual rape is such a turn-on! I forgot. Silly me."

Fritz smiled to acknowledge the performance. "Bravo," he said. "Anything else?"

Pearl finished his wrap, pulled his chair out from behind the desk, and sat. He sighed. "I was just thinking I don't get too many clients like you."

"Did I hire you? I missed that."

"Yeah, a minute ago, I think it was. Anyway, most of the guys I get are mugs. They call me because they got drunk, they got high, they got laid, and they're in trouble. Dumb as mud hens, most of them. They hire Pearl, figuring he's smarter than the dumb prosecutor. Which is correct, but unfortunately, not as much smarter than the dumb prosecutor as the client himself is stupider than the dumb prosecutor. If you know what I mean."

"DP minus C is greater than P minus DP." Fritz found a more elegant way to express the idea. "Doesn't say much for C."

Pearl took a moment to work it out. Was that an insult? Maybe. "Like I was about to say. You're different."

"Must be a disappointment for you."

Pearl said, "Here's this guy Fritz Brubaker from the Marblehead Brubakers, thank you very much, lives in a mansion in Dover, got a house on Nantucket, married to a partner at Elboe, Fromme, got a sailboat worth more than my house, got a bike worth more than my car, plays golf at the country club, got— What is it, Fritzie, two or three mil in brokerage accounts, am I right?"

"Dunno. What kind of car do you have?"

Pearl smiled. For a gentile, this Brubaker was pretty good. He went on. "Turns out, the guy is not actually stupid. Not that you would know this. With his pedigree, all that Yankee inbreeding, to look at him and all, you'd think the guy's got the brains of a golden retriever. Eighth-generation prep and all that. You know? But you'd be wrong. Fritzie's a math major. From Amherst."

"And your point, Mr. Pearl, was what?"

"I ain't *got* a point, Fritz. That's my problem. My point is, there is no point. A guy with all you got, and with your brains, shorts his own company, in his own name, on his home computer?"

"Not as smart as you thought, I guess."

"For, what was it, thirty-five hundred shares? You know, I asked around. Some of the very plaintiff class-action guys who have their jaws locked on this company right now. Very successful guys. Ooh, do they make money." Pearl whistled, closed his eyes, allowed himself a momentary ecstasy, then snapped back to his speech. "But anyway. Your thing? Strictly amateur night. A high school stunt. You short thirty-five hundred shares, even knowing a hundred-mil charge is coming out on a company like Playtime, you might expect two, three bucks of movement. Five bucks tops, my friends tell me. And Fritzie, believe me, these people are never wrong about money. They know. So, on five bucks, you make seventeen five. A great score is fifty thou. You? You melted down the whole company and made, what was it, a little over a hundred thou?"

"That's what the indictment says."

"Right. A hundred thousand, parked in your kids' account. Now, to the jury, that's a lot of dough. Even to a guy like me, maybe, it's money. But to you? Please. It's a boat payment. Your wife makes that in what, three weeks? So, for a boat payment, you commit a federal crime on your home computer. Hi, look at me, folks. The guy trading on inside information, the guy shorting the stock—that would be me, Fritz, in case anybody's interested." Pearl shook his head.

Fritz's face was reacting in small ways around the corners of his eyes and mouth. He'd begun to take on a hint of a frown during this monologue. There were problems, he could see that. He tried to change the subject. "I thought Judge Chandler wanted you to tell me about my rights."

Brubaker didn't want to talk about it. As Pearl suspected. "You know, boneheaded as your stunt was, Pearl could help you. A guy as sophisticated as you does a stunt like this all on his own? A point not without interest. I wonder if—"

"Time does fly, doesn't it, Mr. Pearl!" Fritz made a show of looking at his watch. He rose. "But I have to run. Thanks for speaking with me, as the judge said we should. Send me a bill, will you?"

Pearl stood. "Fine, go. But don't pretend to be missing my point, Mr. Differential Equation from Prepville. You get my point."

"I really don't—"

"Fritzie, read the newspapers! What is the story today? Is the story Playtime's phony books? Or is the story you?"

Fritz stopped at the door. He turned and gave the lawyer a searching look. "What do you mean?"

"Do I have to spell it out for you? Playtime was going to be bankrupted anyway. You're in finance, so you had to know it. The big guys must have known it, too. This restatement of earnings was going to put the company out of whack with its banks, the banks were going to stop lending, and the company was going to get creamed at Christmas. Suppose you're the CEO and you know you have to file bankruptcy for the company. Do you want the story to be that the company's revenues aren't there and its management put out phony numbers, or do you want the story to be that some rogue employee shorted the stock and set off a panic?"

Fritz was still regarding Pearl curiously. "Is that what you think happened?"

"I'm not getting a whole lot of other ideas from you. I give you a chance. I am asking you to explain why a guy who doesn't need the money does something this lame, and what I am hearing is a loud silence."

A bus thundered by outside the window, rattling the glass.

"In a manner of speaking," said Max Pearl.

The judge had liked this guy, Fritz was thinking. He'd even kind of joked with her, and she hadn't bitten his head off. Maybe he should do this the judge's way. With a lawyer. Maybe that would be smoother.

"Fritzie, great white chief look impressive in my doorway, but you gonna go, you gonna stay?"

"Sorry, Max," Fritz answered. "I was just thinking. Is it all right to call you Max?"

"Everybody calls me Pearl."

"Everybody?"

"*Every*body."

"Your wife calls you Pearl?"

"My ex does when she's talking to me. Which, believe me, is rarely."

"Okay, Pearl. Can I ask *you* a few things?"

"Sure."

"First, this conversation we're having, it's privileged, right?"

"Right."

"That means you can't repeat it to anyone?"

"Right."

"That's bulletproof?"

"Only Superman's bulletproof, Fritzie. But the privilege is close. You ask me to help you commit a fraud or a crime, that's not privileged. Anything else, I can't repeat."

"Okay. And I'm the client, right? So you have to do what I tell you?"

"Within limits."

"Do I say whether to go to trial or plead guilty, or do you?"

"You do."

"So if I say I want to plead, it's a plea?"

"Yeah, pretty much."

"What do you mean, pretty much?"

"If I think you're doped out, or mentally incompetent, or don't know what the fuck you're doing, I have a problem."

"Do you? Do you think I'm any of those things?"

"*I* don't know what the fuck you're doing."

"But that's not the test."

"No, the test is, do I think you don't know what the fuck you're doing. And no, I don't think that."

"Good. You're right. Okay?"

"Sure."

"Okay, let me tell you, as my lawyer, what I want to do."

"I got hired? I must have missed that. When did that happen?"

"A minute ago, I think it was."

"Oh. I'm very expensive, by the way."

"How expensive?"

"Three hundred an hour. No, four. I forgot, the firm had a rate change last week."

"I thought the firm was you."

"Don't worry, it's less than what Prentiss Wolcott gets."

"What's Prentiss Wolcott get?"

"Daley and Hoar? Six, probably," Pearl guessed.

"Fine, make it six. Now I want to talk about the plea."

"Six? Really? Nice. For six, you get advice first."

"You can give it to me later. What I want to do now is plead," said Fritz.

"I gathered that on Thursday."

"I want to plead."

"But why? This is what I'm stumbling over, Fritzie. Why are you taking the heat for these—"

"I want to plead."

"You want to plead, you have the right to plead. You may have options, you might want to—"

"I want to plead," Fritz repeated.

"That's your right. But I gotta tell you, Fritzie, you need to hear some advice. And then make up your mind. Because I think—"

"I want to plead."

"Is there an echo in here?"

"I want to plead."

"You're not being reasonable."

"Do I have to be reasonable?" Fritz asked. "Listen, this conversation has been interesting, Pearl, and I appreciate your help. But it's time to move on. Here are your choices. Door number one, I plead. Door number two, you're fired."

"Fired? You just hired me."

"I must have missed that. When did that happen?" Fritz asked.

"A minute ago, I think it was."

"Maybe, but now you're not showing good client skills."

Pearl sat behind his desk, leaned back in the chair, let out a sigh. He ran his left hand through his hair, which was thick around his ears but thinning on top. The dewlap beneath his chin flapped, and his eyes were a-twinkle. "Fritzie, please wait at least ten minutes. Otherwise I got fired in five minutes, like that dope Wolcott. That would be hurtful."

"No, he never got hired."

"I guess that's true," Pearl acknowledged. He considered the matter. "Might be worse for me than Wolcott, though. He only didn't get hired. But I got fired. Think about it."

"It's a problem," Fritz agreed.

Pearl raised his index finger to an imaginary jury. "Nobody fires Pearl in five minutes! Ten, maybe."

"You want to consider door number one instead?"

"That's a problem, too, Fritzie. Door number one, I do something stupid. Bad for my reputation. Door number two, I get fired in five minutes, bad for my reputation."

"But door number one comes with the six hundred."

"You have a point there. A significant point. Six hundred is not to be sneezed at. Still, is six hundred worth my reputation? My ex would tell you you're overpaying. But you know what? What about door number three?"

"Door number three?"

"Sure. Believe me, when you talk *Let's Make a Deal*, this is something I know. There were always three doors on *Let's Make a Deal*."

"All right. What's door number three?"

"Door number three is, before you fire me, you tell me one thing. Privileged. Then you fire me and you keep the six hundred."

"Interesting door. What's the question?"

"Just tell me one thing: why?"

"Why what?"

"Why are you taking the fall for these guys?"

Fritz stared across the hills of paper at Pearl. He did the math. He was still standing a little awkwardly by the office door, and now he folded his hands and appeared to be considering them. Clacketa-BANG went the radiator. He could hear the faint sound of the secretary typing.

"Let's go back to door number one," he said softly. "As your client, I want to give you an instruction."

"Wait, the deal was you would answer the question. Or at least fire me. You don't fire me, you have to pay the twelve hundred."

"Twelve hundred? When did we make that deal? I must have missed that."

"Not bad, Fritzie," Pearl smiled. "You sure you don't have some good Jewish blood mixed in with all that thin blue stuff?"

"Send me the bill and we'll find out."

"Oh, that's cold. But good! And you know what? A guy that good doesn't make a mistake that dumb on October third."

"Pearl, I'm giving you an instruction. This is serious."

"Okay, tough guy. But we should talk first."

"I'm instructing you to plead me out and keep your questions to yourself."

"Fritzie, they go nowhere. But we should talk. Anita!"

"Yes," came the secretary's voice.

"Show Mr. Brubaker out. He's late to polo. And write him up a bill for twelve thousand dollars. And a sandwich."

"But he didn't have a sandwich, Mr. Pearl."

"Write him up a sandwich, Anita. A grilled fucking sea bass on mesquite bread. And kettle-cooked potato chips. Whatever those people eat. He's from Dover. They never read bills in Dover."

Anita escorted Fritz down the hall. At the elevator, she whispered, "He didn't mean that about the bill, Mr. Brubaker. He likes to tease sometimes."

IN HIS OFFICE, with the door closed, Pearl was thinking. Who could tell?

Law was a strange racket. It could surprise you even after twenty-eight years. Some playboy from Dover walks into your office, shrugs, and says, Gee, they got me, I did the trade on my home computer. Pearl wasn't buying that—this thing had to go much higher. That's why the client was in such a hurry to plead guilty. But what did the Playtime gang have on Fritz—why was he covering for them? The guy seemed quick: not like most of the morons Pearl represented. (Also, he could pay—even better.) But could Pearl save Fritzie from himself? That was the question.

THE RED LIGHT atop the television camera came on. RAP! RAP! RAP! went the gavel.

"The committee will come to order," said Senator Jack Oldcastle, although there appeared to be nothing orderly about the proceedings of the Senate Banking Committee. The hearing room in the Russell Senate Office Building was grand, with its pilasters along the wall, its worked ceiling, its portraits of John C. Calhoun and Everett Dirksen, its deep blue carpet, and most of all, its ornate bench raised up in a semicircle of burled walnut, from which a dozen senators would surround their prey. Behind the twelve senators, two dozen aides and pages scurried in and out from the blue curtains, whispering, bearing notes, taking instructions, handing up notebooks. The prey sat at the witness tables in the middle of the room, and beyond the tables were eight rows of oak benches with uncomfortable red leather seats and eagles carved in the armrests at the end of each row. Beyond them loomed an aluminum forest of television-light brackets and camera tripods. The real jungle was right in front of the witnesses—that fifteen-foot swath of carpet between the witness tables and the committee bench that sprawled with photographers.

Oldcastle had meant to wear his best charcoal flannel suit, but there had been some goddamn misunderstanding with the concierge about an unpaid laundry account, a misunderstanding he didn't have time for, so he'd broken out a solid blue pinstripe from the back of the closet, and a photogenic red tie. The jacket was only a little tight, making the shoulders kind of pop up and the sleeves pull back from his wrists.

But only a little. The senator had his gavel in his hand and was feeling powerful. His briefing binder lay before him. He was ready for the room to calm down so he could begin with the hearing.

Ralph Moldy was at his ear. "Here, take this," said Moldy, handing him a black lozenge.

"What is it?"

"It's a BlackBerry."

"What the hell's a BlackBerry?"

"E-mail. It's e-mail, Senator. We'll get CNN, MSNBC, and the others up in the staff room, and I can send you e-mail on how it's playing."

"You can do that?"

"Sure, let me show you." Oldcastle swiveled around, and Moldy quickly showed him how to operate the eensy buttons.

"How do I know when you send a message?" Oldcastle whispered. "It doesn't make a goddamn noise or something, does it?"

"No, Senator, I've got it set on vibrate."

Vibrate? The senator looked apprehensively at his aide. For Chrissakes, was this some kind of gay thing?

Moldy said, "Just keep it in your pocket. It will vibrate if we send you a message."

Armed with his vibrator, Senator Oldcastle swiveled back to the TV lights. The press had one battery of cameras pointing straight at him, and a second toward the threesome at the witness table: Peter Greene, Larry Jellicoe, and Marvin Rosenblatt (who looked, respectively, like a movie producer who'd flown in from the Coast, a soldier's parent who's received a telegram, and a corporate lawyer).

"The hearing will come to order," Oldcastle repeated. "Chair recognizes Senator Slater."

"Thank you, Mr. Chairman," said Dan Slater, the junior Republican senator from Nebraska. He began with a prepared text, so Greene and Jellicoe had to endure about eight minutes of lecture about how the people on the farm assumed that when an accountant said the books were okay, why then that meant the grain was properly counted; and how an honest scale would weigh a steer by just one weight; and other helpful observations of that kind. Greene, who had been schooled to appear down-to-earth and empathetic, was already forgetting his lessons. He began to sneak glances at his watch.

Slater finally wound up his speech and got to the witnesses. "Mr.

Greene, I'd like to begin by asking you some questions about Playtime's restatement of its second-quarter earnings. Are you generally familiar with that subject?"

Greene smiled for his cue. "Senator, I'd like to answer that question and a lot of others. I'd like to set the record straight on a lot of things that have been misrepresented in the media. But I'm afraid that my attorneys," and here Greene gave a rather disgusted nod toward Marvin Rosenblatt, "are telling me that I'm to exercise my right not to testify at this hearing."

In other words, Greene was trying to say, I'm a down-to-earth and empathetic guy, but what else can I do in this nest of thieving lawyers?

"Excuse me, Senator Slater," Oldcastle rumbled. "The chair would interject at this time."

What was this? The attention turned back to the presence at center stage. The TV cameras swung around, the photographers turned. Oldcastle cleared his throat. "I want to advise you, Mr. Greene, that the right under the Fifth Amendment not to testify in this hearing is a right that belongs to you, not some lawyer."

(*Some* lawyer! Just *some* anonymous scrivener with Coke-bottle glasses, *some* obfuscator, *some* pedant Greene had dragged in here to be his scapegoat. The disdain that the senator showed for Marvin Rosenblatt, referred to with such barely concealed contempt!)

Greene didn't have much practice at the receiving end of lectures. He was turning red. This jowly wad of flesh was glowering at the Playtime CEO, and there wasn't a damn thing Greene could do about it except ripen.

"Mr. Greene, you, not your lawyer, will either testify or not, and I will not have it left in this hearing that poor old Peter Greene was prevented by lawyers from setting the record straight. You want to set the record straight, Mr. Greene, you want to speak to the shareholders who've lost their pensions, then you go ahead and straighten it out right now. If you're afraid of criminal prosecution and want to take the Fifth and keep your lip buttoned, why, you can do that, too. It's up to you. But don't come into this committee's hearing and blame things on lawyers."

Oldcastle stole glances to his left and right. The room was silent. He decided to go for the grand finale. "So, you want to take the Fifth, Mr. Greene? Take it. But it's *you* taking it and nobody else. The chair yields."

When Oldcastle said, "It's *you* taking it," he extended his hand and pointed a chubby index finger at Greene. What theater! It's *you*, you weasel! You, you spa-tanned, shiny-shoed, snouting Wall Street pig! You! And suddenly this dramatic *j'accuse*, this finger poking out from Old-castle's blue suit, wasn't just a pork sausage at the end of a fat man's hand. It was Uncle Sam's finger. It was Robespierre's. It was the Ameri-can people's collective indictment of corporate greed, the calling to ac-count by the common man, the righteous force of all the burned little guys, all rising up and gathering into the heroic finger of Jack Oldcastle.

He used his left hand in deference to the angle of the TV cameras. What a boffo opening! A stunner! It's *you* taking it! Get thee be-hind me, Satan! Oldcastle wasn't a fat forgotten farce; he spoke for us. He rocked!

The media had their film clip, the radio and print guys had the dramatic confrontation between the senator and the corporate lizard, and the photograph of the committee chairman fingering Peter Greene would make the front pages of *The Boston Globe*, *The New York Times*, *The Washington Post*, and a few dozen other newspapers.

That no piece of legislation would ever come of this show was only a footnote. Greene would take the Fifth, and Jellicoe, too, and the rest of the witnesses who'd been subpoenaed, and there would be little testi-mony at this hearing. That act was a great one, but people who endured the stifling heat of the room began to grow impatient even before the first day of the proceedings was over. Anybody who stayed around for the entire hearing soon realized that absolutely nothing would be learned about banking, or lending, or finance, or anything remotely rele-vant to the committee's technical duty to draft laws. But television view-ers would not see the whole thing. They would see an eight-second clip, with Jack Oldcastle's dramatic finger point, and then a ten-second clip of Peter Greene taking the Fifth. To them, it looked like somebody in this mess was finally kicking some Playtime ass and taking a few names.

TWO DAYS LATER, just before seven A.M., footsteps echoed down an empty corridor in the Russell. It was before the dawn of the winter sol-stice. A weary Senate staffer appeared, one of the faceless and sleepless preparers of scripts and outlines and notebooks, one of the lads and lasses whisking notes from behind the blue curtain. He stapled the witness list to the board outside the hearing room, then stumbled off to find coffee.

There was only one name on the list.

By 9:45 A.M., the same corridor was full of hurrying people and television lights and chatter. Beyond it the hearing room was packed, buzzing with the rumor that the witness was coming alone, that he would testify without a lawyer. They had arrived early to get a seat so they could hear Old Number 31 excoriate Playtime, and listen as the star witness revealed the company's dark and dirty secrets. The last big party before Christmas, it was going to be a helluva show. The press had mobbed the room. Don Fink had come down from Boston with his lieutenants and sat in the third row of the oak benches, chewing his fingernails and shielding his BlackBerry from the bank of television lights behind him. Nearby, taking notes, was an arresting young redhead. The rest of the seats in the gallery were jammed with Senate staffers, unnamed lawyers taking notes for unnamed clients, and the press.

Senator Oldcastle was primed. He'd attended the training table before the big game, allowing himself a treat in the Senate dining room. Fried eggs over corned-beef hash, sausage, home fries, two sides of Canadian bacon with stewed tomatoes, a cinnamon donut, a pot of coffee, a bowl of oatmeal with brown sugar, six flapjacks with butter and maple syrup, and then a cheese Danish for dessert. In deference to the goddamn doctors, he put butter only on top of the flapjacks stack, instead of in between each one, and stirred only one creamer instead of two into each cup of coffee, but all in all it was a decent meal. The senator was ready for action.

Tension mounted as ten o'clock arrived without a witness. The audience began to gossip and speculate, and a rumor, abetted by the Black-Berries, started flying around that the witness had gone into hiding. The energy in the room was electric, the sense of anticipation palpable. Every neck strained to catch sight of him the moment he came through the door.

The fact was that Fritz had a helluva time trying to park. The garages near the Capitol were full, and there was no chance of a parking space on the street. He ended up with a ten-block walk to the Russell. Fritz had thought about flying to Washington, or taking a train, but he figured he'd get ambushed by press either way, so in the end he drove, staying in a motel in Maryland and coming into the city that morning. Thus it was almost ten past when he made his way, alone, into the hearing room. He felt eyes: all those eyes of senators and aides and reporters and spectators. And he heard all those cameras clicking and swishing away.

He walked to the table in the middle of the room. He'd brought no papers, no briefcase, no lawyer bodyguards, no wife or friend. He looked up into the blubbery face of the senator in the middle. SEN. OLDCASTLE, CHAIRMAN, the placard said.

"Sorry I'm late," Fritz said. "Do I sit here?"

A smile spread upon the fat face of Senator Oldcastle, fifteen feet away. The face, with its wobbly jowls and yellow sclera, nodded at Fritz with creepy courtliness. "Yes, Mr. Brubaker, that's where you sit. It's nice to see you."

Doesn't look like such a bad guy, the chairman was thinking.

God, that senator is *fat*, Fritz thought.

No speeches today: Fritz was sworn, and they were quickly under way. Oldcastle himself took up the questioning. He was warming to the role of scourge of Playtime, and he'd studied the briefing book over breakfast. Oldcastle had even read and marked the transcripts of Fritz's hearing up in that Boston courtroom. The easy thing, the obvious thing, would be to whack the guy. You sold short—whack! You had inside information—whack! But a thinking man, a shrewd sonofabitch, Jack Oldcastle thought, could get much more out of Brubaker. A smart guy could use Brubaker to go big-game hunting. Why he'd sold on inside information was murky, but all the court dialogue made something else clear enough—Brubaker wanted to turn the tables on all the corporate bastards. If played the right way, Oldcastle's astute judgment of human nature told him, Brubaker could be a friendly witness, a means to track down the big cats Greene and Jellicoe, and whack *them*. He would be the senator's horse, and if Oldcastle rode him right, they'd both lead the evening news.

"Mr. Brubaker, we're not going to question you about the stock sales here. You've admitted your guilt on that in the Boston proceedings, and you've accepted responsibility, is that correct?" Oldcastle smiled beatifically. I am your friend.

"Yes, Senator."

"Now, you were in the finance group at Playtime?"

"Yes."

"Working with Mr. Jellicoe and his team?"

"Yes, that's right, Senator."

Oldcastle smiled again. Oh yes, this was going to work out very well. We're going big-game hunting, Mr. Brubaker, you and me. We're going to bag a few trophies before the morning is out, and we're going to lead the evening news at six! Just stick with me, son.

"And did you know Mr. Jellicoe had stock options, Mr. Jellicoe and Mr. Greene both?"

"Yes, I think that's right, Senator."

"And they cashed in some options in 2001, before the stock fell?"

"Did they?"

A bump in the road: no, a pebble. Not a problem. We're a *team*. Oldcastle smiled at the friendly witness. "You don't have the details on that, I expect, Mr. Brubaker?"

"I don't."

"Well, would it surprise you to learn that they did sell?"

"No, not at all."

"It wouldn't." Oldcastle beamed. Our elephant guns primed, we charge off together into the Serengeti! Wouldn't surprise him at all that these scoundrels had been profiting off the shareholders. It wouldn't surprise me, either, the senator's smile seemed to say. And it damn well wouldn't surprise my constituents.

"No, Senator. Senior management with options usually have automatic programs to sell a little each year. It's pretty routine."

Away in the staff room, Ralph Moldy frowned. Maybe the guy was stupid, trying to respond in his insipid way to Oldcastle's softball questioning, but still, Moldy sensed something he didn't like. The guy seemed nice as pie, he wasn't denying anything, but would he slip in counterpunches before Oldcastle could see them coming?

"Would it surprise you to know that Peter Greene made four million dollars in option sales last year?"

"Actually, it would."

Oldcastle gave an "Aha!" sort of look for the benefit of television. Back on the trail again. "It would," he repeated to ram the point home.

"Yes sir, it seems like a pretty small number. You sure he didn't sell more than that?"

Shit, thought Ralph Moldy.

That summed up Oldcastle's thoughts, too. What was this about? Hadn't Senator Oldcastle been nice and polite? Hadn't he passed up the opportunity in front of the television cameras to humiliate this bean counter for his stock swindle? Hadn't he asked easy questions? Oldcastle reddened. The sonofabitch doesn't want to do this the easy way? Oldcastle decided to whack him.

"Four million dollars seems like a *small* number to you, Mr. Brubaker?" he rumbled. "It may surprise you to learn that to my constituents back home in Michigan, four million dollars is still a lot of money." He nodded to the television cameras.

"No, Senator, four million doesn't seem like a small number of *dollars*, but in Greene's case, it's a pretty small number of *options*. Most of Greene's options were ten-dollar options, if I remember correctly. The stock was trading at about fifty, so four million dollars is a sale of about a hundred thousand options. And since Greene had something like seven million Playtime options, his sale was less than two percent of his position. In other words, Senator, it would be like a guy with a hundred shares of Playtime selling two shares. You would think of the guy more as someone who *held* shares than someone who sold them. Did he sell two shares, or did he hold and *not* sell ninety-eight shares?"

Well done, thought Don Fink in the back of the room. He began to type out a BlackBerry message.

Fritz smiled a nice, polite "any questions" sort of smile. But Oldcastle didn't return it: for one thing, he felt a sharp stab in his gut, and for another, this wasn't what he wanted to hear at all. There wasn't anything about this in the briefing book—it just said $4 million. And this witness? The sonofabitch was not staying whacked when he had been good and whacked.

The audience in the hearing room was beginning to stir, sensing a shift in the dynamics of the questioning. Maybe it wasn't so bad for all these management scum to cash in their options—was that what Oldcastle was trying to get across?

In the staff room Ralph Moldy was alert to ETD: extreme television danger. Worse than no sound bite, this thing now showed signs of a bad sound bite—an embarrassing sound bite. He had to get his man out of Little Big Horn. He began typing a quick message on the BlackBerry.

"Don't you—"

"I'm sorry, Senator, but you asked the question, and I'm trying to answer it. What Playtime did wrong is what everybody does wrong."

"What Playtime did was wrong?"

"Yes, of course. They booked earnings they didn't have, and they didn't immediately come clean about it. The company wasn't worth fifty as it was trading; it was probably worth something more like forty-five or -six, on a fair valuation. But what happened to Playtime had nothing to do with senior management selling options."

Shit, thought Don Fink. He stopped typing in the positive news bulletin and began composing a negative one. Meanwhile, away in the staff room, Moldy's fingers were flying across his own eensy buttons.

The sonofabitch, Senator Oldcastle thought. The fact was that these accountants could always sneak around you with accounting bullshit. They could always come up with some detail of accounting principles or SEC mumbo jumbo that he didn't understand and would muddy things up and lead to dull television exchanges. He had to bring this back to some good biting stuff.

"Mr. Brubaker, do you think the captain should go down with the ship or be the first to jump in a lifeboat?"

"Excuse me?"

"Do you think that when the ship founders, the captain should go down with it or be the first to jump in a lifeboat?"

Fritz answered slowly. "You're asking whether those who are responsible for other people should put their interests first?"

Oldcastle had this sonofabitch on the ropes, he could tell! He pressed the point home, demanding, "I'm asking if the captain should go down with the ship!"

"I would agree that a captain of our nation's ship, say, a captain whose political fortunes seem to be sinking, should not be the first to jump into a televised hearing as a lifeboat for his own career, yes, Senator, I would agree with that."

There was a stunned silence in the committee room. Oldcastle rocked back in his chair like an aging fighter staggered by an unforeseen punch, his jaw sprung. A stabbing pain had gotten hold of his gut, and he had to wait for it to pass before he could speak.

Shit, thought Moldy, watching the CNN feed. I knew it about this guy.

Oldcastle got his breath. "I don't think you're in a position, Mr. Brubaker, to bandy words with this committee." The pain was fearful. He winced and seemed to whisper. To the audience, it looked like he was reeling from the blow of Brubaker's riposte.

"But Senator, aren't you bandying words with me? Captains and ships and lifeboats and all that?"

The pain gripped Oldcastle again, and he couldn't speak for a moment. So Fritz went on. "You're not really asking me about lifeboats to get information for a new banking bill, are you? Aren't you just looking to get on television?"

In the staff room Moldy finished his message: "Get off this! Back to restatement!"

"I warn you, you are in danger of being held in contempt of this committee, Mr. Brubaker!"

"Senator, I'm sorry to say that I think it would be an honorable thing to be held in contempt of this committee, because I don't think you're doing anything legitimate here."

"The chair has heard enough!" Oldcastle wheezed. "The witness is in contempt of the United States Senate! I call upon the sergeant at arms to place Mr. Brubaker in custody!"

At that rather thrilling moment, three things happened. First, as to the sergeant-at-arms business, there was considerable confusion. The only guy in the room wearing a uniform was Deke Orstin, a Capitol policeman. He'd never been called a sergeant at arms, and wasn't a sergeant, and didn't have any arms, unless you counted a clipboard, and therefore wasn't sure the chairman was referring to him. Also, he'd never placed anyone in custody, except for the occasional lost child touring the rotunda, and he didn't exactly know how to put Brubaker into custody, since he didn't have handcuffs. (Though down in the basement of the Capitol Building, they did have a box of lollipops for the lost kids.) Then there was the matter of where to *keep* him in custody, since there were no cells. He would have to call the D.C. police, and he wasn't clear on the paperwork involved in being in contempt of the United States Senate. So Deke stood up uncertainly, with a helpless look on his face, as if to ask, "Me?"

The second thing happened upstairs in the committee staff offices. While the Capitol officer was wondering about the paperwork, Ralph Moldy hit the "send" button on his BlackBerry, trying too late to get word to Oldcastle.

The third thing that happened (an instant after the second thing) took place in the bunched-up right pocket of Oldcastle's suit jacket, which lay upon the globe of the senatorial paunch at about the latitude of the senatorial duodenum. Decades of strong drink had pocked this stretch of intestine with ulcers, and one ulcer in particular, about the size of a half-dollar, had worn away the surface to the thickness of gossamer. In the pocket adrift over this nubbin of ulcerated haggis rested the BlackBerry remote wireless, which received Ralph Moldy's message and dutifully vibrated. Maybe it was just bad luck or bad timing, maybe it was some sort of electromagnetic impulse, but the vibration was enough. Pop went the ulcer, and pop went a couple of smaller ulcers to left and right. This was unfortunate, for a geyser of bile and pancreatic juice, only too eager to escape Oldcastle's lower intestine, gushed into the senator's peritoneum, and all around the Oldcastle gut rocketed a thumping jolt of sheer electric agony. The pain was intense enough to achieve liftoff of the massive senatorial buttocks. Oldcastle's elbows went skidding across the bench and launched his briefing book and a jug of ice water over the lip and onto the ruck of photographers beneath. Then the senator himself, great vessel of foul humors that he had become, balancing precariously on his elbows, began slowly to list to windward. The audience watched, stunned. The senators gasped. The aides were frozen. The CNN feed zoomed in for a closer shot. The senior senator from the Great State of Michigan, Old Number 31, his face paralyzed with pain, listed with the quiet grace of a barkentine until he turtled altogether, slipped from view, and tumbled ass up on the carpet.

Pandemonium. Senators and aides came out of their seats. Photographers stormed the bench to get a shot of Oldcastle, who lay beached on the carpet and gasping for breath. Someone was trying to loosen his tie. Aides shielded the fallen man, pushing photographers away. The Capitol policeman grabbed Fritz roughly by the arm—look what he'd done, he'd killed a United States senator! Shouts of "Get a doctor, get a doctor! Call an ambulance!"

And so, as it happened, they were both led away from the hearing room in protective custody; Brubaker, the contemptuous witness, in the custody of Officer Deke Orstin, and Oldcastle, the gasping whale, in the custody of six paramedics (who, at that, had a helluva time getting him on the gurney). Jack Oldcastle would lead the press accounts again, but not in the way he'd hoped. At Walter Reed Army Medical Center the next day, the medical staff were careful to keep the newspapers away from Senator Oldcastle. The overnight press was solidly with Fritz. Just what business is this of Oldcastle's committee, the editorials wondered. What laws are they drafting? It's the *banking* committee, isn't it?

22

A COUPLE OF FIXER-UPPERS

IT IS a small point, but not without significance, that Linda LeBrecque made the initial decision to go to bed with Fritz on the basis of legal research.

Fritz Brubaker and Linda LeBrecque were married on June 26, 1984, in St. Andrew's Episcopal Church in Marblehead, Massachusetts. The bride wore a simple gown without lace or a veil or gewgaws. Like Fritz, she had lost her father, so she walked alone to the altar. For many years afterward, Fritz could quickly summon that image to mind: how beautiful she seemed, walking alone through the crowded sanctuary, moving toward him along the deep red carpet, through the throng of well-wishers. How strong and sure she looked to him, passing through the wedding guests—how they turned to admire her; how they smiled for sheer joy as she passed!

It was a remarkable illusion. Because the overriding impression Linda had taken away from that walk—the memory burned into her mind with each step along the aisle and that, as the years passed, supplanted in her recollection everything else that happened in St. Andrew's Church—was of how much her feet hurt.

They hurt like hell, actually.

She'd bought the shoes only three days before. They were size-seven satin Pappagallo pumps with two-inch heels, and they had looked elegant in the store. Although size seven was the perfect size for a five-foot-seven-inch, 118-pound bride, and Linda wanted to believe she was a size seven, and maybe once ten years ago had worn a size seven, she was really a size eight. It was all right, she'd thought at the time, she was close enough to a size seven and could get by. In any event, the Pappagallos were far more suitable than the size-eight Ferragamo pumps she'd bought six months earlier that didn't look right with the gown. The Ferragamos weren't awful, but they weren't perfect, either, and she had wanted—no, she had demanded—that this wedding be perfect. She had lost six pounds to be the perfect weight, and she had subtly experimented with highlights to have hair the perfect color, and she had gone south to Florida to have skin the perfect hue, and there was no reason for the whole thing to be ruined by not having perfect shoes on the perfect bride she was damn well going to be. So she fretted, and searched, and fretted, and worried until, three days before the wedding, in a boutique in Brookline, she found them: pumps that matched the gown beautifully. The perfect pumps in every way.

Except that they didn't have them in size eight. So she bought them in size seven.

This was a miscalculation. In a store you walk three steps to a mirror. You don't walk the length of the sanctuary in the largest Episcopal church in Essex County. In a store you stand up for thirty seconds, not forty minutes, as you need to do after a wedding to receive an endless line of Brubaker cousins and friends. If the shoes were snug in Sophia's Bridal Boutique in Brookline, they felt like a couple of C-clamps in Manchester on Linda's wedding day. Every step along that carpet sent jolts of white heat from her toes through her instep. The throbbing was so bad she was afraid she might stumble in the aisle. At the altar, she surreptitiously lifted one foot and then the other under her gown. Although it was generally agreed by the many Brubakers in attendance that "the bride was a lovely girl," and by the relatively fewer LeBrecques that "Linda looked radiant," and by all there gathered that "they made a striking couple," for Linda, the entire service was torture.

The sevens from hell rendered the receiving line a particular agony. As time flavored Linda's recollection, the line became, for her, the emblem of the wedding reception. She had never wanted a receiving line in the first place. In the planning stages, she had suggested that the couple circulate among the tables—this was how the matter was handled at all the best weddings. It would be a much sounder way of disposing of the Brubaker relatives. But she hadn't insisted, and Fritz seemed rather stuck on the anachronistic tradition of standing in line, and she had done the reasonable thing, the accommodating thing.

So she stood in line that Saturday in torment. The Shrill Small

Voice, unsympathetic to her agony, observed that if only she had followed her instincts, she wouldn't be in this fix. She could have sat down and maybe forgotten about the whole greeting business altogether. But no, Linda had to grimace through a rack of Brubaker cousins and aunts, shake hands with an endless bastinado of Marblehead friends and acquaintances, all stopping to chatter and fuss and hug and some of them to cry (dripping on her!), and most of all to *linger*, with their vacuous and repetitive expressions of goodwill while poor Linda felt like her feet were in vise grips. While she was suffering torture, what was the groom doing?

Laughing! Hugging and chatting and hail-fellowing and joshing and embracing and looking like the picture of hearty good cheer. Without the slightest concern for the genuine pain suffered by his new wife.

It was the first sign of an insensitivity on his part that would plague the marriage.

She soldiered through, pasting a pained smile on her face. She whispered sidelong to Fritz through clenched teeth, "Let's hurry this up, okay?" Which was the first expression of her married life.

IT WAS PLAYTIME (or, as it was then known, Eastern Recreation) that had brought them together sixteen months before. The star-crossed lovers met on a wintry morning at gate 11 in the B concourse of Boston's Logan Airport, waiting to board a flight to Pittsburgh. Just after seven, a little sleepy, a little hungover, Fritz got into line at the gate behind a striking blonde. She had a rolling cart with two big boxes strapped to it, and she was trying to convince the gate attendant that this horse trailer of material met the carry-on limitations. Fritz recognized the voice immediately.

She was persistent, but the gate attendant wasn't budging. "I'm sorry, ma'am, but it can't exceed twenty-six by thirteen by fifteen."

"Oh, come *on*," said the blonde. "I can't check these boxes. We'd have to tape them and then—"

"I've got some tape," said the attendant helpfully.

"You can't be serious. Look at that man over there—you let *him* through." She pointed at a businessman by the gate holding a carry-on bag and a big accountant's satchel. "And *that* guy." She gestured toward another one, turning to equity where it appeared law would not suffice.

As a junior accountant at Eastern Recreation, Fritz was being sent to scout out a potential acquisition, what they called due diligence: looking over the books, the accounts, checking to see that everything was on the up-and-up. A young lawyer at Elboe, Fromme & Athol had been detailed as his legal counterpart, checking contracts and corporate filings and the like. Fritz had developed a telephone relationship with her, but he'd never met her. Now he was hearing her voice.

That's when he spoke up: "You're my lawyer?"

"Excuse me?"

She turned, and damn, from the front, she was even more striking. "Fritz Brubaker," he said, and extended his hand.

"Oh," she answered, flustered. "Hi, Fritz, I guess you know who I am. It's nice to meet you finally. Can you believe this? I need to review these files on the plane, and they're going to make me *check* them."

He shrugged and turned to greet the attendant. "How about I take one? Would that be okay?" Fritz had only a satchel about an inch thick, and most of the inch was accounted for by the latest *Sail Magazine*.

The gate attendant, who didn't want to give in to this bitchy passenger, was crestfallen. If they divided up the boxes, then it probably was within regulations. Close enough, anyway. And why would this nice, kind of cute guy side with the bitch from hell instead of with . . . her?

"Yes, I suppose so," she said.

"Great customer service!" said Linda a few minutes later, genially (but audibly), as they moved off toward the gate.

"Catch more flies with honey," Fritz answered.

Thus the lovers' first exchange. But Fritz wasn't critical. She had knocked him out. And persistent—by God, she was going to get somewhere in life! From the very first moment, Fritz Brubaker thought there was something damned impressive about that Linda LeBrecque.

AT THE TIME, Linda happened to be on the rebound. Having finally summoned up the courage to dump her law-school boyfriend, she was feeling the redemptive power of freedom, hearing the words of that towering voice of righteousness, Martin Luther King, Jr. For Linda was free at last, free at last—thank God Almighty, she was free at last.

The only blemish in this perfect freedom was the earful Linda was getting from the Shrill Small Voice: "Stanley Mossbach is a very reliable man, a very nice and reliable man, and you go and dump him like a load of garbage."

"It wasn't working out."

"No, not even a load of garbage. A load of garbage you dump with your hands. Stanley you gave the heave-ho on the telephone."

Well, the Voice had a point there. Maybe Linda should have done the deed face-to-face. But she couldn't endure being talked out of it again. Stanley may have been a reliable man, but he was also a whiner. He would have whined and begged and, when all else failed, tried to nuzzle, as though his sheer animal magnetism would overcome her aversion. Yech—she wasn't up for another round of that. So she'd called him. Left him a message on his machine, actually.

"Besides," the Voice went on, "you're not getting any younger."

Oh, the malice of the Shrill Small Voice! Knowing Linda's mind was made up on the Stanley question, it tossed in its reliable parting shot. In those days before her marriage, this was Linda's second deepest fear—the running of her biological clock. (The first was fear of being Subject to Criticism, but Linda was getting to the age where you could be Subject to Criticism for having let your clock run too far.)

When the man behind her in line at the US Airways gate turned out to be Fritz Brubaker, her client on this deal, and when he also turned out to be kind of cute, and even funnier in person than he had been on the phone, was that little shiver she felt at the thought of sitting next to him on the flight all him, or was Linda playing a defense against the Voice? He *was* cute. He wasn't the usual kind of man who's stumped for conversation without his first-person pronoun. He also didn't seem worried about much. He wasn't another one of those tortured souls constantly looking over his shoulder at the professional doom gaining on them. After Stanley Mossbach, that was refreshing.

But not to the Shrill Small Voice. The Voice did not approve. This was not at all the Voice's idea of a suitable replacement for Stanley Mossbach.

"Stanley's going to make partner. He's very smart. One day he'll make a lot of money. He wants to settle down, what's wrong with that?"

"A life of numbing boredom would be wrong with that."

"There's worse things."

"I'm going to be fine."

"Are you? What is so interesting about this Fritz Brubaker that you would dismiss a reliable man like Stanley as boring? I'm telling you, there's worse things than boredom."

"He's cute."

"Listen to yourself," said the Shrill Small Voice.

"What's wrong with cute?"

"Cute is unreliable, that's what."

"He's interesting."

"He's your client."

Well, that *was* a difficulty. Linda even spent a long evening in the law library researching the ethical rule against personal entanglements with clients. The rule seemed direct, and it presented a problem. How could she pull this off without breaking a rule, and how could she break a rule without being Subject to Criticism?

Surely a little courtship wouldn't hurt. The courtship would involve skiing and sailing, and as winter was coming on, skiing first. They made several trips to the Bruhostel, where Linda, flush as she genuinely was with the excitement of wooing, felt the exoticism outweigh the dirt and the outlandishness—but only slightly. You could get a disease if you ate anything off that griddle, and a disfiguring injury if you followed any of the Brubakers to the top of Stark Mountain. She struggled gamely to understand the charm of this experience; she attempted to bond with Fritz's uncle Monty and Monty's wife, Jane, Fritz's brother Hap, and Hap's girlfriend, Becky; but Linda always felt that she was having trouble fitting in.

When the weather warmed up, Linda endured the sailing with a taut smile, but it seemed to her uncomfortable. You were either cold or sunburned. And you were just, well, riding in a sailboat, when it came right down to it. The truth was that neither skiing nor sailing appealed much to Linda on the sporting side. Yet each had about it a different attraction of perhaps greater seductive potency. These Brubakers didn't seem to do much, but they had sailboats and ski houses and, most of all, time. There must be money somewhere.

"Isn't this great!" Fritz would shout over the wind.

"Yeah, great!" she'd answer, smiling broadly, inwardly thinking that she could safely drop the sailing business as soon as they were married.

Married. She was already thinking about it, even though her concerns with being Subject to Criticism had led her to hold off awarding the ultimate prize to Fritz's advances. It was aboard Fritz's twenty-five-foot sloop that the ethical dilemma reached its head. She finally said to him, "You're a client. I can't sleep with a client."

"Why not?"

"Because it's unethical. There's a rule on it."

He smiled at her. "Count on you guys to have a rule. Is there an exception? Lawyers have exceptions for everything."

"Believe me, I've looked."

He kissed her. "Could you look harder?"

So when they'd finished the sail, she drove to Boston and back to the law library and looked at the rule harder. Maybe he wasn't *exactly* the client. The client was a corporation, and he was only a guy working for the corporation. That wasn't the same, was it? Particularly since he was only a midlevel employee. He couldn't sign for the corporation. So he wasn't the client. Maybe.

The next night she went to his apartment and dragged him into the bedroom. He didn't resist.

LINDA HADN'T failed to notice that Fritz was on the indolent side. He didn't have the ambition of most of the men she knew. He didn't seem to want the CFO's job. He didn't care that much about advancing through the ranks at Eastern Recreation. He was fun and pleasant and all, but strangely content with things the way they were. Well, she could work on this with time. Maybe he needed some commitments to discover a greater purpose. Marriage, for example, and a family. In time he would develop that spark, that urgency. The fire of responsibility would forge his ambition.

She could help light it. As soon as he matured a bit. Got the skiing and the sailing behind him. Began to focus on what was important. It was time, he was cute, he was funny, there seemed to be some background protective reserve of money, so she decided that she loved him. Definitely. Fritz was going to be a project, but his fundamentals were sound (or, at any rate, correctable), and there had never yet been a project that Linda LeBrecque couldn't tackle. So that was it. He was the one.

THUS did the Shrill Small Voice seem to lose an important round.

But the Voice wasn't about winning and losing. It thrived on losing; loss was the rich soil in which it flourished, sending out clamorous shoots and caustic tendrils. The Voice abandoned a point only when the point was won, and then the Voice moved on, sometimes to precisely the opposite criticism. It never tired: down through the years after the marriage, its refrain would ring in Linda's ears. There were worse things than boredom. Things much worse indeed, like a lack of material ambition. The Voice developed a catalog of Fritz's faults, which it always contrasted with the values associated with diligent moneymaking. As the years went by, the catalog grew until there came a day when the Voice acquired its own ace: for Linda's marriage had settled into predictability. "So," said the Voice, cruelly triumphant, "he's not so exciting after all—Mr. Unreliable. We're not getting *bored*, are we?"

Stanley Mossbach then made a sort of comeback. Not in person; it was not Stanley himself but mythic Stanley: Stanley the Might-Have-Been. The image of dull, stable Stanley arose anew in the body of dull, stable (and very rich) Marvin Rosenblatt. Fifteen years of the Voice's relentless carping finally had its way with Linda on a steamy night in South Florida, where she and Marvin had gone for a directors' meeting. Dinner had finished, and the clients had gone. The two lawyers returned to the hotel, but as she headed for the elevator, Linda caught the seductive sound of Latin music, and for some inexplicable reason, it stopped her. She looked uncertainly at Marvin; he shrugged; a moment later the two of them were outside on the patio, which was strung with red lanterns and pulsing with the hot brass rhythms of the band. They found a table at the edge of the patio.

The Miami night was hot and close, the music loud and dazzling. Linda gulped the first martini fast, entranced by the singer, whose sheer black skirt was split high on her leg. She shimmied before the band, wailing out Spanish descants to the band's refrain, shaking her hips and driving the bongo man to paroxysms.

The singer's bold eroticism unsettled Linda. She felt dizzy as she sipped the second martini. The beat of the music only intensified. The band's refrain seemed like it would never end. Linda's shoulders began to sway with it. She squinted across the table, examining Marvin in a new way. Suddenly, she shuddered with a revelation. *Marvin was sexy.*

Yes, sexy! How had she missed it before? Marvin was a man of profound sexiness: he was . . . Kissingeresque!

The beat of the bongo drums was relentless. In the hot darkness, it took hold of Linda LeBrecque. She leaned in closer to Marvin. The singer wailed. Marvin glanced in debonair fashion at his BlackBerry. Even that was somehow erotic, she thought: everyone wants him all the time, but only I have him. She smiled. Louder and louder the bongos sounded. Marvin turned to eye the singer, mopped his brow, and drained his martini. He holstered his BlackBerry and looked up at Linda's eyes.

Offer and acceptance.

Upstairs, fourteen minutes later, the deal was closed.

There came another assignation, and another: business trips and hotels in New York and Chicago, Phoenix and Los Angeles. But in these places there were no bongos, and there was no sultry singer. Linda lay awake in strange rooms, more restless than ever, lying in midlife darkness next to a man wearing pajamas. She listened to the snoring. This wasn't boredom; or if it was, there were worse things, right? In the darkness, she yearned for the Voice's ratification.

The Voice, however, was fickle. "Sneaking around with Marvin Rosenblatt is hardly prudent," it said.

THESE UNFORTUNATE EVENTS still lay far off in the future, back on that winter morning at gate 11 in the B concourse. What of young Fritz on that February day in 1983—what had he seen in Linda at the outset, beyond her fabulous looks?

One can't give Fritz too much credit on this point: he was at the time a twenty-seven-year-old male, and "beyond her fabulous looks" was a somewhat theoretical concept. But it would be an error to give him too little credit, either. He thought about what he saw in her—or he tried to, at any rate. Fritz lived in an apartment on the flat of Beacon Hill. He went for long runs by the Charles River. He planned to use these runs to break the Linda issue down to its components, its pluses and minuses—in short, to do the math. The problem was that his train of thought was usually distracted by concerns over his mile split, which was an easier kind of math to do when your heart rate was at 150.

He tried talking to Andy and Hap about her. But they weren't about to take this helping off Fritz's plate. They just nodded and said, "Uh-huh" in a noncommittal way, the way brothers do when speaking about somebody who, while she doesn't seem like the One, nevertheless might become a permanent Thanksgiving fixture. So they answered, "Uh-huh, Fritz, yeah, she's great." Which they did with a smile and an inflection that said, "We might mean this or we might not, and we'll never tell you."

The hell with Andy and Hap. Fritz admired her. That was important, wasn't it? He was in a stage of his life when he admired all those things that were so different about Linda. Her diligence and responsibility. The way she planned things and made lists. Her ambition. Perhaps he was facing up to some of his own limitations, his unwillingness to live a life of lists and diligence. Maybe he was measuring the senior executives, balking at the frantic lives they led, their perpetually harassed manner. Always on telephones, always late for meetings, always bursting out of the jungle to be faced with an unbridged torrent that wasn't on the map. Marrying this woman, Fritz realized, would be acquiring the benefit of his own Army Corps of Engineers. All the pontoons would be requisitioned in time to build the necessary bridges for crossing life's raging streams. You'd never have to worry about anything, because she would worry for two. Funny how, in the early days, he found her worrisomeness piquant and charming. He hadn't any idea then how it would come to wear on him.

Fritz had always been an optimist about projects. He was a guy who could look at a run-down house with peeling paint and imagine it gleaming. Linda was a romantic rehab: that sweetheart of a Victorian that needed a little paint to brighten it up.

But then you move into the house, and the longer you live there, the more of a problem it gets to be to do the paint job. For starters, you have to scrape all that six-edged gingerbread filigree, and that's going to turn up boards that need replacing, and maybe more than a few boards, maybe a rafter or two, maybe shingles and the roof itself; all because you wanted to brighten things up with a little paint. Every time you rip out something to get at one problem, you're going to expose two more. So you start to find ways to make do with the paint job the way it is, just for the short term. Because you don't ever give up on the project. You simply haven't gotten around to it yet.

He was always going to get to it soon. As soon as she settled down after the wedding. And later, as soon as she calmed down after child-birth. And then as soon as she finished nursing and got past that hor-mone rush. And later still, as soon as she got the partnership. Then it was going to be as soon as the kids got older, although "older" was kind of hard to define. But he had never officially given up on the project. He was going to get her in touch with her real self as soon as she calmed down. She needed a boost, a little confidence, that was all.

It hadn't quite happened. Linda became like one of those over-worked cords on the kitchen phone, so impossibly twisted, so wrapped upon itself and highly torqued, that one was afraid of the whiplash ef-fect. He got so he wanted to untwist her but was afraid to try. Years ago he'd thought maybe the laborsaving devices would help, but every new laborsaving device seemed to replace all the saved labor with an exact measure of increased anxiety. She got a home computer so she wouldn't need to be in the office all the time, and then she fretted over the slow modem. She got e-mail so she could stay in touch, and then the e-mail became like a sleeping infant—you always had to check it just in case.

When Linda came home one evening with her new BlackBerry, that was the end. As far as Fritz was concerned, the BlackBerry was the Inva-sion of the Body Snatchers. Her body was there, but Linda was gone.

23

BELLY PIE ON PARADISE

IT WAS ABOUT NOON when Fritz left the police office in the basement of the Capitol and escaped the press massed on the steps.

"Am I under arrest?" he'd asked Deke, who seemed like a nice enough kid once they got out of the hearing room. Deke shrugged. "I'm supposed to keep you in custody," he said. "Whatever that means." They'd hauled Fritz off at about eleven, but within minutes Oldcastle's staff realized that Fritz had become an instant hero. Oldcastle was going to look even more ridiculous on the six o'clock news. They'd be martyring Brubaker if he were still in custody. So a call came from upstairs, and the Capitol cops were ordered to get Fritz the hell out of there immediately.

He hopped a cab outside Union Station, had the cabbie drive around Washington until he lost the press hordes, and finally circled back to the parking garage off New Jersey Avenue where he'd left his BMW that morning.

It was cold. Fritz hunched against a blast of wind as he exited the grimy elevator enclosure on the rooftop. Across the lot was his car, and leaning up against the front left fender, a woman. Fritz approached the car slowly, wondering if the press had tailed him here, staked him out somehow. She was a tall, slim redhead wearing a dark wool coat and black boots. With a bag over one shoulder, she stood smoking a cigarette. As he got closer to the car, she looked up at him. It was that woman he'd noticed in the back of the hearing room. In all this cold, her coat was unbuttoned, but she'd jammed her left hand down in a pocket. She held the cigarette in her right hand but used her elbow to lever the coat in tightly around her. She couldn't have been over twenty-five.

"Fritz? Jesus, Fritz, where have you been?" the woman called out when he was still halfway across the lot.

"I'm sorry?"

"It's not exactly warm up here?" In the mode of her generation, she put it as a question. But it was also a bit of an accusation.

He reached his car. "Excuse me, do I know you?"

"Dude, I'm freezing!"

That didn't seem to be quite responsive. He thought about her predicament, then asked, "Does your coat have buttons?"

Perfectly good question. But she didn't answer, instead crushed the cigarette with her boot, jammed her right hand in the right pocket, and began lightly jogging in place. "C'mon, c'mon, c'mon," she said, beckoning with an elbow toward the door handle. She was going to get in the car. This was a girl who could get into any guy's car she wanted.

Including Fritz's. "Okay, you're in my car," Fritz acknowledged a minute later.

"Some heat would be nice. You got seat warmers in this thing?"

"I just started it. It'll take a minute. You mind telling me why you're in my car? And how you know my name? And who you are, anyway?"

"I'm Ronnie. I'm in your car partly because it's cold and partly because I need a lift. And dude, everybody knows your name."

"Oh, you need a lift. Where to?"

"Massachusetts."

Massachusetts. She needed a three-hundred-mile lift?

THEY SAT in the BMW while the engine idled. Eventually, the heat came on. Up close she seemed even slimmer and longer-legged. The cabin of the BMW 330i was confining for her: she kept shifting from one hip to another, crossing her arms across her chest. She would reach into her pockets, then hunt for something in her bag, then run her hands through her hair, which there was not all that much of, then shift her weight in the seat again.

"Look, Ronnie, nice to meet you and all. I'll take you to the nearest Metro stop, how's that?"

He turned to give her a polite smile and got his first close look at her face. It was striking—strikingly young, for one thing. A long face you would not have said was pretty, but it made an impression on you with its big hazel eyes, a cute little nose, skin that looked soft as a baby's. Her hair was clipped short. A climbing party of silver hoops was making the ascent of her ears, clinging to the lobes and the ridges and the summits.

"The Metro doesn't go to Massachusetts, last time I checked. And don't get all conventional on me now, you know? That's not exactly been your style over the past couple of months?"

For all of her adolescent diction, her voice seemed strangely mature. She had this baby face, and you expected a baby voice, but the voice was a woman's. Sort of husky, almost. It didn't go with the rest of her.

She added: "You know, Fritz, I really admired you for nailing that fat tub the way you did."

"I didn't—"

"Captains and ships and all. Such bullshit. You were totally on it, too, and he was *so* busted. I hate when they do that."

"Excuse me, I . . . Were—are you . . ." Fritz stopped trying. He put the car in drive. Maybe he should get down to the street and let her off there.

"And another thing. What you've done for your family, I really admired that."

The car lurched as Fritz jammed on the brakes. He shifted back to park. Then he turned deliberately to look at her again. He studied her this time. What he did for his family? Who was this woman, and how did she get all these ideas about him? She was smiling brightly back at him.

"How do you know . . . what about my family?"

She shook her head. She leaned down, and he heard, of all things, a zipper unzip. And then another one. This was a very disquieting sound, a very intimate sound. The next thing he knew, she had pulled off her boots and tossed them in the back of the car. She held her knees to her chin and pressed her feet up against the heat vents, kneading them with her fingers. "My feet are freezing?" she explained.

Then she slipped her socks off and rubbed her toes and her bare ankles in front of the heat ducts. She had small feet, for a tall woman, and it was surprisingly disconcerting to Fritz that she would expose herself to him like that, even if it was only her feet that were bare. He felt a Peeping Tom thrill at her unabashed disrobing, this perfect *young* stranger, even if she was only removing socks from her feet.

He thought he'd better take his mind off that. "Ronnie, who are you?" he asked.

"Just an investigator."

"Who sent you?"

"Dude, *I'm* the investigator," she answered, furiously rubbing pink back into her toes. "Anyway, don't worry about it. It doesn't matter, because I've got this problem with the assignment."

"Which is?"

"I started to like you. I mean, at first I figured you were just a suit? But then I got to know you better. And I started to like you, which has seriously compromised my judgment." She continued kneading the toes, then moved up to her insteps.

"How did you get to know me better? We just met. And why is starting to like me a problem?"

She finished with her feet and pulled her socks back on, and he felt a stab of disappointment. "Wicked conflict of interest. Where's Linda, anyway?"

She had that nervous energy about her. All curves and coils in constant motion. She didn't wait for you to finish speaking. She didn't seem to listen all that well to what you were saying. Her hands were moving from her feet to her hair, to the visor flap, back to her hair.

"My wife? I guess that's none of your business."

"Where did you say she was?"

"Is bad hearing a job requirement? I said it's none of your business."

"I'm an investigator. My whole business is none of my business. Anyway, I'm curious—pretty big deal, for you to be subpoenaed for the Senate, and she couldn't come down? That Rosenblatt from her law firm, he came down for this last week. And that Playtime guy, what's his name, Fink? This morning he sat in the back watching you the way a squirrel watches a cat. How come *you* don't have a lawyer? I want you to know I really admire that."

"Who's investigating me, anyway?"

"Don't be nosy."

He let the irony pass. "How do you know all of this?"

"Hello? I wouldn't exactly be much of an investigator if I didn't know all of this. Besides, after what you did to Oldcastle and those other morons, you're like a pop icon, man. You *rock*. You'll be in *People* magazine or something."

People magazine? Was that some sort of hallmark of success? And why was he a pop icon?

"But anyway," Ronnie said, "stop changing the subject. Why didn't she come down for this? Linda, I mean? You did call her, didn't you, after the cops let you out?"

Now it was Ronnie who turned and studied Fritz's face. He met her eye for eye. She didn't back down. God, but she was young. She was examining him very frankly.

"Well, we have kids. She had to . . ." Fritz started to explain, then caught himself. That wasn't exactly accurate. They did have kids, but what Linda had to do was go to some kind of legal convention in New York. And why the hell was he explaining this to a stranger? (Feet or no feet, ankles or no ankles!) "Wait a minute. What do you mean calling my wife 'Linda' as if you know her? This is none of your business, like I said before." He put the car back in drive.

"Oh, right. Like she couldn't get a sitter for Michael and Kristin. Like she hasn't done that, like, at the drop of a corporate meeting for the last ten years. Her husband is subpoenaed to testify before Congress and she can't get a sitter? Pretty lame, if you ask me."

"Nobody asked you."

Ronnie went on as if she hadn't heard. "So, Fritz. Linda's a little nervous anyway, from what I hear, I mean, very mainstream and all. This is probably rocking her life wicked. Don't mind me, by the way, I'm very inquisitive. It's my job. You got any CDs?"

"Did I mention this was none of your business?" He stopped the car again.

"Don't be boring. We need to talk about you and Linda. I'm worried about you. The ramp's over there, by the way." She started rifling the glove compartment.

"Frankly, you worry me, too."

"Ooo," she said.

He paid thirty dollars to get the car out of the garage. The kid in the booth seemed to take his time making change. He kept crouching down to get a better look at Ronnie.

"How old are you?" Fritz asked when at last the car was on the street.

"You know, I really meant what I said. I was glad you said that about the *Titanic* bullshit. That Oldcastle is such a creep—they all are. Captains going down with the ship. I *hate* when they do that."

He wasn't following. "You hate when captains go down with the ship?"

"No. I hate when politicians use these totally lame metaphors, like the whole stupid purpose of the exercise is to get off a one-liner that will make the papers. I mean, you were totally right. The thing is supposed to be about accounting, not icebergs. God, I hate that."

He nodded. He didn't like it much, either. Then he remembered she hadn't answered his question. Any of his questions. "You didn't answer my question," he said.

"I'm outside your formula, let's just put it that way."

"My formula?"

"Yeah. Half your age plus seven. Which, in your case, is twenty-nine and a half. You can be with a woman who's twenty-nine and a half or older. I'm a few years short of that, chronologically speaking."

"I wasn't looking for a date, chronologically speaking. I just wanted to know how old the, uh, young lady in the passenger seat was."

"Yes you were."

"No, actually, I wasn't."

"Yes, actually, you were. It's totally obvious. And as for being a young lady," Ronnie added (a little petulantly, he thought), "I could curl your toes if I felt like it."

For the first time he let down his guard and laughed.

"You laugh. But you wonder, 'Could she?' And I could. If I felt like it. Let's get some music on this thing, okay?"

She gave up on finding CDs and fiddled with the radio until she found a hip-hop station. Thumpthump OOM oom, thumpthump OOM oom, went the beat. Fritz cringed.

Pennsylvania Avenue was busy, the sidewalks bustling with people bundled in winter coats, carrying packages. People were starting to worry about Christmas, to buy the packages, to hide them in the office, to hurry to the stores at lunchtime. Fritz hadn't given any thought to Christmas. He wondered if Linda had. Last year, at a cost of $4,000,

Linda hired an interior decorator to help the family "do" Christmas. The decorator had recommended a firm in Canada that would ship you the perfect balsam fir ($350). He gave advice on certain vital decorations and tree ornaments (total cost: $1,895). All of this was important to help create the right mood.

"You know," Fritz said to Linda at the time, "I think Reverend Mackenzie would consult with us on how to do Christmas if we asked. I think he'll consult for no charge." The young decorator smiled genially at the drollery. Linda just rolled her eyes.

How were he and Linda going to create the right mood this year? Thumpthump OOM oom, went the radio. Outside the car, the crowds hurried past with their bags and their boxes.

ABOUT A HALF HOUR LATER, Fritz had found Route 95 and was headed north toward home. Home sweet home: the angry kids, the angry wife, the lost job, the imminent date with federal prison. Had he really just testified before Congress and practically killed a U.S. senator? What was he *doing*, anyway? The molecule soup was beginning to whiz around his brain again. Fritz felt a dark stirring coming on, an unfamiliar brooding sensation, call it a slipping down the slope, when all of a sudden something caught his attention. Out of the corner of his eye, he noticed that Ronnie had kind of wriggled to get out of her coat. It slipped off her shoulders, and she wriggled a little more to shimmy and ease and slip out of it and . . .

Oh my God in heaven.

No, don't notice this, he thought. Do *not* notice this. Eyes front: on the road. You have enough craziness going on in your life right now.

God, she was . . . sinuous. She wasn't just tall and lanky; there were all these . . . *shapes* to her. She was long and lean but curvy long and lean, like a Ferrari or a bottle of Liebfraumilch, and she had some kind of sheer ribbed turtleneck sweater into which the shapes had been poured, and the turtleneck, the way it lengthened her neck, the way it sculpted those two surprising hills when she arched her back to ease out of that coat, the way the clingy sculpting turtleneck wasn't quite long enough to reach down to her pants, the way those pants were cut so . . . so low . . . just barely clinging to her hips (which she arched and lifted to free the coat, *arching* the back, *lifting* the hips—no, don't think of that!), and finally, the way a pink slice of belly peeked out from south of the turtleneck.

Belly pie—it was a scrumptious slice of belly pie!

She noticed him taking his eyes off the road. "It's kinda warm now?"

Oh yes, it was kinda warm now. But not too warm. Not too warm for a slick chute to have iced up the middle pitch of Paradise. Down, down fell the slope away from Fritz's skis. Bumps and trees and blue ice stretched out below him. A waif half his age who needed a three-hundred-mile lift was in the front seat of his car, curling and flicking and teasing like the tail of a prancing cat. And on her sinuous gorgeousness was one aching, irresistible slice of belly pie. Why hadn't he kicked her out of the car before it was too late?

Because she knew something. Because of the way that gorgeous belly pie had peeked at him when she wriggled like that. Because there is no bailing out of Paradise.

He drove on. She had shed the coat, which lay now in the backseat with the boots. Would any more of her wardrobe end up back there? He remembered what she'd said before, about his looking for a date and her being outside his formula. Was she right? The molecule soup was aboil, firing off at random sleepy receptors. They were sending digitized images to brain pixels, and the brain pixels were illuminating a wide screen at the mental megaplex, the biggest, widest IMAX screen in the biggest theater you'd ever seen, and the whole screen was filled with . . . belly pie! During the drive down to Washington, Fritz had been, for the first time, anxious about what he was going to do next, wondering where this was all headed, but not in the sense Ronnie was talking about. He'd been thinking about how long they would put him in jail for. And what that would be like. And what he'd do next for a living, given that he'd be done with financial stuff. But all those thoughts seemed trivial now. On the way down, he'd shied away from bigger questions, as he'd done all his life. Like what he was going to do about the kids. And what was going on between him and his wife, who had been too busy to come to Washington for his testimony.

"Okay if I smoke?" Ronnie asked, breaking the silence. She reached back around the seat—which gave Fritz another aching portrait of her fleshy elasticity, the curvy, gorgeous flowing length of her, and yes, another perfect wink of belly pie—and withdrew a packet of Marlboros from her coat pocket.

That dampened things. Just for a moment that slice of belly pie was replaced by a vision of . . . a wet ashtray.

"Actually, no, I'd just as soon you didn't," he said.

She lit a cigarette. Maybe she hadn't heard him? The cabin of the BMW clouded up with smoke when she exhaled. "We can crack the window. You won't even notice. Just keep the heat rocking."

She expertly directed the smoke from the right side of her mouth toward the window.

Belly pie . . . wet ashtray . . . belly pie . . . wet ashtray. He drove north, and he kept his eyes aimed at the road, but what his eyes saw was not road at all. They were seeing belly pie . . . and wet ashtray. Alternately. One then the other. One vanilla and warm and ready to melt in your mouth, careless and carefree, just stretching and hovering, inches above those lifting hips, that arching back! The other gray and dank and grotesque, a dirty glass ashtray stained with wet ash, stinking and revolting. The one an invitation, the other the consequences. So it played in the mental megaplex. The belly-pie slice. Then the ashtray. Then the belly-pie slice. But pretty soon it was two slices of belly pie for every one glimpse of wet ashtray. Then three. The belly pie was winning! Even with this cigarette smoke all around him, which he hated, even with his mind going to that dark wet taste of ash, the belly pie was calling him back. Oh, this was terrible, this Paradise, terrible!

THE SUN was setting into the gray west, and dusk already had fallen on the darkest afternoon of the year. Ronnie was rattling on. "On the other hand, Fritz, and no dis on Linda or anything, but it's probably been a long time since you had someone like me. I *could* curl your toes, you know."

How was it, he wondered, that they were talking about sex? When had *that* started? They were still on Interstate 95, northbound, somewhere in southern New Jersey, and he had been thinking of a nice scoop of belly pie, the sweet sleepy taste of it, but he hadn't said a word, not a word. Somehow she took the cue. He'd play along a little. To pass the time. That wouldn't hurt, just making conversation.

"You seem a little young. Would I be your first toe curling?"

"You're right, you *are* pretty old. The question is, would I be your *last* toe curling? If I felt like it, I mean?"

"Are you supposed to seduce the guy you're investigating?"

"No, I'm totally not supposed to seduce you. See, I've been having this problem. I really like you and all. I like what you said about that stupid *Titanic* business. I like what you did up there in Boston. I like a lot of things about you. So I can't really do my job. I thought maybe you could give me some harmless details so later it would look like I did some digging but didn't come up with much. But after yesterday maybe it doesn't matter anymore."

"What I did up there in Boston."

"You know. In the court." She smiled at him tenderly, then reached across the center console and patted him on the forearm. It was a pat of genuine admiration, not a come-on. "That was really cool." Suddenly she shifted away from him and said, "You *didn't* call her, did you?"

"Excuse me?"

"Linda. Fritz, you need to call her. Here, I'll dial."

"She's not home. I told you, she had a thing, some kind of bar-association meeting out of town—"

"I'll dial her cell."

"Dial" being a remarkably persistent verb, when you thought about it. No one dialed anything anymore. They just punched eensy buttons. Which Ronnie did expertly. Before Fritz could say much of anything, Ronnie was punching Linda's cell-phone number (which she seemed to know) into the eensy buttons on her Motorola cell phone. Fritz heard Linda answer.

Ronnie held the phone up to his ear. "Hello, hon?"

"Fritz?"

"Yeah, it's me."

"Fritz, where are you? The kids have been worried sick about you."

How had Linda known what the kids were worried sick about while she was out of town at her convention? Fritz tried to cradle the cell phone on his shoulder, but it was too small for that, so Ronnie held it to his ear. Her fingertips accidentally brushed against his neck.

"Hon, aren't you in New York?"

"Yes, for my conference, but I've been calling them, *of course.*" He'd tripped over another Good Parent Ritual. One of Linda's subtler criticisms was that when Fritz traveled, he did not telephone the children frequently enough. Good parents should spend lots of time (on the telephone) with their children, Linda believed. "Who's Veronica, anyway?"

"Excuse me?"

"You're coming up a strange number on the caller ID. Whose phone do you have?"

His neck was very tingly now, and this was no accident at all. Ronnie was rubbing his neck with one finger, gently, behind the ear, as if she knew exactly where to push. One electric fingertip was brushing the neck control. She was pushing the belly-pie button! Just as he was trying to talk to Linda about—what was it they were talking about? He couldn't remember. Because that slice of pie was rolling up and then down on the IMAX screen, rolling up and down, squirming in and out of view between the turtleneck and the low-low-low cut of those hip-hugging pants, delicious vanilla-peach belly pie. A tasty morsel of lip-licking pie—

"Fritz?"

"What?"

"Fritz, whose phone do you have?"

He reached up and took the phone from Ronnie, and this disengaged the belly-pie switch, which turned off the belly-pie movie and enabled him to concentrate.

"I borrowed a phone. Anyway, I'm in New Jersey, heading home."

"Fritz, are you *with* someone?"

"Yes, actually, I'm with someone named Ronnie, and I have no idea who she is. It's sort of a long story."

There was a frosty silence. Linda was giving him cell-phone tundra.

"Okay," he went on, "maybe I should call home, check in on the kids. Who's with them?"

"The service, of course."

"What's *that* costing?"

"Fritz, I don't think you want to go there."

Oops, he'd landed on another region of the forbidden atlas. It was her salary that paid for the service and everything else. So he asked: "Who'd the service send?"

"Loretta."

The service was Mother's Little Helper, in Needham. This thriving enterprise catered to the needs of double-income executives in the ex-urbs. It provided baby-sitters—women, not teenagers—at a cost of $20 per hour plus $125 for an overnight stay. Since the departure of the nanny, Linda had been mainlining Mother's Little Helper, and a charm-ing grandmotherly type named Loretta was gassing up the retirement tank from the Brubaker pump. Or rather, the LeBrecque pump.

Fritz said, "Look, I'll call you later, okay? I can't talk right now."

"Oh . . . kay. Fritz, what happened down there? Did that senator die or something?"

"I don't think so. I don't really know. I haven't heard the news or anything. What did it say?"

"They said he was in the hospital. Had some kind of abdominal at-tack. Pancreas, liver, I can't remember. You apparently humiliated him?"

"I just answered his questions. Anyway, I'll call you later. Okay?"

"I guess so. But I may be tied up after six or so. I have to go to a cocktail party and then a dinner. So—"

They began the stumble dance of monosyllables. "Okay," he said.

"Oh . . . kay."

"Okay, so . . ."

"Okay. Anyway. Okay. So, bye-bye."

"Okay. Bye."

Fritz handed Ronnie back her phone and drove on in silence, keep-ing his eyes on the turnpike. Ronnie stared at him, waiting for him to ex-plain himself.

"That was, like, a *lot* of okays," she said.

He didn't answer.

"I lost count of them all."

Still he didn't answer.

"How come you didn't say 'I love you'?"

"You know, Ronnie, you're starting to piss me off."

"Dude, it was, like, ten okays or something!"

"Maybe you should make some calls and I'll critique them for you. We can drill down into *your* diction."

" 'Okay' is what people say when they feel awkward. They know they should say 'I love you,' or they even want to be able to say it, but they can't. So they say 'okay.' That's just my experience."

"Which there certainly is a lot of."

It sounded pretty lame, the way he said it. Nya-nya-nya-nya-nya kind of lame.

"I think we should stop in New York," she announced a couple of miles up the highway.

"We should stop in New York? Why?"

"I know some people. I think we should stop."

She left it at that. The sunset had now faded for good, and the shortest day of the year was fast becoming its longest night. The New Jersey Turnpike was picking up rush-hour traffic. What was with this stranger, calling his wife and pushing his belly-pie button at the same time? And what did she want to do in New York? He tried to concentrate on the road, but it was impossible. Darkness was falling, the BMW was blazing northward toward Sin City, and she thought they should stop. Belly pie, belly pie—all he was seeing now was Big Apple belly pie.

"COULD YOU find some music on that thing?" he asked after a while. "Music, I mean, not that other stuff."

She seemed uncertain. "I don't know how to find decent music for a geriatric, but I'll try." She hunted around.

"Geriatric? Who are you, anyway? You never told me that."

"That okay?" She settled on an oldies station but still sounded uncertain.

"Sure," he said. "Doobie Brothers? Great."

She frowned. "The Doobie Brothers? You *are* a geriatric. Want me to turn it up so you can hear it?"

"Funny."

"I think my grandparents listened to the Doobie Brothers," she said thoughtfully. Then she took a breath and sighed. "And I really shouldn't do this, but I'm going to answer your question."

"Which one?"

"Who I am."

He listened to the music until she said, "I'm a snoop for Mel Popotkus. My job is to dig up dirt."

The gentleman who underwrote Ronnie's excavations, Melvin Popotkus, Esquire, was the famous lawyer from Los Angeles. Mel was a genuine celebrity: Mr. Class Action. Corporate America hated Mel. The Republicans hated Mel. All women who had ever been married to

Mel—and there were a number—hated Mel. Most of Mel's associates hated Mel. *The Wall Street Journal* hated Mel with the special loathing it generally reserved for people surnamed Clinton. But Mel had had enormous success suing companies in class actions and now was as rich as Croesus. Already he was mounting a shareholder case against Playtime, and paying Ronnie $500 a day plus expenses to mine for information so he could file more detailed papers than the other lawyers who were vying for court permission to represent the plaintiffs.

"So I'm the target?" Fritz asked.

"No, not really," Ronnie said. "The target is always the same: insurance. That means you have to sue the officers and directors who are covered by insurance. The big boys. They want to get dirt on Greene and Jellicoe and the directors, and they hope you can supply some."

Great, thought Fritz. "What's he like, this Mel Popotkus? Flamboyant trial lawyer?"

"*Trial* lawyer? Mel? No, Mel never goes to court. I don't think he knows where the courts are. Mel's a *phone* lawyer. He's got a bunch of associates who write all the legal papers. He follows the stock quotes, works the phones, and settles cases."

"Just like the shorts, I guess," said Fritz.

DARKNESS HAD FALLEN, hard and mercilessly, and not merely on New Jersey. The solstice brought a strange darkness over Fritz Brubaker, too, as he drove his BMW north on the New Jersey Turnpike, alongside an endless Christmas-tree roping of southbound headlights. Fritz felt himself descending into something altogether dark and risky. He felt surly and mean. It was all a game, and everybody was playing. Playtime's fall had been some kind of Wall Street game, the Senate hearing was a Washington game, and this young snoop Ronnie, who'd attached herself to him like a limpet, she was part of the lawsuit game. What of Linda? Ronnie was right: Linda hadn't even come to hold his hand for his grilling in the United States Senate. She had to go to some lawyers' convention—she was busy at her own game. Right here in the cabin of his BMW 330i, he knew that yet another game was playing out. Games were the one constant in any of this, and so far he'd been the only one not playing. Fritz was doing the math, but it was a colder, more resentful math than he'd done before.

A cold sliver of moon rose and hung in the darkness over the highway. How cunning of the moon to appear in her crescent form! On this dark December night, even she was a mocking slice of lunar pie, beckoning Fritz northward to the City of Sin. Were even heavenly bodies in league with his fall? Why not play the game, chump? Everyone else is, the moon seemed to say. Dark, dark was the way down Paradise now, desperate and intense and rash was Fritz's surrender to the beetling slope. He brooded in the smoky cabin. Was his desire a game, too? He felt its urgency (that was real, all right—at the moment that urgency was jamming his right foot down on the accelerator pedal). What did he care anymore? If it was all a game, why should he go on being the only one not playing?

Ronnie was smoking in the darkness. He glanced over at her enigmatic profile. Maybe he should play. Take the belly pie on offer—what did he care? He was descending, falling down a dangerous Paradise. On the longest night of the year, Fritz Brubaker had lost his way.

PART III

"GO LEFT THERE. He's up on— Shit, it's one-way!"

Fritz and Ronnie were lost in the tangled forest of Greenwich Village—Ronnie barking out directions to Fritz, Fritz trying to dodge the taxicabs and panel vans that swerved at him out of the night, and vaguely wondering what on earth he was doing.

She was hollering into her cell phone, triangulating with some other cell-phone person named Ton. "Dude, where *are* you? Yeah . . . No, go to the corner. No, not you, Fritz, keep driving. It's a BMW. Yeah, we'll come by on West Fourth. Yeah."

Fritz asked, "Where are we—"

"Right. Fritz, go right here. *Right!* Yeah, good. There he is."

He was Ton, and Fritz caught only a glimpse before the wiry young Asian slipped quickly into the darkness of the backseat. But Ton, Fritz quickly gathered, was going to prove a disappointment—he didn't know where anybody was.

"Dude, where's Petey?"

"I dunno."

"Where's Stina?" Ronnie asked.

"She went to Jersey."

Nobody was around. It sounded like nobody was partying. Ronnie and Ton whispered something that Fritz couldn't make out.

"Head east," Ronnie said.

Fritz tried to get a look at this Ton in the rearview mirror, but it was too dark. Dutifully, he made his way east, then headed uptown on Park while Ronnie leaned over the front seat and continued the cross-examination.

"Where's Claire and Catherine?"

"Watching MTV."

"What about Max?"

"Video games."

"Where's Hannah?"

"Asleep."

"Where are we going, anyway?" Fritz interrupted.

"He's got to drop off a package for somebody in midtown," she said. He glanced at her and saw a smile forming. "It's cool."

DESPITE the shame she had suffered on account of Fritz's illegal stock trading, his appalling behavior toward Daley and Hoar, and his shamelessly inappropriate grandstanding before the Senate, despite all the rumors that had flown around the city, despite the snickering hallway conversations that Linda knew were going on around her out of earshot, Linda was still a lawyer and still a delegate to the Business Law Section of the American Bar Association. They couldn't take that away from her. She had been determined to attend the annual year-end convention in New York City and lead the panel on advising troubled companies. Present would be any number of senior partners and prosecutors and judges from around the country, eager to attend and be In the Loop (and not utterly disappointed to be staked by their law firms to a midtown hotel from which they could range to finish up the Christmas shopping). Attend Linda had, right from the coffee of morning registration. Safely free of Boston, she felt for the first time since all this awful business had begun that she could be truly In the Loop.

The panel went smoothly. Linda felt like a somebody again. Her talk was well received; the questions were lively; she was up on all the latest articles and court decisions; they even laughed at her witticisms about the Delaware Court of Chancery. Here at the Waldorf, she wasn't simply the pitiful wife of a felon. Marvin had been most attentive (he was there, too), and now the delegates' dinner was under way in the grand Empire Room at the Waldorf. The delegates were well laved from the bar, the lobster tails and filets were being whisked in by the wait staff, and at this particular moment, the lawyers were socializing. This is to say, with their backs to the maw of the dance floor, they were sending BlackBerry messages while their spouses gamely tried to make conversation.

The maw: for the lawyers, this was what the dance floor had always been. Half the reason these men and women had become lawyers was the memory of events like this—junior and senior high school dances that lodged in the hollows of the subconscious as abiding and painful deposits. In high school, when the dance-floor maw gaped, they busied themselves in brisk maw-corner conversations with guys on the student council, and then purposefully strode along the edges of the maw to other corners where other earnest conversations could be had. Anything to mask the painful fact that they were not the ones *in* the maw: the guys were not and never would be the guys on the dance floor feeling up the girls while standards from Deep Purple played; and the girls were not and never would be the girls being felt up. They weren't then, and they weren't now. That was why they'd gone on to become lawyers, to avoid the social pain of ostracism from the dance-floor maw, to mask it by being professionally engaged to watch the maw. As lawyers, they could earn a tidy and purposeful living watching and tending and minding and fussing over the feelers and the felt, the others who lived and did.

In the Empire Room of the Waldorf, that dread dance floor summoned from the subconscious a deep and Jungian pain. The lawyers balanced by electronic means the need to be In the Loop—which mandated that they attend soirees like this—with their aching memories. In prehistoric times, lawyers spent most of these dinners at banks of pay phones, returning urgent messages, the adult equivalent of the earnest maw-corner discussion. Now, as then, this activity demonstrated that the lawyers had vitally important and cutting-edge things to say and hear, important business that couldn't wait and made it impossible for them to be on the dance floor at this particular moment. (It wasn't that no one wanted to dance with them; they were simply *too busy* for dancing *at this particular moment*.) Cell phones brought these urgent messages directly to the table, although even the lawyers had since joined the consensus of polite society that loud cell palavers at table were a breach of etiquette. The BlackBerry solved all of their problems. They didn't have to stoop at a darkened bank of pay phones by the hotel rest rooms, and they didn't have to offend (or so they thought) the dinner guests by yakking on the cell. The BlackBerry made no noise. They could sit at the table and push buttons to their heart's content.

Which most of them were doing. Five hundred lawyers and half as many spouses were gathered in the Empire Room, and while, to be fair, a minority were braving the maw, gyrating and stomping on the parquet floor to the beat of Danny Gentile and his Orchestra, most of the lawyers were in their seats, working the eensy buttons.

OUTSIDE, on Park Avenue, Ton grunted from the backseat, and the BMW pulled up behind a stretch limo at the side entrance of the Waldorf. "Should we wait?" Fritz asked.

"No," said Ronnie, jumping out of the car. "Come on!" She turned to the doorman and smiled sweetly. "Valet?"

Ton slid out of the backseat and into the cold night air. He punched a number into his cell phone, started speaking in a strange language, and slouched his way into the hotel.

Ronnie seized Fritz by the arm. "Time to ditch Ton," she whispered. "Why?"

"He's dropping off a big load of ecstasy to somebody. Not a good idea to be around him from this point on. I told him he'd be on his own from here. He's cool about it. Come on, follow me!"

In a moment they were inside. The lobby was a sea of evening dresses and tuxedos, washing waves of bedecked and bedizened guests to the left, to the right, this way and that. They rushed, they strolled, they jostled, they gathered in loud tangles of excited flotsam. It was a roomful of people all turning sideways to slide past other people turned sideways, but all frolicsome, all festive. The lobby was loud with laughter. Ronnie seemed to light up around them—no sideways about her, she gaily breasted the surf. She led Fritz through the throng and sat him down on a sofa in the lobby, next to a couple talking furiously on a cell phone with someone about a dinner reservation.

"Dude," she said slyly, "big convention here tonight."

"I can see that."

"No, conventions are perfect for borrowing!"

"For what?"

"Wait," she said with a wink. "I'll be back."

So he waited. Here he was in this crowded hotel lobby, doing what? Delivering illegal drugs, apparently. That would go down well with the U.S. attorney up in Boston. He sat primly on the plush purple velvet and

eavesdropped. The couple next to him seemed to have finally straightened out whether the reservation was for eight-thirty or nine. They
moved off. Fritz waited, he watched, the crowds washed around him,
each with an unfinished sound bite, one overtaking the next. The symphony was tomorrow and Melvin had four mezzanine seats and the
dress was cute but you'd think they'd have it in an eight and George
couldn't get a table at Le Cirque and Jill had a run in her stocking could
you believe it and my cell phone battery's dead and has anyone seen
Marcia?

Fritz thought of belly pie, and wet ashtrays, and bags of drugs, and
prison, and wondered what "borrowing" was. Stealing someone's necklace? Nicking a room-service tray? Why was he waiting here? Why not
just get his car back from the valet? He had the ticket, after all. Hadn't
he succeeded in dropping her off? On the other hand, a wicked instinct
kept his butt anchored firmly to the purple plush. Suddenly, Ronnie re-
materialized out of the crowd. With a smile, but without a word, she
curled her index finger around his and gently led him off to his doom.

The story began to emerge in the elevator. Borrowing—it was the
latest slacker game. Ronnie had cadged a key somehow, right out of
someone's purse, from a table in the Empire Room: cadged a plastic key
card and noted the name tag at the table. She had called the front desk
on her cell, asked to speak to Miss So-and-so in 1217, and been told no,
we had a Miss So-and-so in 1940 but not 1217, and then Ronnie had
apologized and said thank you, and asked to be transferred to 1940,
where there was no answer, of course.

When they reached the nineteenth floor, Ronnie led him down a
long carpeted hall with cream-colored wainscoting, past etchings of old
New York. She was long herself, long and lean—how saucy, how cock-
sure, she looked, striding down that hall past the prints of Tammany Hall
and the Great White Way. Fritz knew this was wrong; he'd had plenty of
time to reflect on that. He knew he was walking that long hall to Paradise. But he followed her. His mind was dark with fear, guilt, and, if truth
be told, a sense of sardonic amusement, but most of all, he was overwhelmed with a craving for pie.

"Whose room is this? Did you get a room?" he whispered when the
door shut behind them.

"Dude, you don't have to whisper."

"Okay. But whose room is this?"

"It doesn't matter—it's *borrowing*. This is somebody else's room. I've just borrowed their key."

"*Borrowing?* Are you crazy?"

"A little. It makes it exciting."

"Exciting? It's burglary! At least I think it is." He frowned. It occurred to him that Linda would know whether it was burglary or some other crime, or what it was.

"We could be caught in flagrante at any moment!" she explained brightly.

"You *are* crazy. You are totally crazy," he said, but he was far enough down Paradise now, helpless and desperate enough, that he had to agree. It did make it exciting. It was a game, but wasn't everybody playing? Besides, he thought, what else can they do to me? I'll be in prison soon enough.

"Danger is a pleasure enhancer," she added.

"You make it sound like a condiment."

But conversation didn't matter anymore. They were squared off in a borrowed hotel room, circling like prizefighters. Somebody else's room, with somebody else's laptop on the desk, and somebody else's array of creams and oils and sprays and perfumes set out on the marble countertop visible over Ronnie's shoulder in the bathroom. Ronnie moved slowly clockwise, her lips parted slightly, a look of amusement on her face. As though they were dancing. But Fritz was a man possessed by visions of belly pie. Circling now, thinking that yes, she was brazen and hungry and, while not exactly beautiful, not in the way Linda was beautiful, she was sinuous and animal and hungry. And *young.* So they circled—but not for long. In the next instant the line between fantasy and reality was crossed. They leaped across it with a grappling, physical urgency. How furious it was, and how impatient Ronnie, as she tugged at his clothes, and how impatient Fritz to be tugged!

Patience is a virtue. Fritz was trying to touch and grasp and unclasp everything at once. In this frenzy to do too many things at the same time, and do them too quickly, Fritz's wing tips were still laced, his trousers half off, and left shoe stuck in the trouser leg, and suddenly, he was—there is no charitable way to say this—hopping. He began by hopping vertically, a crouched hopping man with his trousers around his ankles, and his left shoe stuck, and his hands on the belt. Fritz's hops proceeded, as trousered hops often do, by degrees toward the horizon, and he couldn't quite shake the trousers before he'd acquired the trajectory of a medium-range howitzer shot and launched himself into a Chippendale desk. The desk tumbled over backward and scattered a laptop, a room-service menu, a blotter, a telephone, and a lamp. Ronnie shrieked with laughter, and more magazines went flying from the coffee table. A pillow came sailing across the room and whacked him. The lamp lay dying on the floor, its lightbulb crackling. It fizzled and then went dark.

"Animal!"

She was so long and soft but so strong—that perfect, sculpted figure she had when the clingy ribbed turtleneck was peeled away! He had her on the couch, she flipped him to the floor; then she shrieked and laughed some more, and they coupled on the floor while the telephone receiver, flung from its cradle, protested with urgent beeps. But Fritz and Ronnie, laughing and rolling, rolling and laughing across the carpet, didn't seem to hear it. They crawled through the debris to the bed, still cleaving and grappling, and on the bed she flung him down on his back and took possession of him. He flipped her over; she flipped him back. Oh, the wild gymnastics of Paradise, the gorgeous sin of borrowing, there in the stolen suite. Until at last came a giggly shudder, and an outcry, and Fritz's explosion, and then collapse, and release, and petit mort and . . .

A lot of gasping and panting is what it was.

It was 8:43 by the clock. There they lay, in a borrowed king-size bed on the nineteenth floor of the Waldorf-Astoria, in midtown Manhattan, panting. She panted out a question: "How're your . . . toes?"

Between breaths, he choked back, "Curled."

"Told you."

"Maybe permanently," he panted. "Maybe never . . . walk again."

There they lay catching their breath, laughing as though the whole thing were a big practical joke. Giggling. But the giggling died down and, as they lay quietly and normal respiration returned, stopped altogether. That uneasy feeling began to steal right back over Fritz—that bad morose feeling.

The otherworld of Paradise that had seized him so urgently now began to dim and fade out of suite 1940. Paradise blurred, and out of its blurry images of belly pie, out of its lusty promise of romping and releasing and long, soft limbs, the hard, unforgiving Planet Earth came back into laser-sharp focus. Fritz was staring vacantly from one side of the bed, and out of the background popped the sharp edge of a lamp shade. Then a desk upside down, and a pillow on top of the television, then a terry-cloth robe on the floor, lying by a lamp, and then another lamp, which seemed to be broken (how the hell had *that* happened?), a phone off the hook, shoes, twisted sheets, the fiendish trousers wrapped in a woolen smirk, next to them a spavined room-service menu and a laptop lying upside down. All with sharp lines and square corners. Finally, next to Fritz in a hotel bed, the red hair and climbing earrings of a young, toe-curling stranger.

What was he doing in bed with this kid, closer in age to Michael than to him? Much closer—outside his formula!

While he was skidding along this path of reflection, and while the sharp rock formations of Planet Earth were coming keenly into relief, the redheaded stranger rolled back over on top of him.

"Oh no," he said.

Ronnie nodded firmly. "Oh yes." And yes it was.

Well, yes and no. Or, to be precise, Oh yes! And then, Oh no!

THE LOVERS dressed in silence. Partly this was because Fritz now looked less like a Don Juan than a weary prizefighter (the one whose limp arm isn't being held up by the referee). He was wrung like a dishrag. But mainly his exhaustion was emotional. Fritz was feeling empty. He leaned over and purposefully relaced the wing tips. It was all a game, and he was just another cheesy player like everyone else, and on top of that, he was a losing player.

He stood, a little bowlegged, and looked around at the carnage. "Do you think we should . . ."

Tidy things up? It seemed hopeless, and besides, who could remember where everything went? She shrugged, so he followed her to the door.

Not so fast. Because right there in the corridor, fumbling through her purse for her room key (which she could swear she had put there before dinner but now for some reason she could not find) was the woman who actually had rented suite 1940, in lawful tender of the United States, and who was there not to borrow the suite but to use what she'd paid for (although she would be reimbursed for this expense, and thus in a metaphysical way was also a borrower), and whose suit bag was actually in the closet, whose laptop had been on the desk (before . . . well, beforehand), and whose toiletries were spread out next to the marble sink. She wore a maroon cocktail dress with sequins, and thin spike heels, altogether rather a sexy-looking number for a woman who seemed a trifle old for duds like that. Next to her was a man in a dark worsted suit and an even darker tan, absurdly dark, considering it was December, wearing a smile that was 50 percent concupiscence and 50 percent middle-aged stoner (a smile you could say, at that moment, was ecstatic, thanks to the attentions of a young Thai). Still going through her black leather purse, the lady nearly jumped out of her sequins when the room door opened.

It threw Ronnie, too. Ronnie and the woman peered at each other across the threshold, their hackles up, like dogs held barely apart, straining on leashes, keen-eyed dogs that haven't quite decided whether to sniff.

"What are you doing in my room?" the woman demanded.

Ronnie managed a halfhearted smile. "We got confused?"

"Confused? Confused about what?"

"We're in twenty-forty and got off on the wrong floor. This is, like, nineteen?"

"How did you get in my room?" This, you could tell, was a woman used to having her questions answered double-quick, and not with bullshit. Her stoner companion nodded vaguely but remained silent. Good question, he was thinking. On the other hand, the redhead was a babe.

"The weird thing is that the key worked? But once we got in we were like, this is someone else's room." Ronnie flashed her key. "See?"

No sale. Sequin Woman was not buying any of this. "I'm calling security," she said. It was then that she noticed Fritz hovering behind Ronnie. "Wait—don't I know you?"

"I don't— Wait a minute," said Fritz.

They peered at each other. Oh Jesus, Fritz thought, I *do* recognize her from somewhere. She is definitely very familiar, something about her face and eyes—

"Gotta go—sorry!" said Ronnie brightly, gave a firm tug on Fritz's stunned, dazed arm, and brushed past Sequin Woman into the hall.

"I'm calling security!"

Ronnie turned and waved. "Dude, if it was me, I'd call house-keeping—it's a *mess* in there. But go for it!"

And in a trice Ronnie was giggling and urging her bowlegged lover down the corridor.

I know her from somewhere, Fritz was thinking. Cottage Street in Dover? Playtime? The Chaney School? He couldn't place the face. He shuddered—he had the sinking feeling that he not only knew her but had seen her recently. Car-pool lane? Was she at the wheel of a tank some morning last week? Or was she some Linda pal from Dover or Wellesley, a face recalled from the grain-bin aisle at Bread & Circus. Maybe a lawyer from Linda's firm. He tried to concentrate, tried to flip through the mental Rolodex under "Linda," but his brain was so besotted that he couldn't make it work. Anyway, Ronnie was towing him at a brisk clip, and he had to be careful not to bump into the ornamental tables in the corridor. The next thing he knew, they were stumbling, running, running and giggling down the corridor at the Waldorf, escaping from whoever that very familiar person was.

Meanwhile, in shock and disbelief, the woman in sequins peered through the doorway at her ravaged hotel room. She wasn't besotted, not yet—she hadn't trysted with the exceedingly brown gentleman, and she knew exactly who the burglar was. (It was, indeed, burglary, as she well knew.) Fritz Brubaker, that was who. With some kid, in her hotel room. She turned and watched him stumbling down the corridor, then had an "Oh my God" moment of her own. What had Brubaker noticed about her companion, and what might he say?

"Friends of yours?" the man asked.

"*His* name is Fritz Brubaker. I don't know the teenager."

At the end of the corridor, Ronnie and Fritz headed left with a last sprint to the elevator bank, where Ronnie pushed the button and then leaned, laughing, against the elevator door. Fritz didn't know whether to laugh or cry. Who the hell was the woman? He couldn't place her, but she sure as hell looked as though she recognized him. He'd screwed this girl in a hotel room belonging to a friend of Linda's, then left the room looking as though the defensive line of the New York Jets had just finished a full-pads practice there, and now he couldn't place the face! This wasn't good.

The tone sounded, and the elevator door slid open. Still giggling, Ronnie fell into the elevator, tugging Fritz by the hand. Shaking his head, confused and dazed and feeling cheesy and fearful and racking his brain to figure who in the hell that woman in the sequined dress was, Fritz stumbled in behind her and came face-to-face with . . .

The wages of sin.

Linda. And next to Linda, Marvin Rosenblatt.

The door slid shut with a sedate tone, and there they stood, surrounded by the dark oak and mirrors of the Waldorf elevator: Fritz, Ronnie, Linda, and Marvin. A nice little foursome. His wife's elevator: could Paradise get any worse than this?

"Fritz?"

"Hi, hon!" he defaulted automatically to standard chipper-Fritz greeting tone.

But Linda didn't seem very chipper. Fritz nodded at Marvin, who bowed solemnly, like a valet waiting for you to advise whether you will require your topcoat this evening. Fritz's head hurt.

"Fritz, who is this, and what are you doing here?" Linda demanded.

God, did his head hurt all of a sudden. "That's what the woman in the sequin dress wanted to know," he said.

"The woman in the sequin dress?"

"Long story."

"It's *Linda*?" Ronnie asked.

"Excuse me? Do I know you?" Linda turned to her husband. "Fritz? Who is your friend? And what is she doing here?" She pointed at Ronnie without looking at her, as though she weren't quite there.

"What are the odds?" Ronnie asked.

Fritz said, "Well, hon, this is Ronnie, whom you met, or whose phone you met, sort of, before, and as to what we're doing here, I guess . . ." His voice trailed off.

"Yes?"

"I guess that's pretty obvious," he said quietly.

"What are the odds?" Ronnie wondered again.

Fritz said, "Of all the elevators, in all the towns, in all the world."

"You walked into hers," Ronnie agreed.

The couples stood on opposite sides of the elevator, although it wasn't very big and didn't allow for much separation. Fritz was studying Linda. He wondered about the etiquette for meeting one's wife in an elevator when in the company of a woman with whom one has just been unfaithful. Should he kiss his wife? Ronnie was still holding his hand. Should he at least remove his hand from Ronnie's?

Ronnie was studying Linda, too. "You look great," she said to Linda.

"Excuse me?"

"For someone, you know, who's that— I mean, you look great, you know? Fritz, she really looks great."

Then Fritz noticed Marvin. He'd noticed him the moment he'd stumbled into the elevator, had even nodded politely, but now he really *noticed* him standing next to Linda, staring down at the carpet in the elevator, on closer inspection looking less like a valet and rather more like the spouse of a disgraced politician giving a farewell speech. The *spouse* of a disgraced politician . . . Fritz stared at Marvin. Then he looked back at Linda. She began to flush, whether from anger or some other emotion wasn't clear. He looked back to Marvin. "So, Marvin, what are *you* doing here?"

What Marvin was doing there was adjusting his glasses and examining the carpet and trying not to turn red, with as little success as Linda. But before he could say anything, Linda interrupted.

"Don't change the subject. We're finishing up from the seminar, Fritz. And I think it's *you* who's got the explaining to do."

"Hon," Fritz pointed out, "you and Marvin are on the down elevator."

"I'm sorry?" Linda said.

"Was the seminar somewhere above the nineteenth floor? Isn't it just hotel rooms up there?"

Good lawyer that he was, Marvin thought this question both leading and compound, and therefore in all respects objectionable. But he didn't say so. Linda couldn't come up with an answer.

Ronnie interjected, "Dude, are you, like, *doing* this guy?"

Linda turned, stunned, to face the astonishing young woman. Apparently Marvin also had an objection to this question. He began to say, "I really don't think it's appropriate that you—"

Linda summoned all of her righteous indignation. "Excuse me, young lady?"

Ronnie turned to Fritz and raised an eyebrow. "She's doing him," she said. "Wow."

"That is outrageous. Outrageous!"

"I'd agree with that," Ronnie said.

Furious, Linda turned away. She folded her arms and stared at the elevator buttons.

Conversation might have flagged at this point were it not for a startling development. Three weeks earlier, the Waldorf-Astoria had completed its new and improved electronic security program, a state-of-the-art installation of software and electronically activated alarm systems to secure the hotel doors and elevators in the event of terrorist attack. Cameras had been mounted at all key locations and an electronic override panel installed in the command center behind the front desk. This command center happened to be about fifteen feet from the west wall of the Empire Room. It was at this particular moment that more than 130 of the lawyers at the ABA dinner dance were pressing the "send" button on their BlackBerries. Unfortunately, the combined amplitudes of 130 infrared signals tripped an override sensor on the security command module, which caused all the street doors instantly to lock, and the elevators in the old hotel to issue a metallic clunk, then stop running.

Including the elevator in which Fritz, Ronnie, Linda, and Marvin were riding. It halted somewhere between the sixth and seventh floors. Then the lights went out.

Not just darkness but black black darkness fell on the elevator. Not even the emergency light, not even the buttons. There was no light at all, there in the elevator suspended in its Waldorf elevator shaft. In the distance, an alarm bell was ringing.

"Oh my God," Linda said.

"Well, *this* is interesting," said Ronnie.

Marvin got out his cell phone and began to call 911. The phone gave off greenish light that lit up Marvin's busy fingers. They looked like elf fingers, disembodied and hovering in the blackness.

It took the Waldorf-Astoria command center two minutes or so to trace the problem and override the security cutoff. Any two minutes can be longer than you think—a man can run half a mile in two minutes and have a few seconds left over to catch his breath. But two minutes in a blacked-out elevator suspended between floors of the Waldorf-Astoria is, even as two minutes go, a long two minutes. Linda used them to invite God's intervention. Marvin, being a more practical sort of lawyer, reached the call center for New York City 911. (The call center was having some difficulty understanding exactly what he was saying, since the cell phone was cutting out.)

And Fritz? In that darkness, Fritz felt the great weight of his own foolishness bear down on him like a lead suit. With all the Playtime mess, he'd been trying to stay true to himself—to reject corporate dishonesty, to do the right thing, whatever the consequence. In an instant, he was living the very life he'd rejected. What was the difference between cheating on a stock sale and cheating on your wife? And now Professor Vorblen, with his tweedy green suit and his blue bow tie and the light reflecting on his glasses, had popped into the blackened elevator. He began to let fly with his Socratic cross-examination: "If you were capable of cheating on your wife, shouldn't you also carry on a life of financial fraud and other convenient frauds? Would it not be less responsible to let your family suffer the financial consequence of your criminal punishment than to hire a lawyer and do the usual dance?"

The professor wasn't the only interloper. Others began to join the elevator. There was Hap's face in the blackness, scowling at him. Next to Hap appeared Andy, saying, "Jesus Christ, Fritz!" Then Michael and Kristin were in the elevator, too. They had something to chime in, something important. They interrupted Andy, they tugged at Fritz's arm. (Or was that Ronnie tugging? It was hard to distinguish the flesh and blood from the poltergeists.) Michael and Kristin gave him that look, then sang out in juvenile bisyllabic harmony: "Da-ad!"

Boy, was it getting crowded in there! Between Marvin, with his green elf fingers hovering in the blackness, and Linda, and Ronnie, and Professor Vorblen, and Andy and Hap and Michael and Kristin, it was getting hard to breathe. Then the woman in the sequined dress, the woman whose name was on the tip of his tongue, she was in the elevator, too, fumbling in her purse and trying to find a room key.

"What are you doing in my room?" she was demanding.

"Jesus Christ, Fritz!" Andy was saying.

"Da-ad!" the kids were going.

The professor added, "You can't simply take love. Love is an investment. And you haven't made it. Remember the parable of the wasted talents—"

And then *he* was interrupted. Because that wasn't all, there was someone else. Who was that new person frowning in the corner?

Cabot Brubaker, Fritz's father, had joined them. The elder Brubaker—who seemed to Fritz only half alive even before the 6:20 express from Rockport had transported him to a better place—calculating, cold, perpetually frowning, and long-dead, now made an appearance with his clear horn-rims and his blank, bloodless, unsmiling face. That stern patrician whom Fritz had disappointed throughout his whole life. Whom Fritz disappointed with his ordinary grades, his lack of ambition, and his jocular attitude. Cabot, who probably never laughed at a joke in his life and certainly never told one. Whose brother, Fremont, known as Monty, inherited all the sense of humor and zest for life. Cabot, who rode the 6:15 train in to the office every morning from Beverly Farms and the 5:45 train out again in the evening, and worked right up until the day of his death. Who never made a mistake in his whole life (certainly never balled a stranger in a hotel room!) right up until his seventy-fourth birthday. Who, on that birthday, in almost perfect health, trim, fit, vigorous, seemed entirely impervious to age, with the sole exception of his hearing, which had begun to go, and for which, with Brubaker pride, he had refused to get a hearing aid. Who, on that very day, returning from work precisely as he always did in his vigorous, unfailing routine, was distracted by a note in *The Wall Street Journal* about softness in the commodities markets, and stepped briskly into the path of the 6:20 express. Cabot, who worked the first half of his life to set up his sons in trust money and then, throughout the second half, seethed with anger at them for spending it. There it was, brooding over the blackness of the now crowded elevator, the face of Cabot Brubaker.

It was a particular likeness that Fritz remembered well. Cabot was looking down at his son Fritz, that awful first day the seven-year-old had tried the Chute from the top of the single chairlift at Stark Mountain. Fritz had wiped out badly on a mogul, bruising his temple. His hat and skis had gone flying. He lay in the snow cold and blubbering, humiliated, choking back sniffles, while gentle mortifications rained down from skiers passing overhead on the chairlift. "You okay, son? You all right?"

No such solace from Cabot Brubaker. Into the frame of Fritz's vision, blurred with snot and tears and snow, came his father's frowning face. The face that from that moment on had haunted the boy, came to haunt the man, repeating the words Fritz had never forgotten:

"Son, stop sniveling. When you fall down, it's usually your own fault."

Thus Cabot Brubaker, hovering there in the Waldorfian darkness, pronounced judgment on his son again. Cabot, whose instinct had always been for fault rather than compassion; who had embraced with all conviction Micah's injunction to do justice but never read on to the bit about loving mercy; whose face seemed to Fritz as bloodless as ever. Cabot spoke to his son from beyond the grave:

"Son, stop sniveling. It's your own fault."

"Love is an investment you haven't made," Professor Vorblen chimed in.

"What are you doing in my room?" added Sequin Woman.

"Da-ad!" said the kids.

It was a quintet, right there in the elevator at the Waldorf. God, his head hurt, trying to keep up with it, until suddenly Linda's live voice sounded her elevatorial refrain. "Oh my God."

What of Linda? How had things gone so far awry that on the very day of his Senate testimony, she would have abandoned him for a fling in a hotel room with Marvin Rosenblatt? Was that some cruel accident or the inevitable result of his own lack of attention to her? Love was an investment he hadn't made, the professor was saying. And there was Cabot's grim message. The messages hit him with a one-two punch. This was his fall, not hers, the fruit of his own selfishness and self-absorption. He had neglected her, he had left her to provide for the family, he'd been a sailboat playboy, he'd gone on this self-important frolic and detour over the Playtime business, and he himself had betrayed even that not ten minutes before. He had been lazy and complacent. This was his own fault.

But Marvin Rosenblatt? Were things that bad? It didn't make any sense, except in some melodramatic Baptist way—as in God would punish you for sinning, and boy, would He do it quick! (And boy, would He have a sense of humor.)

Fritz was in the midst of these weighty ruminations when the lights came back on and vaporized the various shades who had peopled the elevator a moment before. Only the four living persons remained. The buttons lit up. Linda glared at Fritz, then punched the one marked "L." The elevator clunked again and began to move.

"Linda," Fritz said.

"We will have to discuss this some other time."

"But Linda, I—"

"Not *now*, Fritz."

"But I just need to ask you one thing, hon."

The elevator reached the lobby. The chime sounded, and the door opened. Suddenly, the time travelers had returned to the real world: the festive lobby of the Waldorf-Astoria Hotel, with its throngs coming from the theater, its merry crowds of lawyers issuing from the Empire Room, and its two security men ready to board the up elevator for the nineteenth floor, where some sort of problem had been reported.

"Thank *God!*" Linda said. Without a further glance at her husband, or at that ghastly woman with all the earrings, she frog-marched Marvin out of the elevator and into the crowd.

"But hon," Fritz called after her. "Marvin *R*osenblatt?"

THE NEW YEAR was not off to an auspicious start: in fact, Dr. Helga Schadenfrau was worried. The patient was in crisis. She'd demanded an appointment, insisted on seeing the doctor on an emergency basis. Now she was sobbing reflexively and uncontrollably, right here in the Wellesley Hills sitting room. Dr. Schadenfrau had seen Linda's sniffles before—she'd choked back a few on occasion—but never anything like this heaving, racking mess. On this January morning, the patient was bawling, and her tears were running muddy with eyeliner, and some of the mess looked as if it might drip onto the immaculate pale blue linen of the easy chair. Dr. Schadenfrau wondered if she should call for help. Then she remembered—Dr. Schadenfrau was the help.

"They're firing me—they're firing me!" Linda wailed, then fell back into sobs.

As far as Dr. Schadenfrau could tell, Linda had gotten about halfway through the pitiful details of that cruel morning the Thursday before Christmas—the morning after the New York City seminar—before breaking down completely. She'd told how Barry Fisher, the managing partner, had called her and asked her to come see him. How she'd almost skipped down the hall to the elevator, not suspecting a thing, still feeling a high after her New York trip. (Yes, there had been that astonishing business at the Waldorf with Fritz, but what else was new? She had given up on him. Most important, Linda had shone on the afternoon panel and been gloriously In the Loop.) She'd smiled brightly at the secretaries on thirty-six as she trotted unsuspecting into the abattoir.

For Barry Fisher's corner office, with its commanding view of Boston Harbor, and its elegant chrome and glass desk and its Chagall prints, was to be Linda's slaughterhouse. The betrayal of it! They were lying in wait—on one chrome and leather chair sat Fred Van den Hut, the head of Elboe's business department. Behind the glass desk was Fisher, the managing partner. And there, on the other chrome and leather chair, with eyes averted, was Marvin Rosenblatt. *Et tu*, Marvin! Her lover of only twenty-four hours before had assembled with the others, taken his place, then summoned the prisoner for sentencing.

Linda knew how things like this worked. This meeting must have been meticulously planned. She shuddered as she realized that Marvin must have been deep in BlackBerry consultations about this very meeting *even as he was with her in New York*. It had been scripted and worked carefully through preproduction, and Linda had been left entirely and completely Out of the Loop.

How alone she felt when the door clicked shut behind her. How falsely solicitous the three men were, the way they looked at her (two of them, anyway: Marvin wouldn't look at her, the weasel). Fisher beckoned to her to take a seat on the couch, the lowest position in the room, her back to the wall, her face to the firing squad that was mustered left, center, and right. Would she like coffee? Would she like tea? Would she like a blindfold, or would she prefer to see the bullet coming? Poor Linda. Confrontation had always been her weakness. In an ambush, three on one, male on female, surrounded in this office, she never had a chance.

"Linda," Fisher began. Then he frowned and shook his head. He would show his empathy by having a little trouble getting started. Oh, how difficult this would be for Fisher, his attitude seemed to project. How his heart rebelled at this painful duty of firm management, this cup placed before him. Then he said it: "This is difficult." He shook his head again, to show the weight of the difficulty.

After this initial pause for empathy came Fisher's sonorous platitudes and the earnest nods from his toadies. Playtime was the biggest client of the firm and, even in bankruptcy, the source of special-counsel corporate work; on its board were various muck-a-mucks who ran other corporations that were key clients, and so on. They were sure, absolutely sure, that Linda had nothing to do with this disturbing insider-trading business, everyone was sure of that, no one doubted that, no, not at all. Not for one minute!

"But . . . still." That was what Fisher said, with a wince, and then he turned to the window overlooking the harbor. It was like the crack of a carbine ringing out at dawn: "But . . . still." And then the wince. And then the head turned, and shaken. Followed quickly by a forlorn half smile, striking the attitude of corporate compassion.

It looked bad, he explained. Or it might look bad. Surely she could see that. How it looked—or might look. We would all have to face facts. For the good of the firm. And then Linda saw how, with cruel irony, *the good of the firm*—a carbine she had trained on other victims over the years—was now trained on her. How many times, in earnest discussions about the necessity of firing Abe or transferring Betty or cutting Chuck's pay, had she herself locked and loaded *the good of the firm*. Now the barrel was aimed at her. How convenient the weapon, how elastic the phrase! They were all partners in the firm, but *the good of the firm* never lined up with the good of the partner on the couch. Fisher reprised his phony empathetic smile. Van den Hut nodded in agreement (he had momentarily been distracted by incoming vibrations on his BlackBerry, which required a brief check, but he came back to the matter at hand with a brisk, supportive nod). And Marvin? Linda kept trying to catch Marvin's eye, but he was staring at the floor.

These successful lawyers all spoke the same language, and they had followed the same path to success—each must never be Subject to Criticism. It was not that they were criticizing Linda themselves, no, not that they doubted their partner for one minute, certainly not! It was just that somebody else might. And if somebody else did, then Linda's presence might render *them* Subject to Criticism. And that was intolerable.

Fisher leaned across his desk. Surely she understood?

"But," she said, "it's . . . it's almost Christmas!"

It's almost Christmas. Oops. How about let's forget that particular remark, okay? Rewind the tape, positions everyone, take two. Except no one could forget a line like that, not one that offered such comic potential. The instant it left her lips, Linda cringed. She could almost hear it scored *vivace* for snickers and guffaws, performed to the rousing bravos and huzzahs of the steering committee. *It's almost Christmas!* Was that all she could come up with? How lame!

In the account of her execution rendered to Dr. Schadenfrau, punctuated here and there by descants of sobs, this was the melodramatic climax Linda had reached when she could go no further. That she had been so humiliated, that she had burst out with so pathetic a remark to these men, she simply couldn't bear it. Her sobbing graduated to outright bawling and took over the session.

"It's all right," said Dr. Schadenfrau. "It's all right."

Linda bowed her head; she held her pretty hair in her hands. Her shoulders heaved, her head shook. She wiped her eyes. It was Rachmaninov playing over the Bose speakers this morning, and Dr. Schadenfrau tried to concentrate on the music, waiting for Linda to calm herself. Which, in a moment, she did, enough to speak, anyway. "These people are supposed to be my partners. My partners! They're supposed to owe me a fiduciary duty!"

"It's terribly upsetting," Dr. Schadenfrau agreed. She thought she'd better do some validation, and quickly, or she'd have a big dry-cleaning bill for that easy chair.

"A punctilio of an honor the most sensitive!" Linda dissolved into more sobs.

"Yes." Dr. Schadenfrau made notes. She wasn't sure what the last remark meant. Punctilio? Some legal thing, apparently. But it was sort of poetic.

"A leave of absence!" Linda sobbed. "You don't recover from something like that. You leave, all right, but you don't ever come back. It's over for me, all over! I gave everything to that firm!"

The doctor made a note of this interesting observation. She thought it might be quite significant, clinically. Also, it sounded like the sort of thing that could bear on the continued availability of Linda's BlueCross BlueShield coverage, and conceivably on the patient's ongoing ability to cover her copayment. "Do you really think it's over?" the doctor asked.

Little by little, remark by remark, Linda was recovering her composure. She dabbed at her eyes again. "Oh yes, I know how this works. It's a paid leave of absence, in theory, but what they pay you is the base only. And then, when compensation time comes, you get the maximum cut. If they ever let you back, you've become a Typhoid Mary. Everyone in the firm knows about it, all the clients know about it. You don't get work. You're totally Out of the Loop. You never recover."

The doctor nodded. This didn't sound very encouraging. She thought it might be best to bring the conversation around to something more agreeable. "Do you hold Fritz responsible?"

The subject of Fritz would be good for another fifteen minutes, and fifteen minutes was about what was left of this session. Besides, they probably could both agree that Fritz was totally responsible for all of this, and begin to feel better about things.

At the mention of Fritz's name, however, Linda reverted to sobbing and could do nothing more than nod in an ambiguous way. "I'm sorry," she whimpered.

"It's quite all right, Linda." Dr. Schadenfrau handed her patient some more Kleenex, trying to dam up the facial effluvium.

"Thank you. I'm so sorry."

"It's all right. It's all right. It's important to let these feelings out. In order to get in touch with them."

Just as long as they don't get in touch with the chair, she was thinking. There was more sniffing and sobbing and more tears, and by the time it was over, a big wad of Kleenex sat in a mound on the coffee table next to Linda's untouched cup of chai, but when Dr. Schadenfrau later checked her notes of the session, she didn't find in them an answer to her question about whether Linda held Fritz responsible. Interesting.

As Linda was leaving, the doctor offered her earnest end-of-session smile, her best consolatory look, and said, "I expect that things may get better."

BUT THIS was not an accurate prognosis. Things would get worse for Linda, much much worse than the simple leave of absence. Thirteen days later a messenger would pull up the drive to the Palazzo and hand a stunned Linda LeBrecque a default notice. This was the first notice that all of the mortgage debt and the home-equity line on the house and the Siasconset house—all of the debt that the bankers at Boston Private Bank and Trust had been so good as to provide on a signature basis—was about to come tumbling down.

When the man had gone, Linda stared at the certified letter in disbelief. She had drafted papers like this for other people, but to receive one herself was a different thing altogether. It meant there was no time to lose. Sure, she and Fritz had equity in the two properties. But she could hardly refinance them now, with her on leave of absence and Fritz heading for jail. They would have to sell. Not that the houses would be hard to sell: news of her misfortune would race around a grateful Dover at light speed. ("Did you hear about the Brubakers? Terrible shame! Just awful! But Jill Snoring said their place is coming on the market.") Linda had already noticed more than one slow drive-by on Cottage Street, which she suspected was the real estate brokers, circling. No, the place would sell over a weekend, if she wanted it to. But the family would have to move. The shame of it! The snooping, voyeuristic real estate women who would paw through her home, who would find grease underneath the range hood and dust bunnies in the corners, who would poke their busy little eyes into closets and cupboards and drawers and the kids' rooms and her bedroom, into shower stalls and under toilet seats! Who would paw through the medicine cabinet, slyly noting her prescription medications. Who would have quite the titter in the office afterward about the goat and the tree stump. And that flagpole (which was perfectly charming in concept but frankly a little amateurish for a place like this).

The *shame* of it.

But there was no choice. Her houses would have to be flogged off, or she'd risk losing the equity in a bank foreclosure. She wouldn't have to be present for all the snooping, thank God, but she would have to bear the unspeakable humiliation of walking into one of the town's real estate offices. She would have to feel the stares of all those busybody women while she filled out the listing agreement. So the job was gone, and soon the house would be gone, and the Nantucket house with it. And a week from now Fritz would be sentenced amid some enormous, ghastly Roman circus.

But that wasn't all. Three weeks later would fall yet one more blow. This one would arrive with the FedEx man, a letter from her partners at Elboe, Fromme & Athol—a punctilio of an honor the most sensitive.

WHAT A WEIRD CASE, Max Pearl thought as he ordered his usual bucket of coffee with six creamers from the ground-floor canteen at the John Joseph Moakley United States Courthouse. First the comedy routine at the initial hearing, then the guy seeming pretty smart in his office, then the craziness in New York, then last week that strange pretrial conference with Chandler.

Pearl met Fritz on the first floor of the courthouse. He sat his client down at one of the tables by the cafeteria. They were looking out at Boston Harbor through the grand sweep of glass that served as the courthouse's seaward face. In the pale light of the January morning, the harbor was gray and forbidding. A stiff breeze sent whitecaps scudding toward the airport. One determined water taxi held her bow into the wind and fought gamely across the gray chop.

"Fritzie, I gotta tell you, this is one for the scrapbooks."

Fritz was staring at the harbor panorama, focused on the intrepid water taxi. He didn't answer.

"Pretrial order, don't leave the commonwealth, and you—"

"They subpoenaed me. I had to go to Washington."

"Sure. But did they subpoena you to the Waldorf, too?"

"Oh, that."

"Yeah, *that*. *That* went down big with probation, I can tell you. Very big with the U.S. attorney." He slurped from his coffee bucket.

"Is it going to be a problem this morning?"

"Oh, no," Pearl said. "Chandler loves it when guys violate her orders. Particularly when . . ." He shook his head and took another hit. "Let's just say it's a good thing they don't have the death penalty for insider trading."

Pearl worked his coffee for a while. They both looked out the window. Over at Logan, a jet lifted off from runway 22R and banked left out to sea. It would be nice to be on it, Fritz thought. Wherever it's headed.

What a terrible morning. Michael had barricaded himself in his room, refusing to go to school. He wouldn't come out or even speak to his father. "Just go!" he said. "Go!" Linda, hearing this, stared at Fritz angrily. Fine for him to jaunt off to prison to prove whatever infantile point he was proving. Look at the mess he was leaving behind. He'd cost Linda her job! They were going to lose the house and Nantucket, too! The boy was crying!

And not the boy alone. Next had come the dreadful parting with Kristin, right in the car-pool lane at the Chaney School. Kristin was going to school, but in the Lincoln Navigator she sat taut as a bowstring, a little Linda, twanging with anger. For all to see, her mother noted—including that busybody Mavis Potemkin, who was working welcome teacher that morning, and the SUV immediately behind, and who knew who else.

"Peanut, I'll be back home sooner than you think," Fritz had said. He leaned toward the backseat to embrace her.

Kristin stiffened like a plank and pulled back from him. "DON'T call me PEANUT!" she snapped. She grabbed the door handle and pushed open the door.

"What a lovely winter morning!" sang out Mavis Potemkin.

Kristin tumbled from her seat and then turned around, glaring at her father. "And *don't* say anything out the window in front of my friends!" she hissed. She hurried over to Fielding, her shoulders stooped.

Oh yes, what a lovely winter morning. How frozen, how windblasted and empty the tundra that followed the car-pool lane as Linda drove Fritz in to Boston. Not a single word passed between them the entire trip. When she finally pulled up to the cement caissons that blocked off the courthouse's main entrance from the street, he'd looked over at her and realized she wasn't even coming in with him. She was dropping him off like a wife dropping a husband at the train station. Have a nice sentence, hon. Just dropping him off to go to prison. He'd tried to say something, but she'd shaken her head—she wouldn't even look at him.

"Linda . . ."

Would there be one good-bye kiss, at least? A taxi honked. And then another. Linda's face was locked forward, and she shook her head firmly. A kiss? Forget about it: she wouldn't even speak to him. So he climbed down out of the SUV into the cold, alone, pulled his jacket around him, and watched her drive off.

"It's your own damn fault," the voice of Cabot Brubaker had reminded him as Fritz watched the Navigator being swallowed up in rush-hour traffic.

"But there's another thing," Pearl was saying.

Fritz blinked, and Linda vanished from his thoughts. He came with difficulty back to the present: to Pearl, the table, the bucket of coffee, the sweep of glass showing off Boston Harbor, and his imminent date with doom. "What?"

"Fritz, I'm wondering, trashing hotel rooms, okay, it's kind of a rock-and-roll thing, I guess, a movie-star thing. And you're a big star after that business with Senator Oldcastle, which personally I loved, I have to admit. That was sensational cross-examination."

Fritz couldn't smile, not even for Pearl. Senator Oldcastle seemed like a long time ago.

Pearl leaned over the coffee cup. His eyes danced. "But Fritzie, can I ask you something?"

"Yeah?"

"What exactly was the percentage in trashing the judge's hotel room?"

It took one half of an instant for the import of the question to sink in, and the other half of that instant for the terrible, adamantine "Oh, shit" to form in Fritz's brain. It formed like a mighty pestle of lead, then began crushing out whatever life remained in the Brubaker mortar. Oh, shit. Oh, shit shit shit shit shit! The *judge's* hotel room? *That* was who was in the maroon sequined dress?

Pearl nodded as though reading his mind. The gotcha eyebrow went up and down. Yup. That's who that was.

"She didn't look the same," Fritz tried to explain. "Without her robe and all. I . . . I only saw her once, and was up there on the, the . . ." He held up his hands hopelessly, sawing the air with them, as though sawing hands could explain what words could not. "Sequins, all these sequins." He shook his head. "And she was so . . ." His hands kept flailing, trying to pluck a word from the air.

"Short?"

The strange little lawyer grinned at him over the coffee. Fritz's eyes widened, and his hands stopped sawing because that was exactly it, that was exactly right. "Yeah."

Pearl nodded. "They always look short off the bench."

"So damn short," Fritz repeated.

"An excellent reason to trash her room, by the way. Some guys would pick, you know, a taller judge's room to trash," said Pearl. He drank some more coffee and reflected. "Or at any rate, another judge's room to trash," he went on, "other than the one who's about to sentence them, but hey, to each his own. Whaddayagonna do?"

"No, I didn't know it was *her* room when I—when we—oh, shit."

"Fritzie, maybe you did know it wasn't your room, whosever room it was, when you did whatever you did? It's just a detail, I know."

Fritz grimaced, shook his head, and went back to looking out the window, and thinking about how goddamn short the judge was, and how icy the Linda tundra had been in the car, and how vicious was the martian who had taken possession of his daughter's body.

"This whole thing, it's hard to make sense of," Pearl said. "Judge Chandler was very cold in our pretrial last week. Not like her usual self. It was like an informal pretrial. She calls in me, Feingold, just the two of us. Usually a pretrial, you know, it's in court, the defendant's there, the court reporter's there, the clerk, it's on the record. But no, she just wants me and Feingold off the record. So we go to her chambers. Now, in chambers, they like to shoot the breeze before getting down to the case. Mr. Pearl this, Mr. Feingold that, Judge Chandler, how ya doin'. You know? But not this time. No chat, we go right to business. 'Straight plea, Mr. Pearl,' she goes to me. 'No funny business?' Like a question. And I go, 'Sure, Judge. Funny business, no, it's just a plea. He doesn't even want me to negotiate with the government. Whatever it is, it is.' And you don't, right?"

Fritz nodded. He didn't. Whatever it was, it was.

"She goes, 'Play it by the book, Mr. Pearl.' Just like that. 'Play it by the book.' So I go, 'Sure.' End of conference. Feingold, he never says anything. Very strange."

This got no response from Fritz, so Pearl continued, "Fritzie, my point is, that was a weird conference from her. It wasn't an accident. She was asking me or telling me something, I don't know what. It was like she was worried about something, something I might do at the plea, I don't know." He blurted out, "What the hell happened in New York?"

Fritz thought back to it, to that meeting on the nineteenth floor of the Waldorf, that moment at the doorway of room 1940 with Ronnie and the judge in the maroon dress with all the sequins. And then he remembered. There was that other guy. There was that other guy, kind of leering there, behind the woman in the sequined dress. Fritz did some quick math.

"Is she married?" he asked.

"The judge? Married? Sure. Why?"

"Ever met her husband?"

"He's a public defender. I know Harry for years."

"What's Harry look like?"

"What's he look like? Fritzie, I got a bad feeling."

"What's he look like?"

"Where you going with this?"

"Pearl, what's he *look* like?"

"Well proportioned. Good-looking guy, a real sexual animal. Short, fat, stylishly bald. Kinda like me."

Fritz stared out the glass at the harbor, as though he didn't want to see Pearl's face when he put the decisive question. "Is he tan?"

"Is he tan?"

"Yeah, you know, tan. Like TV-makeup tan. Cocoa-butter tan. Like you painted it on. That kind of tan."

"Harry? In December? In *July* Harry isn't tan. He wears a wool suit to the beach and a big straw hat in case he would get skin cancer. In December Harry's as white as a herring."

Fritz nodded. All a game, it was all a game, and even the judges were players. He didn't want to play this particular game anymore. Pearl, who had a sense of where things might be headed, and who had to practice in this particular court, in front of this particular judge, in front of this particular judge's other judge friends, and who knew Harry for years, he was happiest to let this one go, too. So, that was that. What a shame this case had turned out to be or, less than a shame, what a *routine* case it had turned out to be. But Pearl was still curious about one thing: "The babe, Fritzie. She was who, exactly?"

"Never mind. It's complicated."

"One of those little details that cries out for minding, you gotta admit."

Fritz shook his head.

"It's congenital with me, Fritzie. My guy trashes a judge's hotel room with a mystery woman, I like to know. Maybe she's a hooker, but I'm thinking, no, that doesn't sound like Fritzie. C'mon, are we sharing?"

"She's not a hooker."

Another hit from the coffee. "This is progress."

Fritz sighed and shook his head. "Pearl, it won't make any difference. It's like the judge said, a straight plea. Let's leave it at that."

At this point Pearl unleashed his most effective cross-examination technique: silence. Silence and a boyish smile that seemed to say, "Oh, c'mon." But that didn't work, either.

Pearl waited and at last shrugged. Whaddayagonna do? At some point in most of his cases, he had to shrug and ask the question. Pearl knew—he accepted—that guys did unaccountably stupid things. ("Thank God," he liked to say, "or how would I make my alimony payments?") A guy would sell drugs to a narc. Or slug a cop. Or a loser wouldn't do much of anything except be stupid enough to be around other losers, and some prosecutor full of testosterone would get a hair across his ass. Shit would happen. So Pearl filed this peculiar information in the same file. The client trashes the judge's hotel room in New York? That's a little unusual, but hey—whaddayagonna do?

Still, it was a disappointment, particularly when you thought about what had really happened back in October. Which Pearl had a new theory about. He lingered with his coffee. They had a few minutes to kill before the court hearing. Pearl had liked this guy's attitude before. He'd seen a lot of things, but he'd never seen a guy stand up the way Fritz did in that first hearing. He hated to have it end so clownishly, as just another whaddayagonna do.

"You know, Fritzie, we had an insider trade here, guy with no record, the sentencing guidelines give you a little time, probably, but with co-operation, early acceptance of responsibility, knock off a point here, a point there, work the right deal, you might have been looking at restitution, a big fine, and some probation. You want to take your lumps, okay, that's honorable. Not to mention three points on the guidelines. But it didn't have to be time, you know what I mean? You could have paid your debt to society without doing time. Maybe some community service.

"Now you've violated the terms of bail, you and the mystery babe who is not a hooker apparently destroyed the judge's hotel room, I dunno, what the hell am I supposed to do with you? You're probably looking at some time now."

Fritz nodded, still staring out through the majestic sweep of glass. Another plane took off. He thought of flying away, or sailing away, or even zipping up his coat and walking away. Right outside the window were people getting away. But he wasn't going anywhere without handcuffs on, he knew that now. When you fall, it's usually your own fault.

"I understand," he said.

"Fritzie, can I ask you one more thing? I know it doesn't matter anymore, but I keep thinking about the case—you know, the real case, before you pulled your boner in New York. It wasn't Greene, Jellicoe, or any of those guys who did the short trade. I was wrong about that, wasn't I?"

Fritz remained silent, staring out the window.

"I figured out that I had that wrong. That's why you hired me, isn't it? You were about to walk out of my office that day, and then you realized I was sniffing down the wrong trail, so you said, okay, I'll go with this guy."

Pearl could see Fritz was listening. He could see it in his eyes, although his expression remained blank.

"Remember I said your stunt was very high school?" Pearl's eyes were narrow and twinkling.

"Let's go upstairs and get this over with," said Fritz.

Pearl shrugged. Hey, the guy had paid his fee in advance. He was an adult and could do as he liked. Whaddayagonna do?

As they walked to the elevator, Pearl said, "I gotta tell you one thing, Fritzie."

"Yes?"

"You're a mensch. Dumb, maybe, but a mensch."

THE PROCEEDINGS would prove a great disappointment to the press in the gallery, for there was to be no more of the high comedy they had come to expect of this case. There would be no dialogue, no one-liners, no defendant chiming in with funny stuff. The judge was businesslike and frosty; the plea was accepted with antiseptic formality. The prosecutor made a short proffer, the judge raced through the rote questions, and bang: $115,000 in restitution, a $1 million fine, and a year and a day.

"A year and a day, a huge break," Pearl whispered. "You can get forty-seven days off for good time. She sentences you to a year, one day less, you gotta serve the whole thing. You know what, she must like you."

The other break was the location. Before they led Fritz away, Pearl added that the federal penal camp in Deer Path, Pennsylvania, was as good as it got.

"Club Fed," he explained.

But there was no public banter that cold January morning; there were no lawyers hired and fired, no give and take. There was no wife to storm out of the room—Brubaker's wife didn't even show up, the press noticed. As for Brubaker, he didn't say much at all, not until it was almost over. Neither did the judge, and neither did the prosecutor, and neither did Pearl. They all sent him to jail as quickly and coldly and efficiently as you could imagine.

The only human moment came right at the end, and it flashed by in a couple of seconds. Ker-chick! the cuffs went on. Just then Chandler looked at Fritz with something that might have been compassion, the angry compassion of a parent for a particularly wayward child.

"Mr. Brubaker, you need to get ahold of yourself," she said.

He nodded. "Your Honor, I appreciate that. I agree completely."

HE MAKES ME
DOWN TO LIE

FEBRUARY HAD COME, and a pall hung over the gray lands in the Play-time Tower. The cubes stood empty, their cloth walls picked clean of photos and cartoons and calendars and kindergarten finger paintings. Many of the offices were dark, too. The layoffs had swept like plague through the fourth floor, decimating cube and office dwellers alike, leaving behind dark computer screens, unplugged phones, and desks empty of everything except paper clips and dead ballpoint pens and old Advil bottles that rattled when you opened the drawers. When fluorescent lights began to flicker in the corridors, no one replaced the bulbs. They flickered for a while and then died, and then other lights began to flicker. Boxes of files lined the halls, the lower courses crushed, the higher courses leaning crazily, and as the lights failed, the box walls grew more forbidding. In offices and conference rooms, papers still lay on tables where they'd been abandoned in midmeeting, like the lunch bowls at Pompeii that hadn't been cleared away before the volcano erupted. The framed corporate mission statements hanging in the elevator lobby acquired a thin coating of dust.

Outside, the tower itself was dingier. Dirty snow lingered in the flower beds; trash blew against the brickwork and gathered in mean little piles. Exhaust particulate washed south through the air from Route 128, as it always had. But now there were no window cleaners. The windows slowly darkened with grime.

From the lonely spaces below the ninth floor, where the retention bonuses had not percolated, morale had fled. When the layoffs came at New Year's, only the management people on nine were spared. Some of the other floors had lost half or more of the employees, and a silent resignation hung about these spaces. The cubescape was still inhabited, but only in the way that ruins are always inhabited, with here and there a survivor picking through the box courses, looking for something. Occasional lamps shone where one of the silent rearguard worked over the bankruptcy crisis of the day: the schedule or affidavit that must be filed tomorrow, the projection that the suits needed for the creditors' meeting on Tuesday. But no one stopped at a cube to chat; no conversation echoed from the lobby. It was so quiet that whenever one of the management people came down from nine, the lonely cube dwellers still eking out an existence on four would start at the sound of the elevator bell, then listen to the footsteps off the elevator.

Those few who remained avoided eye contact.

Luce was one of these. Here among the ruins, Fritz's assistant had survived, holed up in the cube across from his old office. She worked for three managers now, including Frank Pitts, who still stalked his morning lap around the office, investigating which employees weren't getting in early, even after he'd laid half of them off. Through that winter, Luce waited mutely for Pitts and two other managers to call with assignments. She dug through the box piles to find what they'd lost; with grim efficiency, she delivered the financial summaries they asked for. By February the new reality of bankruptcy had settled on the suits as something they could live with, but it had not settled on Luce. She declined their pleasantries, their jocular efforts at gallows humor. Her face was dutiful, blank, hardened. The one point of honor she reserved to herself was this: she would not be their friend. She would do what they said and no more.

Those boxes along the south wall could be organized better in all this empty cube space, Luce knew. Arthur was still down in support services: she could hit him up for a few lightbulbs. In the old days she'd have done jobs like these without waiting for someone to ask, but now there didn't seem any point. She wasn't going to invest any more life in this place. Pitts and the rest of them didn't deserve it. So Luce waited for the phone to ring and studied the want ads and Internet job sites.

In her desk Luce kept the newspaper articles about Fritz: his arrest, his arraignment, his testimony in the Senate, his conviction. For some reason she'd clipped these from *The Boston Globe* and saved them in a manila file. She hadn't known quite what to do with his things: she'd put the photos and bric-a-brac into boxes, which she'd stacked in her cube. On top of them was his sail bag, still holding his gym clothes.

On a cold February afternoon she was going through the classifieds. From time to time she looked over at Fritz's darkened office. Had he really done what the suits on nine kept saying? He'd pleaded guilty to it, but cynical instinct is a Bostonian's birthright, and Luce was Boston born and bred. Her bet was that the guys who gave themselves bonuses and then fired half the company must have had something to do with this, too. Maybe they'd all been in it together, the stock business. You couldn't tell about anybody.

Whatever the reason, Fritz was gone, and she had to forget about him and find the next job. Luce shivered, rubbed her arms, crossed herself instinctively. She could swear they had cut back on the heating. It was always cold in the afternoons. She checked her watch. Four-fifteen: forty-five minutes to go. Before, she'd been the kind of person who couldn't find enough minutes in the day; now she'd become a clock watcher. She looked again at a want ad. "Office administrator needed for start-up," it said. "Tremendous growth opportunity!" Sketchy, she thought. But she put a red circle around it anyway. She had to get out of Playtime. The place felt too much like death.

THREE HUNDRED MILES to the south, death stalked Nell Hasty's ground-floor guest room as well, where the old bed presser made his last visit. They would have kept the senator at Walter Reed indefinitely, but he couldn't take the quiet of it, the brusque professionalism of the nurses, their appalling and blank disinterested youth. Also, he couldn't get a goddamn drink. Just their look in the morning when they came around with the meds told him that he was nothing to them, a senator they'd never heard of from a state they didn't care about. From the first, Oldcastle had a terrible fear that he'd die there among people silent and stiffly courteous, people who never knew about Old Number 31. He would die among strangers who would stay by his bedside up until the moment of his death, unless that came after shift change. So in his final triumphant act of will on this earth, Jack Oldcastle roused himself to a semiprone position, coughed up sputum, roared at the attending physician, and got himself the hell out of there.

Nell took him to Georgetown one last time.

For years it had seemed like his belly had been getting tighter. Bigger, but also tighter, more swollen. Something was haywire in the intestines. Since the summer he'd been passing more gas than a New Orleans pipeline. This wasn't just the steak dinners. The goddamn plumbing had sprung lots of fluid leaks, the doctors said, and it was too far gone to patch. The diagnosis was grim: ruptured duodenum, sclerosis of the liver, pancreatitis, and partial renal failure. Translation: a massive plumbing breakdown.

How bad was it? Bad enough that each of his kids made a visit to Walter Reed before Oldcastle abandoned it for Nell's. First Dolores came and fussed with the nurses. Didn't they have any Saint-John's-wort? His feet were cold, did he need another blanket? She'd get it, preferably from the linen closet a quarter mile down the hospital corridor. Did somebody need to find the nurse? She'd rush after one. Oldcastle could tell that she was looking for an excuse to get the hell out of the room. God, he thought, how old and matronly his firstborn had become! It was a relief when she had to leave. The kids had games and recitals on the weekend, she explained, but she said she'd be back soon. His grandchildren—Jesus, he wasn't sure he could remember their names.

On the day she departed, Butch arrived. He didn't fuss or fetch, he just sat silently in the chair in the corner of the room for a long, awkward day. That was even worse, for Chrissakes. Like having the undertaker himself show up, smiling coldly at you and checking his watch. Then Butch left and John Jr. came. It was at this point that Oldcastle realized they had divided him up—divided up the bedside watch so that they wouldn't, God forbid, all have to be together. John Jr. actually spent the night, but he spent most of it on his cell phone.

Once he'd reached Nell's, he slipped quickly, and now it wasn't so much shakes as terrible fevers that left him delirious for hours at a time. Soon he couldn't get out of bed. He tossed and trembled and kept pulling the catheter out and pissing himself. Nell had to put a rubber sheet on the daybed, but it was too late, and soon after that, the mattress started to stink.

Fat as his body remained, his features seemed to sharpen as the end came on. His nasal bone began to stand out like a hatchet, and his cheekbones popped out of his face. "Gimme a drink, a drink, for Chrissakes!" he cried out, then slipped into mumbling something incoherent. Delirium came on. "My glass! A glass!" he yelled. "Overflowing, Chrissakes! My glass, goddammit, my glass! Make me lie down. Lie down! I'll—"

The night nurse shrugged at Nell. There was nothing to be done now.

"In the green pasture!" he shouted. And then: "Where's my staff?"

Nell wondered if she should call Ralph Moldy.

"Staff," he mumbled, "staff, rod and staff . . ."

The last time Nell saw Old Number 31 alive came just before midnight on February 11. The nurse had gone off to get some sleep, but Nell woke and thought she'd better go downstairs and check on him. When she looked into the guest room, he was tossing and turning. The light was off, but a full moon was shining in the window, and she could clearly see in the pale light the dangling hose of the catheter. Suddenly, Oldcastle began clutching at his sheet, picking at the hem, then holding up his fingertips and staring at them with an unearthly smile. He shouted out Lancaster's name, and then his voice trailed off. Nell sat near him in the chair by the foot of the daybed. The old hulk grew calmer and settled some. And then it was quiet, and Nell nodded off.

Sometime after one, she awakened. The moon shone through the window, illuminating one fat leg poking out of the sheet at a crazy angle. She touched his foot. It was cold.

Only later would Nell wonder whether Oldcastle's last delirious snatches had come to him, via some indirect and improbable route, from the Twenty-third Psalm.

IT WAS the letter that did it. Having some drone in human resources send Linda a letter like that? Lacking even the decency to sign it themselves? First she raged, but when Linda LeBrecque's rage cooled, it hardened into steel. Linda unholstered her cell phone and called the loyal aide-de-camp who had always acted as her chief quartermaster. If they wanted war, war it would be.

"Linda, where have you been?" Richard demanded. "And what is this awfulness I'm reading in the papers about Hunky-Boy?"

Richard manned Linda's armory, and Hunky-Boy was his pet name for Fritz, whom he'd met only once, on a Saturday when Linda had dragged Fritz into the Armani boutique on Newbury Street to pick up a suit. Richard had Linda's numbers (all of them) on his speed dial, and he regularly phoned her with breathless news about recent arrivals. Linda was one of Richard's annuities: in a good year she might amount to 3 percent of his revenues.

"Richard," Linda said, "things are pretty bad. I'm working through some difficult issues right now."

"I read."

"He's gone insane. I mean, absolutely insane. I don't even know him anymore. Richard, I'm married to a prisoner in a federal prison, okay?"

"Oh, darling . . ."

"My husband has a number. He's a con, Richard. Right now the father of my children is an inmate at a place called FPC Deer Path. FPC, Richard, do you know what that stands for?"

A pause. "I'm thinking it's not 'First Presbyterian Church.'"

"Federal penal camp."

Another pause. "Interesting."

"Richard, please, no jokes."

"I'm sorry."

"I'm at my limit. I get a letter a day from him, full of philosophy."

"Linda, I'm speechless." (This was a figurative expression. Richard was never without speech.)

"But I'm not calling you about that. I've got a bigger problem now. I have two children, as you know, who are totally dependent on me, their father being a felon. My law firm is trying to throw me out. I'm going to have to go in and confront them."

Richard digested this bulletin. "It sounds very dangerous," he said. "Linda, listen to me. You need to go *shopping*."

TWO HOURS LATER Linda was downtown, in the back of Armani, mapping out the objective of her planned assault. Richard was a tall, slim fellow in his early thirties, about whom everything, from his short hair to his trimmed beard to his suit, was aggressively neat. He had an angular face accented with slim rectangular glasses. His navy suit was neatly pressed, as was the silky aquamarine T-shirt he wore underneath. His shoes were shined. There was the subtlest suggestion of aftershave when Richard leaned down to buss Linda. It was his usual cheek-bussing embrace, followed by a gentle scolding about not calling him or coming to see him in positively *ages*.

Linda expanded on the tale of horrors.

"But why are they being so bitchy?"

"Because they think they can get away with it."

Richard nodded. He well knew about people being bitchy because they thought they could get away with it. He was a little bitchy himself sometimes, when he thought he could get away with it, but that was another story. Richard understood the mission. His jaw was set and determined: he was all business, a Patroclus girding up his Achilles for the climactic contest before the battlements of Ilium. It was a wonder to see how he sprang into action, whisking suits from the back and spreading them out on the couch. "All right, I'm thinking navy for the suit, spring is coming, it's almost March, but you know? This isn't bad, it's just come in. I sold one to Dianne Purcell at Daley and Hoar, she's *such* a witch.

Here, give me your arm." He began nipping and tucking. She tried it on, and Richard stepped back to consider her in the mirror.

"It's nice," she said.

The words hit Richard as though fired from a cannon. "Oh, God! What am I thinking? What is wrong with Richard's little brain today, people?" (There were no people in the boutique other than Linda; Richard asked the question rhetorically.) "Richard missed his mocha triple shot, and the brain simply is not working! Navy, for a meeting like this!" He shook his head. "I'm sorry, Linda, I have been wasting your time. I cannot permit you to buy that suit. Please take it off your body at once! I'm covering my eyes."

(Which Richard did, although it looked like he might be peeking.)

"But—"

"Linda, do as I tell you. The suit is nice, but nice is not appropriate for us to meet the dicky-faces in. For this meeting only one color will do."

Presto! Richard vanished to the back of the store. Presto! He returned with another suit. This one was jet black, it was tapered, and in the morning light of the Newbury Street boutique, it gleamed like a weapon. Richard gasped with reverence when Linda put it on. "God, it's *gorgeous* on you. It's *Garbo*."

"I'm going to need it—"

He waved her off. "I am having this fitted today, Linda. *Today*. You will have this suit tomorrow morning. This thing will be *illegal* on you!"

He clapped his hands; his manner became brisk. He began to pace around the boutique in the manner of a field commander giving orders to his colonels. "Right. We have the dark suit. I'm thinking simple and powerful for the blouse. A silk blouse—I have something in cream. No, cream is recitals and opera, it won't do." He paced, his hand to his chin. "Blue? Too predictable. Red? Too dressy, too old-lady. Pink? Too weak. Wait!" He rushed to the back of the store, returning in a flash with a lemon-colored silk blouse. "We are black and gold in this meeting, black because we are remorseless and fearsome in crushing the bad bad dicky-faces, gold because that's what they have to pay us to make it better. Right?" He held the blouse up to the suit. "You like this?"

She did, actually. Now the master appraised her critically, assembling in his mind the entire package. "Okay, let's pull our hair back this way"—he reached around her neck and gathered her hair in a ponytail—"draw it tight from the head. Sunglasses, we'll wear Chanel, I think, on the hair, like this"—he slipped a pair of his own out of his breast pocket and up on top of her head—"black, please. All right now, jewelry. We're not to do pearls, pearls are far too congenial. One gold strand on the necklace, not too fine, not too goopy. Simple gold hoops for the earrings. What do we have for a watch?"

"Cartier."

"I didn't mean to doubt you." He gestured at the Swatch she'd worn that morning. "We'll leave that, whatever that thing is you're wearing today, we'll leave that at home, sweetie, with the other gardening tools? Yes, that's fine. Wear the Cartier, a bracelet or two, not too many.

"Now, Linda, please sit." He sat her on one of the couches, put his hands on her shoulders, and looked at her severely. "We have to talk about shoes."

"I've got plenty of shoes, I've got some Ferragamos that would—"

Richard looked stricken.

"No?"

A blast of scolding trochees: "No no, No no, No no, No no, NO! No little-girly pumps, Linda, promise me!"

"What do I—"

"Linda, we are going into this meeting to *kick* the nasty little dicky-faces, aren't we? Kicking the dicky-faces is a job for *boots. Boots!*" He stood up and put his hands on his hips. "What do you have?" he demanded.

"I've got some Pradas that I could—"

"Are we a Japanese tourist? If you wear Pradas to this meeting, I will never speak to you again."

"Well, what should—"

The commander began to pace again. "I'm thinking we could go Gucci. We could. But no. It's not quite edgy enough. We need something that isn't quite over the top but is teetering on the edge. We are going in to kick some ass, and we need to be a piece of ass. So let's really go for it."

"How do you mean?"

"Darling, look at me. This is serious." He had stopped and adopted his gravest expression. "You have to go Manolo."

"Go Manolo?"

"Forget the Pradas and the Ferragamos and the Guccis. Leave them in the closet. You're going Manolo."

"Richard, aren't those kind of—"

Richard waved it off. "Of *course* they're expensive. You could buy my Vespa for a pair of Manolo Blahniks. Richard's little brain was a little slow to get rolling this morning, you don't even want to *know* what kind of a party Richard was at last night, Linda, but the brain is finally switched on now. I'm getting to work on the suit, you go straight to Neiman's, you talk to Edward on the second floor at the back, you know where it is, Edward has big brown eyes and a dimple and he wears a little earring, very elegant, and he's *completely* gorgeous, I'm calling him on the cell the *moment* you leave and I'm telling him to drop everything to put you in the perfect pair of Manolos. I want them quite snug on the calf—Linda, listen to me, this is *important*—quite snug on the calf, the Armani is very fey, but it's not a pair of cargo jeans, we understand? Edward will know. I'm going to call him. Do not talk to Sylvia, she works in women's footwear, too, but she's a cow. Promise me! Oh, and Linda, bring the corporate card, because we're going to max it out, darling. And promise me one more thing."

"Yes?"

He lowered his voice. "Edward is a dreamboat, and I have the utmost confidence in him, but he can be, sometimes just a little, I mean, I don't *know* this, but I have just a little suspicion—anyway, a little mercenary. I don't think he'll—but—Linda, if anyone tries to sell you anything less than a three-inch heel, call me on my cell *immediately*."

SHE DID bring the corporate Amex card. A decent regard for ironic justice compelled at least that, and so, when Richard and Edward had completed their work, Elboe, Fromme & Athol would be $6,280 poorer. But it was worth it. In her battle gear, Linda shone like a black knight. She was a phenomenon of nature, like Mediterranean heat shimmering over black sand, an apparition in black and gold: the Armani suit a gleaming jet, the necklace and golden hair and lemon blouse blazing fire.

And Richard was right: when, without warning, she stormed the downtown battlements of Elboe, Fromme & Athol two days later, it would be the $1,895 Manolo Blahniks that would knock out the rank of secretaries on the twenty-eighth floor, and the associates staring out of their office doorways. They were sharp-toed black boots in the softest leather, with three-inch stiletto heels: kick-ass boots. Tie-'em-up-and-whip-'em boots. Her boots, her purposeful walk, her gorgeousness with a mean streak, it all announced, as she strode into Elboe's offices, that ass was what she'd come to kick: specifically, the skinny hindquarters of Marvin Rosenblatt.

IT WAS right before eleven A.M. when she swept into his corner office and trapped him behind his desk, like a squirrel cornered in the basement. He stood there, startled and frozen, his fingertips on the desk.

"Oh, Linda, how nice to see you . . ."

"Is it, Marvin?"

"Of course, Linda. Of course." Said with a forced smile, a smile of terror. "I'm a little tied up right now, but I'd love to get together and—"

With an electric shimmy, the Armani of Doom slid into one of his chairs. "Better get untied, Marvin."

She was dark and dangerous, she was long and cool, she flamed like gold foil. Marvin would be no match for her. She left him no escape. She was Elizabeth I with a page, Catherine the Great with a serf, a cat scolding a very naughty mouse.

"Marvin," she began, shaking her head, "Marvin Marvin Marvin. We really need to talk."

Marvin gave her his best "I can't imagine why" look. Then he started to say, "I'm afraid now isn't a good time, Linda, but I'm sure—"

She shook her head and leaned forward. "We need to talk *right now*, Marvin," she said. "Sit down."

So he sat.

"Marvin, let's see what you guys have done to me. Let's take inventory, okay? Item one: my clients. Item two: my career. Item three: my future. Item four: my partnership. Item five: my house. That about sum it up?"

"Linda, I—"

"Oh no, sorry, I missed an item, Marvin. Item six: my body. You took that, too. You used me. A personal betrayal, to give the stew flavor. The others were only money, after all. But you were hot-wiring me during our adventure in New York—you were, to be blunt, fucking me while you were arranging to fuck me, weren't you, Marvin?"

Linda smiled coldly. She had spoken with a calm control, without visible or even audible anger. This new coolness scared the hell out of Marvin. His mind was racing—how could he extricate himself from his office? At a minimum, he'd be late to his meeting with the steering committee, which could lead to being modestly Subject to Criticism. Marvin started to stand again, but her withering glance froze his glutes and left him hovering between sitting and standing, like a guy in a bathroom stall taking aim at the seat. God, she was so totally sexy! And so malevolent! With a last effort, he popped back to his feet and began stammering that this wasn't the appropriate time. "I know how upsetting all of this must be, but you have to understand that for the good of the firm—"

"Marvin, a little advice. Don't say 'good of the firm' around me again."

He tried again: "I, I, know how you must—"

"You don't know anything. And don't even think about leaving your office for steering committee. Not till I'm done." She smiled brightly.

"Linda . . ."

"Marvin, I'll tell you something. I may seem calm to you, but don't be misled. I'm capable of quite a scene. Screaming, hysterics, the whole thing. I might open this door and start doing a nutty about the *affair* we had." Oh, the coldness of her, the implacably icy coldness. She said the A word out loud! Marvin had never seen her like this.

Linda went on. "Frances would get a kick out of that. Then I'd give it, oh, six or eight minutes to be on every e-mail in the firm. Marvin, darling, if I were you, I really would sit down." She gave him another frosty smile.

Marvin froze behind his desk. She wouldn't! Would she? He slowly eased back into his chair.

"That's better, Marvin. Now we need to have a conversation about this letter I got the other day."

The letter—he knew it must have been the letter. He'd told Fisher not to have them send that letter. Very ill advised. It had gone out from HR and told Linda that the firm was going to continue her monthly draw but, while she was on administrative leave, suspend any distributions until year's end, in conformance with policy statement twenty-six under the partnership agreement. Translation: she would get $10,000 a month.

Linda removed the letter from the breast pocket of her suit. She tore it into pieces, and Marvin watched them flutter to his desk.

"I don't care about you being a weasel, Marvin. And I don't care about being out of this place. But I do want you to know one thing. If any more fallout from this mess hits my kids, I bust an ugly on you. Ug-*leeee*. With twenty years left before retirement, on the curve I was on, I think I can come up with a number that looks like twenty million dollars. But I can do something to *you*, Marvin, much worse than that."

She wouldn't, he thought; she couldn't.

"Marvin, my kids have lost their house. Their father's gone to jail. I have a tuition bill coming due in ten days, and you are going to cause that bill to be no problem to me. Am I clear? My kids are off to expensive camps this summer, and they aren't going to feel any more pain out of this thing. That ten-thousand-a-month draw that you had Joanne"—Linda referred to the assistant HR director—"send me? With the idea being that I hang around on tenterhooks until the end of the year, waiting for you to do the right thing? I don't think so, Marvin."

"We should get Barry for this discussion, Linda, and I—"

"You don't want Barry for this discussion, Marvin, not for what I am about to tell you."

This caught him up short. He waited. Linda leaned back in her chair and, in a gesture of sheer contempt, swung her $1,895 Manolo boot heels onto the desk. Marvin stared at the soles.

"You want a leave of absence, Marvin, you're going to pay for it. You are going to get with Barry and the rest of the weasels, and you are going to get me a check for sixty thousand dollars. I want it in five days. You will get me sixty thousand dollars a month for as long as I feel like it. Think of it as a deposit against the considerably larger sum that we will settle upon later. When I get around to it. If there is any question in my mind about that check coming, I'll sue, and I promise, Marvin, I promise that in the lawsuit, I will be dirty. I will be low. I will be nasty. I will stop at nothing. *Nothing*, Marvin." She swung her legs down and leaned over the desk, close to him. A teeny gulp escaped, try as Marvin did to stifle it.

"I will throw all the mud that I know. I'll be launching mud from howitzers, Marvin. Because I've got a lot of mud. How you guys screwed Latham in last year's comp, for example; how Fisher funneled his love nest through the firm's accounts as 'visiting lawyer's housing' in New York. But that's all window dressing, Marvin, because the main item, count one, in big italics, Marvin, on page one of the complaint, is going to be the Marvin affair."

"Linda, I know you're upset, but—"

"Sex discrimination gives it such flavor, don't you think? How you screwed me; how you worked to cut me out of the Playtime account; how you conspired to get me fired when I tried to call a halt."

"That's not accurate, Linda, and I—"

"Marvin, I will get you screwing me on the front page of the complaint that I will file in Suffolk Superior Court, where no one from the *Globe* will miss it. And on the interior pages? Steam—whistling, scalding steam. Marvin, believe me when I say your marriage will go down in flames over this. *Flames*, Marvin."

"Linda, you're being irrational, I think, and—"

"I'm being irrational? Try Cheryl when she picks up the newspaper and reads about our romps in the Fordyce Hotel. You want irrational? *That* will be irrational. Who do you think will end up with the house in Newton, Marvin?"

"Linda . . ."

"Marvin, you have no idea what irrational is. No clue. You want to see irrational, then let me think you people are going to play money games. Let me think that five days from now."

Marvin's face was white as a bratwurst. His mind raced with fear, its circuits overloaded with the madwoman's direct assault on the principle of "I must not be subject to criticism." Linda had gone crazy! She would do that to his marriage?

But Linda, who could read his mind, smiled her you-bet-your-ass-I-will smile. The meeting was over. The black knight had swept the field and trounced the enemy. She'd even left two little half-moons of black shoe polish on the Carrara marble. She rose and went to the door.

"Bye-bye, Marvin," she said. "Think it over—for the good of the firm."

"I'M TELLING YOU, Fritzie, every once in a while you should listen to your lawyer" was what Pearl had said. "It's a big mistake not to self-report. You get stuck on the *Elreno Express*, you don't know what could happen."

Boy, would Fritz remember that advice over the next two weeks. A nonviolent first-time offender usually had the right to check himself in to the penal camp, as though it were some kind of retreat. He could take thirty days after the sentencing hearing to wind up his affairs, then be driven there by friends or family. But Fritz had passed on all of that, which seemed like more deal cutting to him. They've sentenced me, let them take me, was his attitude. Let's get this over with.

Which proved to be a mistake, just as Pearl warned. Because they took him, all right, via a roundabout route that would make sense only to a border collie herding scattered sheep, or a federal bureaucracy. He spent four days in the county jail in Plymouth, Massachusetts, wearing a dark green jumpsuit, before the Bureau of Prisons turboprop (the *Elreno Express*, as they indeed called it) was even available. And as he shuffled up the gangway to board the plane at the local airport, hobbled and shackled, with the dozen other hobbled and shackled prisoners, he realized that the *Elreno Express* simply flew from prison to prison, taking on a few here, letting out a few there. They'd get to yours eventually, but they didn't seem to be in a hurry about it.

The *Express*'s next stop was FCI Columbia, South Carolina. There Fritz would spend five days in a holding cell in a maximum-security prison. The cell was stark and small, painted a dingy green. He was released for only two hours a day, to a bleak concrete yard that bristled with surly prisoners. One look from them made him long for the cell with its rickety bunk bed and rust-stained toilet. Almost every prisoner in the yard was black—did they send any white people to jail in South Carolina? he wondered. They stared at him with blank faces. Except for those two electrically apprehensive hours in the yard, the South Carolina days dragged slowly, ponderously, into lonely South Carolina nights. A year and a day, he mused, is going to take longer than I first thought.

Until one morning, as he lay on the bunk, a fat old cracker in a gray uniform appeared at his cell door.

"I hear you've drawn Deer Path time, Brubaker." It took just a moment to translate (*I heahyee drone Deeuh Path tom, Brubakuh*).

"That's what they told me."

"Must be your lucky day," he said. "The *Elreno Express* is back in town. Time for you to move on" (*Thale reeno spress back in tayown. Tom fuhyee t'move own*).

But the lumbering turboprop once again moved not on but farther away from where Fritz was supposed to be going. The turboprop flew west, over the Smoky Mountains, and over Tennessee, and— Damn, wasn't that the Mississippi he saw beneath the wingtip? The plane didn't put down until Springfield, Missouri. Same cell, different prison. With one important exception.

The exception's name was Steve Jessup. A blond bantam rooster from the Oklahoma panhandle, he was assigned temporarily to bunk with Fritz while, as they said, "they got his permanent assignment organized." Nervous as a hog on ice, Jessup slept about four hours a night and spent the rest of the time pacing the cell. He'd gotten the idea that Fritz's name was Bluebaker, an error Fritz didn't feel obliged to correct.

"So, what'd you *do*, anyway, Bluebaker?" Jessup kept asking as he paced.

Fritz guessed he was in his early twenties. He had thin blond hair and pale, blotchy skin and the limp outlines of a goatee around a chin that sloped softly toward his neck. But did he ever have arms. His pumped arms bulged with tattooed muscles: death's heads and screaming eagles and knives and scorpions, and right where the left biceps bulged, the open mouth of a rattlesnake. Jessup had a habit of flexing his muscles as though they had too much power and he had to release some of it. This contraction and expansion made the rattler spread its ugly jaw wider and appear to strike. Jessup had a cocky bantam strut, too. He sprang up and off his back foot as he paced, his thighs as uncontainable as his biceps.

"Securities thing," said Fritz vaguely. "You?"

Jessup nodded, not quite certain what securities were but knowing they had something to do with big business. As for him, he and two of his buddies had graduated from an apprenticeship in gas stations and convenience stores. "Me and some guys hit a bank," he said.

He tossed it off nonchalantly, in a practiced way, as if hitting banks was just something guys did, like hitting golf balls. No big deal. He strut-paced from the wall to the bars, then back.

Jessup had hit the Sun Country Bancorp branch in Guymon, Oklahoma, and thereafter enjoyed nineteen minutes of exhilaration, feeling like Jesse James himself. But in the twentieth minute he was in custody, and he'd been in custody every minute since. Although Jessup had visited county lockups in western Oklahoma since just after his eighteenth birthday, this was his first trip to a maximum-security hellhole like FCI Springfield, and that fact had him agitated.

"So where you from, Bluebaker? Where you live? You some kinda businessman?"

Fritz hesitated. "Back east," he said.

"Where exactly back east?" Spring went Jessup's stride, spring-spring to the cell door. He stopped, turned, flexed, then sprang-sprang back.

Fritz thought about Jessup showing up on the front step someday, flexing his rattlesnake biceps, and asking if Kristin might be free for the evening. "Doesn't matter," he said.

The bantam stopped pacing. "You fucking with me, Bluebaker?"

"No."

"Anybody fucks with me in this place," Jessup continued, pacing quicker now, "I'll fuck them up bad." He glared at Fritz. "You sure you ain't fucking with me?"

Fritz stared back. Jessup had reared himself up, his face now reddening. He inflated his chest so his arms didn't touch his sides. He was small, this Jessup, but he sure was pugnacious. And he had those arms. "Don't show fear," a voice told Fritz.

Fritz forced a smile.

"You fucking with me?"

"Just following orders."

"Whaddayou mean, orders?"

"Did you have a lawyer? When they sentenced you?"

The bantam glowered, pondered, decided he could answer maybe that much without being fucked with. "Yeah. 'Torney Costello. Gonna take care of that fuck the first thing I do when I get outta here. Another guy that thought he could fuck with me." He shook his head, contemplating darkly the vengeance that awaited Attorney Costello. His rattlesnake biceps seemed to hiss as the snake's mouth inflated and deflated in rapid, involuntary flexions.

Jessup looked up again. "What's that got to do with you?"

Trying to seem unruffled, Fritz carried on from his bunk. "He say not to answer questions?"

"What again?"

"The lawyer? He say you don't have to testify, don't have to answer questions?"

"Sure. What am I, stupid? I know that."

"That's what mine said, too, Jessup. So I do what I'm told. I don't answer questions." He smiled politely.

"Don't answer questions?"

"Nothing personal," Fritz explained.

Jessup considered this explanation. He strut-sprang to the bars and back. "Long as you ain't fucking with me, Bluebaker," he said.

"Wouldn't dream of it."

"It would not be advisable. No sir."

For three days Jessup paced back and forth in the cell, strut-springing and flexing, pursuing a soliloquy on his imminent cell assignment, and generally reinforcing the theme of the inadvisability of anyone fucking with him.

"And they better not 'sign me with no fuckin' Ricans, that's alls I can say, Bluebaker."

"Ricans?"

Jessup stopped and stared at Fritz. "Don't you got no Ricans where you come from?"

"What's wrong with Ricans?" Fritz asked carefully.

"What's *wrong* with fucking *Ricans*?" Jessup shook his head as he repeated the question, as if to assure himself someone had really asked him something that stupid. "What's wrong with fucking Ricans?" His whole muscled frame seemed to tremble with the inanity of it. "Can't *stand* the motherfuckers, that's what's wrong with Ricans. They 'sign me with a Rican, I'll fuck him up!"

Having explained what was wrong with Ricans, Jessup now gathered steam on the subject of other people they'd better not assign him with. Strut-springing rapidly, he allowed as how they'd better not 'sign him with no queers, Chinks, wops, kikes, dot-heads, camel jockeys, spicks, niggers, or wetbacks, neither, because if they did, Jessup would be obliged to fuck them up, too.

"And Indians," added Jessup, realizing he'd forgotten a category. "I hate fucking Indians."

"Kind of particular, aren't you?" Fritz asked.

"I don't mind micks too much," Jessup allowed.

The temporary cell to which Jessup and Brubaker had been assigned was in a row of cells along a corridor between the infirmary and block one of the prison. As Jessup pursued his argument over the course of several days, from time to time, noises were heard off in the bowels of block one—a vague clatter and the rumble of voices. This indistinct but alarming racket was unearthly, like a roar from the nearby dragon's lair to which Jessup, after this hiatus, was going to be sent. The noises always got him going. "Bluebaker, I don't fuck with nobody, nosir, but the fuckers fuck with me, I'll *fuck* them up!"

He spat out the word with a terrible gusto. But then the indistinct clatter, the distant crashes and shouts and yammering, would break out more loudly, as if the dragon had heard him and didn't take him seriously (and was fucking with him even now), and the affront would agitate Jessup even more.

By his third day at FCI Springfield, Fritz had made a curious observation. The more jittery Jessup became, the more his sobriquets began to take on a black cadence: he began to slur "motherfucker" and opted for a jive emphasis on the ultimate syllable.

"I'll fuck some muhfuckers *up*, they fuck with *me*!"

Jessup's notion of tough black jive seemed unconvincing. The combination of geography and passionate race hatred had kept him so far from any actual black people that his only source was made-for-TV movies. Jessup flexed and paced and fired off his painful clichés until he was promising a world of hurt and sorrow for any muhfuckers who even thought about fucking with him.

Came again the shouts and clatter, the roaring dragon of FCI Springfield.

"I'll fuck some muhfuckers upside the *head*," declared Jessup, pacing.

Fritz watched politely from the bunk. He felt weirdly sorry for the bantam. If anything, Jessup seemed like he was getting whiter.

Jessup was still pacing the cell when, at last, a guard appeared at the door.

"Brubaker, grab your shit, sunshine."

"The fuck?" asked Jessup. "*Bru*baker?"

"You'll stay put, son," the guard said to Jessup. The guard was black, maybe in his late forties, grizzled and broad across the chest. Soft-spoken but tough: the kind of guy bored by the Jessups of the world; the kind who, while not particularly interested in people who bored him, didn't take any shit from them, either. His voice had an authority that instantly chastened the Oklahoman.

"*Bru*baker?" Jessup tried to appeal to the guard in what he thought was his native tongue. "Muhfucker told me his name was *Blue*baker!"

"I said you stay here, son," the guard repeated.

"Fine, fine," Jessup said contritely. "Fine. I ain't fucking with nobody."

Fritz hopped down from the bunk. "Good luck, Jessup."

"Let's go," said the guard.

"Go? Where you going?"

"*Elreno Express*," said Fritz.

"The fuck's that?"

The guard led Fritz out and slammed the door. Fritz last saw Jessup clinging to the bars, flexing like mad, his biceps bulging, his rattlesnake hissing, his eyes narrowing with the recognition that he had been seriously fucked with. As the guard led Fritz down the corridor, Jessup yelled bitterly, "Muhfucker told me his name was *Blue*baker!"

Maybe. But at last Bastille Day had come. Binghamton, New York, had shown up on the itinerary of the *Elreno Express*, and Fritz was to be liberated.

AT CLUB FED, there were no high walls, no razor wire or prison yard, no gun turrets; there were no Dobermans baying for you, no searchlights plodding lazy laps at night. Deer Path sat out in the hill country of north-central Pennsylvania, separated from the surrounding dairy farms by horse fences. There was one guard shack by the entrance road.

Nobody was going to fuck with you at this place. Hell, Playtime had about as much security. Deer Path didn't even have cells.

Nevertheless, Fritz was at a penal camp, not a country club, and the first order of business in any federal institution is rebirth. They made that clear as soon as he arrived at receiving and discharge—R&D, as they called it. They took everything from him: his clothes, his wallet, his watch, $5.85, a pen, his shoes, his belt. Everything.

"You have to take my wedding ring?" Fritz asked.

"It's contraband," said the guard, a beefy fellow with a crew cut. He wore a gray uniform. C. HARDY, read the nameplate on his pocket.

"It is?"

Apparently so. C. Hardy took the ring and put it in a gray envelope with Fritz's wallet and watch, then packed the envelope in a Bureau of Prisons pouch with the shoes and belt and clothing. In place of these items, the guard handed Fritz a thin beige stack of neatly pressed prison clothes and a duffel jacket. Then he led Fritz in sock feet down a corridor to the shoe room, where they fitted him in steel-toed leather boots and a pair of cheap canvas sneakers. He would also be issued an identity card, a small toothbrush and razor, and a pen.

"You can upgrade at the com," said C. Hardy.

The com, Fritz would learn, was the commissary, a kind of prison general store, where all kinds of things were for sale, including fleece jackets, Nike sneakers, serviceable plastic watches, paperback books, magazines, and that most important obsession of the camp, food. Prisoners could establish an account with money sent in from the outside. The prices were exorbitant.

"My stuff," Fritz asked, "do I get that back when I leave?"

"Negative," said Hardy. "We ship it home. You get it there."

When Fritz had dressed and finished with R&D, Hardy packed some papers into his aluminum case with a clipboard on the top, grabbed his jacket, and led Fritz outside. Fritz followed through a quadrangle where the snow had been neatly shoveled from the paths. He was wearing his new clothes: beige khakis and shirt, prison-issue duffel coat, black leather boots.

It was midafternoon, and the light was beginning to fade. Hardy led Fritz across the quad to a large brick building about three stories high and as long as a large milking barn. A UNIT, the sign said. Fritz followed Hardy up the stairs to a landing, then through a swing door and onto a sort of balcony. It overlooked a cavernous space divided into cubicles. They didn't seem all that different from the cube spaces in the Playtime Tower.

He followed the guard down six steps and along the corridor that bisected this large room. To each side were open doorways, or entrances, rather, because there weren't any doors. They went past four or five of these, and inmates looked up as they passed. Almost all were middle-aged white guys wearing the same uniform. It was scary how much it resembled Fritz's memory of prep school.

Hardy glanced at his clipboard and stopped. "This is you," he said.

Fritz peered across the threshold into an eight-by-ten box. On the right side was a wooden bunk bed whose bottom bunk looked like it had been slept in. The top was acting as a credenza, holding stacks of papers, magazines, and journals. Along the left wall of the cube was a fiberboard module with hangers and shelf space and a built-in writing cubby on each side. And leaning into the far cubby was Fritz's cube mate.

Just as Jessup did, Fritz had worried most about that—the prospect of a cell mate. Sometimes he pictured a white supremacist with a hair trigger, a buff World Wrestling Federation castoff in sleeveless leather with a bald head and biceps like cantaloupes, hungry for violation. Sometimes it was a lean angry black, young and smoldering, with the muscles of a prizefighter, in whom two centuries of racial injustice had bubbled like molten lava and was about to explode. Fritz had, after all, seen the movies, and he'd been to Columbia and Springfield.

But Fritz's flesh-and-blood cube mate would disappoint these fears. He was a slight man of perhaps fifty-five who wore thick horn-rimmed glasses. As Fritz would discover soon enough, he did have an urge to violate his fellowman, but only conversationally.

The man had been writing when Fritz arrived, listening through headphones to a CD of the Stokowski Bach transcriptions. If this guy is in the WWF, they must have a flyweight division, Fritz thought. He introduced himself, extending his hand.

"Yes, Brubaker, I know. They told me. What are you here for?" the man asked.

Fritz gestured toward the guard. "They assigned me."

"Take the top bunk," the guard ordered. "Esperance, you'll have to clear that shit offa there. You know you're supposed to keep it in the library."

Fritz would learn that rigid hierarchies applied at FPC Deer Path. The top bunk was the lowest rank. You couldn't graduate to a lower bunk without seniority. Esperance sighed with a pained look and blinked at the guard. "Do you find there are insufficient nouns in the language?"

He did seem to have a little hostility, or at least impatience, but it wasn't the physical kind, at least.

"C'mon," said the guard.

Esperance got up and began gathering his materials from the top bunk. "Papers, sheaves, sheets, pads, notes, foolscap, journals, magazines, writings . . . it's not like there aren't words available," he mumbled.

"College professor," the guard explained to Fritz.

As he gathered his papers, Esperance renewed his question. "What was your crime, I meant?" he said.

"My crime?"

"Or perhaps I should say your mistake. You'll be encouraged here to acknowledge your mistake. Everyone's made one." The fellow had finished bundling his materials onto his cubby. He smiled ironically, then blinked, waiting for an answer. He blinked a lot, Fritz noticed.

"Johns and showers are through that way, at the end," the guard said, indicating. "TV room to the right. You can buy headphones at the com. Next count's at four. Be at your bunk for count."

"Terrible sin to miss count." Esperance shook his head. "The whole community atones."

"The professor here will show you to the cafeteria at six. A Unit eats second this week."

There would be seniority even in eating. For the sin of untidiness, A Unit had this week yielded pride of place—the five-fifteen dinner slot— to B Unit.

"Compound's closed at nine," Hardy was saying. "In the cube at ten-thirty, lights out at eleven. It's in your materials. Welcome to camp." The guard glanced at his watch and then left.

Fritz looked down at the pamphlet he'd been given in processing. Orientation, they called it. Just like prep school.

A minute later the guard returned. "Brubaker, I forgot. You got this." He opened his aluminum clipboard and withdrew a letter.

"Stock fraud?" Esperance asked.

"Excuse me?"

"Your crime. Stock fraud?"

Fritz was looking at the envelope. He recognized Kristin's hand. She had written out "Mr. Phineas A. Brubaker" in purple felt-tip marker, with a little heart over the *i*.

"I was accused—"

"No, you were convicted," Esperance corrected him. "Or you pled. Otherwise you wouldn't be here." He blinked.

All Fritz wanted to do was read the letter. "Right," he answered, a little distracted. "Ah, what was your name?"

"It was and is Gerard Wright Esperance, professor of biochemistry, University of Washington. I pleaded guilty to criminal trespass on a federal facility. I already know your name. Phineas A. Brubaker. They told me yesterday you were coming."

"Nice to meet you," Fritz said. He sat on the corner of the bed and tore open the letter.

"Ah, Brubaker . . ."

"Oh, sorry," he said, at once understanding that at Deer Path, you didn't sit on another inmate's bed, not even a college professor's. Privacy was scarce. He climbed up to the top bunk and began to read.

Dear Dad,

I'm really sorry for the way I acted the morning you left. I was sad. I love you Dad. I hope you are okay in jail. Write soon.

Love,
Kristin

p.s. Sorry I didn't kiss you goodbye and I'm kissing the letter right here XXX so if you kiss the letter then thats my goodbye kiss. Au revore (= until we meet again in French) and love Kristin.

"So, your mistake?" Esperance insisted. He had resumed his seat at the cubby and was looking up at his new cube mate, who seemed to be kissing his letter.

"Excuse me?" Fritz looked up, his eyes glistening.

"Your crime. What was your *crime*?"

"Insider trading."

"Figures," said Esperance with evident disappointment. He turned back to his writing.

ON THE WHOLE, Fritz thought, FPC Deer Path's accommodations weren't quite up to prep school. On the other hand, prep school had more psychopaths.

The cubicle walls went up five feet and then stopped, which Fritz supposed was to help them do the count. "Count" was the four P.M. head count they conducted each day. You had to be by your bunk for count, and there were no exceptions. If even one guy blew it, they'd count the whole camp again. Counts were also conducted at night, while the inmates slept, by guards using flashlights, but the big one was at four P.M. Missing count, even being in the john during count, was a big deal. It could get you a serious sanction.

Sanctions were available in great variety, to accommodate the endless resourcefulness of the inmates. At the top of the hierarchy was expulsion, which was the ultimate sanction because it meant reassignment to a real prison. It rarely happened. Beneath expulsion was the hole, an actual cell reserved for recidivist bad actors. Short of the hole lay a Byzantine litany of lesser penalties, from forfeiture of headset rights (headsets were necessary for television watching, which eliminated a huge source of noise, a real blessing) all the way down to Goose Shit Detail. Many of these lesser penalties were imposed for one variety or another of thievery. The camp trafficked heavily in stolen food, chiefly eggs, vegetables, and potatoes nicked from the cafeteria, which enterprising inmates would use to spice up microwave meals purchased at the com. Being caught with a potato, for example, would get you an afternoon of Goose Shit Detail.

The camp was laid out like a campus, with A, B, and C units; the hospital; Detox Unit; and the command center, surrounding a quadrangle and a pond. (At the far end was Detox Unit. The real source of the problem for many of Deer Path's inmates was alcoholism or drug addiction, and many would begin their stay in detox.) The pond and the neighboring lawns were home to a flock of geese whose extravagant regularity supplied light punishment for wayward inmates.

At night, lying in his bunk, Fritz could hear the guys on either side, and the guys on either side of them, and so on for about six cubes in each direction. Once the snoring kicked in, A Unit got like a symphony orchestra warming up, with trills and blats and gasps and wheezes all over the hall, some pitched for bass, others for treble, this one a toot, that a honk, the other a percussive explosion. Fritz slept in a crowd, in the morning he shaved and showered in a crowd, and three times a day, in the cafeteria, he ate in a crowd.

So mainly, Deer Path was about loss of privacy. Loss of freedom was actually less pervasive. For a man of forty-five, incarceration—of the peaceful sort—was not a wholly alien idea. Fritz had grown accustomed to thinking of long-term obligations: ten years to fledge Michael and Kristin, fifteen years to repay the mortgage, twenty until retirement. By comparison, a year-and-a-day sentence would be relatively short, almost like a retreat. A guy he vaguely remembered from Amherst had left the real estate business and joined a monastery. For men of Fritz's generation, freedom had long since devolved to a relative concept, and incarceration was one more form of obligation, different in degree but not in kind.

After lights out that first night, he lay wide awake in his top bunk. Reading the short lines from Kristin had brought relief, and the rest of the day's orientation had passed in a kind of dizzy irrelevance. He had seen showers and johns and sinks, Ping-Pong tables and basketball courts and two libraries, one with law books and one without; he'd been shown a strangely silent TV room full of beige inmates wearing headphones, a woodshop, and a cafeteria; he'd sat in a classroom and listened to a recitation of rules; he had even eaten something, although he couldn't remember and didn't much care what it was. Because he had the letter.

Two lines could blot out a lot of detail. He realized, however, that the letter didn't let on much about how Kristin was bearing up, about how any of them was bearing up. It didn't say anything at all, and this worried him. It had been a long time, he thought, almost twenty days— longer than he had ever been apart from his family before.

Below him in the darkness, oblivious to Fritz's thoughts, Esperance was speaking. It was a quiet voice that nevertheless had a sharp pedagogical tone. Esperance seemed to love statistics. "At the Hanford nuclear site, over six million gallons of medium-to-high-level U.S. nuclear munitions waste are stored in underground tanks. The half-life of the radioactive material exceeds five hundred thousand years, and contaminants in the cooling water rot through the tanks at approximately half a centimeter of material every twenty years—"

A voice sounded out in the darkness. "Good luck, Brubaker! Last guy in that cube begged for the hole!"

Laughter in the darkness. Esperance ignored it.

"Another half a million gallons of material has been transferred to HICs—so-called high-integrity containers, although the name is a gross misnomer. Neither DOE nor USEC nor any of the other agencies has any credible plans for dealing with that material. The HICs are not high integrity in any meaningful sense, given the half-life of the materials they contain. They will probably outlive the political career of all current congressmen, but they will not outlast the lifetimes of your children. At Cal Tech, they have done studies about the decay rates of the stainless-steel alloys currently in use, and the findings extrapolated to significant degradation at fifty years—"

Another voice: "Esperance, you're killing us!"

Laughter.

"No, your ignorance will take care of that," the professor responded evenly.

"Just nuke me now!" someone shouted.

More laughter in the darkness. Whoever had been snoring before must have awakened to join it.

They didn't slow Esperance down. He cited statistic after statistic about the compromise of the aquifers in eastern Washington, the inevitable contamination of the environment, the millions of people exposed to the Columbia River watershed, the effects of radioactivity on childhood development, the government's refusal to acknowledge any reliable studies—which is to say, Esperance's studies.

The blinking professor had led a class of undergraduates from Seattle in his Volkswagen microbus to conduct a sit-in at the Hanford nuclear munitions–treatment facility in eastern Washington State. It was his third trip to Hanford, and the feds had lost patience with him, so he was serving an eighteen-month sentence for criminal trespass.

Fritz would see over the course of the next few weeks that Esperance wasn't so unusual: the inmates at Deer Path were an eclectic mix. There were various prisoners of conscience: criminal trespassers, Unitarian ministers who'd staged sit-ins at military bases or the Pentagon, one or two of the legalize-marijuana crowd. There were a few counterfeiters. There was a judge. Marshall, a peppy young kid, had run an identity-theft ring. He worked in the Dow Chemical mail room, stealing checks, depositing them into DBA accounts. Then there were the Wall Street guys, who looked vaguely familiar from the newspapers. In the cafeteria one day, Fritz met Jerry Plotkin—*the* Jerry Plotkin, who'd been extradited from Switzerland after bilking millions from an elaborate investment scam. There was even comic relief: a crazed Czech who was in for manufacturing drug paraphernalia and kept up a vain crusade to line up support for a hunger strike.

That first night Fritz lay awake on his top bunk for what seemed like hours, thinking of Linda and the kids. It had begun, whatever he'd been waiting for. His atonement. Esperance's voice faded to background music, and faded some more, and at last passed out of Fritz's consciousness.

THE KIDS were off at school, and Linda sat alone at the kitchen counter, staring at the package. Discordant music was playing on the radio: the classical station was well into its late-morning program list, and the music wasn't helping Linda's mood. It had been an extremely trying morning. After car-pool lane, she'd gone down to the Dover post office and endured a ghastly public humiliation. You would think the postal staff would have been trained to behave discreetly and professionally, but no. "Never seen one of *these* before," the clerk said as he handed over the box. He might as well have shouted it out—there were three other people in line, and they all stared at the screaming BUREAU OF PRISONS stamps on Linda's box as she hurried from the window. As if the clerk hadn't been mortifying enough, who should have picked that precise moment to walk into the post office but Anne Shermerhorn, the biggest gossip in town. Anne set up a blockade in front of the door. She was *so* glad to see Linda, and had been *so* worried about her, and *hoped* she was doing all right, and *promised* to call her so that they could get together and talk, and had *heard* her house was on the market, her eyes all the while darting greedily to the red-stamped box in Linda's hands.

Linda had practically run to the car.

Alone in the Palazzo, she'd tried to calm herself with a cup of tea, but it wasn't working. Which of Anne's dozen committees was hearing about the box this morning? It sat on the counter, mocking her.

The Shrill Small Voice commented, "He's gone a week, and not even one phone call. They can call collect, you know."

Linda took a sip and rubbed her forehead. The real estate agent had scheduled a showing at eleven, which meant that she had to have the house immaculate by ten-forty-five. She'd better get this over with.

Inside the box she found a pile of folded clothing. His pants, his shirt, his parka, and underneath, his shoes. She rooted farther into the box. Was that it? Was he sending home laundry? She hunted—surely there must be a note—and discovered a gray envelope at the bottom of the box. But when she opened it, she found that it contained no letter, either. Just Fritz's wallet, loose change, key chain, watch, and . . .

"Charming," said the Voice.

Linda's face darkened. Her hands were shaking. This was the last straw. After fourteen years, this box was how he was going to do it? Without a call, without a note, without warning, without even a word of explanation, he'd just sent home his wedding ring in an envelope?

Later that afternoon, Linda went to Barnes & Noble and bought a

book on the nuts and bolts of divorce law, and six others on its psychological dimensions.

ON FRITZ'S FIFTH DAY at Deer Path, a Saturday, he was having lunch at
one when a guard came and found him in the cafeteria.

"You've got a visitor."

"Really?" Fritz put down his tuna sandwich.

"Relax," the guard said. "She's filling out the forms. You can finish
your lunch."

But Fritz couldn't. It had been a long time: almost a month. Fritz
hadn't seen Linda since the morning she'd left him standing in front of
the Moakley Courthouse. He hurried out of the cafeteria and across the
quad to the visitors' room, which was on the south side of the command
center, whose glass-fronted turret rose up like an airport tower.

The actual visitors' room would disappoint another preconception,
which had to do with Plexiglas and microphones. The reality was more
like a high school cafeteria, furnished with small Formica tables and plastic cafeteria chairs, and surrounded by soda machines and a hamburger-
and-hot-dog grill. The guard led Fritz in, and he sat alone at a table, and
other lucky inmates came and went to other tables. The wives, the girl-
friends, and the mothers with little children filed in to find their men
and take them by the hand, to embrace, to small-talk.

This was better, much better. He wanted to hold Linda, at least to
feel her hand again. He began composing things he wanted to ask her
about when all of a sudden—

"Dude, you look terrible."

Ronnie leaned over and gave him a peck on the cheek.

She stood over him like a cocky waitress, sure of her order. But she
was dressed much more formally: she'd worn a pale blue blouse, and a
white sweater with cream-colored buttons, and a long skirt of dark blue
wool. Like she might have worn to church. Only a single earring adorned
each ear. She sat down and reached across the table, gave his hands a
squeeze, then settled back into her seat very correctly. "You not getting
too much sun here?"

"Ronnie," he said. He smiled at her, wondering if she sensed his disappointment. He didn't want to be rude.

"Surprised?"

"Ah, yeah. A little."

"Disappointed?"

"No . . . no," he lied.

"They treating you all right?"

He nodded. "Yeah, sure." He looked around at the array of vending machines. "You want something?"

"No, thanks."

"Like an arcade here," he said. "I had no idea. Thought they'd have Plexiglas."

She brightened. "Am I your first visitor?"

He nodded.

"It's only a year, Fritz. You have to remember that," she said. "You have to take it a day at a time, okay?"

"Right," he said. "I know."

"So how is it? How's the deer camp?"

He hadn't expected to see her again. That night at the Waldorf was so surreal that it hadn't even been filed in the history section of his memory. As though it never happened. She looked pretty, he thought. Older. It was good to look at a woman up close again, to catch her scent faintly. She was not in costume, like she had been in December. On the other hand, maybe for her this was more of a costume. Had she dressed this way to try to please him?

Ronnie forged ahead with conversation, although she wasn't getting much help. "You have to admit, for a prison, this isn't so bad. They were very nice in the whatever you call it—reception area? They did lecture me about not bringing in any . . ."

"Contraband?"

"Yeah."

He nodded. "They have a thing about contraband."

"Well, I didn't bring any. This time." She smiled.

Ronnie kept up a battery of relentlessly cheerful questions, undeterred by his silence. She reached across the table and squeezed his hand again. "It's nice around here, the countryside, I mean. Pretty hills and farms with the snow on them. Did you notice when you drove in? Who brought you here, Linda?"

Linda? he thought. Not exactly. He looked up and caught Ronnie's eye. She shifted gears.

"Saul Herzog wants to sue the officers and directors," Ronnie said.

"Saul Herzog?"

"You know, that lawyer in the bankruptcy. The one with the silk suspenders and the matching handkerchief? He wants to sue all of them, Greene, Jellicoe, the directors, the accountants, everybody. Mel's crazy with it because he wants to sue them first."

Oh yeah, he thought, Playtime. That one *had* been filed in the history section. Ancient history.

Although it was a cold February afternoon, the visitors' room was a little warm. Ronnie unbuttoned her sweater and placed it carefully on the back of the chair. At some of the neighboring tables, heads turned. Fritz felt a tingle.

She told him some more about the Playtime news, and Mel Popotkus, and the rumors that Greene had backed some other syndicate to buy the company out of bankruptcy. Ronnie tried to get Fritz interested in it all, but it was like overhearing a conversation in an airport in a foreign language. Whatever it is, he thought, it just can't be that important.

As Ronnie went on about the latest hijinks in the bankruptcy court, he remembered a story he'd seen just the other day in *The New York Times.*

"I read that senator died," he said.

"Oldcastle. Yeah, he was pretty sick. Forty years an alcoholic. It blew up on him all at once, I guess."

"I can't believe that."

"It wasn't your fault."

It didn't seem like it could have been, but on the other hand, what good had come of his being such a smart-ass? Of all his so-called principles?

Ronnie seemed to read his mind. "Listen, Fritz, you were right about the guy. He was just chasing cameras. He didn't care about Playtime or its shareholders. He was reading a script his staff had written him, and you were right to call him on it."

He didn't respond.

"So you're sure everything's okay?" she asked at the end of the hour. "I guess that's a dumb question, huh?"

"No. Not dumb. Sorry. I'm fine. It was nice of you to visit. Really."

She had to go. They stood and she hugged him, hard. He responded limply, embarrassed by the attention. He knew he should hug back, but on the other hand, he also knew he shouldn't. "It's all right," she said. "It's all right."

THE ABSOLUTE SOMETHING-OR-OTHER RULE

ALL THROUGH FEBRUARY, the New York lawyers had been telling Peter Greene they had to get together to discuss a plan of reorganization to take Playtime out of bankruptcy. Everyone was nervous. First Playtime had filed, and then Global Crossing, and then Enron, and every day brought rumors of more shoes to drop. The media was raising hell about the SEC, and the SEC was raising hell about accounting, and each Monday it seemed like somebody else's books turned out to be inflated. The markets had tanked. The lawyers needed to get this case reorganized quickly, they were saying, before the creditors got too skittish. Already there was talk from Saul Herzog of kicking out management and bringing in a bankruptcy trustee. That would spoil everything and get everybody sued.

As Peter Greene took the anxious calls on the ninth floor of the Playtime Tower in Burlington, he had a more immediate problem. Micah Fensterwald, the company's bankruptcy lawyer, wanted a meeting in New York, but how would Peter get to New York? The banks had taken away the corporate jet. What was Peter supposed to do, go to Logan Airport? Where God knows who might see him, reduced to shameful penury, enduring the snaking security lines to ride the Delta shuttle? Was Peter Greene supposed to hail a cab at La Guardia? It was unthinkable.

"Micah," Greene had explained, "we're very busy here at the company, and I'm not sure how much time I can carve out for this meeting."

The banks hadn't taken away Peter Greene's car service, so he could still travel from home to office without humiliation. So instead of Peter going to New York, six lawyers and four financial advisers agreed to come up to Burlington, at a net additional cost in airfare and billable hours of approximately $22,000.

The other problem wasn't so easily solved. It emerged three days later, as Micah's junior partners stood at one end of the vast slab of New Hampshire granite that served as the table in the boardroom on the ninth floor of the Playtime Tower. They were going through the blue and green PowerPoint slides, laying out the proposed bankruptcy plan, explaining what would be given to the banks, what to the bondholders, what to the taxing authorities and trade vendors and so on, how the exit financing would work. The bubbles and arrows and graphics multiplied on the screen.

Peter Greene drummed his fingers on the granite slab. Finally, he said, "Look, Micah, I've got eighteen percent of this company. I didn't hear what provision was made for that."

The junior partners down at the end of the room stopped talking.

Micah was an articulated man, very tall and thin, and configured mainly of elbows and knees and ankles. He had a long face, the slender fingers of a pianist, and the distracted air of a philosophy professor. Chairs didn't accommodate him well; his joints shot out at unusual angles. Even at the height of the dot-com bubble, he had not succumbed to the tyranny of dress-down. He liked navy suits with a wide chalk stripe, and he kept the suit jackets on even when seated, so that they rode up his arms and gathered at his shoulders.

He was holding his fingertips together at his lips, staring down the long fingers at the polished granite slab, his forehead wrinkled in thought. At length he nodded to one of his partners, who flipped the lights back on. Then he leaned back in his chair.

"That eighteen percent was before bankruptcy, Peter. If you don't pay the creditors what they're owed, the original shareholders can't get anything. Unless we can invoke the new value corollary to the absolute priority rule."

Sitting across the table, flanked by his colonels, Larry Jellicoe and Don Fink, Peter Greene didn't think "shareholders" quite captured the importance of his contribution. It seemed dismissive. This was his company, wasn't it? He turned to Don. "You familiar with this rule? Absolute . . . what was it?"

Fink nodded vigorously to demonstrate his familiarity with the rule, whose name he was trying to remember. "Absolute, er . . . value rule, Peter. The absolute value rule. But I believe there are some exceptions that Micah can tell us about. Micah?"

"Exceptions?" Greene leaned forward. That sounded promising.

Micah smiled. "Actually, there's been a scholarly debate about an exception to the absolute priority rule for over fifty years—"

"Priority," Don Fink said. "Meant to say that. Absolute *priority* rule."

Micah continued, "There is—or there isn't, depending on which scholar you subscribe to—something called the new value exception to the absolute priority rule. Actually, it's more accurate to refer to it as a new value corollary, because . . ."

And the long lean lawyer was off, leaping from his gate like a racehorse. One of Micah's favorite things was to talk about the absolute priority rule, and the new value exception, or corollary, to the absolute priority rule, and whether it existed, or didn't exist, or might exist, or should exist. He always began with the nineteenth-century railroad decisions and proceeded to the footnote in Justice Douglas's *Case* v. *Los Angeles Lumber* opinion, then paged through judicial snapshots, lingering over each case with the loving attention of a young mother showing off her firstborn's album. The rule went right to the heart of corporate finance, right to the enduring struggle between debt and equity, between the owners and the owed. Nothing suited Micah better than a good seminar about the new value corollary to the absolute priority rule, and he occasionally confused client meetings with seminars. As he was doing now, leaning back in his chair while, right across the massive slab of granite, Peter Greene got more and more steamed.

Greene stared out the window. Tap-tap went his fingers on the tabletop. This absolute whatever-it-was was drowning him in needless detail. He tried a pained smile, but that didn't seem to slow the lawyer down. The meeting had been late getting started, because one of the $650-per-hour financial advisers had missed his flight. They weren't under way until past eleven. Now it was well after twelve, and the ninth-floor kitchen staff (who somehow had emerged unscathed from the January layoffs) had been in to heap the credenza with platters of designer sandwiches half wrapped delicately in wax paper, and designer water and bowls of elegant rotini. The $650-per-hour financial guys, and the $450- and $550-per-hour lawyers already were sneaking glances at the spread. Greene himself had to be in a car at one-thirty if he was going to make his two o'clock. He looked for an opening, a pause in the delivery, a natural cutoff point. Finally he lost patience.

"I don't care about that."

Micah had just arrived at the question of Justice Souter's jurisprudence in the *North LaSalle Street* case, really one of the most fascinating chapters of the whole saga. "I'm sorry, Peter?"

"I . . . don't . . . care . . . about . . . that . . . absolute corollary . . . thing. Or whatever it is. Okay?"

Micah was taken aback. Not care about *North LaSalle Street*? About the underpinnings of Justice Souter's analysis?

Apparently not. Because Peter looked like a guy stuck in the slowest line at the tollbooth. "Listen," Peter said, "let's get to *my* priority value . . . thing. I've got a company to run. I've got a lot of expensive guys from New York sitting in my boardroom, and I have other things to do." (Specifically, he had to meet his wife, Bunny, and the historic-reproduction contractor at two o'clock to talk about the kitchen remodeling, and it had taken almost three weeks to get this meeting.)

"So let's get to my priority, which is to understand how you guys plan to protect my eighteen percent. Let's get to that."

The PowerPoint speakers remained silent. The financial guys looked over at the lawyers, and the lawyers looked over at Micah. Micah looked down the length of his long fingers again.

The great bankruptcy guru considered whether Greene needed a gentle reminder that Micah's client was the company, not Peter, and that it was not Micah's job to protect Peter's 18 percent. Then he reflected further on the $6 million in attorneys' fees he had budgeted for the first year of the Playtime bankruptcy alone, and the fact that the CEO still had the nominal power to hire and fire the company's lawyers, and he decided there was no need to embarrass Greene publicly. They could talk about it later.

"How do you keep your eighteen percent, Peter? We could start with paying the creditors."

"What do you mean, paying the creditors?"

"Pay the creditors in full. Then the shareholders keep the company."

"It would kill the model," piped up one of the $650-per-hour financial men.

"No room in the projections," added a $450-per-hour assistant.

"Yeah," said Greene. "Pay them with what?" He shot a sharp glance at Fink. This Micah Fensterwald wasn't making any sense. Greene had trusted Fink to get the right guy to handle the situation, and Fink had come up with a professor type from New York who had some kind of obsession with the absolute value rule, or the absolute rule of priority, or whatever it was called. And here he was suggesting they pay the creditors. In full!

"Micah, you can't pay the creditors on these numbers." Greene gestured at the fifty-page handout Larry Jellicoe had distributed. "Right, Larry?"

"No, you'd have to adjust the model. There isn't room in there to pay them more than about fifteen cents on the dollar, and to be frank, these numbers are on the aggressive side."

"Aggressive" was a Wall Street euphemism, generally employed where other streets would use a synonym like "bullshit." The investment bankers had prepared lots of projections, and the spreadsheets looked nifty, but they had fine print in there that said it was all based on what the company told them. Which was aggressive. That is to say, bullshit.

The chorus line of financial advisers was nodding. Definitely on the aggressive side. Full of aggression, these projections. The financial guys had charged hundreds of thousands of dollars for the projections, and had the name of their firm printed on the lower right-hand corner of every page, but they wanted one thing clear: these weren't *their* projections.

"Right," said Peter, "so let's be a little more practical about this, Micah, all right?" Greene shot another glance at Fink, as if to say, "I trusted you to get someone *practical*, for Chrissakes."

Micah was unmoved. "You asked how you keep the company, I'm telling you the ways you keep the company. The first way is the company pays the creditors. The second way, which may or may not work, is you make a contribution of new value, and we shop it to the marketplace to see if someone else will offer more."

"What do you mean, 'new value'?"

"I mean money, Peter."

"*Cash?*"

There was an awkward silence at the intrusion of this rude concept. The junior partners looked at the financial team. The financial guys stared longingly at the bowls of rotini, wondering if a call to lunch might disperse the unpleasantness. These were Wall Streeters: people who paid for things with convertible subordinated debentures. That was one of the beauties of bankruptcy. You could use all kinds of PIK notes, warrants, and stock to deal with people. (The one exception to this commendable flexibility was the lawyers, who had to be paid in cash.) Creditors would be given fine print, all of which came down to one thing: we'll pay you later. Sometimes much later. With interest being earned (but not actually paid—the polite word was "accrued") until later came. So throwing around tacky concepts like cash was unsettling. And besides, they were hungry.

But cash was precisely what the New York lawyer meant. This guy who was the head of Pladd and Tweed, and wore a chalk-stripe suit, and was supposed to be on Peter's side! "Not promises, not notes, not borrowings, not guaranties," Micah said, his scolding index finger aloft. "Money. Real honest-to-goodness money. The idea is, you give the company some new capital, you get stock."

"I already *have* stock!"

Micah smiled but shook his head. "That's old stock," he said.

Greene shot another eye dagger toward Don Fink. *Old* stock? After all Peter had done for Playtime, his own lawyer wanted him to buy new stock? After all he'd suffered? "You're suggesting," he said, "that I put more money into this company when I've already lost—how much is it, Larry?"

Jellicoe looked a little lost himself. It sounded like Peter was asking how much he had invested in Playtime when he had not in fact invested anything. Peter had pulled down over $8 million in salary and cashed out options worth over $65 million.

"I'm sorry, Peter?"

"My vested options."

"Oh," said Larry. By "lost," Peter meant how much more might he have cashed out in options had the price held. "About two hundred million in options," Larry said.

"Look, Peter, my job is to tell you what the rules are. You don't like the rules . . ." Micah shrugged. "Call your congressman. The exception says the contribution has to be money. You want the equity, you put in money."

"There must be another way."

Micah rubbed his long fingers along the side of his face. He stared at the ceiling, thinking. At the other end of the room, eyes were drawn to the credenza. Mr. $650-per-hour's stomach gnawed at him. He spotted a roast-beef-and-Boursin wrap that seemed to be puckering at him lasciviously. Ms. $450-per-hour had her eye on the tomato-pesto-and-mozzarella wrap.

"We might try to be creative. But there are no guaranties here, Peter. Saul Herzog is already screaming for a trustee."

"Does he want a trustee?"

"No. He wants money. Like everyone else." Micah sighed. It was always the same in bankruptcy. Everybody wanted money and there wasn't enough.

"Let's be creative, then," said Peter. "Guys, I pay you a lot of money to be creative, so let's be creative. Why don't you carry on with the plan. Have some lunch and kick around the creative thing. I have a meeting to get to. Larry, I'll catch up with you tonight."

AWAY to the southwest, in Deer Path, Pennsylvania, Veronica Pettibone had another kind of priority. In her mind, it was no less absolute.

She strode into the visitors' center as she had on that first Saturday afternoon, with a brisk cheeriness. She was like a nurse determined to cure the patient by brute jollity alone. She'd dressed in the same oddly formal way. Before Deer Path, there'd been only that one day of the winter solstice, so it wasn't as though Fritz knew much about how she usually appeared. But it didn't seem natural to see her in wool trousers, a turtleneck, and a Fair Isle sweater. It seemed altogether preppy. She sat primly on the plastic chair. There was no belly pie on view, but still, she turned heads.

She also spoke too loudly. It made Fritz hunch down at the table. But this time, he thought, it was good to see her. He'd been thinking about it all week. He'd even pressed his prison chinos back at the prison laundry this morning, put a nice crease down the front.

"You want something?" he asked. "Coffee, a burger, anything?"

"No, thanks," she said, "I'm fine."

"Finest in prison food," he said. "I've got my Deer Path Visa." He held up his ID card, which they could swipe at the com, or here, to access his account.

"Dude, it's cool. Sit."

Two hours passed in animated conversation. He told her about Esperance, and Goose Shit Detail, and the count. "They make you stand by your bed and count heads," she asked, "when they don't even have a wall around this place?" He answered: "At least it's honest accounting. They don't accrue inmates, or expense them, or footnote them, or pull any of the usual accounting tricks. They count heads. Nine hundred fifty-two heads equals nine hundred fifty-two inmates. Not one more, not one less." That kind of straightforward accounting was refreshing to him now.

She had rented a car in New York. It was a six-hour drive. That was pretty impressive math, when Fritz thought about it. Twelve hours in a car just to visit him? Linda certainly hadn't made the drive. She hadn't even written. They sparred, they even laughed. That was *fun*, he thought afterward, as he trudged along the icy walk back to A Unit.

THEY HAD PUT Fritz to work in the camp laundry, operating the steam presses on the sheets and towels, and running the inmate and guard uniforms through the huge drum washers. He was paid fifteen cents an hour. It was hot work, and dull, but once you got the hang of the machine, not difficult. They told him if he did a good job, he might be able to go on outside release when summer came, mowing grass.

"Many of the inmates prefer mowing," Esperance explained. "Operating the big riding mowers gives them the illusion of power."

"That what you do?"

"No," he answered, "I requisition plumbing supplies for the maintenance department. I'm afraid mowing would excite my allergies."

Spring seemed a long way off to Fritz as he walked to the camp laundry each morning. The laundry lay across the quadrangle from A Unit, past the cafeteria and the asphalt basketball courts, on the other side of the six-lane running track. They had a heavy snowfall that winter, and his duffel coat provided little protection against the cold.

By early March the snow began to melt. When the track reappeared, Fritz developed a routine during the hour after count and before dinner. He'd stretch, jog a few miles, then run some sprints. Quite often Marshall was there, stretching, jogging a few laps. Marshall always seemed sunny.

"Brubaker, you slow, man. No hope for you!" He'd laugh.

"I'm an old-timer, Marshall."

"You ready for the wheelchair, man. I could get you some vitamin supplements from the infirmary or something."

"You could?"

"Yeah. Just give me your social!" Marshall laughed and ran on.

Fritz demurred. Marshall's check-cashing scam, he'd proudly confessed, required not much more than small banks and borrowed social security numbers.

South of the running track, the ground gave way to field, which rolled gently down to a pasture fence. When the snow receded, a few flower beds reappeared beyond the track, with frozen rosebushes and stalks of peony. Beyond them stood a stand of maples that would, in the summer, give shade to a cluster of picnic tables. Except when the weather was really bad, Fritz tried to spend a few minutes each day at the picnic table farthest from the track. He'd sit with a newspaper or a magazine under the bare tree. He'd return to his picnic table to study the tree, its stepladder branches and silky gray bark. He waited, as spring came on, for the tree to bud out.

It grew warmer. Spring arrived. Each evening in his cube, Fritz would finish the letters he'd started that morning. Writing in longhand was something he hadn't done since college. He usually wrote a letter to Linda and one to the kids. Sometimes he wrote separate letters to Michael and to Kristin. It was a little hard to concentrate, because it was in the evenings that Professor Esperance got rolling on the nuclear-waste problem.

"One hundred seventy-seven tanks, rotting in the earth, within two and one half miles of the Columbia River watershed!" he'd say. "One of the great American rivers! And do you know how many people live within the Columbia River watershed?"

Esperance did. He knew a lot of other useful facts, too. Fritz had made the mistake, early, of mentioning to Esperance that people in the East didn't hear that much about Hanford.

"It is amazing, shocking, that people do not know what Hanford is," Esperance answered. "How can we mobilize real action when nobody even knows what it is?"

By March Fritz knew that it had been the site of the nation's largest plutonium factory, originally developed during the Manhattan Project. There they made the key ingredient to nuclear weapons, but the by-product of plutonium manufacture was low-to-medium-level radio-active waste. Now the factory was shut down, leaving behind over six million gallons of waste in underground tanks. At first they said the tanks would never leak. Then the local towns started picking up levels of cesium and iodine-131 in the local aquifers.

"The Department of Energy talks about cleaning it up," said Esperance. "But all they do is talk. And chase will-o'-the-wisps. The latest thing is this vitrification business. They've hired a big engineering firm to turn it all into glass, ship it to Yucca Mountain in Nevada. It'll never work. Don't they know glass breaks?"

At night Fritz turned in early, lying in his top bunk, while most of the guys were off watching television. When it got dark, sometimes he'd start to think about sex, but it was hard to do that with the biology professor lecturing him about the imminent end of the world, and half a dozen other guys making a racket like a class of kindergartners sawing violins. Deer Path saltpeter, Fritz called it. The other niggling problem was making out the face of his imaginary lover, which always faded into shadow.

ON A MAPLE BRANCH about twelve feet from the ground, in a tree near the tables, a single yellowed leaf had survived autumn and winter and clung to a twig right through March, even after the first red buds appeared. Each afternoon Fritz would look for it and, finding it, wonder what would happen when the branches budded fully. In a breeze, it would whirl around the branch, first one way, then the other. But it never blew off. How long would the leaf last?

One sunny afternoon early in April, Fritz sat beneath the tree with the latest issue of *Sail Magazine*. The idea of sailing away was an enticing one during that spring of 2002, but the magazine's technical articles also kept his mind busy. He was reading an article about techniques in sail design for maximizing the airfoil. Sails had always fascinated him, the way they used wind to create shape, shape to create lift, and lift to move a heavy object across the water. All that weight in a boat, yet the lift created by the passage of air across a curved cloth could generate enough power to move it. The physics of wind weren't so remarkable when the winds were strong (no one who'd ever been out on Nantucket Sound in a big blow doubted the power of strong winds). What always struck Fritz, as a sailor, was what a sail did when winds were light. Right above the point of calm (where a sail lost its shape and ceased to function), at the level of breeze that could fill a sail, that sail would power a boat—which, after all, weighed thousands of pounds. This had always amazed Fritz—how you might go out to the saltwater ponds on an afternoon when the wind was barely noticeable ashore, and before you knew it, the sails on the sloop bellied out, the hull began to heel, and off you went.

He was thinking about this when a fluttering distracted him overhead. It was the yellowed leaf up in the maple, still clinging, whirling about its twig. As he watched, it blew off.

One determined leaf, one sail, as it were, up in the tree, where the best wind was . . .

And that was when Fritz Brubaker came up with an absolute priority of his own. Jim Feeney hadn't been able to design a propeller that would work in a class-two wind zone. But a sailboat could sail in six knots of wind. Who ever saw a sailboat with a propeller attached to its mast?

The next morning, when Fritz presented his request, it seemed like an odd shopping list. The assistant warden studied it and even asked to know what the components of an anemometer were. "Will it fit in your locker?" he asked. Each inmate had a locker next to his cubby. Most were used to store food and commissary soap.

"My locker?" Fritz thought about it. "Yeah, why?"

"Contraband," the warden said. "If it isn't locked, it gets stolen, knocked down, the bits and pieces sold. What are you going to use this for again?"

Fritz explained it a second time. The assistant warden still looked skeptical.

"It's a rehabilitative purpose," said Fritz, who'd read the regulations. "It's vocational. I'll be prohibited from another finance job when I leave here."

"So you planning on being a weatherman?"

"No. I'm going to design sails."

There was one dilemma for him: to whom should he send the list? If he sent it to Ronnie, she'd have the items back to him by return mail. Yet it seemed to him that making the request of her might be as big a betrayal as he'd committed. In the end, he sent it to Linda, who decided, on review, that her husband really had gone nuts. An anemometer? Handkerchiefs? Model airplanes? A sewing kit? Tinker Toys? But then came another letter, and another and another. So she bought the items and sent them in a big box to FPC Deer Path.

On May 21, the box arrived and was inspected, and that afternoon Fritz got busily to work. Almost from the beginning, his project attracted attention, and other inmates would come by the picnic table to watch him building his foot-tall Tinker towers. At the apex of the first tower, he used aircraft glue to affix a propeller to a dowel. The dowel turned a wooden donut. Into the donut he'd carved a groove, and in the groove he ran a string loop that connected to a second donut suspended loosely from another dowel. To the dowel end he could add more donuts for more weight. Next to this contraption he placed the anemometer. By counting rotations and varying the weight of the donut axle, he could measure the turning power of the propeller-driven dowel at various wind speeds.

Fritz built a second Tinker tower, identical in all ways but one. Affixed to the top was not a propeller but a rig built of a hub and three dowel spokes. From these spokes Fritz hung three tiny sails.

He wasn't looking for much of a breeze. He wanted just the opposite—winds between five and twelve miles per hour, the power of the class-two wind zone, which happened to encompass most of Massachusetts and Connecticut. Deer Path was right in the middle of one. When there was a light breeze, Fritz took a reading from the anemometer. If it was within class two, he set up his contraptions on the picnic table. He had some trouble with the sail rigging (which was only thread) but, after some trial and error, devised a system of tiny sheets that worked well enough. At his picnic-table observatory, Fritz made careful observations in a notebook. He reengineered his Tinker sails several times, trying to develop constants as to propeller and sail weights. He recorded pages and pages of data and, at night, in his cube, studied and tabulated the results onto graph paper.

What most interested Fritz was the performance of the contraptions at the lowest wind speeds. He knew that his controls were rough and unscientific, but the results he tabulated were dramatic. A low wind would turn both the sails and the propeller, but at wind speeds between five and ten miles per hour, the sail turbine generated almost twice the power of the propeller.

THE SAILS were slowly spinning, the cups on top of the anemometer revolving in a light June breeze. He'd been taking down readings in his notebook, wondering whether he should belly the sails more, when he looked up to see the professor approaching.

"Planning a career as a weatherman? You've got the looks for it," Esperance said dismissively.

Fritz smiled. "You know, Gerard, you should lighten up a little."

Esperance harrumphed. "What do you think you're going to accomplish with all that?"

"Gonna power the suburbs."

Esperance stood in the chilly sunshine, blinking. "A noble goal."

Fritz stopped the apparatus and removed one of the sails. He unwound the thread. "I think we're slipping wind at this corner," he said. He looked up at the professor. "Gotta grab all the wind you can."

Esperance seemed vexed. "Even if you reduced household dependence on fossil fuels, that would represent less than twelve percent of the usage. Out in Hanford, one tank alone could represent—"

"Gerard," Fritz interrupted, "it's not going to clean up any tank waste to be mad about it. Some of us tilt at dragons, and some at windmills." Fritz smiled and unfurled his sail on the Tinker mast.

"Well, it's all very well to talk," said Esperance. "What's needed is *action*."

THEY WERE in the visitors' center again, on the last Saturday afternoon in June. Fritz seemed distant. And thinner. It had been five months. Ronnie leaned across the table and took his hand. "How's the family, Fritz? The kids?"

He didn't answer. When he thought about the family, it was often to valedictions that his mind turned. Valedictions such as "Best wishes, Michael Brubaker," which was how Michael had closed the three lines that constituted the only letter he'd sent to his father.

There had been maybe a dozen letters from Kristin, each in a different felt-tip marker, and these were the best valedictions. Smiley faces. Hearts. "I love you" with three underlines. The letters reported, in a kid's reassuring diction, on the breaking news. Shea had been returned to Mr. Feeney, and Kristin had actually biked over from Wellesley to check up on him. (That's a six-mile ride, Fritz thought. Good for her!) The goat was doing fine. However, he'd gotten out of his paddock into Farm Street and jumped up onto the neighbor's car. This was a problem because the car was a convertible, and Shea didn't realize this until too late, and he put a hoof through the top when the lady screamed. It wasn't his fault—the neighbors should have left the top down, but the neighbors were still upset. There was a new petition. Michael, too, had committed various high crimes and misdemeanors. School had ended, thank God, and Field Day was hot and boring except they would have won the relay race if Myra hadn't fallen down. Ms. Potemkin was going to be Kristin's lead teacher, although Kristin felt Ms. Potemkin ill suited for the demands of the seventh grade. Alison didn't invite Michelle to her sleepover.

And so on.

When Fritz received news of this kind, he would lean back against the silvery maple, shutting his eyes tightly and trying to remember the Alisons and Michelles, but often he couldn't.

Kristin's most recent letter had arrived the day before, bringing with it the best valediction yet:

I MISS YOU DADDY!!!

Love,
Kristin (aka Peanut)

p.s. don't get in any trouble that puts you in the "cooler" or lets them keep you in jail for longer.

p.p.s. 219 days and counting!

"Daddy" again, he thought.

But the matter of valedictions was most ambiguous when it came to the four letters he'd received from Linda. There had been one in late February, brief, correct, acknowledging receipt of his clothes, giving him the address of the Wellesley house she was going to rent starting April 1, and passing on other news in a clipped, businesslike way. Months went by before her next correspondence, but that was simply a cover note explaining the extreme inconvenience to which she had been put coming up with his package of Tinker Toys. Another letter had come a month or so ago. He had read and reread every line of this single piece of paper, searching it for nuance like a spy hunting for invisible ink. But Linda remained severely correct. Again she reported the news in a businesslike manner; she passed on the results of a doctor's visit and the final report cards; she summarized the negotiations for closing the Palazzo sale (sale of the Palazzo—Jesus! It was hard to think about, even for him). The letter went on to advise that his signature would be necessary on the deed, and he wondered with a sinking heart whether that was why she'd written. Her letter simply ended without a valediction. As if she didn't want to face the issue at all. Just "Linda." Your wife, Linda? Your lover, Linda? Your fond Linda? Your forgiving Linda? Your business partner Linda? Your correspondent Linda? Your implacably pissed-off Linda? It was a mystery. You'd have thought she could be more direct about what she was thinking. Was that too much to ask of her when he was stuck at Club Fed?

Ronnie was saying something that he hadn't heard. He looked up, confused.

"You were daydreaming."

"I'm sorry." He lowered his eyes.

"If you don't want to talk about it, I understand."

"I don't," he acknowledged. "Let's talk about something else."

In his tone was a hint of sullenness. She caught but ignored it, to keep everything upbeat. "Okay. I've been going to Delaware a lot, to watch the fun. More fights with that lawyer for the bond committee.

The company won't sue its own directors and officers, so Herzog's made some motions to the judge to let *him* do it. The judge doesn't know what to do. He keeps having more hearings, and—"

Fritz interrupted, "So Ronnie, why are you here?"

The sharpness of the question took her aback. "Because . . . just because."

"Need more dirt for Mel Popotkus?"

It stunned her. The blood drained from her face, and she tried to say something, but nothing came. She turned from him. "I don't know what I did to deserve that."

He didn't answer.

"That was really, really harsh, and I don't know what . . ."

He knew he ought to say he was sorry, but he was too morose to get the words out.

"It takes six hours to drive here, Fritz! If you don't want me to visit, then . . ."

She had given him the opening, and he knew he was supposed to fill it, but he hesitated.

"I'm going to go now," she said. She rose from the table, erect, resolute. In silence, he watched her leave the visitors' center. She was play-acting, maybe, but then wasn't he?

That night he lay in his bunk and dwelled again, as he had many nights before, on their hour together in the Waldorf-Astoria Hotel. For the first time in his life, Fritz Brubaker admitted to himself that he was really, really lonesome.

IT WAS JULY, and the day had come: the official turning post that tells an inmate he has rounded the halfway point and is headed home. Except that Fritz had never felt further from it. He wrote:

Dear Linda,

Today I've finished half the sentence. It's been six months since the last time I saw you. I think about the children a lot, but I find that I think most about you. During the first couple of months, each day would begin the same way, with me hoping maybe I'll have a letter from Linda today. The few that came I read hungrily, but it was hard. There was such a wall in them. They were like business letters—no, they *were* business letters. I couldn't tell whether you loved me or hated me or were indifferent to me altogether. That was the hardest thing. Anger would have been much easier to understand.

Now I don't think about your letters so much anymore.

But I'm whining, and I don't mean to. Except for one thing. It's important that I see you. I know that you are on your own and things must be difficult, with the kids, and the job and house problems. On the other hand, I have all kinds of time to think, to deconstruct, and to imagine us starting over. I want to talk to you about it. Please bring Michael and come for a visit.

Please.

I love you,
Fritz

P.S. I miss Kristin very much and would love to see her as well, but maybe it is better for her not to see me here. But I need to see Michael. Please.

He finished the letter and sealed the envelope. Over in his cubby, Esperance was writing another paper about tank waste. The tinny sound of headphone Bach leaked out from his headphones. Fritz picked up another piece of paper and began to write a second letter.

He wrote that he was genuinely sorry for his insult. Ronnie was right, she had done nothing to justify it. He said he was very grateful for her visits. He'd snapped at her out of irritability, but his irritability was difficult for him to fathom; in fact, he had been delighted and relieved by a note he'd received that week from his daughter, Kristin, and ought to have been in a much better mood. He looked at the words on the page, "my daughter, Kristin." A mild rebuke—a faint suggestion that Ronnie might not know who Kristin was? Or a painful reminder that there would always be Kristin for him, and Michael; that there were parts of him in which Ronnie could never share. He stared at the paper. He hadn't meant any harm by this note, just the opposite. What to say? *You were a lovely girl*, he wrote, then put the pen down again. Hmm, he thought. He wondered what he'd meant by "were." She still is a lovely girl.

The past tense seemed too definitive, when the fact was he no longer could define anything. So he resorted to the comforting vagueness of the imperfect. He crossed out what he'd written. *You have been*, he wrote, and then he stopped. He listened to the soft melody of the cantata, faintly audible from Esperance's headphones. There was the ink upon the page.

He completed the sentence: *a true friend.* He wrote some more, then stopped with the note unfinished, holding his pen poised in midair. He was thinking that he missed her, too, and would like to see her again, and plain and simple that he wanted her. He wondered if he should write that down. Was it better to be honest or kind? He stared at the page for a long time.

"WHAT, PAY THE GUY? Myself?" asked Peter Greene on the Thursday after Labor Day.

It was an intimate gathering in the CEO's office: only Greene, Greene's privilege shield, Don Fink, and Micah Fensterwald, whose knees and elbows had not been successfully folded into the Hepplewhite. A painful conversation had finally reached this bottom line. Greene would actually have to pay his lawyer. Himself. And with money—not with the usual stuff Peter Greene used to pay people, stock and warrants and other bits of paper.

This was Micah's imperfect solution to the hell that Saul Herzog was raising over the absolute priority problem. The bankruptcy plan wouldn't give Peter anything for his 18 percent. But the company would do a long-term employment deal with him after the bankruptcy. And the deal would involve stock options. Depending on how the options were priced, this might give Greene a way to get his stake back. But the details, the terms, the option strike price, that would all have to be the product of a negotiation, and for that, Peter would need his own lawyer, a lawyer he paid himself.

"Doesn't the company have to indemnify me?"

"For buying it? I'm afraid not," said Micah.

"Isn't there D&O insurance?"

Micah shook his head. "It won't cover this."

"It sure as hell ought to! If there's no insurance for this, Don, god-dammit, then I want to know why—"

"I could check, but—" said Don Fink.

"Peter," Micah interjected, "Don! Listen to me. Don't bother. I'm telling you, there's no such thing as insurance in case you have to hire a lawyer to negotiate a sweetheart employment deal. Trust me. You have to pay Arthur yourself. That's the way it is." Micah had contrived to cross one long leg over the other, which revealed seven inches of hairless calf, a skinny shank the color of Sheetrock gleaming above the lawyer's black sock.

Peter had met this Arthur Lutz. He seemed affable enough, a popinjay with a bow tie who worked in a Boston firm and had a squeaky laugh. He understood all about warrants and convertible preferred and stock options. Arthur Lutz could write the instruments in his sleep; that wasn't the problem. It was this payment business. Arthur Lutz had come to meet with Peter in the executive suite last week, making his require- ments clear. He'd been offered all the usual warrants and percentages, but he just laughed his jolly squeaky laugh and demurred: he had no in- terest in getting his legal fees in anything other than anachronistic cash, and he wanted a healthy slug in advance. Now Micah was saying that the company wouldn't reimburse Greene. He suspected something was up. All these lawyers knew one another, and they were in cahoots.

"Why can't *you* do it?" he demanded.

Micah's calf bobbed in front of Peter, pale as a lawn grub. Greene straightened his own legs. Perhaps by power of suggestion, he could in- duce the guy to cover that thing up. But the leg only bobbed more.

"Because I represent the company. You want to do a deal with the company. The court would say that's a conflict."

Peter frowned. Count on the court to raise quibbles of this kind— what the hell was the court, after all, but another lawyer! Conflicts? The company, Peter Greene—the two had meant pretty much the same thing before all this bankruptcy business. He hadn't had these problems before, not with Don Fink.

"I would think that if the court is going to raise some sort of legal technicality, then it ought to provide a person in my position with reim- bursement for his trouble. The banks get their fees. The committee gets theirs. You get paid."

Why Peter Greene should pay his own way was proving harder to explain that it ought to have been, considering he was a CEO and sup- posed to be sophisticated. Micah wondered how he should proceed. The eminent lawyer entwined his skinny fingers about his knee and pulled it toward him. This had the effect of liberating three more inches of grub-colored leg.

Micah was distracted: he was thinking about conflicts in bankruptcy cases. Maybe, he mused, he should give a brief disquisition on some of the latest legal precedents. The committee and the company lawyers were looking out for the company itself, that was the idea. The banks, well, there was a special rule that said they could get their fees paid if they had collateral. Which they did. (Did they ever! You name it, they had filed on it.) But Peter Greene was only a shareholder. He didn't have the interests of the company to protect. His shares were now worthless, and he couldn't get any value back without, in some way, buying the company.

Micah looked over at Greene again and changed his mind, wisely deciding to keep it simple. "Peter, I assume your interest would be in pricing the options as low as you could, and the company's interest would be in pricing them as high as they could, so that's where you'd have the conflict."

God Almighty, Peter couldn't look at the sonofabitch's naked leg anymore. He stood up abruptly and strode over to the window. None of this was computing for him. Why would the company want to price them higher? He was interested in having the options fairly priced, that was all. Peter wanted what was fair, what made sense. He wanted to avoid confusion—that was in everybody's interest, surely. What the hell was Fensterwald trying to do, create an auction? Let other people start bidding on options? That wouldn't be in anyone's interest. It would just create . . . confusion.

"God knows who might buy options, and then where would you be?"

His hands still clenched around the knee, Micah shrugged. "Depends on how much money God knows who has," he said. "If he's got enough, then where the creditors would be is . . . paid."

Boy, was this guy irritating. Peter struggled to contain himself. How could a guy supposed to be so smart be such a simpleton? Screw the company for the sake of paying a few creditors?

Peter Greene was a CEO in America. He had a position to maintain. Like most CEOs in America, he believed that no matter how much money he got from Playtime, he shouldn't have to offend any of it with personal expenses. He should never have to pay for his membership at the country club in Brookline. Nor for the Mercedes sedan that he drove there, nor for his greens fees, nor for the three-bedroom apartment in the East Sixties that his new wife used on shopping trips to New York. Nor for the chef who prepared sushi lunches for him at Playtime. He should not have to pay for life, health, or disability insurance, nor for his personal trainer, telephone, personal computer, fax machine, or BlackBerry. He must never never fly on a commercial aircraft; a self-respecting executive flew only on a company jet, even if flying the family to a week's vacation in Aruba. And while it was true that he might not be able to expense quite all of the vacation bills, he could work that out with his personal financial planner, whose fees should be paid by the company.

In Greene's mind, it wasn't about cost: it was a question of honor. A CEO was of such value to his company, devoting so much of his energies to its well-being, that the company had a moral obligation to cover these trivial personal expenses. Any failure on its part to do so would be a moral failure and, when you got right down to it, a kind of insult. You wouldn't expect the president of the United States to write a check for his meals at Camp David. Was Greene any less important to the creditors and shareholders of Playtime than the president of the United States? In America, the more money you had, the less of it you should have to spend on your personal needs.

However, try as he might, Greene couldn't get the point through to the lawyer from New York. "Peter," said Micah, at last releasing his knee. "Write the man the check. You get your options priced, we get the case done, one day this all seems like so much cab fare. Okay?"

"YOU'LL BE OUT in a hundred days," said Ronnie. It was warm in the visitors' center that Saturday afternoon in October. Indian summer had come and confused the central heating at Deer Path. She was wearing a clingy Izod shirt and capris. What was this? She'd dressed so formally before, had made herself so prim and correct. She seemed more like her original self today, and playing about her in the warm air was a hint of the old delicious belly pie. The shirt was a little small. Oh, for that peek of unutterably lovely pie, Fritz thought. God, what a body!

He shouldn't be looking, he knew. Or even thinking. It wasn't fair to her. And it would distract him from what he'd decided he needed to do. He needed to get this done before he left Deer Path. What had she asked him? Oh yes.

"If I play my cards right, it's fifty-three. I've got some good time coming, as long as I'm on my best behavior."

"Are you?"

"I salute everyone in sight and never miss count."

"Dude, you're *such* a brownnose."

She was part of a conspiracy. The weather, her cute clingy clothes, her bright conversation, and most of all, thoughts of the end of his term—it was a conspiracy of pleasantness to distract him from his mission. With difficulty, Fritz brought himself around to task. He caught a mental flicker of belly pie—but no. It was time to lay the cards on the table. He took a breath. Damn, she looked good. Damn, it had been a long time. No, he scolded himself again—the mission. He had to stick to it.

"Ronnie, how are you managing to get up here every week? It's a long trip."

She could tell now that something was coming. "Told you a dozen times. I drive—"

"No, I mean the time. How do you get the time?"

"I take a day off here and there."

"Let me ask you something. I'm forty-five, forty-six in a couple of months. I'm a married man with two children. I'm outside your formula, remember? I'm also a prisoner in a federal penitentiary."

"Dude, I noticed. I'm the one who has to go through intake before every visit."

"So what are you doing here?"

"You fishing for a compliment?"

He'd spoken too sharply. He hadn't meant to be sharp, only firm. But the words kept coming out that way. "No. I'm trying to get you to face facts. Look, Ronnie, you've got options."

"Every option has a price," she said. This was making her upset, and she had to look away. "Do I have to spell it out, Fritz? What if I . . ."

She had a determined expression, almost a fierce pout that he could watch in profile, along with the delectable rest of her, as she stared at the

wall of vending machines. He started to answer, but she cut him off with
"Don't you say it!"

"Say what?"

"Don't you say it!"

"What!"

"Don't you say I don't know what love is, or I'm too young to
understand, or whatever you were about to say."

"I didn't—"

"I can tell. I can *tell* you were about to say it."

He resisted the urge to point out that if she could tell, maybe it was
because that was what she thought, too. He looked over at the table to
his left, saw that they had an audience. Ditto the right. Still, how could
you not look at this woman?

"Ronnie," he said quietly, "whatever you know, you don't know
what it's like to have a wife and two kids. If you love me, then you love
a forty-five-year-old felon so tangled up in history and obligation that
you can never untangle it. Why would you do that?"

"Love isn't something you *do*."

"You know what I mean."

"Don't think I haven't asked myself the same question. You aren't
the only guy available."

"No. I appear to be the only guy *un*available."

"Well, that's a matter of choice," she sniffed.

"Where do you see this going?"

"Look, at least I *do* love you. Isn't that worth something?"

It was an elegant way of bringing Linda into the debate without
mentioning her name. Ronnie never asked whether Linda had come to
visit. She never had to.

"You know, Fritz, it wouldn't kill you to be a little nicer to me."

"We need to be frank."

"Instead of attacking my interest in you, maybe you could say it's
nice to see me."

"Okay. It's nice to see you."

"Great. I feel better already."

It *was* nice to see her. And today was it ever! She came almost every
Saturday, and occasionally even to the evening visiting hours during the
week, and it was true, he counted the days. He liked to see her walk

through the door. How lean and confident she seemed. That young, handsome body she seemed to ride like a proud horse. That smile she had, the way she seemed to float around him. And how glad to see him she was!

"Fritz, why are you fighting it?" she implored.

But he dodged her with a question. "Why aren't *you*? Ronnie, as your friend, I'm telling you you've got options. Better options than this."

SUMMER HAD ALWAYS BEEN the season of Fritz. It was Fritz who orga-nized the sailing, Fritz who loaded up the car for the trips to Nantucket, Fritz who strolled around the lawn in Bermuda shorts, his legs tawny, the hair on them silky and filigreed with gold, his smile broad, his eyes squinting in the sun. But in the suburbs west of Boston, the summer of 2002 had come and gone without him. Gone were the tennis-court an-tics that in past years could excite a laugh from Kristin at will, and even on occasion from the more somber Michael. Linda used to resent that it was she who made the family trains run on time while Fritz got the party going in the club car. As she lay alone in bed during those warm August nights, a party in the club car no longer seemed like such a bad thing. The family train had become a commuter, chugging along to its next stop with all passengers correctly silent, each studying his own newspaper.

The family train had become very like the real commuter train that thundered through Wellesley Hills, three blocks away from Linda's new home. The rental house was not a step but a whole flight of stairs down from the Palazzo. It was a real person's house. A regular guy might eat in its kitchen, watch TV in the living room, have a beer on the small deck, sleep in one of the upstairs bedrooms. A regular guy wouldn't have overwhelmed the deck the way Linda did with the wrought-iron garden furniture from the Palazzo, and the postage-stamp yard with the lawn furniture from the tennis court, but where else could she put all this stuff?

It was a McHouse: a small, clean three-bedroom colonial painted in eggshell, with a pressure-treated deck out back standing on ugly stilts. Downstairs was one room in each corner, centering a staircase that led straight up from the front door to a landing. Three small bedrooms and a bath fed off it. Michael's room was on the other side of Linda's bedroom wall, instead of off in a different wing.

The noise took some getting used to, and it wasn't just the trains. Trucks, too, rumbled down Route 16, which followed the tracks through town. Inside the house, through the thin walls of the bedroom, Linda heard the blasts of Michael's computer games late into the night.

Linda passed solitary days in the McHouse that summer: the kids went off to camp, the commuter trains thundered past on their way to the city, and she was left alone. Across town she was hammering the checkout line at Barnes & Noble with divorce and self-help books. By studying the divorce textbooks, she recognized her regret for what it was. It was just a stage, a form of grief, something everyone went through, even if the marriage's end was a good thing.

In the fall Kristin turned twelve and started the seventh grade at Chaney. But Chaney went through only eighth grade. Last spring that fact had presented the increasingly worrisome question of what to do with Michael when fall came. Unfortunately, his grades were poor, and not even Harriet Tichenor could be induced to pull strings at Milton or Nobles. She just shook her head sadly and said, "I don't know if private school is right for Michael, Linda, and with all the . . . you know, the problems . . ."

"You mean Fritz?"

Harriet nodded.

"They won't take Michael because of Fritz?"

In May Linda took Michael out to St. Mark's School for an interview. It lasted twelve minutes by her watch. The boy emerged sullenly from the office of the admissions director, who gestured at Linda from his office. After the door closed behind her, he shook his head, too, much as Harriet Tichenor had done.

Michael climbed into the backseat of the Navigator and flipped on the new DVD screen, which Linda had replaced.

"Michael, please turn that thing off."

He turned the sound down. She glanced up at the rearview mirror.

"Look, Michael, I'm trying to help you."

"Don't worry about it."

"If you don't take this seriously," she snapped, "you're not going to get in anywhere."

"Don't worry about it."

"Michael—"

"The guy was a dork, Mom."

"It's an *interview*, Michael. You have to at least be civil."

She glanced again at the rearview mirror, but he was looking away.

"If you're not going to cooperate with this, I can't do it myself." When he didn't answer, she added, as ominously as she could, "You'll end up in *public school*."

In the backseat, Michael adjusted the joystick, giving the video game just enough sound for his mother to hear. "Whatever."

She'd done what she could. In September, Linda enrolled Michael Brubaker in the ninth grade at Wellesley High School.

With Labor Day gone, Linda decided that she needed to get moving. Standing still opened a woman to depression—all the books said so. Fritz had left her with this mess, and she couldn't trust him, or the weasels at Elboe, Fromme & Athol, or anyone else. So she got busy with new beautification projects for the McHouse: a new hanging plant, a newly scrubbed kitchen floor and painted bathroom wall, a window box, a set of curtains. By mid-September she was driving the librarian of the Chaney School crazy. She kept showing up to volunteer, then trying to reorganize the shelving plan.

Linda had passed through perils previously unimaginable. The Palazzo was gone, Fritz was gone, the partnership at Elboe, Fromme was gone, and yet she carried on. Although she didn't understand it, something much more profound was happening to her. At forty-six, she was being liberated from the fear of being Subject to Criticism. She began to catch the pungent whiff of freedom.

After long confinement, a prisoner may show erratic behavior, and Linda was no different. Ever since her triumph over Marvin Rosenblatt (followed by a hasty letter from HR explaining that a mistake had been made, accompanying a fat check), the fear of criticism had lost some of its potency. She'd survived Anne Shermerhorn in the Dover post office, and she'd put her son in a public school. Then, one September afternoon as she picked up Kristin from Chaney, Linda ran into that art teacher again, Philippe, the one she'd had such an intriguing meeting with last winter when Michael was having his problems. Three days later, on a reckless whim, she telephoned him. That led to a drink downtown, three blocks from his gallery on Newbury Street. Which led to a brazen dinner at Ginger Blow's, Wellesley's tony new restaurant. Which led to fierce and furious gossip all around the grocery aisles and post-office lines of Wellesley and Dover. Which led to Linda not giving a damn about it anymore. Which led to— Well, you've met Philippe: you can guess what it led to.

Linda had gone from fearing criticism to courting it.

After that first furious tumble, Linda rose from Philippe's bed like an NCAA wrestling champion springing from the mat, her face the picture of triumph. This young man's desire had been terrific—he'd been a hungry wolf! This was no Marvin in pajamas—this was a *lover*! (If only Fritz could have known about this, then Linda's satisfaction would have been complete. Send home his wedding ring without explanation? Then write a lot of philosophical letters?) It was midnight. She drove the Navigator back to Wellesley with the radio blaring. She was not to be kept down, not by the weasels at Elboe, Fromme, not by Fritz's inane stunts.

The hell with Fritz's letters. She felt liberated from his criticism, too. She didn't need to wait around for him anymore. Lord knows she'd tried hard enough. During that midnight drive back to Wellesley, she dressed Fritz down. Talk is cheap, Fritz, and a house in Dover isn't!

The second tumble, while lacking the pure fire of the first one, was vigorous, at least. It was still exciting, and Linda still exulted. It was a chance to feel again, to be suddenly alive, when she'd been dead for so long. The only real problem was that Fritz still didn't know about it.

There was, however, a frisson of embarrassment that second time. Philippe had a one-track mind—the moment he had his arm around you in greeting, he was unhooking your bra strap. That was gratifying enough, but afterward, the Shrill Small Voice returned to provide some color commentary. The Voice had recovered its equilibrium after the first heated rush and was now beginning to insinuate that maybe Philippe was just horny, and that he was rather young. The Voice was suggesting that people were going to say the whole thing made Linda appear ridiculous. "You do look silly," said the Voice. Unlike Linda, the Voice had not been liberated from fear of criticism—indeed, the Voice *was* criticism.

"*Silly?*" Linda shot back. "*I'll give you silly. I have a husband in prison who wants* Tinker Toys." Exercising new independence, Linda gained strength to give the Voice the brush-off, at least on the Philippe question. The hell with criticism, Linda thought: it served Fritz right.

It was funny how Fritz kept popping into her mind during those late-night drives back to Wellesley.

But the Voice kept after her. "So which part of that conversation did we find intellectually satisfying?" asked the Voice after one date with Philippe. "And why are *we* driving back to Wellesley? Why isn't *he* in Wellesley driving back to Boston? Why are we keeping him away from Michael and Kristin?"

Count on the Voice to pose a tough question. Even though a piece of Linda came back petulantly (why couldn't the Voice just back off, let her have a little fun?), another piece of Linda began to wobble. Honestly, what *am* I doing? She occasionally wondered. The third tumble had been lackluster and ho-hum, it was true. He was snoring within seconds. And this business of Philippe rolling over while she had to get herself up and out of the city and back to her children—it gave Linda a moment or two of genuine nagging self-doubt.

The Voice had gained a couple of sets, but Linda rallied. What was the alternative? Philippe was an artist. He was tired. He'd been firing a kiln, and that was demanding work. Her "serves Fritz right" side scored a few more points of this kind, and by the time she reached home, that side had prevailed in a wearisome tiebreaker. No longer exultant, perhaps, Linda nevertheless was grimly determined to go forward with this. Although she wouldn't admit it, part of her worried about Fritz's return and searched out a Rubicon to cross before he showed up on her doorstep again. Why not this one? Philippe was youthful and interesting (or, if not interesting per se, interesting to look at), he seemed smitten (at a minimum, horny), and the accounts for his art gallery were in serious need of attention. Linda needed a project. Why not this project as much as any other?

The Voice remained critical. As far as it was concerned, Philippe was available, that was all, and Linda had a history: there was never even a brief hiatus between her men. She had to go directly from one to the next. Remember Stanley? "What is with you that you can't be without a man for two seconds?" the Voice demanded.

"Is a little comfort and understanding too much to ask for? With all I'm going through right now?" Linda rejoined.

"You should have higher standards."

"Oh, shush," said Linda to the Voice.

LINDA'S LONELINESS wouldn't go away. The Philippe business was an occasional rush, but it didn't cure the loneliness, because she couldn't even begin to bring him into her real life. There were no more work colleagues, her old friends were dying to get together but busy just at the minute, the kids were embittered and distant, and she didn't have a regular companion in life anymore.

Michael wasn't making friends at Wellesley High. Nobody came back after school to the McHouse with him, and he wasn't off to friends' houses, either. Every day at 2:45 he walked in the door alone, guzzled milk from the fridge, and went to his room.

Kristin was doing all right at Chaney, but at home all she did was sit in her room, watching music videos and reading *Glamour.* A typical conversation would go something like this:

"Good morning, honey!"

Silence.

"How'd you sleep, okay?"

A glower. "Fine."

"Are you still working with Amy on that science project?"

"Mother, I *told* you yesterday."

"Honey, I don't know if that top isn't a little—"

SLAM.

Like all good mothers, Linda snooped diligently through her daughter's things. (Good suburban mothers and daughters had evolved an elaborate communication ritual. Things too awkward to say to one's mother were written into journals or other private records and hidden for mother to find. Daughter knew she was writing for mother, mother knew that daughter knew, but mother and daughter would never acknowledge what was going on.) Linda soon discovered that Kristin kept her father's letters under her pillow in a bundle tied up with a red ribbon.

Most mornings, after the kids had gone off to school, Linda would go to Kristin's room. Sometimes she even curled up on the Laura Ashley coverlet on her daughter's bed, untying the ribbon and reading Fritz's letters, hearing his voice again. On the small writing desk, Linda would prospect for Kristin's half-completed compositions. They almost burst with all the chatty girlishness that Linda now never heard and so longed for. It occasionally upset her to see smiley faces and hearts dotting every *i*, and to think that she never got that kind of affection anymore; but a bigger Linda, a better Linda, was reassured. It meant that part of the old Kristin was still there, and that lifted Linda's spirits, even if she had somehow lost that relationship with Kristin herself.

She was even calling him Daddy again.

Thus a strange virtual correspondence developed. Linda rarely wrote to Fritz, and she didn't even read his letters to her closely. But she lingered lovingly over every word he wrote to their daughter, then over the words Kristin wrote back. A smile would play across her face, and her eyes might tear. Curling up in the bed like a little girl, she occasionally dropped her guard enough to indulge the fancy that she missed Fritz herself.

GAME OVER

BACK IN NOVEMBER OF 2001, during the first days, you could almost smell it in the Wilmington air: the savor of a succulent joint of meat, crackling with fat, oozing with juice. Playtime was a huge roast, one of the hugest ever seen, and it would bear millions of carvings for the professionals before anyone noticed. So they all thought, at the beginning.

"Carve out" was a favorite expression of the bankruptcy lawyers: it referred to that part of the roast reserved for their fees. In a case like Playtime, scores of knives were sharpened—knives of lawyers and accountants and investment bankers and appraisers and financial advisers and restructuring specialists; there were counsel and local counsel and special counsel. That was a lot of carnivores, and it meant a lot of carving.

But there was plenty of marbled beef for all, everyone thought, plenty for heaping second helpings. Because at the beginning, they figured Playtime needed only the security of bankruptcy to get the Asians shipping. Once that happened, the toy business would get the jump start it needed. It may have sounded odd to talk of security and bankruptcy in the same breath, but it was true: a court watching over a company usually gives the vendors confidence. The Asians would get court orders to say that their Action Men would be paid for, they would ship, the toy chains would buy, and the roast would continue to turn on the spit.

That's what everyone thought.

Things were bad at the VD unit, but people figured those losses wouldn't drag down the rest of the company. The heart of the VD unit consisted of young men from San Mateo and Seattle with pierced tongues and goatees and poor hygiene, with Birkenstocks on their feet and dreadlocks on their heads, young men in their twenties who understood two things: software and stock options. (Some of the artists were women, but artists weren't as hard to come by as programmers. Only the rarest of women had much interest in cranking out the miles and miles of computer DNA necessary to bring gore to life in games like Death Vault.) These young men didn't know anything about bankruptcy other than it put their options out of the money, but that was all they needed to know. As soon as their options disappeared, they disappeared, vanishing like Bedouins in the night, leaving screen savers tracking across their computers and cold cups of Starbucks by the keyboards. The unit still had contracts and licenses and patents, it still had leases and office equipment and computers, and it still had games in development. But without the twenty-four-year-olds, the VD unit was toast.

No big deal, thought the lawyers at first. The hell with the VD unit. The rest of the company—the strollers and Action Men and Big Trikes and Bad Boyz and Boobie dolls—why, that was a Manningtree ox. So when this horde of fee carvers smelled the joint of roast meat on the table, when they got a whiff of its aroma, their saliva glands took over. The negotiations escalated to motions, the motions to court fights, all over the subject of who could carve what. While the professionals were busy carving and brawling, something far more important was happening, far from Delaware. It was happening half a globe away, where Herman Trabbert had organized a tour.

Herman Trabbert rarely left the northern suburbs of Kansas City, Missouri. Those suburbs contained all of the key institutions of Herman's life: his home on River Terrace, Zion Baptist Church, where he was a deacon and elder on the stewardship committee, and the world headquarters of International Leisure, where Herman was chairman. Since that wonderful day when his chief competitor had erupted in flames, he often thought about bidding for a piece of Playtime's business. He'd even had some investment bankers look at it. But one Sunday afternoon in Advent, after services, he took his usual roast pork dinner with his wife, Carol Ann, and then his usual nap in front of the television. It was later that afternoon, while watching a football game, that God gave Herman Trabbert a revelation. The Kansas City Chiefs had an end named Juwon Brown whose pass catching had terrorized the league, but for some reason, the Chiefs weren't throwing the ball to him.

"They've got to get him the ball," the announcers kept saying. "Juwon Brown may be the best split end in football, but if the Chiefs don't get Juwon Brown the ball, Juwon doesn't hurt you!"

Herman Trabbert smiled. He had conceived his plan. You didn't need to beat Juwon Brown. Or trade for him. As long as Juwon doesn't get the ball, Juwon doesn't hurt you.

The next spring, a team that might have been made in Herman Trabbert's own image, looking for all the world like a half-dozen Bible salesmen, was dispatched from Kansas City to the Far East. They went canvassing China and Malaysia and Korea, gathering Chinese and Malaysians and Koreans into conference rooms, shutting the doors behind them, then preaching about hellfire and damnation: specifically, how damned American bankruptcy was—particularly for foreigners.

In hushed and fearful tones, Herman's team asked, "How much exposure do you have to Playtime?"

What did this mean? The Asians knew their receivables were iffy, but they'd been told they'd be paid for any new shipments. There was no problem with that.

The Bible salesmen shook their heads. "You think some American bankruptcy judge is going to favor you above the American creditors? I'm afraid they just want your Action Men."

"We have coat odor! We have coat odor!" the Asian manufacturers protested.

But the International Leisure team sighed and rubbed their hands, sorry to have to bring this news. They looked around the table at one another and wondered how their fellow Americans could have been so perfidious with these poor Chinese and Malaysians and Koreans. To have so flagrantly misled them about the perils of doing business with a bankrupt—why, it was a scandal, that's what. "Is that what they told you?" they asked.

"We have coat odor!"

The gentlemen from Missouri asked very gently and kindly to see it. They read with interest the photocopies of the court papers signed by Judge Shoughler. Then they nodded gravely and, in low, compassionate voices, asked, "They said these would get you paid?"

"Is signed by judge!"

Was there no depth to which Playtime would not sink? "We're afraid," said the lead Bible salesman, "that this court order isn't worth the price of the fax paper. Not to foreigners. See where it refers to vendors in here? Vendors will be paid in the ordinary course and so forth? That's *American* vendors. It's a nuance of the case law."

This was the cue for the deputy Bible salesman who was in fact the traveling attorney to nod sagely. "*Galardi* versus *Hanks*," he said. "A case decided under section three-oh-four of the bankruptcy code."

Nods all around.

"Right," the leader added. "*Galardi*. It's their secret weapon. Didn't they tell you about *Galardi*?"

The Chinese or the Malaysians or the Koreans, as the case might be, exchanged helpless glances. No one had told them about this Galardi. The Chinese and the Malaysians and the Koreans were stunned by this news, this dreadful perfidy, this hidden trick of the Americans. What could they do?

"We're here to help," said the men from Kansas City, smiling. "*We'll* take your Action Men."

"You have coat odor?"

"Even better." Out of their satchels the Bible salesmen pulled their gleaming file folders, and spread them on the table, and fished from them the crisp documentary letters of credit. With the stamps and seals and everything.

"Ooh," said the Chinese and the Koreans and the Malaysians. "Citibank."

Citibank was better, much better, than a court order. In the Far East, hands were shaken, and containers of Action Men contracted for shipment, and dinner was ordered, and then drinks (which the Bible salesmen politely declined), then more drinks (which they declined again). And then the smiling Missouri entourage moved on. City by city, they picked off Playtime's suppliers.

And so while the lawyers in Delaware were bawling about carveouts, and filing papers, and arguing in court, and charging $600 an hour to harangue one another on the telephone, six gentle Bible salesmen from Missouri were driving a stake right through Playtime's thorax. But nobody noticed until the fall, and by then it was too late.

ONE SATURDAY in October, Linda at last drove Michael to FPC Deer Path to see his father. Michael's brooding had become so intense that maybe it would do him some good to see Fritz, she thought. At least it would get him off the computer for a day. Linda couldn't understand why Fritz insisted on seeing Michael rather than Kristin, when it was she who so longed for her father, but Linda secretly agreed it was for the best.

It didn't look like prison to Linda as she steered the Navigator up the drive. The fields had been mowed that morning, and the lawn tractors had blown the fallen leaves into big drums, and the smell of autumn suffused the air. The place looked more like a campus on top of a hill. Where were the high concrete walls, ugly yellow and topped with barbed wire? ("Just like Fritz," the Shrill Small Voice commented, "to get sentenced to a country club!")

"This doesn't look so bad," Michael said.

They parked and entered the lobby, and then there were forms to fill out at the desk. Michael waited nervously, trying not to catch the eye of any of the other visitors. They were women, mostly.

"Come with me, son," said a heavyset man in a gray uniform carrying a big set of keys and a walkie-talkie. It was one P.M. Michael followed him through a set of double doors, leaving Linda behind. The doors swung shut, and Michael began to grow alarmed. Squeak-squeak-squeak went the guard's shoes as he led Michael down the hall to the visitors' room.

His dad was waiting at a table.

Where was the jumpsuit with the number on it? His dad was wearing all beige, but the shirt was the button-down kind. There were dozens of tables scattered around, and most of them had on one side a guy who looked like a dad, and on the other a visitor who looked like a mom. The visitors were all women except for Michael and this one old man who'd come with an old lady. They were speaking softly. But Michael was the only kid in the room.

Fritz stood when his son was led in. Michael seemed lankier than Fritz had remembered. He hugged the boy, who hugged back as perfunctorily as he could before sitting. Michael was all in black—black cargo pants, black Vans sneakers, black T-shirt with the logo of the rock band Stiletto on the front. Along his jawbone and under his sideburns grew the first hint of a dark furze. Michael sat at the table across from his father, averting his eyes.

"How've you been, son?"

"Fine." Michael's voice honked a little.

"You're taller."

"I guess so."

Michael felt his father examining him in that way that embarrassed him so much. Michael had worn, in addition to the T-shirt and cargo pants, his adolescent carapace for the visit. He'd retracted his neck, turtle fashion, so it was almost with the hooded eyes of an amphibian that he peered out, occasionally regarding Fritz from protective cover. But the shell was thinner, and that vulnerable boy more visible, than Fritz could remember having seen in years.

"This doesn't seem so bad," Michael honked again, trying to sound adult.

"It doesn't?"

"No, I mean, like, there's no walls or fence or anything."

"Michael, it's a federal prison. People are here because they broke the law."

He'd just been trying to make conversation. "Whatever."

Fritz thought he'd better change the subject. "How's Kristin?"

"Pain in the ass."

"I guess it's lucky she has a big brother," Fritz said.

Michael shrugged.

"Let me show you something." He spread the graph paper out on the table. "Know what this is?"

Michael shrugged again, but Fritz could tell he was interested. The boy looked at the drawing. "Windmill?"

"Yes. Remember Jim Feeney? Oh, that's right, you didn't meet him. Anyway, he's been trying to design a wind turbine—a windmill to generate electricity. Mainly, he's been trying to develop a propeller that will work in low wind. I think I've come up with a better idea."

They talked about Fritz's experiments. Michael even studied the graph of results, nodding with interest as his father showed him a drawing of the sail turbine.

"But what if the wind changes?"

"Sorry?"

"You know, if the wind's, like, out of the south one day and out of the east the next, how would you keep the sails filled?"

"Well, you, you . . ." Damn. A simple thing like that, all these months of experiments, and he hadn't thought of it. You couldn't hang around and readjust the sail sheets all day.

"I need to work on that some," Fritz admitted.

Michael was studying the drawing. "You could, like, put it on a swivel," he said, gesturing. "Have the turning gear stick up like this, and have the thing rotate."

"How do you mean, rotate?"

"I dunno, like bike handlebars or something, you know? Three-sixty." He pointed at the drawing again. "This post here could turn through three-sixty degrees. It should work automatically and swivel to where the sails fill."

Fritz studied the drawing. "That's a good idea." Maybe, yeah, something like that. He'd have to work on it. But Michael was on to something. Fritz rubbed his son's arm appreciatively, and the boy shrank a little.

They sat together quietly, listening to the faint whisperings at the other tables. Florence had had a birthday. Uncle Mort was worse again. The doctors had increased the medication. The landlord wanted them out at the end of next month.

"So," Fritz said.

"So," Michael answered.

"Listen, I didn't just want to talk about the wind turbine. I asked Mom to bring you here for another reason. I think you know what it is."

Michael looked down at his hands.

"What do you think about all of this? I need to know what you're thinking."

Michael lowered his voice and looked briefly out through his hooded eyes. "Why did you say you did it?"

"You don't know?"

Michael looked away. "No, it's stu— I mean, no."

"Stupid, right?"

He looked up again. "Yeah."

"We didn't have to go through all this bullshit, right?"

Michael agreed but suspected a trap. He nodded warily.

"Suppose we'd told them the truth. What do you think would have happened?"

He shrugged. "I dunno."

"Sure you do," his father said. "You know exactly what would have happened."

"They would have, I dunno, sent me to—"

"Bullshit, Michael. They wouldn't have sent you anywhere."

"Right, so, why would you, I mean, I don't get it," Michael said. Then he shrugged again. "Whatever."

Fritz lowered his voice. "They wouldn't have sent you anywhere except maybe to a shrink. You know what would have happened. They would have called in the counselors, and they might have sentenced you to sit and talk. And you would have sat there with the shrink asking you how you felt about everything, and you would have spun them some story or other and smirked your way through the whole thing, thinking how stupid they all were. Wouldn't you?"

Michael hung his head.

"Wouldn't you?"

"I dunno."

"They'd have made you the victim in this thing. And pretty soon you'd have thought you were the victim, too."

"But I still don't get why you—"

"Because you *don't* get it. Because you never would have gotten it."

"What?"

"They'd have been so busy worrying and fussing over you that you never would have gotten it."

"Gotten *what*?"

They'd spoken in louder tones. They looked around at the other tables, then settled down again.

"That what you did was wrong," Fritz said. "That it was cheating. That being smart on the computer is no excuse for cheating."

"I didn't mean anything," Michael said.

Fritz knew what Michael was trying to say. It was a childish stunt, a fit of bravado. Right from your own computer terminal, to move money around, to borrow your parents' social security numbers and open accounts, and purchase options, and earn a huge profit, all without leaving his room. It was cool. Fritz knew all of that, but he didn't let his son off the hook.

"You didn't mean to put a hundred thousand of someone else's dollars into your own account? Don't lie to me."

"I said I was sorry—"

"No, you didn't. You made an excuse. Which is just what they would have done—all the shrinks. They would have helped you make excuses. By the time they were done with you, they would have had you believing it was your parents' fault, or the Republicans' fault, or your fourth-grade teacher's fault, or television's fault, or too much sugar in your diet. They'd have felt so sorry for you that you'd be feeling sorry for yourself. You never would have gotten it that when you fall down, it's usually your own fault." Fritz caught himself too late. "I can't believe I just said that."

The boy was silent.

"This isn't complicated, Michael. What you did was wrong. It was illegal and wrong, and there's a price to pay when you do things that are wrong. And I know you. I know how smart you are. I know that with you, it wasn't just the thrill of proving that you could pull off this hack. That wasn't hard, not for you. There was some bravado there, but you were also in it for the money."

The boy's eyes were glued to the floor.

"Listen to me: insider trading isn't a victimless crime. When you make money selling, it's because someone else lost money buying. People buy and sell the stock of companies based on the information we put out. If we know something that the public hasn't been told, that's inside information. If we use it to make money, we're taking that money from the people who don't have the information. So if you overhear your dad sitting in the living room one night, talking about problems in Playtime's accounting, then you know something all those other people don't know, and you make your hundred thousand right out of their pockets. And it's wrong.

"This time I'm paying for it. But next time it'll be you."

"I'm sorry," Michael said.

"Do you understand that? They won't let someone else pay the price next time. It'll be you."

"I said I'm *sorry*."

"I know you are," Fritz answered. "Now."

"But I still don't see why you—"

Fritz's voice was beginning to rise again. "So you would be sorry. Really sorry. Not regretting you were caught. But *sorry*. That's what I wanted. I couldn't think of any other way you'd get it. I felt like if you didn't get it, you'd do something like this again, only next time it would have been worse.

"You know what a lot of the guys in here say? They say, 'I was stupid.' That's what they say: 'stupid.' And what they mean is, 'I got caught.' They don't mean, 'I was wrong.' Do you understand the difference, son?"

Michael wanted to be anywhere but there, with his father speaking too loudly, so that other people might be hearing. But Fritz wouldn't stop.

"I've been kind of a lazy father, I admit it. And I really want only one thing from you. I don't need you to play lacrosse or to be an A student. I just want you to get away from a world where you measure things by whether they are smart or stupid. I've been there, and that's a bad world. You've got to divide things by right and wrong, not smart and stupid. Can you get that?"

It was two o'clock. One of the guards stood up from his desk and came over to the table to escort Michael back to the outside world. There were couples at each of the adjoining tables, and three guys at the end of the room. With Fritz, Michael, and the two guards, there were eleven people in the room. In a loud voice, Fritz said, "I love you, son."

Michael had inherited his mother's fear of any scene, and he shrank into his carapace. But he nodded, and it looked almost as though his eyes glistened.

Fritz had a word with the guard, who nodded and escorted Michael out. Then Fritz sat alone at the table, staring at his drawings, waiting, hoping. For a few minutes, anyway, the boy could wait in the car. She could come in to see him, if only for a few minutes before the long drive home. He wanted to show her his drawings, he wanted to talk to her. Maybe to hold her hand again, to ask what she was feeling.

The minute hand inched around the clock. Well, it would take them a few minutes. She'd have to put Michael in the car. Then maybe there was a form to fill out. It got to be 2:12, 2:13. Maybe she hadn't filled out some forms? Or was on the cell phone, yes, couldn't get off right away. Or had to wait in a line somewhere. The hand clicked around to 2:20. He'd wait a little longer, in case, maybe . . . Maybe, he thought, she's just . . .

At 2:35, Fritz rose and left.

What he didn't know, and wouldn't learn until months later, was that Linda had planned to come in and see him after he'd talked to Michael. She'd worked up the courage and, in a sneaking way, had even looked forward to it. She'd been all set to do so when, just before two, that woman—that tramp from the Waldorf, that Veronica Pettibone— walked into the lobby at FCI Deer Path.

Linda froze. The two women stared at each other across the room. Then Ronnie flushed, bit her lip, and approached slowly.

"I, I didn't know," Ronnie said. "Sorry. I can visit some other time." She turned around and retraced her steps.

As the door shut behind Ronnie, Linda felt her anger rise. So this was what had been going on! While she was left alone to look after the kids. While she was busy driving their son all the way from Wellesley to this godforsaken corner of Pennsylvania, he'd been cozying up to that little tramp! And the tramp thinks she can visit some other time?

No, Linda thought angrily. No need for that. You can visit anytime you damn well want. When Michael emerged a few minutes later, she seized him by the arm and hurried from the building.

ANGER was the prevailing mood in Delaware, too. Micah was trying to get Peter Greene's option deal done as part of the bankruptcy plan, but everybody in courtroom 6 was throwing up on the deal. Herzog was raising hell. The committee was raising hell. Every damn time Micah went to court in Delaware, some nickel-and-dime creditor nobody had ever heard from would pop out of his seat to raise hell. *Your Honor, Morton A. Shnick representing Nobody, Inc. I'm just here to second all that hell the others raised.*

And every time, Micah had to get up and argue more mental gymnastics for this guy Greene, whom, to be perfectly frank, Micah didn't much care for. Now the wagons were circled. The financial experts were writing long reports about what the company was worth and what the options were worth. The depositions were being taken, and the camps were massing for the big court fight. Late into the night, the lawyers' phones were ringing.

"Micah, I'm telling you, the bondholders need to see something much better than this!" Herzog was saying on line one. "Much better!"

Irv Klein was on line two. "Micah, the banks are getting nervous. Can't you get with Saul and get this deal done?"

Micah's litigation partners stood in the doorway of his office wearing long faces. "We don't know about this. The expert reports don't look so good."

"Be patient," Micah said to himself. "It always goes this way. The CEOs are always a pain in the tuchis. This case will be like all the others. It gets settled in the hallway outside courtroom 6."

Micah had been around a long time. He wasn't usually wrong about bankruptcy cases. But he was wrong about this one.

UP IN BURLINGTON, the wound left by Herman Trabbert's stake through the abdomen had shown up on the financial CAT scan, all right. A hole gaped from the monthly numbers spread on his desk. The company simply couldn't get product. He had $150 million of Chinese goods that he couldn't get shipped, and that was just China. Forget the court fight over Peter's options. If they couldn't get the Chinese to ship Action Men, it was academic. Peter could have all the options he wanted because they represented the right to own a worthless company. The bankruptcy filing was supposed to stabilize things, to make for a decent Christmas sell through in 2002, but inexplicably, Jellicoe had some kind of Boxer Rebellion on his hands. What the hell had gotten into Asia?

He called Greene. "Peter, I need to talk to you about the numbers."

"Relax," Greene said.

"No, Peter, I really think—"

"Listen, Larry, a little downward spike in the numbers will give this Saul Herzog some religion. He'll back off, and I'll get my—er, we'll get our deal done."

"Fine, Peter."

Fuck it, thought Jellicoe as he hung up the phone. What the hell do I care about it anymore?

ONE NIGHT at about ten, Linda was nodding off to the usual muted accompaniment of bleeps and blasts when she heard Kristin's voice through the thin McHouse bedroom wall.

"Michael, turn it *off*! I can't sleep!"

"Shut up, you little jerk."

"You're the jerk, jerkface!"

Linda sat up in bed, listening in the dark. They were fighting all the time now. They had always fought, but since Fritz had gone, the conflict had intensified. They couldn't speak to each other without angry insults. Linda heard louder blasts and computer splats, then the irritating computer melodies. Michael must have turned up the volume.

"I said *you're* the jerk!" Kristin repeated.

"Get out of my room, dickwad."

Linda was swinging her legs off the bed when she heard Kristin say, "*You're* the jerk for what you did to Dad!" Linda stopped to listen. Michael said something that she couldn't quite make out.

"*You* did it! And got him in trouble. It's not *fair*!"

"Shut up, you don't know what you're talking about."

"If it wasn't for you, Dad wouldn't be in prison. And Mommy wouldn't be with stupid Philippe the Creep, and *we* wouldn't be poor. You ruined everything!"

"Poor" being a relative concept, as far as the youth of Wellesley and Dover were concerned. But Philippe the Creep? Linda cringed.

"I saw the cookie on your computer. I know what time you were home. I saw it, Michael!"

At this point a strange thing happened. The computer sounds ceased. Michael must have turned it off. She heard next only a quiet mumbling when he spoke.

"U-Trade, U-Trade, U-Trade!" Kristin chanted.

A mumble that Linda couldn't make out.

"*You* got him in trouble. So Mommy would think it wasn't you. And now we're poor. You're selfish and stupid and I hate you!"

The door slammed.

Linda lay wide awake in bed for hours, until long after the last commuter train had chugged by. Dear God, she thought. The whole insider-trading business wasn't Fritz . . . it was Michael? But Fritz had pleaded guilty! What an idiotic stunt for him to have pulled—look what it had done to the family. Why hadn't he just talked to her, why hadn't he just explained? They could have gotten Michael some counseling. And this all wouldn't have happened, and she wouldn't have been forced to turn to Philippe the Creep! Yes, Philippe was Fritz's fault!

"Honestly," the Voice scolded.

Linda was crying. Was there, deep down within Linda LeBrecque's instinct to criticize, a tiny note of admiration? But why hadn't he said something to his own wife?

"Maybe you should have been nicer to him," said the Voice.

The world seemed to have been stood on its head—was the Voice on Fritz's side? Linda turned her face to the pillow lest the children hear her.

PETER GREENE was on his cell phone to Micah Fensterwald. "Did you get them to take the deal yet?"

"Peter, I told you already, they're not going to take the deal. Five percent, tops."

"Tell them business doesn't look good."

"That doesn't help anybody. Just gives all of you less to fight over."

"Tell that loudmouth Herzog we'll litigate forever."

Micah stifled the urge to respond. That would be effective, he thought. Like telling a hungry Bengal tiger you're going to keep shoveling meat at him until he stops eating.

"These creditors don't know what they're doing. Once they see the EBIT trail off, they'll get scared and make our deal."

"Okay, Peter," said Micah.

But he didn't call Herzog to tell him any such idiotic thing. Instead, Micah called Larry Jellicoe. "Larry, what are you seeing in your numbers?" he asked.

And Jellicoe spilled like a secret lover who's longed to confess. The suppliers wouldn't ship. Sure, Playtime could sue them, but Christmas was a bust for the second year in a row. They were going to trip every bank covenant. And then who knew what. The projections that the plan had been based on were all toast. They'd never make it.

Micah sat, stunned, at his desk. Then he said, "You need to get the cash out to pay my firm's interim fees. That needs to be done right away. Otherwise we'll have to withdraw."

Micah hung up the phone and called Saul Herzog. But not to carry on with any more of Peter Greene's bluster. Micah and Saul were part of the same union. This was only one case, and there would be others.

He sounded weary, not himself, Saul noted instantly. Micah worked through awkward pleasantries, then said: "Saul, I've known you a long time."

What was this about? Herzog wondered.

"Some of those vultures you represent, I've seen them treat their lawyers badly in the past."

Saul waited. But Micah said nothing else. "What are you telling me?"

"Saul, I've known you a long time."

"What's going on with the company?"

Silence.

A quiet tone, with no histrionics. "Does my firm need to get current on our fees?"

"That's none of my business. But it wouldn't be imprudent."

There was a pause as Saul digested this. "You mean . . ."

"We're off the record."

"I understand, I understand." They were both silent. Then Saul said, "Micah, I appreciate this."

"Let's talk about my carve-out. It's about a million light," Micah said.

"I'll call Irv and take care of it," said Saul Herzog.

BECAUSE MICAH KNEW. And Saul knew. And in ten minutes Irv would know. Although Greene would watch the numbers spike downward, and lay in bed at night dreaming of getting his equity back, the bankruptcy veterans knew this was no spike. The lenders would never stomach another failed Christmas.

And soon the world knew. By Thanksgiving 2002, the writing wasn't just on the wall, it was in the court filings. The cash had dried up. The Asians were refusing to supply. Irv Klein's banks called in their bankruptcy loans. The chapter 11 reorganization of Playtime and its subsidiaries would be converted to a chapter 7 liquidation. Shut the stores, cancel the orders, lay off the employees, and bring in the auctioneers. It wasn't just a flameout of the VD unit. It was game over for Playtime.

ON DECEMBER 10, 2002, two days before Fritz's sentence would finish at Deer Path, Ronnie's last letter arrived. This one was all business, containing a set of very specific practical instructions such as you might leave for a child. How she wanted to meet him in New York that weekend. How he should call her on the cell phone on Saturday because she would be flying into La Guardia. How she had checked on the Internet and there was a bus that ran from Deer Path to Scranton, where you could change for New York City. How she knew that he would want to get home and see his kids but it was important that they "spend some time together" first. How she knew that he felt this, too.

Fritz was tempted. He sat for the last time beneath the maple, whose limbs were naked again against the coming winter. He leaned back against the tree, closed his eyes, and watched belly pie on the mental IMAX. He revisited suite 1940. It had been a long time since Linda had wanted Fritz with such fierce determination, and he was only human. Mmmm, he thought. How nice that would be. Another romp with Ronnie.

There had been no letter from Linda in many months.

But the problem with suite 1940 was that he kept remembering the end, the sheepish dressing and the bowleggedness and the woman in sequins. And the teeming elevator. He'd try to force his mind back to the sexual tornado that had preceded it, but he kept getting stuck on the elevator.

What about Kristin and Michael?

Saturday morning came, Fritz's last at Deer Path. He rose early. He packed up his notes from the wind project. He shook Professor Esperance's hand and wished him luck with the nuclear polluters.

"There's no *luck* about it," Esperance said sharply. "You've got to take action!"

Fritz smiled. Five minutes later, Marshall stopped him on the quad. "Yo, Brubaker, best of luck, man. Hey, give me your social before you go!" He winked.

Fritz waved at a few other guys he saw on his way out. And then he followed the guard across the quad to the processing center.

It was a gorgeous winter morning in central Pennsylvania. At 11:08 A.M., Fritz Brubaker stepped out into the sunshine. Fifteen minutes later, he was sitting in the back of a blue taxicab, heading down Route 11 to the bus depot in Deer Path. Cold as it was, he rolled down the windows and drank in the breeze.

"Beautiful morning, isn't it?" he said.

"A little cold," the cabbie answered. "So how long were you in for?"

"Year and a day. Less good time."

"Heading home?"

"I guess so."

"Must feel good to get out," said the cabbie. "And just in time for Christmas."

"To be honest with you, I'm not sure what to expect."

The cabbie was voluble, a chubby fair-haired guy in a baseball cap and a Pittsburgh Steelers warm-up jacket. He seemed nice enough. "You live around here?" Fritz asked him.

"Over in Sayre," the cabbie said. "Name's Dave, Dave Hobson. Guys call me Butch."

"Nice to meet you, Butch. I'm Fritz Brubaker."

"I've met all kinds of famous inmates up at the camp," Hobson said. "That Reverend Solomon Wilson, the Harlem preacher who did those sit-ins, remember him?"

"Sure," said Fritz.

"He was my fare. Took him to the bus, just like you. He was laughing and carrying on that day, I'll tell you. And that Fred Thodal, the Wall Street guy, you hearda him?"

"*The* Fred Thodal?"

"Yessir. Rode right where you're sitting. Guy like that, made five hundred million dollars, the papers said, didn't have no limo or nothing to pick him up. Took a cab to Deer Path and waited for the bus."

"Really?" Fritz asked.

"Five hundred million dollars and he tipped me fifty cents. Imagine that!"

Outside, the sun flashed brightly off the snow on the hillside. "You know what buses run through Deer Path?"

"Sure. You've got choices. There's the Greyhound runs from Williamsport to Binghamton, Albany, and on up to Boston. That goes about twice a day, I think. And then there's a Peter Pan that'll take you to Scranton, and you can change for New York. Three or four of those, probably."

Those were the choices. Hobson's choices, on a clear and chilly morning in December, when a man couldn't be sure of anything, not even that little feeling, that sensation down in the center of his gut that said, Dammit, I have an instinct about this, I've *always* had an instinct about this. Not even that. Because you couldn't trust your instincts anymore. You couldn't be sure of anything except that it was a fine morning in December—a morning when a man's whole future might turn on which of two buses he would board at a depot in Deer Path, Pennsylvania.

"AT THE OUTSET of this course, I put the question, and now, as the course comes to its close, my greatest fear is that you think we have answered it. Do you remember the question?"

Let us call to mind springtime in Amherst, a morning early in May when the daffodils are past but the tulips are rioting, the grass greening up, the Frisbees and shorts and flip-flops back, the windows in Converse Hall flung wide to the world. We are in that happy prehistory before hip-hop; the sounds blasting from distant dorm rooms are the laments of the Temptations or the Four Tops, the singers croon for love, instead of spar—difficult to imagine, now. Let us imagine a breeze washed by sprays of lilac as it enters through the open windows of the lecture hall. All outdoors beckons to these students, but out of respect, none of them has skipped this final lecture. We fancy they will soon be heading east to Boston and south to New York, the graduates for careers, the undergraduates for summer jobs, and they will bring with them their understanding of economics, their new finance key ring. They are excited by the future, they are intoxicated by spring; life for them is about as glorious as it ever will be. For this last hour, they have come to pay respects to the odd little man who has shown them the mysteries.

How fitting that Professor Vorblen is wearing that same three-button suit of dark green tweed, the one he seems to wear whatever the season. How appropriate that he has on the same dark blue silk bow tie. The same glasses. Their memories of him at the end will be as they were at the beginning. Is there one lanky undergraduate whose brown curls we might recognize, whose young smile we would instantly place— one undergraduate in Bermudas and an Izod shirt, whose legs are bronzed already, who slouches comfortably in a seat halfway up the left side of the hall? Has he been there all along? Was he there for the beer and then for the yellow liquid? Was he the first to sell that day they shorted the grades?

He was, and as tempting as it was for him to cut class—any class—on this gorgeous day in May, he, too, has come out of respect for the last meeting of the course.

The professor's diction has about it the usual brisk clip. He welcomes them, thanks them for coming to these lectures. He hopes they have been useful. And yet is something changed? Does the voice sound different, somehow less sure, like that of a great Shakespearean actor backstage, after the performance? It's the same voice, but it seems to lack its earlier force, almost as though (and it sounds absurd to say it) the professor has lost confidence.

He looks out at the Red Room in Converse, where every seat is filled, and says, "The question was 'What is value?' "

Nods all around the hall. Yes, they remember. What is value? And then the bit with the beer. That was cool. It made a definite impression.

"Last fall we learned about a financial concept called 'present value.' Remember? Present value was the reduction of all enterprises to a future stream of cash, and the process of discounting those predicted streams to a dollar amount today. What would you pay today to have the right to receive that stream of cash tomorrow? That's how people value a Treasury bill, or an Acme bond, or an office building on Fifth Avenue. Nothing but an expectation of money in the future, with all the attendant risks that the fellow who owes the money may or may not go broke, that the United States may go to war, and Acme may file bankruptcy, and the building may burn down. All of that reduced to a dollar amount. Present value, we learned, has nothing to do with the present—it really is a bet on the future. There is no present where value is concerned. Nothing lasts. Nothing stands still.

"What is it that proves out all of this guesswork about the future? Strangely, not the future itself. No one waits to see what actually happens. The place to test our expectations for tomorrow is the marketplace of today. Because everything's for sale today, even the bets on the future—*especially* the bets on the future. Thus we learned in this course that commerce was the only crucible in which to test the future predictions inherent in present value.

"And in commerce, where we measure these predictions, everything is relative. A function of bargain and exchange, of supply and demand. We discovered that value is purely relative, that there are no absolutes."

Nods again. It is a good point. These students have fully endorsed the themes of capitalistic economics. Everything is relative. And everything is for sale. Which is a good thing—isn't it?

"Fair-market value, we said, was what a willing buyer would pay a willing seller, each being knowledgeable and neither acting under compulsion. That is, what someone will pay today for a bet on tomorrow. Then we found that the marketplace was everywhere. Let's consider this class's favorite commodity and Molson Companies Limited, which bottles it. First, Molson makes beer, and you can sell the beer. Next, you can sell the assets of the company—its breweries and delivery trucks, its inventories of ale and its brewing equipment. You will set the price on these assets based on a guess as to how much money the enterprise will make in the future. Or the owners can sell the stock of Molson, so that Molson carries on unchanged under new ownership. The price of that stock? Another guess as to future returns to stockholders. But there is more. Suppose Molson borrows money to finance its beer production. You can sell those borrowings. FirstBank can lend Molson a hundred million dollars, then whack the loan into a hundred pieces and sell them off. You or I can buy up lots of debts of lots of Molsons and repackage those debts into a new company and sell the stock of that company. And so on and on, ad infinitum. All of that buying and selling is guesswork about how much cash may or may not come tomorrow. In short, it goes far past the beer. In our society, everything is a bet on the future. And since everything is for sale, the future, too, is for sale.

"So if value simply describes a relative function, a moving target between supply and demand, and if everything is for sale, and if all sales today are merely predictions of what streams of cash may come tomorrow, then what have we proved?"

Silence. Heck if they know. Although he's making it sound like they've proved something pretty grim.

"We have proved that the only constant is relativity. Exchange, give and take, buy and sell—in other words, commerce. Ladies and gentlemen, we have proved that commerce itself is our only truly present 'value.' "

This gets big smiles from the audience. Something's coming. They know this professor now, how he beckons them into a grand avenue that seems to lead logically into a pleasant street that turns sensibly to a quaint lane that then empties inexorably into a dark alley where they get mugged. Commerce itself is the only present value? Sure, he sort of proved that in some clever way, but that doesn't apply to *us*. We can continue to hold dear real values, true values, moral values, but at the same time, through our understanding of economics, not to be too crude about it, get a job in an I-bank next year and make a shitload of money. Because we can operate on two tracks.

"You think you can operate on two tracks?" he asks.

There he goes with the mind-reading thing again. Sheesh, that's creepy. But now, at the end of the course, they have to smile about it. He's done it to them too many times.

"Let me make a confession. *I* can't."

This is starting to feel like they're stuck in that alley behind the Dumpster. Like they're in the shadows, waiting for the goons to appear. They wish the professor wouldn't be so dark on the last day of his lectures.

Meanwhile, the professor has taken out a book from behind the lectern and is turning the pages, hunting for something. They can see the gold foil glint. What is that, a Bible? Heads turn, one to another. Is he wigging out on us? He's gone . . . Baptist, or something!

"Luke talks about this," he says. "God and mammon, you remember the bit." He's leafing, mumbling that he thinks it's Luke, anyway. Of course they don't remember that bit, or any other bit, because no one reads the Bible anymore, at least not that he'd admit in polite society.

The professor looks up. "Yes, it is Luke, after all. 'Lay up your treasures in heaven.' *You* remember."

The professor smiles, looking out at his students for any sign of recognition. But if they remember, they aren't showing it. "Now, I don't propose that you do that. Heaven has little place in this course, heaven knows!"

The joke gets no reaction: the faces in the audience remain blank. They have that embarrassed look people get when somebody starts quoting the Bible. They wonder if they will need to call for help.

"But whatever your faith, Luke's got it right about one thing, I'm certain of that. The Gospel says, 'Where your treasure is, there will your heart be also.' Your heart will be in one place, not two. So, can you operate on two tracks? I don't think so. And Luke doesn't think so, either. You won't be able to keep your hearts away from your treasure. Will commerce itself be your treasure?"

This is pretty dark, although at least the students may now conclude that Vorblen hasn't gone starkly evangelical on them; he's just making another one of his points. But it's an awfully gloomy point for the last lecture. It had been such a good course—why not break out the beer again? Have a little fun!

"But you'd rather talk about beer," says the professor. "Let's return to the Molson brewing company. What about the man who goes to work for Molson? Is he relative, is he a pawn of this commerce god? It would seem so. We pay him based on what we can get away with paying him. How little will the unions take? If he's in management, what's the going rate for managers? Is this not measurement? Is this not a value?

"Life is for sale. We insure life, and then we measure values; we pay settlements for wrongful death that we measure in dollars. We compete in burial costs, and then we sell shares in the burial companies. There are markets in people, just as there are markets in aluminum futures or prune juice. How much do you have to pay a computer programmer, or an opera singer, or a Major League pitcher, or a lawyer? Or, for that matter, a college professor? What must you pay his widow if he is hit by a runaway truck? How much would someone charge to insure against the risk of his death?

"It depends on how good he is, you might say." (Nods. Yes, sure, we might.) "But what does that mean, how good he is? Isn't that just shorthand for still more of our commerce, more of our relativity—isn't how 'good' he is a function of how many people need his particular service, which in turn is a function of the current demand for computer programmers or college professors, which in turn will be a function of dozens, or scores, or perhaps thousands of other shifting and imponderable facts? And when we use a word like 'good' to describe this computation, what are we saying about our values?

"This is commerce, ladies and gentlemen. This is our present value, and it absorbs everything, all things, all relationships. So can you really exist on two tracks? Do you think that if you go to New York and join the Goldman Sachs investment banking program that you will exist on two tracks? That in your lives you will trade only soybean futures and never love?"

Of course we will, they are thinking. Won't we? Heads are turning as the students look around the hall for support. But the professor seems to be heading off on a different tack.

"Is economics just? We economists always stumble on that one. We like to say that economics is *efficient*. That its ruthless forces lead people to make 'efficient' decisions. And that is sound. Take the elements: life depends on light, and life depends on water. Yet experience teaches that you can't sell sunshine to a man in Riyadh. He has all he needs. Put the right photograph of it in a travel brochure, and you can sell it in February to a resident of Minneapolis. On the other hand, you can't sell a desalinization plant to our Minnesotan—he has ten thousand lakes at his disposal, while the Saudi gentleman is very interested in water.

"Since no one needs more water in Minnesota, the laws of economics will punish the investor in a Minneapolis desalinization plant. This is efficient, we say. It leads to better outcomes in the next investment.

"Yet we are uneasy. The man who made that investment was a flesh-and-blood human being. He suffered financial setbacks. He became moody and morose. He beat his wife and succumbed to alcohol. These are terrible things. Our minds tell us these results are inevitable and that at what we economists like to call the 'macro' level, the result is efficient, but our hearts tell us that nothing so measured can have any 'value' at all, and that deriving such a value is not valuation at all. It is math, perhaps, but it is in fact empty of anything of real worth.

"So what is value?

"Let me propose a definition. After forty years in this field, I find it profoundly dispiriting although, unfortunately, accurate. The definition is this: value, in economics, is the precise opposite of real value. That is, economic value is only that which has no intrinsic content at all. It is only commerce—only process."

He sums up: "It is the opposite of treasure."

The students look perplexed. Professor Vorblen's eyes twinkle just a little. "Real value, by contrast, is that which defies economic laws. To illustrate, I propose three real values. Love. Constancy. Faith. None of these has value an economist would understand. You cannot sell love—

if it is negotiable, well, 'Love is not love / Which alters when it alteration finds.' And yet love is the most profound incentive we know. Love is the reason so many of you are now staring out the window."

Smiles. They are indeed. They are fond of Professor Vorblen, but it's May!

"Faith—if this is measurable, it is not faith. Constancy—if salable, it is inconstant. Yet we prize these things above all else. We *value* them above all else. These things are not merely present. They are not bets on future market movements or cash flows. They are not relative—they are not commerce. Perhaps finding big-V Value consists of rejecting all that you have come to understand about little-V value in this course.

"And this is a deeply dispiriting thought for me. The investment of my life has been made, and it has been made in this field: economics. I realize that one has to invest in something. You cannot hedge your life as though it were a mutual fund. Where will you put your treasure? Will you invest in constancy or commerce? Will you invest in love? Love isn't some coupon you clip for free. It's an investment, but you have to choose to make it. Will you reach my age and realize that love is the investment you haven't made?"

Love? What's all this talk of love in an economics course? And how sad the eyes! The students hardly dare look at him.

"You are young. For you there is still time to determine where you will put your treasure. As you leave this course, as you consider the question that I posed on the first day—'What is value?'—now it is you who must ask yourself a question. Did learning something about economics, about commerce, about present value—did listening to an economist give you any tool to understand real Value, or did it give you nothing at all?

"Class dismissed."

IT WASN'T EXACTLY the sort of December day that puts one in mind of Christmas. In fact, it was pouring.

He found her in Cerabesque, Philippe Iskandar's gallery in Back Bay, eight steps up from the sidewalk in the most outrageously priced rank of galleries on Newbury Street. The room was narrow, with white walls and a high ceiling, and at the front of the gallery, sunbeams would dance across the blond wood flooring, but not on a day like this. From front to back, on black and white plinths, were the sculptures—a rolling ceramic sea of breasts and bottoms, rounded, flattened, half-mooned, arching, winking, sly, bulbous, bountiful, overflowing: some orange, some gray, some with traces of lime or cobalt or ocher. At the back of the gallery, hanging on the wall and centered, as it were, by these ranks of ce-ramic flesh, was a gigantic ceramic torso—the unrolled shell of a prodi-gious woman with a pregnant belly and pendulous breasts. The torso hung headless and legless on the wall. A discreet card identified this work as *Peeled Venus*. (Next to this torso was a much smaller wall sculp-ture that, on closer inspection, proved to be a mottled pink and white penis. An even more discreet card identified it as *Vealed Penis*.)

On this bleak, gray, dreary December morning, with the rain lash-ing down outside, Linda sat at a desk beneath these wall-mounted sculp-tures. Before her was a stack of papers and a calculator. She was trying to make sense of Philippe's accounts. Not that she knew much about book-keeping or accounting, but what she knew was more than Philippe did, and the more she'd thought about it, the more she thought she could turn this gallery of his around with a more businesslike approach. (It was important to be turning something around, to be intently and minutely focused on getting *something* organized and productive and moving forward, lest she stop for five seconds to reflect on how truly desperate her life had become.)

It was about ten-thirty. Except for Linda and the ceramic sculptures, the gallery was empty. She heard the bells tinkle on the door, and looked up, and there he stood, stamping his feet and leaving a big puddle at the front of the gallery.

He looked at her and winked. "Got any teapots?" he asked.

FOR DAYS Linda had lived in dread of this moment. Fritz had been released from prison last Saturday, but he hadn't called her or e-mailed her. She'd found out after the fact that he contrived to see the children, without seeing her, by appearing unannounced at the Chaney School and Wellesley High on Monday of this week. He'd taken them out of school—what could the teachers do?—over to the Brigham's in Wellesley Hills, and they sat in the front window, eating hamburgers. Where anyone could see them. The poor children, displayed in front of all kinds of people who might be going through the center of Wellesley in the middle of the day: Michael, Kristin, and the jailbird. She had wrung every word of this conversation out of the kids afterward, then discussed it at length with Dr. Schadenfrau. It had gone something like this:

"What do you guys want to do about all of this?"

(Asking *them* the question, as if "all of this" was their mess to clean up!)

"Whatever." Michael shrugged.

"Could we just forget it all and go back like before?" Kristin asked. When she reported this account to her mother, she confessed that she might have been crying a little. (He made his own daughter cry, right in front of people driving by in the middle of Wellesley!) "Could you both just stop being so stupid?"

"What do you think?" Fritz had asked Michael.

"You know, if you and Mom wanted to get back together, it would be, you know, okay with me. No big deal. Whatever."

"We won't be able to go back to the Palazzo."

"Ah, that was bullshit anyway," Michael said bravely.

"You guys have to realize something," Fritz went on. "I don't think we can ever go back like before. You kids have to ask yourselves, what were we before? A big house in Dover, and a lot of money, and a TV and a computer and a DVD player in every room, and a house in Nantucket, and all of that. That's gone now. If that's what we were, then we can't go back like before."

"No." Kristin shook her head. "Not that kind of before. We mean *before!*"

LINDA HAD PREPARED herself for anger, for shock, for bitterness, for every kind of inappropriate male behavior, even for . . . physical violence. She made sure to keep her cell phone and BlackBerry with her at all times, just to be safe. (She generally kept those items with her at all times, anyway, so this wasn't difficult.) She had thought through all the scenarios. She was careful where she went at night. She peeked out the door and checked up and down the road before exiting. She kept expecting to find him lingering by her car in the morning, or in the cheese aisle at the grocery store, or at the alcove of the Chaney School.

She hadn't readied herself for the obvious thing: a *joke*. There stood Fritz Brubaker, dripping all over the entrance of the gallery, a soggy cardboard box under his arm, and grinning like a madcap, looking like the same old Fritz, wearing khakis and a dark rain jacket, his curls wet, his face on the thin side, but his smile the same old Fritz smile. And he was making a joke! He was not brooding or threatening; he did not look violent or even upset. Once again he insisted on behaving inappropriately.

"Why is it always a joke with you, Fritz?"

He took that for an invitation and walked toward her slowly, threading his way through the breast pots down the length of the narrow studio. He was surprised by how poorly she looked. She was too thin, her skin drawn too tightly across her face and far from its usual unguent-aided perfection. It was blemished along her hairline and back around her ears. And pale. There was one chair by her desk, reserved, as he imagined, for big art spenders, where they might sit down to close a deal.

He didn't look bad at all, she noticed as he came toward her. ("He's leaving puddles on the floor!" the Shrill Small Voice commented.) But she wondered about that box—what did he have in the box? Could he have brought a weapon?

Linda realized she was trapped here, at the back of the gallery on a rain-lashed morning when no one was out shopping. She was at the back, where no one from the street could see. There was no one else in the gallery. She reached for her cell phone.

But when he drew close, she put down the phone. Because she could tell. The look on his face told her that whatever he had in his box wasn't a weapon. It was probably shopping or something. It embarrassed her, so she turned to avoid looking at him. And then he was there, right across from her desk. After, how long had it been—almost a year? She tried not to tremble, but that only made her tremble more, which made her nervous, which made the trembling worse, and so on. Why must he make her feel so awkward? Why couldn't he have just sent an e-mail like a normal human being?

Fritz leaned over the desk, clumsily, to kiss his wife, but she turned so that his lips would brush only her cheek. Cold rain dripped off his hair and onto the stack of invoices on the desk.

"May I sit?" he asked.

"Fritz, there could be customers, I don't know if—"

But there weren't any customers, and on Newbury Street, a part of town where nobody wakened much before nightfall, it didn't seem likely that a crowd would soon materialize in this filthy weather to make a run on breast pots. So he sat. He put the box on the floor under the seat.

He didn't *seem* violent, at least. But she held the cell phone in her hand, just in case.

"It's nice to see you again," he said. "I've missed you."

She nodded, tried to say something but didn't know how. So she managed a clipped smile, the smile of a civil servant. A noisome thought intruded: hadn't she missed him, too? ("No!" hissed the Shrill Small Voice. "You haven't missed him at all! Get ahold of yourself, for God's sake!")

"How are Michael and Kristin doing?" he asked.

They had been doing terribly, both of them. Fighting like tomcats, angry and resentful at both of their parents: at their father for going to jail, at both of them for losing the house, and at their mother for betraying their father and for making herself, and thus by extension them, ridiculous in the eyes of the whole school by having an affair with

Philippe the Creep. To Linda, Michael seemed even more morose than ever. Except for Monday night, when she recounted Fritz's visit, Kristin had refused to speak to her mother for most of the previous week.

"They're fine," she said. "You should know."

He nodded. Smiling at her that way, staring at her that way.

"As good as can be expected, given . . . Dammit, Fritz, why did you do it? Why didn't you just explain to them what happened? We could have gotten Michael some counseling and . . ."

Poor Linda. She broke down even as the Shrill Small Voice hissed at her not to be such a blubbering fool. She began to sob. Forty-six years of hard work to avoid being Subject to Criticism, and he had undone it all in fourteen months. She had sunk so far from being above criticism as to be almost beneath it. Running around with Philippe the Creep (as the Shrill Small Voice had come to call him, too). What was she thinking! She held her head in her hands. Fritz reached across the table to stroke her hair, but she shrank from his touch.

"Excuse me," she said. "This is very upsetting."

"It's okay. It's okay. I've missed you, too."

("What does he mean, 'too'?" hissed the Voice. "That was presumptuous!")

"The *kids* have missed you terribly," she said. "Still, I don't see how forcing them to display themselves in the middle of Wellesley, on a school day, was really the best thing for—" And then she started sobbing again.

("For heaven's sake, get ahold of yourself!" the Shrill Small Voice demanded.)

Meanwhile Fritz rose, as if to come behind the desk and kiss her.

She held up the cell phone. "Please, Fritz, not now."

So he sat again. But she was even more confused than before. There was something about the way he looked that had been so familiar in her life for so long. "Too" was right. She'd missed him, too, damn him. And damn the Shrill Small Voice, too.

She softened. Her eyes slipped their leash, and Fritz and Linda began a wary inspection. "Nice place," he said, glancing up at *Peeled Venus* and *Vealed Penis*. He thought he detected the slightest inclination on her part to join in his wry amusement, before she quickly caught herself.

"It looks like prison didn't disagree with you too much," she finally said, grasping for something pleasant.

"It was actually a very positive experience," he said.

("Classic!" hissed the Shrill Small Voice. "Classic! Prison, a positive experience!")

"Not like you read about at all, these minimum-security prisons. Or camps, as they call them. Not scary or any of that. Can be very dull, but my time was so short, it was more like a sort of retreat. I spent a lot of time reading and thinking. And working on my little project."

She smiled. "You got your Tinker Toys all right?"

"Yes," he said. "They worked pretty well. I'd say on the whole, the experience was an excellent opportunity."

Only Fritz could refer to prison as an excellent opportunity! She gave him that "Fritz the nutcase" look, then caught herself. Maybe he was right. Maybe it had been an opportunity.

"So, what's it like to have an affair with a twenty-five-year-old art teacher?" he asked. He put the question without edge or irony but with kind of a genuine interest.

"He's twenty-*six*. And what's it like to boff a hotel hooker?" she shot right back.

"She wasn't a hotel hooker. That's not fair. But to answer your question, it was, well, I guess it was okay as lust goes. For a little while. She's a very nice and sort of mixed-up girl. And a true friend. She was awfully good to me while I was down at the camp."

"Did you think I could just pop down to Pennsylvania for a visit? Someone had to look after the kids."

"I know," he said. "I know. I was trying to tell you that although she was a nice girl, and a beautiful girl, I never stopped feeling . . ."

"What?"

"To be honest with you? Goofy."

Linda thought, Just like him to *answer* a rhetorical question. You're not supposed to answer rhetorical questions, you're supposed to be shamed by them. (She hadn't answered his question, for example. Which had shamed her with its maddening curiosity.) Why couldn't he be resentful? What right did he think he had to summarize her feelings in his own? To have a randy young man hungry for her, that had been comforting, reassuring, even, given all the other disasters going on in her life.

But this avenue of breast pots she found herself in, this companionship of Philippe the Creep? That was exactly the word—it felt a little goofy. And here Fritz was again, not angry, still charming, the father of her children.

They reprised the Stumble Dance of Monosyllables.

"And so . . ."

"So . . ."

"Ummm . . ."

"I, uh . . ."

"Did you . . . ?"

"No, you?"

"Umm . . ."

And so it went for a while until he said, "Look, Linda, what if we just drop all the stuff that distracted us the first time, all the playing up to the world's expectations, and if it were just you and me, and Michael and Kristin? I believe we—"

"The world's expectations have been adjusted."

"Exactly. And that's a liberating thing. The hell with the world, whoever the world is. We're the world! I'd like us to be our world. I liked that world. You see, hon, I never loved what you wanted to become. I just loved what you were already. I think you still *are* what you were already."

She smiled a sad, weary smile. "Fritz, I'm hardly what I was already."

"You sure?"

She didn't feel like she was any longer. Was she ever the lover of a pot boy, a washed-up ex-corporate lawyer, working at a desk beneath these ceramic things? "The career's gone, and my kids hate me," she said.

"The hell with the career. As for the kids, you're wrong. I checked. They don't hate you. They're just mad at you. Mad at us both, actually. It's never too late for anything. Before it was too early, maybe."

Such confidence! The emphatic way he said it, you could almost believe it. She felt that tingle, that magical, delightful something. But . . .

"Anyway, you think it over, see how you feel. I gotta go. I have a meeting with Jim Feeney. I have to get out to his place." Fritz looked at his watch. "I'm late. But think it over." He stood, started to leave, then turned. "Almost forgot," he said. "Brought you something."

He put the box on her desk, then turned back around and walked up toward the front of the gallery.

A puddle began forming on the desk around the spongy cardboard. She looked at the box, then up at this strange husband of hers as he walked slowly away. That word had come into her head suddenly— "husband"? Why had she thought of him that way instead of as "Fritz"? Now, of all times? There he went through the file of breast pots, receding from her toward the front of the gallery. She lifted the wet cardboard top from the box and looked down at its contents: a pair of Pappagallo silk pumps.

Size eight.

She stared at the shoes. Then lifted one out and turned it in her hands in disbelief. "Oh, Fritz," was all she could choke out. "Oh, goddammit, Fritz!"

But the door jingled shut, and by the time she got up to it and peered out, he'd disappeared in the rain.

THE WORST
CHRISTMAS EVER

NEAR THE BOTTOM NOW, Paradise has opened up a dozen feet or so, but you've picked up crazy speed, bouncing recklessly in the bumps, tired, going too fast, too *fast*, punch-drunk, almost; skis chattering and sloppy and careening over the ice, and you are muscling the turns, dodging the trees, and just trying to get down somehow.

Below you can almost see the bottom—almost. But the last steep glade of Paradise can kill you as surely as the first pitch at the top.

CHRISTMAS MORNING comes to the McHouse. Michael and Kristin are agreed: this already is the worst Christmas ever. Already, even before today. Nobody had wanted to decorate anything all week. They hadn't gone out with Linda to get the tree, she'd had to do it herself, and nobody had helped her put it in the stand, nor string the lights, nor hang the family ornaments. No one helped her take the crèche out of the old encyclopedia box and unwrap the wise men and the shepherds from the ancient yellowed tissue paper. She tried to buy Christmas CDs, to get simple carols performed a capella, and they were all horrible, goopy with strings and harps. The children derided them.

Now, in the corner, the tree kind of leans. It is a pathetic leaning Christmas tree, mocked cruelly by extravagant heaps of packages.

Linda is the first one in the living room on Christmas morning. The sun is up, and she is there before the children, alone. This has never happened, not since Michael was three. A terrible chill is on that house, with no children to shake and poke packages and crawl under the tree prospecting. No one is impatient for breakfast to be over. No one even stirs in the bedrooms, though Linda knows they are awake behind those closed doors. She is alone on Christmas morning with the packages.

And there are far too many. Extravagant heaps of boxes jeering at her, as if loot could replace what is missing.

Eventually, the children come down, diffident feet on the stairs, late in the morning. Linda is determined to be cheerful. She is department-store merry, full of phony brightness, but Kristin will cut her to the bone. She sniffs at breakfast. Not hungry. When the time comes, she will look blankly at the extravagant heaps and say, I don't want them.

Linda's face clouds, and she bites her lower lip. Then she is in the bathroom and running the water so the children can't hear. A while passes before she is back. Kristin's cruelty is uniquely potent: only a daughter could be so cruel, and only to her mother. Kristin fishes for her father's present and, finding it, opens the box. The green ski jacket is the wrong color, Linda knows it is the wrong color, but Kristin pronounces that she loves it.

And puts it on.

Linda wavers but holds. Wonderful. Wonderful that Kristin loves it, the words brittle in the air. Excuse me, something to check in the kitchen.

She seems to be cracking, and Michael is fearful for his mother now, hissing at his sister. Can't you just open the fucking presents? For Mom?

Why won't she have him over, Kristin hisses back.

The day limps forward. Linda hides herself in the kitchen, cooking and cooking, everything they like. It will be Christmas dinner, it *will* be. The big pot is for the potatoes whipped with butter, Kristin's favorite, and the saucepans simmer with the creamed onions and the green beans, and a warm roasting smell suffuses the kitchen, for the top round is in the oven.

Linda is alone and busy and determined. It will be Christmas dinner. The oven grows hot and the pan smoky for preparing the Yorkshire pudding that is Michael's special favorite, and she is trying, it will be a wonderful dinner, warm and wonderful. We will hold on to some traditions even today.

The pudding pan is in the oven. It smokes darkly with hot fat. You must wait until just the right moment, with the pan drippings dark and blazing in the oven, and then pour in the pudding so that it will bubble and squeak and brown, as it did in those old Christmases everyone remembers. In another minute or so, when the fat is hot enough, smoky and succulent in the dark oven, she will pour in the pudding. And then—

My God! God, can't *somebody* stop it! That sound! Throbbing in their skulls, drilling into them, making them shrink and writhe and panic. Waving the towel frantically and throwing open the windows, and the damp frigid air pouring in, and still it won't stop.

Stop it stop it stop it stop it STOP IT!

Until Linda is crying and Kristin is crying and the oven is still smoking and the kitchen is cold and Michael savagely rips the smoke alarm from the skip-troweled ceiling and it lies smashed on the kitchen floor and the red wire and the black wire dangle from the hole. It is silent again in the McHouse.

But not completely silent. From the living room come the strains of thick treacle: Mantovani butchering "O Holy Night."

Early afternoon and shadows lengthening. No one hungry now. And everyone fearful of that table with three seats, with one gaping empty unlaid place, in plain view of the mocking heap of unopened packages. Not even Linda wants to sit there. But she must. She must have Christmas dinner, and this will be all right. Wipe briskly at the corner of her eye. Force a laugh; won't this be funny to remember years from now? But everyone knows it won't, that it will never never be something you could laugh at, not a hundred years from now.

The dining room is still cold as hell while the worst Christmas ever is lengthening into gray afternoon. It cannot lengthen and fade and die soon enough.

Kristin refuses to eat, refuses even to sit down, leaving the two of them at the table. She's not hungry. Kristin, sit down, honey. Angry words ring like hammer blows. No! I won't! You will! I won't!

She rushes down the back stairs and pulls her bike out of the laundry room, and the door slams behind her. Kristin, what are you doing, where are you going? Kristin is gone, disappeared, a runaway on this horrible afternoon, vanished into the fading gray, and Linda is holding her head in her hands.

Michael gapes—he doesn't know what to do or what to say. He feels his mother's brittleness, as if she might break and lie shattered on the kitchen floor with the smoke alarm. He is the oldest, he is the only one left at home, a vague awareness that he is supposed to do something about this, and realizing that he'd better not go off to watch TV. So he sits in silence next to his mother. And then, with transparency, tells her he didn't really like Yorkshire pudding that much anyway, Mom, don't worry about it, it's not a big deal, and she has to leave the table again.

But she keeps trying. She is like a wounded mouse staggering away from the cat until the cat casts a languid eye and flicks a claw to bat it back to the starting point. She keeps playing the stupid Christmas CDs, and she gets more and more frustrated because they make everything goopy. Why can't they just sing the carols? It is Christmas, and Linda actually says: "Why can't they just sing the goddamn carols without violins!"

Her knuckles are white and enlarged. The blue tracework shows on her shaking fingers, and her eyes look red, and she is crying again. Michael is behind her, afraid to touch, his half-extended arm frozen in the air.

BY THIS TIME Fritz agrees that it is the worst Christmas ever. His day is stumbling by in the rough apartment at the back of Feeney's barn, where Fritz is a lodger. A dozen or more Feeneys are in the house. The lights are on and the stove is busy and the cats are cozy in the warm kitchen corners and the family is loud and merry. Kids and grandkids have returned. A happy throng of Subarus and minivans is parked in front of the barn, all giving a festive hood salute. Nan comes out to the barn and calls to Fritz at intervals during the day. She's worried. She's instinctive. Won't he come in and sit with them? "Have Christmas with us, Fritz. Or a Bloody Mary, at least."

"No, thank you, Nan, I'm fine. Don't you worry about me. Merry Christmas! My best to Jim and the family." His jolliest greeting. He pokes his head around the door and smiles at her. "You enjoy yourselves!"

He is full of sadness, the contagious kind, and it would only infect the Feeneys.

He would have gone up to the North Shore, seen Andy or Hap or something, sat in their living rooms watching his nephews and nieces tear into packages, but it wasn't to be. The BMW crapped out the night before, deader than a post, he and Jim leaned over it long into the night while the goats watched with curiosity. They couldn't jump it, some kind of short in the electrics, Jim said, his breath coming in clouds, and Fritz had to agree.

Just as well, the way the streets glisten with black ice. Cars skid off into the verges, and three of them ding the stone walls along Farm Street. The barn is poorly insulated. Fritz goes out to the shed behind the barn and gets an armload of maple logs. He looks for the goats, and they are huddling in the front of the barn, none of them on the cars today. He heads back in and stokes up the old Vermont Castings top loader, his breath still faintly visible even indoors. On the stove handles, the porcelain is all cracked so that you have to use vise grips, or when the stove heats up, you will burn yourself. But the stove takes a while to heat up. The room is dank and cold over toward the barn wall but warm by the stove. Fritz sits by the hearth with a book in his hand that he is not reading.

Didn't think he'd get this sentimental. It is just another day, after all.

Maybe they will call. But they don't call. Not in the morning, not at noon, not as the shadows of the naked maples grow long and gray outside the window at the back of Feeney's barn. He could call *them;* he could go in and ask to borrow the phone and, in the midst of all that family cheer, lay bare his desperation.

Better not to disturb them.

He remembers the shoes and how he thought surely she would be touched, but they hadn't worked. Too much time has passed. His typical cute ploy, just a stunt, and it must have backfired. He wonders about that ski parka. Probably Kristin already has one. He wonders about the Orvis rod, sure to be a dud. What made him think Michael ever wanted to go fishing?

Everyone says the holidays are the worst time. He'll get through this all right. One step at a time. One step . . . toward where?

A phone rings in the house, and he waits, and waits, and waits for the sounds of a door opening or footsteps coming outside. But Nan doesn't come. The call is not for him.

The day fades away into dusk and then disappears altogether. Still he sits by the woodstove. Maybe he was wrong about the whole thing.

It feels like it was wrong, but dammit, he doesn't think he was wrong. He keeps doing the math, and it doesn't come out wrong. He sits and sits by Feeney's old Vermont Castings top loader, and the chunks of maple burn down to coals, and then they simply glow. He opens the stove door to watch them, and the oxygen lashes a lazy flickering tongue up from the dark red coals, and then it disappears until there is just a red glowing from the black, and more black than red.

A bicycle comes silently up to Feeney's. At the back of the barn, staring at the coals, Fritz doesn't hear it.

Into the barn she rides, then rushes through to the back, and Shea bleats at the sight of her, and this he does hear. "Merry Christmas, Daddy!"

Kristin? Have they come over to visit? No, she is alone. But how? "Did you ride your *bike* over here?"

She nods proudly.

"Come in and get warm, Peanut! Come on in here, girl, and get warm!"

A big squeeze, holding her close with his face averted, lest she get some idea, because it is contagious, contagious.

"Merry Christmas, Kristin."

"Me and Michael got you a present."

His sweet sweet girl. She has brought him herself, that is present enough.

"But we got you one."

"Okay, sit by the stove and then let's see it."

"It's in Wellesley."

Oh. A shrug. A sense of resignation, a glance outside where it is black darkness. "I—"

"If you want it, you have to come over."

A gentle smile. "That's awfully sweet. But my car died."

"You've still got your bike here that Mom said cost, like, five thousand dollars, don't you?"

"It was thirty-five hundred."

"Well?" Kristin doesn't seem to be taking off her coat. She stands fierce and determined. With her hands on her hips, wrists reversed.

"I'd have to pump up the tires. It's dark. I dunno, Peanut, your mother . . ."

"You chicken?"

◆━◆◆◆━◆

CHRISTMAS NIGHT. Cold, cold is the road from Dover, the asphalt gleaming black with invisible, deadly ice, and almost empty now. All outside is dark and cold and slick. Everyone is home with family. Merry lights are in the windows as they pedal by, but the windows and doors are shut up tight. Only a few cars race past. Coasting down the long hill to South Natick, the wind bitter and penetrating, and then riding along Route 16 in the blackness past the bottle-glass windowpanes of the Eliot Street Church, past the Hunnewell Farm. Jesus, it's a long way. Pushing upwind now, another mile or more to the hill by Wellesley College, where the President's House is so festive, so bright with lamps and fire-light. Up another hill—steep, you have to stand on the pedals—and into the darkened square. Fingers stiff with the cold and faces numb. Fingers not working well at all.

But anxious now, picking up speed on Route 16, pedaling hard. Not far to go, the road flat now, soon be there.

They are in the back door at seven-fifteen, stamping and rubbing their hands. Then up the stairs.

At first awkwardness. Staring at feet and fingers. "Merry Christmas, Linda."

She hesitates. But it is Christmas, and the look on Kristin's face, on Michael's, too. "Merry Christmas, Fritz." A hug with cheeks averted, stiffly courteous.

Nervous, both of them. But she is not angry to see him. She is flushed and relieved. And he is relieved.

It comes to him like an old familiar habit. He is Father Christmas and he is late to the house and the house needs cheer. "Let's eat! Hungry as a bear," he says. No one sees Linda slip another table setting in, she does it so subtly. They sit. It is warmer in the dining room. She reheats the roast and puts the mashed potatoes and the gravy in the microwave.

"God, these are good."

"Daddy, stop hogging them."

"No way," he says, mugging, and holds on to the bowl with both hands. " 'Gravy and potatoes in a big brown pot! Put them in the oven and—' "

Kristin sings out: "Serve them very hot!"

A glance stolen at Linda, whose lips moved subtly, repeating the nursery rhyme she read to the children years ago.

Linda has opened a bottle of wine and poured four glasses, even for Kristin. Yet it doesn't seem odd. The wine warms them all.

"Let's open the rest of the presents," says Kristin.

Fritz, crestfallen: "I didn't bring any."

"We opened what you sent, Dad. They were great." She loves her ski parka, Linda is explaining now. "And Michael got a fishing rod—a beautiful Orvis fly rod—and you know what? He likes it. He thinks he wants to go fishing, maybe. Strange."

"What's so strange about that?" Michael wants to know.

Now it is time for Linda's presents: boxes and boxes of them. There are computer games and CDs and skirts and sweaters and pants and roller blades and a fleecy bathrobe and a backpack and socks and under-wear and cute puzzles. Boxes and boxes of clever gifts from Linda.

Michael is the miner. He crawls under the leaning tree, unearths one, then another. For his father, an envelope. *Merry Christmas Dad*, it says. A computer-generated design of a self-correcting sail fan, swiveling through 360 degrees. Fritz has already designed a similar mechanism, but he'll never mention it. "What a wonderful thing!"

Done yet? "Yes," Linda says at last, after the boxes and packages are torn open, "now we're done." Fritz and Linda sprawl on the couch, the paper in heaps around them. Wine swirls in the glasses. How much bet-ter this was.

"I don't have anything," he tells her. "I'm sorry."

A squeeze to the arm. "You gave it to me last week. It was . . . it was a lovely lovely gift." She smiles and turns her head.

But Linda is wrong. We still aren't done. One present remains under the pathetic leaning tree. It's a big one at the back. A long rectangular package, wrapped clumsily in green wrapping paper.

Merry Christmas Mom AND Dad, love Kristin and Michael. With a smiley face.

"It was Kristin's idea."

"Yours too."

Michael doesn't contradict this.

Fritz gropes the package with a mime's fingers, mugging again. It yields to the touch. "It's . . . long," he says.

"Open it TOGETHER," Kristin orders.

"Yeah," says Michael. "Together."

The package sits across their laps. Gingerly, she lifts a length of Scotch tape from one end. He does the same from the other. She tears gently. "Aw, the hell with it." He rips. And there it is, revealed, a single long . . .

"How . . . odd. Did you guys get this from a catalog?" Turning it over in their hands, not getting it at first. A bolster? No, a pillow. A four-foot pillow. Then the penny drops and they understand. Kristin folds her arms firmly. "And no," she snaps, "there isn't another one."

She says one more thing that makes them all laugh. How they laugh—even Michael joins in. How the heart wells in Fritz Brubaker, for his son and daughter, his daughter like him, and his son—like him, too. How Linda cries and cries—and cries. The thing about Paradise is this: it can kill you, but if it happens not to kill you, then it ends. If you don't die, you will get to the bottom eventually. Gravity is infinite, but Paradise isn't. And as you emerge from the birches on the last pitch, and look back up that impossible slope, the trail seems to vanish within the trees so you can barely tell where you've been. You can barely tell there's a trail there at all, or that you were on it. You've made it. God, you looked like hell up there, and you had a few close calls, but maybe you even skied Paradise. Survived it, anyway.

You stand on a midmountain boulevard, an easy avenue that meanders to the lodge at the bottom along groomers with names like Periwinkle and Bunny. Anyone can ski them. Linda's done it herself, lots of times.

ALONG THE DARK STREETS they go, where the sidewalks are lacquered with dangerous black ice. Careful where you walk. No one is out except for them. Only a few minutes of the Nativity remain. Close under the faint streetlights they pass, huddling together, stepping gingerly so as not to fall. When it's this slippery and cold, you can't tell whether it helps to walk with someone, or you are better off alone.

They are talking a little, not much. Mainly there is the sound of their footsteps and breath. Linda, in particular, is feeling an emotional exhaustion. She knows, as he does, that Christmas Day, with its packages and wrapping paper and Christmas dinner, comes but once a year. The rest of the time you are staggering around on familiar streets where something treacherous may lurk. You are clinging to a companion but secretly thinking the footing might be better if you walked alone.

"I'm glad you came. I almost lost it today."

"Me, too."

"You?"

"Sitting in Feeney's barn. Never felt sorrier for myself."

On a night like tonight, judgment is clouded, and it's easy to be sentimental. Each of them knows this. That's why it's better not to talk too much. They walk up into Wellesley Hills, along the dark winding streets, past the big Victorians and Tudors and rambling Queen Annes, along the rows of colonials, into the darkened lanes and the quiet circles. Slowly they begin to loop back toward town.

"Fritz, tonight . . . We have to be honest. Tonight didn't solve anything."

They are both thinking the same thing. It was a wonderful gesture the kids made, but let's be honest. This is no time to make decisions. They turn back toward town, the railroad trestle downhill from them. Below, the road glistens black in the pale yellow light. Their breath makes clouds. She leans against him and puts her right hand out on his forearm.

"Gotta hand it to Kristin," Fritz says. "It's what we said to them all their lives, right?"

"I didn't think they'd ever heard us, to judge by the way they fight."

Kristin had stood before the pathetic leaning Christmas tree with her arms folded. "Learn to SHARE," she'd said.

Their steps are quickening as they come back into town: the cold is penetrating. They have reached Route 16 and the row of shops across from the train station. It was funny the way Kristin said it. As they hurry along past the shopwindows, they are both smiling to think of the children conspiring on this gift.

Linda's fingers are freezing, and she jams her hands into her pockets. An idea begins to germinate.

Face it, sharing isn't easy. Learning—relearning—to share gets harder when you're old. And the gift is not the kind of thing one usually shares. Still, as Kristin said, there's only one. Maybe they can learn to share it after all. Time will tell.

They're past the shops now, almost home. One turn off of Route 16, a block and a half from the McHouse. Fritz has made the turn, when Linda stops at the corner, hesitating by a trash basket underneath the streetlamp, her hands still in her pockets.

"You know," she says, "that gift—it's the only thing I've ever seen *them* share."

And that is the point upon which there can be no argument. That those two kids should agree on anything—it must be significant. Linda cannot get past that idea. One gift to their parents; to both of us, she thinks, looking over at him. At his curly hair, poking out from beneath a ski hat, his blue fleece jacket, the old zippered one, the fleece all matted down and the cuff torn, an old familiar thing like all such things: something gone ratty with wear but that you love too much to get rid of. He's hunching over, eager to go home. That look in his eyes, so familiar. To both of us.

Still she lingers at the corner. The house is only fifty yards away. She has the oddest look on her face. "Fritz, I have a present for you, too."

She fishes it out of her pocket. In the pale light, he can't tell what she's holding. He takes a step toward her, then recognizes it, and it puzzles him. Another gag?

That smile, it's one he's never seen on her before. Reckless. Not herself at all. A little unscrewed, like she might laugh out loud. God, she's beautiful. She slam-dunks the gift into the trash basket.

"I can't believe you did that," he says.

"I can't believe I did that either."

After midnight now. They hurry the last few yards to the house. He takes her by the hand and promptly slips on the ice but doesn't fall. She lets go but quickly takes his hand again. They reach the door.

"This was maybe the worst Christmas ever."

He answers: "But maybe the best Christmas ever."

"Yes. Maybe that, too."

So the worst Christmas ever comes to a close. The kids are where they were at dawn: behind the bedroom doors, listening. The CD with its Christmas horrors has finished, and the McHouse is quiet. The living room is dark except for the Christmas lights on the pathetic leaning tree. The ski parka is on the couch, and the fishing rod stands in the corner. The kitchen is dark, the sink piled high with dishes. Linda's shoes are upstairs, tucked into the back of the bedroom closet. The four-foot pillow lies on the bed. The best Christmas ever, too—maybe. Time will tell.

Two blocks away, underneath the streetlight on the corner of Route 16, Linda's gift to her husband will lie in the basket for thirty-three hours, until the next trash pickup. In the cold December air, the plastic lozenge will even vibrate a few times before the batteries fail—vibrating with urgent messages that nobody will answer.

PRESENT
VALUE

SABIN WILLETT

A Reader's Guide

Questions for Discussion

1. *Present Value* takes a swipe at the "eensy button" devices upon which so many of us have come to rely. Is the criticism fair? Do these devices improve communication? Do they simplify work and life, or supplant them? Why?

2. The stress of the "have-it-all" lifestyle is hardest on Linda. After all, Fritz has no Shrill Small Voice to bedevil him. Is the portrayal accurate? Why?

3. What has changed about the way we raise children? Do we do the job better than did our parents?

4. Is there hope for the Brubaker/LeBrecque marriage once the book ends? Should there be?

5. At work, Fritz is not a team player. Does that absolve him from responsibility for what happens to Playtime, or to his marriage? Or does it make him more responsible?

6. In the Waldorf-Astoria Hotel, Fritz falls. On a moral scale, how does his fall compare with Linda's? If we make a distinction between them, should we?

7. Senator Oldcastle is a pale imitation of a famous comic character. Can you spot three places where the text pays homage?

8. Ultimately, what sacrifice should a parent make for a child? Did Fritz make the right one? Was Linda right about Michael? Shouldn't they just have gotten him a little counseling?

9. Consider the viewpoint of Chapter 16 ("Did You See It? Were You There?"), where the account emerges only from anonymous rumor. How effective is this as an approach to storytelling? (If you find it effective, read the master, Joyce Carol Oates, in *Broke Heart Blues*. If you do not, consider why not.)

10. Lay up your treasure in heaven, says the Gospel, for where your treasure is, there will your heart be also. Why does Professor Vorblen quote this passage in his farewell lecture? Can a system of ethical values operate simultaneously with a system of economic values?